BLACK CIPHER

ALSO BY
PAYNE HARRISON

STORMING INTREPID

THUNDER OF EREBUS

BLACK CIPHER

PAYNE HARRISON

CROWN PUBLISHERS, INC.

NEW YORK

Published by Crown Publishers, Inc., 201 East 50th Street, New York, New York 10022. Member of the Crown Publishing Group.

Random House, Inc. New York, Toronto, London, Sydney, Auckland

CROWN is a trademark of Crown Publishers, Inc.

Manufactured in U.S.A.

Design by Nancy Kenmore

Library of Congress Cataloging-in-Publication Data
Harrison, Payne.
    Black cipher / by Payne Harrison.—1st ed.
    1. Intelligence service—Great Britain—Fiction. I. Title.
PS3558.A6718B53   1994
813'.54—dc20   94-9849
                                                            CIP

ISBN 0-517-58753-X

10 9 8 7 6 5 4 3 2 1

First Edition

This book is for my sister,
Karen Harrison,
who helped me decipher many
of life's mysteries

ACKNOWLEDGMENTS

A great many people assisted me with this book, but I felt it best not to disclose their names because the nature and level of their assistance might be misinterpreted. Suffice to say, to those who did lend me a hand, I hope they will accept my profound gratitude and genuine respect.

There are, however, three people I do have to thank publicly. First is my brother-in-spirit, Thomas Frederick Sharp III, who gave me the title of *Black Cipher*. Next is Prof. Desmond Ball, whose knowledge of Soviet/Russian signals intelligence is nothing short of encyclopedic. Finally, there is Prof. Tom McElmurry, whose advice and counsel has been valuable beyond measure.

And as for the women in my life—Wife, Daughters, Mom and Sis—thanks for all your help in bringing this volume to a successful conclusion.

Men at some time are masters of their fates:
The fault, dear Brutus, is not in our stars,
But in ourselves . . .

— Cassius, from Shakespeare's
Julius Caesar, Act I, Scene II

We have met the enemy and he is us.

— Pogo

BLACK
CIPHER

CHAPTER  ONE

The long, black Jaguar Sovereign emitted a throaty growl as it motored along the tree-lined ribbon of Gloucester Road. It was a gray morning in Cheltenham, where a lingering mist draped a damp chill over the Cotswolds. Pedestrians huddled into their coats and eyed the elegant car with envy as it splashed through the shallow puddles. Sporadically, the Jaguar triggered its timed wipers, cleansing the windshield of dew as it prowled along like its feline namesake—changing lanes, then executing a harsh sling-shot maneuver round the roundabout. Peeling off at Princess Elizabeth Way, it surged forward the last hundred meters before turning left into a toll-booth-like entry, past an old wooden sign with faded fine print. With an electronic hum the driver's window slid down, allowing the uniformed guard to inspect the proffered identification card. After a look, two gloved fingers motioned the Jaguar past.

At first glance, it might appear the Sovereign had driven through the gates of a prison, or one of those depressing institutions where society houses those it wishes to forget. It was something of a compound, ringed with an eight-foot Hurricane fence and topped off with several strands of barbed wire. Within the fence was a five-story office building and a mélange of dingy, hutlike structures laid out row upon row. But three things betrayed what sort of place this truly was. To the west of the main building, on a large pasturelike plot of open ground, was an antenna that resembled a giant hairnet tossed upon the ground. The second clue was a large satellite dish behind the main building. And the final and most telling clue was the barbed-wire ribbon on top of the fence. It was canted *outward*, not inward, meaning it was designed to keep intruders away—not to prevent escape from within.

The Jaguar pulled across the tarmac and slid into one of the cherished reserved parking spaces near the main administration building. The sleek Sovereign looked distinctly out of place amongst the Fiats, Fords, Vauxhalls, and Toyotas that populated the lot. It wasn't the type of transport a civil servant's salary could underwrite, and you might say it was something of a rarity.

Like the driver.

He emerged from the Sovereign wearing a double-breasted camel-hair overcoat, then reached back in for his Hermès briefcase. Deftly closing the door, he locked the car with an electronic key ring and moved toward the entrance of the building. He wasn't tall, perhaps five feet seven, but his frame was symmetrical so you couldn't perceive his true stature unless you were up close. Like the coat, the suit was from Gieves & Hawkes, the shirt from Turnbull & Asser, and the tie and pocket scarf from Sulka in Paris. The angular features of his face were softened by a generous mane of hair colored gunmetal gray, but with a sprinkling of salt. His skin possessed that shade of tan milky white tourists lusted after on their summer holidays in Brighton; and his walk, like the car, had a feline character about it. Easing through the entryway of the administration building, he stepped out of the cold and made his way to the guard desk in the foyer.

"Morning, Doctah Shaikh," said the guard in greeting, pronouncing *Shaikh* like the second syllable in *milkshake.*

"Good morning, Henry." The embossed identification card was extended once again. "Has your new grandchild arrived yet?"

The white-haired Henry looked at the card perfunctorily as he had through the years, but was now too close to retirement to really care. "Two weeks late. Told my daughter the bairn must be 'avin' second thoughts."

Shaikh chuckled. "It must know life is simpler on the inside than on the outside."

"No doubt."

Shaikh checked his watch as Henry passed judgment on another piece of plastic. Normally he would have taken the stairs to his fourth-floor office, but the clock was approaching ten-thirty, so he walked into the lift. Shaikh typically went to bed late and rose late—an atypical schedule, but one that was forgiven due to his rarefied talent and senior position. But duty required him to rise early on Tuesday and Friday mornings, much to his discomfort. He exited the lift and walked along the threadbare carpet toward his office at the end of the hall, nodding to the random staffer who passed by. The walls of the passageway were painted a dull beige and punctuated by a series of poorly done portraits of academic-looking men. At the base of each portrait was a small brass plate, denoting the individual's identity. Names like Alan Turing, Marian Rejewski, Nigel de Gray, Gordon Welchman, Meredith Gardner. Names that wouldn't mean squash to a society enthralled with sports figures and film stars, but names that were legends on the fourth floor of Government Communications Headquarters (GCHQ).

At the end of the hallway he entered his office where the departmental secretary, Geneviève Monson, rose to help him off with his coat. Geneviève was approximately five foot naught—by horizontal or vertical measure, whichever you preferred—with white hair, bespectacled eyes, and the most hideous makeup Shaikh had ever seen. He was quite certain she'd come into government service about the time the Zimmermann Telegram was deciphered. Her redeeming feature was that she ran Shaikh's office like a Scots Guards sergeant major.

Geneviève tossed Shaikh's camel-hair coat on the rack and pointed to the adjoining office. "Burdick, and you've got fourteen minutes."

He entered his office with time counting down to the PM's brief. His domain was surprisingly well-appointed for one of Her Majesty's humble servants. The carpet was government-issue drab, but the desk was large, made of cherrywood and obviously hand-crafted. Built-in shelves held a small library on topics like number theory, statistics, chess, and the stock market. A computer terminal was on the credenza, along with bits of memorabilia. A striking thing was the tidiness of the room. The books were all dusted and flush with the edge of the shelves, the papers on the desk stacked in neat piles and properly weighted down. Two Parton landscape paintings (on loan from his personal collection) adorned the wall. He had always been entranced by the subdued elegance of Parton's style. It imparted a peaceful, pastoral feeling that was impossible to find elsewhere on the fourth floor.

Standing over Shaikh's cherrywood desk, leaning on his palms with a sheet of paper entrapped between them, was Jamie Burdick, a man who was as unkempt as the room was tidy. Plaid shirt open at the collar, knit tie pulled down, and sleeves rolled up, Burdick wore his blond hair combed straight back and almost shoulder length. There always seemed to be a cloud of Player's smoke enveloping his head, as there was now, and the sheet of paper between his hands absorbed every dram of his attention.

There was no greeting between them as Shaikh set his attaché case on the credenza and asked the younger man, "What's the brief?"

Burdick looked up, his face appearing older than his thirty-six years, and with a crisp movement he slapped a file of papers in front of his superior.

"First off, China. Little Sai Wan in Hong Kong snagged an intercept on a freq traditionally reserved for high-priority traffic two days ago. It was short and sweet and put the traffic boys in heat. I yanked the Purple Gang and got them onto it straightaway with the China Clippers. Then I stroked the in-laws to bump time for us on the Paradox machine. Remember that plaintext crib the altar boys flagged to us last week? Damned if it didn't work! Struck gold. Seems that General Wang, commander on the Vietnamese border, is being sacked. He's to be replaced with a chap named Fong."

Shaikh scanned the message. There was a simultaneous English translation below the verbatim printout, but Shaikh preferred to read the original Cantonese.

Jamie Burdick knew there must be a language that Faisal Shaikh couldn't read or speak. Burdick just hadn't found it yet.

"And who is this fellow Fong?" asked Shaikh.

Burdick slapped down a fax printout. "Lifted the dossier from MoD. Seems our General Fong is the hardest of the stonehearted. He was the on-scene commander at Tiananmen Square. I would say his appointment indicates Beijing means business. My guess is an invasion is imminent."

Shaikh looked up with a paternal smile. "Why, Jamie, that's analysis. I thought you knew. We are not in the analysis business. We only decipher the traffic."

Burdick pursed his lips. "Like hell we aren't. Angelfish and Toad couldn't find a rhino in the Royal Mews if it weren't for the decrypts we hand them on a platter."

"Quite right, Jamie. And this is gold, indeed. Has it been put on Platform yet?"

"Negative."

"Has SUSLO been notified?"

Burdick shook his head.

Faisal Shaikh smiled. "Excellent, Jamie. The timing is quite"— he searched for the right word—"sublime. I'll drop this into the PM's brief. You set it up for transmittal on Platform so we can get it out immediately after the brief. Attention to director, NSA. Copy to SUSLO here and SUKLO at Meade. Then subsequent distribution to the Canadians, Aussies, and Kiwis on approval of the director."

"Right."

"What else have we got?"

Burdick handed his superior some more papers. "Ivan can't seem to make up his mind on the Crimea. The defense ministry at the Kremlin keeps sending 'eyes only' messages to the theater commander to go in and restore order, but the local commander keeps balking. Asks for clarification of his mission. Complains his rules of engagement are unclear. MoD says the local CO was a battalion commander in Afghanistan and seems content to let the rebels and the Ukrainians shoot each other and keep his troops in the barracks. Nothing new on the fighting you couldn't catch on BBC last night."

Faisal drummed his fingers on the cherrywood desk as he

scanned the intercept. "Do the in-laws have this Crimean transcript?"

"Of course. It already came across on Platform. The transmissions were encrypted on Ivan's RSG-nine-seven-nine machine, your basic open book. The in-laws had it before us."

Faisal rested his chin on his hand and considered whether or not to place this particular kernel into the PM's brief. The Crimean flare-up was one of a half dozen rattling around the old FSU (Former Soviet Union). And bickering between the Kremlin HQ and military commanders in the field had become commonplace. The PM only had so much time for her briefing, and presumably she watched the BBC news. Faisal pondered for a few more seconds and decided to include it anyway. Perhaps she missed the BBC last night. "What else?"

Burdick plucked the Player's from his mouth and muttered, "Nothing spectacular. Our Nippon friends at the Ministry of International Trade and Industry have cabled their delegation at the GATT renegotiation talks in Singapore not to give an inch on rice-import quotas, but they know we can read their cables so the message could be a plant. . . . Oh, and the Don Juans say Paraguay's military seems to be on a slow boil and a coup may be in the offing. They don't seem to like the reforms implemented by the new president. Encrypted traffic between midlevel Army commanders has a conspiratorial ring to it. If the PM remembers where Paraguay is, perhaps she might be interested."

Faisal shot his subordinate a scornful glance. Jamie Burdick had that streak of intellectual arrogance that was difficult to rein in. He was the kind of man who didn't suffer fools gladly, if at all. Left unchecked, Burdick would commit a career-imploding blunder with his mouth one day, and the heir apparent to Shaikh's cryptanalysis division would be lost. Faisal couldn't afford to lose him. Better to rap his knuckles now. Hard. So he'd learn. "The PM knows damn good and well where Paraguay is, Jamie, and she is the constituency we work for. Don't forget that."

Chastened by his master, Jamie tossed his blond locks back and assumed the pose of a supplicant schoolboy. "Of course, Faisal. I withdraw that remark."

"Now then, anything else?"

Burdick cleared his throat. "A little gem for the last. An A-level, eyes-only message to all German ambassadors from the Foreign Ministry. The in-laws broke it almost in real time and put it on Platform about"—Jamie checked his watch—"seventeen minutes ago. The newly appointed German foreign minister is resigning today. Turns out he was an East German Stasi agent for most of his career."

"Hmmm," murmured Faisal. "Rumors have been in the press for weeks."

"Yes, but this is the first confirmation. The announcement will be made in two hours' time."

The fingers drummed again. "Very well, I will lead with the German's resignation, follow up with the Japanese GATT—with a disclaimer of course—then the Russians, Paraguay, and save China for the last."

"Nothing like a big finish."

"Exactly. Route the German data to the Foreign Office. Set me up to lunch with the China Clippers and Purple Gang, and tell them 'well done' on the Beijing intercept."

"Consider it done."

Faisal looked at the clock. Six minutes to go. "Now, Jamie, if you don't mind, a moment alone to collect my thoughts for the PM."

"Certainly, Faisal." And Jamie left via the private entrance to the hallway.

Once again, Faisal scanned the Russian, Japanese, Paraguayan, Chinese, and German messages in their original text, then he read the English translations. The translations were not done by people. Instead they were generated by computer, translated by the most advanced language recognition, translation, and text-editing software on planet Earth. There was nothing quite like it in the realm of the "outside world," but within the barbed-wire confines of Government Communications Headquarters it was commonplace. Yet Faisal didn't quite trust the machines completely, so he did his own comparison, taking time to make little notations on the English script until Geneviève appeared at the door.

It was time.

■ ■ ■

All of GCHQ's firepower was massed together every Tuesday and Friday morning on the fifth-floor conference room of the admin building. Here the senior division chiefs assembled to reveal their pearls of wisdom to the director of GCHQ, who would decide which of those pearls to polish and pass on to the PM.

The former director of GCHQ was Sir Reginald Bloom and a master of the PM brief. He would lay out the critical items for the Prime Minister, then finish off with a spicy intercept of, say, Raisa Gorbachev cursing out her dressmaker through her Zil limousine car phone, or a U.S. senator leaking juicy intelligence data to *Time* magazine on his cellular phone (yes, GCHQ spied on its friends; but then, so did the Americans. It is what spies do). But Sir Reginald was gone now, and a new regime was in power at Cheltenham.

Shaikh checked his watch as he hurried down the corridor to the conference room. Three minutes late. Not good. He hated not being prompt and was reaching for the door when he heard a whispered yell behind him.

"Faisal!"

Shaikh turned and saw Jamie Burdick—blond locks flapping, file in hand—jogging down the hallway toward him, his face radiant with excitement.

"What is it, Jamie? I'm late already."

Burdick slapped open the file and yanked out the script. Breathlessly he said, "This just came in from Platform. The algorithm you put together on the Tempest Two machine, damned if it didn't work!"

"You're joking," gasped Faisal as he seized the printout.

"No joke," said Burdick with the giddiness of a schoolboy. "You broke the bastard to hell and gone."

Shaikh shook his head in disbelief. "It is sometimes better to be lucky than good, Jamie. Stoneleigh is supposed to be here to talk about the Tempest Two machine today. Oh, my, this text . . . how delicious."

Burdick could hardly contain himself. "Beastly. Absolutely beastly. Go in there and saw the bastard off at the knees."

Shaikh clapped Burdick on the shoulder. "Now, now, Jamie, that's no way to speak of a colleague. Rest assured, however, I shall use a dull saw." A smile passed between the two men as Faisal pushed through the door.

The fifth-floor conference room had no windows. It was an interior chamber of the admin building dominated by a large, oval-shaped table. The lighting was dim, giving the room a conspiratorial air. Small lights in the ceiling illuminated the Queen's portrait at the head of the table, and similar lights shone down on other portraits along the walls. Again, little brass plates were engraved with names virtually unknown outside the barbed wire of GCHQ—Alastair Denniston, Brian Tovey, Peter Marychurch—all former directors of GCHQ and knights of the realm. Behind a partition in the room was a small kitchen where private luncheons were served to visiting officials from the Defense Ministry, the Foreign Office, the intelligence committees, and, on rare occasions, the PM or the royal family.

Four men were already seated when Shaikh arrived, but he was glad to see the chair at the head of the table was empty, indicating the punctual director was behind his own schedule. As Faisal took his chair, a tinny voice on the opposite side said, "A bit late, aren't we, laddie?"

Faisal forced himself to smile at Graeme Stoneleigh as he raised his hands in mock surrender and said, "Guilty."

Faisal remembered when he was an adolescent in school. There was always that little smart one in class who would tease, complain, whine, and take special care to point out your transgressions to the headmaster. He was an irritant to the entire class and would always take pleasure in your discomfort. Faisal Shaikh knew that Graeme Stoneleigh had been just such a child, for he was exactly that as an adult. About the same height as Faisal but chubby, Stoneleigh wore expensive clothes that never seemed to fit. He viewed the world through oversize, tortoiseshell glasses, while his thin, straw-colored hair was combed straight back with a generous helping of hair cream. Never without his public-school tie (Faisal guessed he wore it in the shower), Stoneleigh seized every opportunity to discreetly remind people he was a graduate of Eton, just like his father and grandfather. Faisal was not impressed.

On Stoneleigh's left was a gentleman who was thin, perhaps a shade toward the anorexic. Well over six feet in height, his slender body was encased in a dull blue suit, and he wore the regimental tie of the Royal Corps of Signals. His bespectacled face resembled an angelfish out of water, so of course his nickname was Angelfish, and he was the chief of J Division.

J Division had long been the favorite son inside Cheltenham, for this was the arm of GCHQ that monitored, processed, and analyzed signals intelligence of the Soviet bloc. Now it collected SIGINT on the remains of the Soviet bloc. When the Soviet empire imploded, J Division's stock had fallen with it, and the carte blanche days of budget largesse were over. Yet J Division still remained the largest division within GCHQ, and with good reason. The remnants of the Soviet bloc still possessed thousands of nuclear weapons, and such an arsenal required the attention of Cheltenham, however benign the old adversaries might seem at the moment.

Seated to the left of Angelfish was the man called Toad, who could've passed as the long-lost brother of Benito Mussolini. He had a thick chest, virtually no neck, and a hairless football of a head that was punctuated by black eyes and a Roman nose. His lips were thin and bloodless and cast in a perennial frown—like a toad. He was chief of K Division.

K Division dealt with "general SIGINT," which was all signals intelligence scooped up outside the old Soviet bloc. With the Russians taking a fall and China heating up, the stock in Toad's K Division was very high these days—very high, indeed—and it was continuing to rise.

On Faisal's left was Dickie Bartholomew. A born salesman, Bartholomew dressed with panache. He sported a double-breasted Italian suit, a Perry Ellis tie, a silk pocket square, and a gold chain on the wrist with DICKIE engraved upon it. He was in charge of Z Division.

In the highly classified organizational manual of GCHQ, Z Division was in charge of "assessments, requirements, and liaison." That meant Dickie's division looked after the care and feeding of the spy committees and cabinet departments that were GCHQ's customers. That's what his department did, but 80 percent of Dickie's personal time dealt with the care and feeding of the Americans, and insuring the in-laws were kept happy.

Dickie pulled out his tobacco pouch and began filling his trademark meerschaum pipe. Faisal followed suit, reaching into his jacket pocket to retrieve his onyx cigarette holder, his malachite Cartier lighter, and gold cigarette case. He lit the tip of his latakian cigarette as he held the onyx holder underhanded, Russian style— a habit he'd picked up during his posting to Moscow.

The conference room door opened and in walked the director of Government Communications Headquarters, Sir Vivian Mittleditch, all nineteen stone of him, followed by his eellike male secretary, Anthony Beekman. Sir Vivian was wearing a somber black suit, and Faisal thought it gave him the appearance of a dirigible in mourning. When the director sat down at the head of the table, his chair seemed to groan, and Faisal could've sworn the room tilted slightly in that direction.

Beekman was the director's éminence grise, who took copious notes during the PM's brief.

Sir Vivian Mittleditch had arrived at GCHQ twenty-three months ago, and in that period Faisal estimated his own private contact with him was less than two hours. Mittleditch had come from the defense industry, the former managing director of a firm that produced landing-gear components. Billed as a financial wizard, he'd contributed mightily to Tory causes for years before selling his company to British Aerospace for a fortune. A knighthood had followed, and then the appointment as director of GCHQ.

Faisal found Sir Vivian impossible to read. The little communication that passed between them came at these briefings and through written memoranda. He seemed to manage by noninvolvement. In face-to-face sessions Mittleditch would simply sit there, like a sea lion on the beach, wrapped in massive layers of blubber that made his unremarkable face impenetrable. Faisal had often looked for Sir Vivian's chin, but could find none. His neck simply extended up in a column to a bald head, where his thick-lidded eyes remained half-closed.

Impenetrable.

So here they were, the inner sanctum of Her Majesty's royal eavesdroppers. Public servants who scanned the globe for secret communications vital to the defense of the realm. The information harvested by the massive institution below them, and the fruits of the special American relationship, all percolated up the chain of command to this meeting so they could lay their pearls of wisdom before the director.

Sir Vivian nodded to Beekman, who pointed his pen at Angel-fish, and the PM's brief was under way.

The bulk of the prime minister's brief went through on the nod, offering little more than amplification of BBC newscasts the previous evening. But when Faisal's turn came to discuss China, the attention level around the table went up noticeably. He recapped the message announcing the appointment of General Fong as the new theater commander on the Vietnamese border, then he concluded his remarks with, "I would say the situation has become very grave. General Fong's appointment may portend that an invasion is likely, if not imminent."

"Confirmation, old boy?"

Faisal was the picture of innocence as he turned to Dickie Bartholomew. "I don't believe the in-laws have broken this one yet, Dickie."

Bartholomew rapidly wrote down the particulars in his notebook. He would spring this gem on the American liaison officer at lunch. There was nothing he liked better than spreading his feathers like a horny peacock in front of the in-laws. It earned their respect.

Faisal continued, "We have a transcript of the message queued up on Platform and are prepared to transmit to Meade on the director's approval."

"No."

Every head turned. Sir Vivian had spoken and Faisal was

stunned. He couldn't understand why Mittleditch would stop the transmittal of such a gem to the in-laws.

"No," he repeated. "Do not place it on Platform until after I have briefed the prime minister."

Beekman scribbled in a frenzy.

Score one for the codebreakers! thought Faisal. Apparently Sir Vivian knew a true gem after all.

"Then send it eyes only, director of NSA."

Even better, thought Faisal. *Close it now. Go out a winner.* "I have nothing further to submit for the prime minister."

Sir Vivian nodded and his countenance changed. His face became a bit energized, perhaps even benevolent, as he turned his head toward Graeme Stoneleigh and graced him with a smile. "Now then, Graeme," he said in a singsong voice, "what do you have for me?"

Graeme Stoneleigh was the head of L Division, the branch of GCHQ responsible for communications security for the British government. To insure that Foreign Office cables, military orders, Special Branch terrorist alerts, submarine navigation orders, and the like were impervious to eavesdropping from foreign codebreakers, L Division had been created. It was L's responsibility to design, oversee manufacture, distribute, and monitor cryptographic and secure voice/data equipment for the military and civilian branches of government. It was a heavy responsibility, both in the criticality of its mission and the size of its cost; for to put a cryptographic machine into service, on a worldwide basis, was a vastly expensive process.

For years, Graeme Stoneleigh had been a minor midlevel official in the communications security (COMSEC) L Division. Then the new director had taken over twenty-three months ago, and for some unfathomable reason he'd taken a shine to Stoneleigh—sponsored him, mentored him, promoted him. Even forced the old chief of COMSEC into early retirement to make a place for Stoneleigh at the senior level. It was puzzling.

Stoneleigh assumed a supplicant posture and began. "Sir Vivian, we at L Division are pleased to report our upgraded Tempest Two encryption machine is ready for manufacture and field deployment. Testing is virtually complete, and"—a smirk here—"despite the best efforts of our codebreakers, the machine has remained impregnable. The vendor's revised contract is on my desk ready for your signature. I am delighted to report that upgrading the old Tempest One machines to Tempest Two will save Her Majesty's government some sixty million pounds in procurement costs while sacrificing nothing in communications security." Stoneleigh beamed. Sir Vivian beamed. It was a win-win for them both.

Faisal sensed there was some sort of chemistry between the two men that went beyond the professional, and it made Faisal uncomfortable. Nevertheless, he ignored his discomfort and turned his attention to the issue at hand.

The Tempest I machine had been the high-level encryption workhorse for Her Majesty's government for a dozen years. It could be found in British embassies abroad, on Royal Navy ships at sea, at regimental headquarters of the British Army, at various ministries in Whitehall, and in the communications complex of No. 10 Downing Street. A gray, boxlike object about the size of two car batteries strapped together, the Tempest I was state-of-the-art when it came on line over a decade ago. It had kept the government's Teletype traffic secure for years, remaining impervious even to the Americans' attempts to break it. But as the science of cryptanalysis and the power of computers continued to advance, the Tempest I became vulnerable. To the point that the previous GCHQ director, Sir Reginald Bloom, had ordered a new machine designed, developed, and prototyped. This new machine was codenamed Bloodstone, and Faisal and his department had found the damned thing utterly impregnable. The Americans took a shot at cracking the Bloodstone prototype, and they, too, ran into a brick wall. The machine simply could not be beaten. After a half dozen prototypes were built and tested, it was set to go into production. But then Sir Vivian arrived on the scene, and as the Berlin Wall crumbled and the Red Menace retreated from Europe, a costly new encryption machine held less appeal.

Yet in spite of the Soviet Union's crumbling, Faisal thought the new Bloodstone machine absolutely essential to protect Her Majesty's communications, regardless of the prevailing political climate. Faisal hoped Sir Vivian would follow Sir Reginald's lead and deploy Bloodstone, but instead the new director did two things. First, he made Graeme Stoneleigh chief of the COMSEC L Division. Then he let it be known all division chiefs would be judged by their ability to "control costs." In response to the new Holy Grail of cost cutting, Graeme Stoneleigh hatched a scheme to retrofit the old Tempest I machines with a new internal-logic circuit board, at a quarter of the cost of the new Bloodstone program. Sir Vivian had bought the idea lock, stock, and semiconductors; and much to Faisal's chagrin, his codebreaking H Division had been unable to break the revised logic of the Tempest II machine. But instinctively, Faisal knew the Tempest II was a rotten idea, so he took over the testing personally. He worked himself and his Purple Gang to exhaustion trying to defeat it, but ultimately Faisal had to admit they were beaten and couldn't crack it . . . until a few minutes ago, when Jamie Burdick had caught him in the hall. It was with shameful relish that Faisal now cleared his throat and said, "I'm afraid you may want to rethink the deployment of the Tempest Two, Graeme."

Stoneleigh failed to soften the tone of his voice as he replied, "Oh, and why is that, Shaikh?"

Faisal was the very picture of a sympathetic colleague. "Because my division broke it earlier this morning."

Stoneleigh was raising his teacup to his lips when Faisal's words froze him in place, as if he'd looked upon the face of Medusa. There were several moments of silence, with no sound in the room but the low hum of the central heating. Cup suspended, Stoneleigh emitted a barely audible, "What?"

"I said my division broke your Tempest Two machine this morning."

The silence continued to hang over the table, screaming at Stoneleigh for a response. Slowly he lowered his teacup, and there was an abrasive clatter as he fumbled to get the base of the cup into the recessed circle of the saucer. Stoneleigh was now like a butterfly impaled on a hatpin. His new stature at GCHQ, indeed his very career, might hang in the balance at this moment. His mind raced, searching for some way to blot out the simple statement that his Tempest II machine had been "broken." In a voice that was part whisper, part whimper, he said, "You're bluffing."

Casually, Faisal pushed the file across to Stoneleigh and in a friendly tone replied, "My people attacked the simulated text provided by your COMSEC people. There are some of the results."

Stoneleigh grabbed the file and extracted the printout. He held the paper tightly, as if trying to asphyxiate the evidence. But then he read the deciphered text, and Faisal saw his grip loosen as his face turned a deathly, ghostly white. Stoneleigh became paralyzed as Faisal waited for a response. As the room waited for a response. As Sir Vivian waited for a response.

In his sympathetic voice, Faisal prodded, "I think you will agree, Graeme, that we should shelve the Tempest Two idea and move on to the manufacture and deployment of the Bloodstone machine."

Stoneleigh robotically closed the file and slid it across to Faisal. More silence ensued until the chief of COMSEC choked up a guttural reply. "In view of this . . . this development . . . I feel my division should . . . reassess the deployment of the Tempest Two."

Sir Vivian fixed his pet with the harshest glare, but Stoneleigh's ghostly gaze remained on Faisal, his eyes transmitting the unspoken plea: *Bury the file. Bury it deep. Name your price, but bury it in the bowels of the earth. Please.*

The silence remained until Beekman asked, "Do you have anything further?"

Stoneleigh's head gave a minute shake.

"Very well," said Beekman crisply. "Sir Vivian, we must get on to your meeting with the Northern Ireland Working Group before we depart for Number Ten Downing Street."

The director of GCHQ said nothing. He only glared at Stoneleigh again, then hefted his girth from the leather chair and lumbered out the door. No one else in the conference room was part of the Northern Ireland Working Group—that was a select division of its own within GCHQ—so they departed leisurely. Angelfish and Toad stood, gathered their papers, and exited out the far door, while Faisal and Dickie Bartholomew closed their briefcases and left through the near exit. As the door was swinging shut, Faisal caught a glimpse of Graeme Stoneleigh staring at him from behind those tortoiseshell glasses with a look of blind rage.

As they walked toward the lift, a strong arm came across Faisal's shoulders, and Dickie Bartholomew's silken voice said, "Our friend, Mr. Stoneleigh, looked a man who's been castrated without anesthetic. What exactly did you do to that bugger?"

Faisal exhaled a cloud of gray smoke and queried, "Just between us?"

Bartholomew had a crooked smile of perfectly straight teeth. "But of course, old boy. Dickie knows how to keep his trap shut."

Which was true, mused Faisal as he reached into his briefcase and handed the file to Bartholomew.

Greedily, Dickie took the Tempest II test message and scanned it. It was a limerick. Just a simple limerick typed over and over. And it must have captured some of the COMSEC Division's feelings about the director of GCHQ:

> Sir Vivian's cheeks are pretty and pink,
>> Not much upstairs 'tween the ears, we think,
> He sits on his duffy,
>> His eyes oh, so puffy,
> Clouded by sins of excessive drink.

Bartholomew smiled as he reread the text. "My, my, I'd no idea we had such literati in our COMSEC Division."

But Faisal didn't hear him—his mind was still occupied with the searing rage he'd seen in the eyes of Graeme Stoncleigh.

Then the lift came and he plucked the file from Dickie's grasp.

CHAPTER TWO

For the uninitiated, which includes most everyone beyond the barbed wire, it is difficult to grasp the size and scope of the enterprise known as Government Communications Headquarters. Nestled in the sleepy town of Cheltenham in the Cotswolds region of Gloucestershire, the barbed-wire enclave of GCHQ is merely the head of an octopus whose tentacles stretch around the globe, under the sea, and into outer space to intercept a vast cauldron of electronic signals. On a given day the prodigious talents of GCHQ and the American National Security Agency will snag low-frequency submarine communications from Polyarny, missile telemetry over Kazakhstan, OPEC ministers' cellular phone calls in Dubai, Swiss-bank wire transfers, radio chatter of Indian fighter pilots, facsimiles of medical records on Japanese cabinet ministers, encrypted German Foreign Ministry cables, and so on and so on. Such sensitive communiqués are intercepted at remote venues, such as Dhekelia, Cyprus; the Seychelles; Ascension Island; and Pine Gap, Australia. Then the signals are sorted, collated, deciphered, translated, analyzed, and finally routed to the end consumer in Whitehall. To execute this massive undertaking, GCHQ employs a population of about six thousand electrical engineers, software designers, experts in signals processing, cryptanalysts, linguists, radar and telemetry analysts, plus all the clerks, typists, secretaries, administrators, janitors, and groundskeepers that go hand in glove with an institution of such magnitude.

Yet even GCHQ was dwarfed by the mammoth National Security Agency of the Americans, or the "in-laws" as they are known at Cheltenham. The NSA was perhaps ten times the size of GCHQ in terms of payroll, budget, and plain gut-level horsepower. For an investment of £500 million a year to keep GCHQ operating, the British government gained access to all—well, almost all—of the signals intelligence captured by the giant American spy machine. There are secret agreements in place between the two governments and with the Australians, Canadians, and New Zealanders, outlining each party's responsibilities and what SIGINT would be shared among them. Britain's assets in this agreement were its remote pieces of real estate, such as Ascension Island in the South Atlantic, Cyprus, or Little Sai Wan in Hong Kong, which were the remnants of a dismembered empire. At each locale was a barbed-wire enclave that bristled with antennae of every size and description, pulling in signals from around the globe.

Pound for pound, GCHQ could match the Americans, but the sheer scope of NSA's reach, manpower, and technical prowess were so overwhelming that the mission of maintaining the "special relationship" with the in-laws was paramount. And through ups and downs, highs and lows, storms and tides, scandals and schisms, this special Anglo-American relationship remained intact. To the point that the bond between GCHQ and NSA was much stronger than with other agencies of their own governments. GCHQ and NSA swapped personnel freely, engaged in joint research programs, exchanged senior-level experts and envoys, and cross-fertilized each other to a remarkable degree. Indeed, at jointly operated field stations the lines of authority were, at best, blurred.

The intelligence harvest they shared was linked together in a secure worldwide satellite network called Platform, and so awesome was their joint power it would be difficult for Her Majesty's taxpayer to fathom. Case in point: say GCHQ and NSA had made the communiqués of a certain Russian Army commander on the Sino-Russian border a high priority. Say the Russian general sends an encrypted signal to the Defense Ministry in the Kremlin. After reaching Red Square, however, the signal does not stop. It continues to bounce off the ionosphere until it's snagged at Ascension

Island. There the signal would be automatically digitized, analyzed by computer, and sent to Cheltenham, where it would be screened by the extraordinary data-processing power found in the basement of the admin building. Automatically, the computer would compare the signal to historical "traps" in the data archives and ascertain the type of encryption device used. The message might be attacked then and there by GCHQ's codebreaking software, or, if required, routed via Platform to the NSA's basement at Fort Meade, Maryland. Here it would be compared to historical signals to ascertain if a broken "key" was already on file that could break the cipher. Assuming this was the case, the broken message would then be processed through a simultaneous translator and routed back to Cheltenham via Platform, where it might be flagged on a codebreaker's video screen for examination or automatically converted to hard copy via a high-speed laser printer. So advanced was the state of the art within the barbed wire of GCHQ and Fort Meade that the interception, analysis, transmittal across half the globe, decryption, and printout of the Russian general's message could take place in the time it took you to read this page. Indeed, the commander's message might be rolling out of the laser printer at Cheltenham before it was dropped into the IN basket of the proper addressee at the Kremlin. However, after being processed by such exotic, hypersecret technology, the intelligence analyst might experience a big letdown, because the decrypted message could be a complaint by the lonely Russian general that his shipment of vodka from Moscow was two weeks late.

But not always. Sometimes there were messages of vital importance to the security of Her Majesty's realm, be it SIGINT related to the Falklands conflict or the Persian Gulf War.

Faisal Shaikh rose from his evening prayers and stepped to the window of his fourth-floor office, taking a moment to ensure his waistcoat was straightened properly. He was a man who cared about his clothes and took pains not to rumple them. It was late Friday afternoon, already dusk, and from his office window he could see the GCHQ staff begin their exodus toward hearth and home. Since Faisal had no family to go home to, this part of the day was the interlude he used to reset his internal compass. Soon an evening meal of ghastly food would be brought up from the canteen and placed on his desk. Then the parking lot would empty, leaving only his Jaguar Sovereign and the cars of the night-watch staff.

Shaikh wore two hats within GCHQ. He was administrative head of the codebreaking H Division, as well as chief cryptanalyst. Therefore in one and the same man Faisal was the rarest of species—a managerial and technical wizard rolled into a single soul. Not many of his cloth could use both hemispheres of the brain to their fullest. But Faisal did, and that peculiar talent gave him an edge in career firepower. An edge that had catapulted him over his peers. Yet no one in H Division seemed to mind. There was really no one to match his skill in the arcane science of cryptology, or his talent for bending GCHQ's ponderous bureaucracy to his will. His days were taken up by the tedious administrative chores of his management post: winnowing through his IN box, and putting a bit of stick about when the need arose. But once the normal workday came to a close, he would relax, take off his shoes, fill his cup with Darjeeling tea, and shift mental gears from paper shuffler–manager to technical genius. The tea acted as a kind of lubricant, allowing him to refocus his Athenian powers on the complex science and seductive art of codebreaking (also known by the technical term of cryptanalysis).

Faisal returned to his desk and pushed aside the administrative prattle, then pulled a stack of technical papers toward him. On top was an article on the development of holographic memory devices for computers. Quickly he scanned it, for in this business one had to keep up with the cutting edge of technology. The next one was a monograph that dealt with the Chor-Rivest knapsack cryptosystem, and he scanned that as well before placing it aside. The following piece was an announcement about the upcoming Eurocrypt Society convention in Lyons. He was looking forward to that, for he would be presenting a paper on elliptical-curve cryptosystems. He marked his calendar accordingly. Next on the pile was the latest issue of *Cryptologia*—a rare scholarly journal devoted to the science and history of codebreaking. With relish he thumbed through its pages before selecting the article "Transposition Ciphers With Pseudo-Random Shuffling." He had just started to read when . . .

"I'm calling it a day, Faisal. See you on Monday."

Faisal looked up to see a weary-faced Jamie Burdick at the door. He graced his understudy with a paternal smile and said, "Off to the home fires? And how is our little Nigel doing?"

Burdick barked a laugh. "Like an armored tank on winter maneuvers. I had no idea a three-year-old could cause so much property damage. I was fixing the bloody drainpipe last night when he came up behind me and lifted the hammer out of my tool kit. The next thing I know there's a thumping sound in the stairwell, and, well . . ."

Laughing, Faisal said, "I see."

Burdick shook his head, then tossed a file on his superior's desk and pointed. "This surfaced in the hopper last week. The Riding Hoods and Purple Gang broke their knuckles on it and thought you might like to take a shot."

During his tenure as chief of H Division, Faisal had assembled teams of cryptanalysts to tackle different "flavors" of message traffic, according to their country of origin. The China Clippers focused on the People's Republic and Taiwan. The Red Riding Hoods focused on what used to be the Soviet Bloc, while the Don Juans were Latin America, the Arabian Knights were the Arab countries, and the codebreakers specializing in the dark continent were known as the Zulu Spears. Each team was collectively familiar with the languages, ciphering equipment, message formatting (very important), syntax, nuances, and other "cribs" related to the message traffic they were trying to break. But above the country teams was the Purple Gang—a select group of cryptanalysts (which sometimes included visiting Americans) that Faisal had assembled to attack ciphers that were singularly difficult or juicy or important, or all three.

The "hopper" was a repository for all encrypted signals that were intercepted but without an on-line key to break them. The hopper was always brimming because encryption keys changed frequently, some keys were unbreakable, and many simply did not warrant the attention of GCHQ (a flash message from the Kremlin to its London embassy always generated more scrutiny than an encrypted message from Mauritania to its envoy in Bombay).

"Found it in the hopper, you say?" asked Faisal as he reached for the file.

"Right. The S and T fix says it came out of the Siberian Strategic Rocket Force base at Aykhal. The Hoods say it's unlike anything they've seen before."

Faisal thumbed through the file and examined the encryption format. "Hmm. Seven-letter code groups. That's unusual."

"Isn't it? Ivan has never used a format like that before."

Faisal nodded, then asked, "Sequence?"

"Twelve messages all together. Eight originating in Aykhal. Four replies from Moscow. It's in the file, but the spacing was tight early on, then it spread out."

"Collateral traffic?"

"That's even stranger. Angelfish's division says security tightened up around the rocket base during the early transmissions, then there was a commo blackout for seventy-two hours, except for the traffic in that file. Aykhal is remote and relies on a Raduga satellite for its primary commo link with Moscow. It has a microwave relay for backup. Angelfish said the Americans had both links covered by Magnum and they both dried up."

Faisal thumbed through the file. "Then how were these transmitted if not on satellite or microwave?"

"That's the queer thing. They were snagged at Ascension on high-freq radio."

"Hmm," mumbled Faisal as he held his onyx cigarette holder. "That is odd. The HF radio must be a secondary backup system. Curious. Very well, I'll have a look at it tomorrow."

"No chess tourneys this weekend?" queried Burdick.

Faisal leaned back in his leather chair and stretched again. "No, not this time around. No significant competition. Next month I'm going to Barcelona. I may have a chance to square off against that young Czech phenomenon. Teenage girl named Polgar. Youngest grandmaster in years. But don't keep your young cyclone waiting, Jamie. Go home."

"Right," came the reply, and with a raised hand his understudy was gone.

As he watched Jamie disappear toward home and family, Faisal was struck by a pang of envy.

He lived in the fashionable area of Battledown Estates, which overlooked Cheltenham from the eastern hills. In this area the homes were imposing, the grounds and gardens immaculate, and the pace of life slow, sleepy, and peaceful. Faisal lived in a four-bedroom, two-story, Tudor-style home on Stanley Road. It was absurdly large for a single man like himself who rarely entertained, but he drew solace from the fact it was appointed strictly to his tastes. The living and dining areas were large formal rooms, which he only used for the rare GCHQ social functions he hosted. The rest of the house was functionally generic—bedrooms, bathrooms, etc.—except for two chambers that gave him particular pleasure. One was a large dressing room where his considerable wardrobe was kept in paneled closets, while the other was his library/study. He had knocked out the walls of a bedroom and combined the space with the den to make one large chamber that functioned as a retreat within a retreat. It was paneled in beachwood, and the bookshelves were filled with tomes on cryptology, history, biography, mathematics, chess, and the stock market.

Faisal had been married once. It was a relationship that might have made an enjoyable weekend at the Chewton Glen Hotel, but instead had ground through seven long years of bitterness. And it was during those seven years his career at GCHQ shifted into afterburner. As his duties made more and more demands on his time, he gave the time willingly to avoid the more painful aspects of going home. Finally Margaret (that was her name) had left. Returned to her native Glasgow, leaving Faisal to his three remaining passions: cryptology, chess, and the financial markets. At forty-seven, he was leading a monastic life and starting to realize how passionless his passions had become.

That Saturday Faisal had slept late, almost to noon, which was late even for him. Upon rising, he pulled on a warm-up suit and walked (he didn't jog) to the bottom of Harp Hill. Then he climbed back up in the brisk November air. Upon returning to his home he collected the *London Times* from the doorstep and went inside. During the week his housekeeper, Mrs. Wheatland, prepared his muffins and tea before he departed for work at eleven A.M. But on the weekends, Faisal had to fend for himself. He put the water on to boil and placed the muffins in the oven, then he entered the marble-lined bathroom to shave and shower. Once cleansed, he threw on a terry-cloth bathrobe and returned to the breakfast room to eat and quickly scan the *Times*. Then he retired to his dressing room.

With studied precision he draped the bathrobe on a hook and opened one of the paneled closets. Carefully he withdrew a cream-colored *kurta*, a garment native to Pakistan that is a kind of caftan worn over slacks called *shalwar*. Faisal had about a dozen *kurtas* and *shalwars*, all fashioned by his tailor from imported Egyptian cotton. When he wanted to swath his body in pure comfort so his mind would not be distracted, he would don the *kurta* and *shalwar* and slide his feet into a pair of leather slippers that were hand-crafted by Lobb's bootmaker in London.

He retired downstairs to his library/study, where he walked across the Herez Persian rug to the walnut desk set into the curve of a giant bay window. In the spring and summer the window provided a lovely view of the courtyard and garden, but on this November day the grounds were brown and barren. Faisal flicked on his computer atop the credenza, and with rapid familiarity he commanded his modem to dial up and retrieve Friday's closing share prices on the companies he was tracking. He found that Midland Pharmaceuticals had moved out of the price parameters he'd set for his broker. He called up his electronic mailbox to ensure his personal program-trading instructions had been carried out.

They had; and he calculated he would clear a tidy profit of thirty-eight hundred pounds on the transaction.

Faisal bettered his own salary each year from his share plays. He enjoyed the stock market, and his prudent investments had provided this opulent house, the clothes, the Sovereign, and other comforts that were beyond the pale of a civil servant's remuneration.

His financial transaction completed, Faisal picked up the speech-scrambler telephone and called the watch officer at the GCHQ situation desk. Had anything changed on the Chinese-Vietnamese situation? Negative. He rang off and stretched, then turned his attention to his agenda for this Saturday.

He stepped to the fireplace and fired up the logs with a flick of the gas starter, then pulled back a panel of simulated books that revealed an electronic safe. He punched in a code on a keypad, and with a hum and a click the door opened. He withdrew the file Jamie Burdick had given him the day before—the one with the intriguing cipher from Siberia. After the Geoffrey Prime spy scandal at GCHQ years ago, staff were forbidden to take work papers home. But with his senior position Faisal had clearance to do so.

The file had a red, diagonal stripe across the cover, and in black letters was the admonition:

MOST SECRET:

IMPROPER DISCLOSURE OF THE CONTENTS OF THIS FILE TO

UNAUTHORIZED PERSONS IS A CRIMINAL OFFENSE SUBJECT

TO PROSECUTION UNDER THE OFFICIAL SECRETS ACT

After twenty years of handling such files, the warnings had a muted impact on Faisal. Security was a necessary inconvenience that was always underfoot.

At one corner of the massive library, past the chesterfield sofa that faced the windows, was a leather recliner. On one side of the recliner was a coffee table with reading lamp, and on the other side was something that could only be described as a monstrosity.

It was a giant hookah waterpipe made of ornate glass, with double smoking tubes. Faisal had used the pipe innumerable times as he reclined in this corner of his study for hours, focusing his intellectual powers on the mysteries of cryptanalysis. He carried the file to the recliner and snapped on the reading lamp as he leaned back and made himself comfortable.

Opening the folder, he recapped what he knew about the seven-letter cipher. There were twelve messages altogether, and he re-examined the S & T (traffic analysis) Division's report on each one. Using sophisticated sensors, the S & T Division could locate the source of an emission. They had determined eight of the messages had originated at the Strategic Rocket Forces base outside the town of Aykhal in Siberia. The base was slated for closure, and its missiles were to be destroyed under the new strategic arms treaty between the Russians and Americans. Four of the messages had originated from Moscow. The Greenwich mean time, date, latitude and longitude coordinates, and the radio frequency of each message was printed at the top of each intercept. Faisal arranged the messages in the order of transmission, and the sequence was Aykhal-Aykhal-Aykhal-Moscow-Aykhal-Aykhal-Moscow-Moscow-Aykhal-Aykhal-Moscow-Aykhal. All of the messages were brief, except for the next-to-last transmission from Aykhal, which ran for three pages. Faisal looked at the Greenwich mean time notations, then did some mental time-zone computations. He figured these messages went back and forth between 1:39 A.M. and 5:42 A.M. Aykhal time. That seemed odd, but not improbable if it was military communication. The first three transmissions out of Aykhal were tightly spaced together, only minutes apart, while the first reply from Moscow was brief. An acknowledgment perhaps? Then the timing grew successively longer to the final transmission.

What Faisal was doing, in essence, was examining the envelope before he tried to steam it open. An envelope can yield surprising information about the person who sent it. What kind of stationery was it? Expensive? Cheap? Printed letterhead? What about the postmark? What was the date and location? The handwriting? Was it a man or a woman? A trace of perfume perhaps?

Having studied the nuances of the "envelope," Faisal now

turned his attention to the messages themselves, and this is what intrigued him the most. They were arranged in seven-character cipher groups. Seven-letter groups were not unheard of. The Swedes used such a format several years ago, as did the Taiwanese, the Italians, and the Israelis, and even the Bloodstone prototype was based on a seven-character format. But no known Soviet encryption machine generated seven-letter groups. At least, not until now. This made Faisal wonder if a new type of encryption device was in service.

He took a pad and pencil from the coffee table, fired up the hookah, and began to focus his Athenian powers on the symbology in front of him. Unlike codebreakers of old, Faisal would not crank out possible solutions by hand. The computer would do that. Modern codebreakers designed mathematical and statistical software programs, or algorithms, to "attack" the encrypted texts.

With the onset of eventide the library grew dim, and smoke swirled over Faisal Shaikh's angular features like a highland mist caressing the face of a craggy cliff.

Jamie Burdick held his morning cup of coffee with one hand and some staff papers in the other as he made his way down the hall toward the office of his superior. Burdick was an early riser, which seemed to dovetail with the more nocturnal habits of his boss, Dr. Shaikh. GCHQ never really slept, and their overlapping schedules kept, as the Americans were fond of saying, "the bases covered" for fifteen of twenty-four hours each workday. It was 8:17 A.M. on Monday morning, several hours yet before Faisal would appear with his brimming briefcase. Burdick wished Faisal would take more time off. Take up fishing. Play croquet. Find a girlfriend. Or do *something* that would make him a little less obsessive about his profession. His chess and financial wizardry helped, but they weren't enough. Burdick had to turn himself into a pretzel day after day to try to match, measure for measure, a genius who had no family responsibilities. Still, Faisal was an incredible fellow to work for. Burdick had learned more about higher mathematics in six months under Faisal Shaikh than he had in four years at Cambridge. Yes, to keep pace with his boss was a lesson in high-pressure dynamics. That's why Burdick treasured his mornings. It allowed him time to catch up before the Master of the Game appeared.

Geneviève Monson had already arrived. For Burdick, it was too early in the day to cross swords with the white-haired battle-ax so he used his hard-earned privilege of access through the private entrance. Stepping inside, he stopped dead in his tracks. Burdick rechecked his watch, then looked up and said, "Faisal? What are you doing here? It's not even half-past eight."

Faisal turned away from the credenza, the whites of his eyes resembling a Michelin road map of the Midlands. Faisal raised his arms in a tired stretch and replied, "I worked over the weekend on an algorithm for that cipher you gave me Friday evening. Thought I'd come in early and get some time on the Paradox computer."

"Any luck?"

Faisal shrugged. "Not so far, but it's early days yet."

Burdick deposited his load of paper in the IN box, then cradled his coffee cup as he sat down on the desk. "Never saw a seven-letter cipher group in all my days of working with the Red Menace," mumbled Burdick as he yanked down his worsted tie and unbuttoned the collar of his plaid shirt. "Think we've got something new?"

Faisal was contemplative as he reached for his tea and mulled over Jamie's question. "Possibly," he murmured between sips. "Probably . . . but there's something else that puzzles me."

"What's that?"

Faisal stared at the computer screen but did not see the characters, for his mind was focused on a different dimension of the problem. He was silent, and Burdick didn't interrupt him as he entered one of his "séance" modes for perhaps twenty seconds. Finally, Faisal said, "Why, Jamie? Why was this traffic transmitted out of a Strategic Rocket Force base over a high-frequency radio, when we know each SRF installation has its own satellite and microwave links with the Defense Ministry in Moscow?"

Burdick shrugged as he plucked a packet of Player's from his shirt pocket. "Maybe they were afraid the satellite wasn't secure. Figured we were wired into that link."

Faisal shook his head. "But even if we had the satellite link covered, which we did, sending an encrypted signal over the air via radio is just as likely to be snagged. And the signal wasn't hopped or wrapped or anything. It came out clean. Makes no sense at all."

"How did we snag this one? Slipped my mind."

"Ascension. And the time of the transmittals. From one to six in the morning, local time. That's an odd way to debut a new encryption machine, wouldn't you say? One in the A.M., in the icebox of Siberia."

Burdick pursed his lips. "Maybe so. Let's break the bugger and see what we've got. Then maybe the altar boys or the in-laws can bring things into focus for us."

"Perhaps so, but in order to do that I'm going to require more traffic to work with than I've got here."

"Hmm. Perhaps this machine's been around longer than we suspect. Maybe Angelfish would do a historical search on the tapes . . . if you ask him nice."

"Umm. Perhaps." Faisal's gaze returned to the screen and the séance veil came down again, as if he were communing with someone in another dimension about the mystic patterns on the screen. To bring him back to current space and time, Burdick asked, "So, how are you attacking this one?"

Faisal sighed. "The Red Riding Hoods and Purple Gang ran the standard gambits with some Boolean twists, but I decided to try a chaotic algorithm on a random-shifting matrix. I've run it through Paradox at Meade, but the first three passes came up trash." He paused and sighed again. "But like I said, it's early days yet. Perhaps you're right about having Angelfish do a search. Maybe it's been out there for a time and we've just missed it until now."

Burdick smiled knowingly. He could tell when his boss had the bit between his teeth and wouldn't let go until he'd cracked the puzzle. He'd seen it before. A regular bullterrier. Long nights. Chain smokes. Tea by the bucket until it was broken.

"I was wondering," said Faisal wistfully, "if maybe there was a shift in the groupings that—"

"Ahem."

Faisal and Burdick turned to see Geneviève Monson, all five feet by five feet of her, standing in the doorway in a pink wool suit.

"Yes, Geneviève?" queried Faisal.

Imperious as always, Geneviève folded her hands in front of her pink midriff and announced, "I thought you two gentlemen would like to know. We just had a departmental flash from J Division. You'll see it on BBC tonight, no doubt, but as you two like to get a jump on things, I thought I would pass it on straightaway."

Burdick crossed his own arms, trying to match her imperious air. Without success. "And what flash message is that, *Miss* Monson?" He always emphasized the *Miss* to point out the fact no man would have her.

But Geneviève remained unruffled and said, "Chinese troops have just invaded Vietnam."

CHAPTER ✛ THREE

Ah, oil.

Since economics, not ideology, drove governments these days, a basic truth had evolved that Vietnam had won her wars but lost the peace. Legions of boat people took to the sea, fueled by the utter despair of their economic lot; and Western capital shied away from the small, backward country that had brought the American superpower to its knees. Vietnam had languished—until something spectacular was discovered. An oil field, bigger than the Prudhoe Bay find on Alaska's North Slope, was discovered straddling the Chinese-Vietnamese border, with about 90 percent of the reserves resting on the Vietnamese side. The Vietnamese latched onto this extraordinary find as the engine that would, at long last, drive the transformation of their economy. They would export oil. Perhaps join OPEC. Finally join the Community of Nations.

Meanwhile, the Chinese economy was overheating, just as their demand for fossil fuels was outstripping supply. The massive oil find could only make them salivate. Vietnam had barely sunk their first production well in the Lao Cai field when the Chinese started rattling their sabres about the theft of "their" oil. If this sounded like a replay of the Iraqi-Kuwaiti dispute over the Ramallah oil field that led to the Persian Gulf War, it was.

Chinese troops had massed on the Vietnamese border and the U.N. decried the provocative action—but there was precious little it could do because China had a veto in the Security Council. The U.S. response was muted, as with Tiananmen Square, because the Americans didn't want to lose their listening posts in China, they didn't like Vietnam anyway, and kicking Iraq out of Kuwait was a lot different than going toe-to-toe with a billion Chinese. But Britain was having great angst over the oil-field dispute because the Royal Crown Colony of Hong Kong was coming under the People's Republic flag in a short time. Therefore GCHQ was turning its electronic ears on the Orient to follow closely the troop movements of Beijing and Hanoi.

Faisal Shaikh and Jamie Burdick sat in the backseat of the Vauxhall estate wagon as it pulled away from Victoria Station.

When the news of the Chinese invasion flashed through GCHQ, the institution immediately began turning its resources toward the conflict, including Faisal Shaikh's cryptanalytic H Division. He had put the mysterious cipher from Aykhal on the shelf and immediately took personal charge of his China Clippers team as they focused on encrypted traffic emanating from the war zone. The Little Sai Wan listening post in Hong Kong had become even more critical because the Chinese had seized the American listening posts at Quitai and Korla along the Russian border.

So much for the China card.

After a short drive along the Thames, the chauffeur wheeled the Vauxhall down a ramp that emptied into a basement parking garage. The garage lay beneath a gleaming new edifice of green glass and honey-colored stone that was built at a cost to the British taxpayer of £200 million. This was Thames House, the new headquarters building of MI-6 (better known as Her Majesty's Secret Intelligence Service), and Faisal had traveled here in search of a crib.

In cryptologic parlance, the term *crib* is simply another word for "cheating." The Svengali-like art of codebreaking has always relied heavily on cribs because breaking an error-free encrypted message is a difficult thing to do. Therefore the cryptanalyst looks for cribs that will provide a toehold and establish the "key" for the encryption. Cribs might be an often-used plaintext word that appears in many messages—such as *ambassador, foreign minister,* or *negotiation* in diplomatic traffic, or *tank, missile,* or *attack* in military messages. The "To" and "From" heading of a message may be standard, or the Teletype operator may make some error in formatting the message that may tip off the codebreaker.

Cribs came from a number of sources—happenstance, luck, trickery, and, on occasion, spies.

The driver, whom Faisal guessed was a shot-putter in his spare time, said, "This way, gentlemen," while gesturing toward the lift. They walked over, then stopped as the shot-putter looked up at a camera suspended on a steel arm. He pushed a button beside a speaker and said, "I have two visitors." After a pause a voice from the speaker said, "Watermelon." The shot-putter responded, "Lolita."

The lift opened, allowing Faisal, Burdick, and their escort to enter.

Watermelon and Lolita.

Faisal didn't grasp the connection.

The elevator opened to a small reception area where a uniformed guard offered a sign-in sheet and queried, "Shaikh and Burdick?"

"That's us," said Jamie.

"Identification, please."

Faisal and Burdick displayed their GCHQ IDs, signed in, and were given green visitor badges "to be worn so they are visible at all times."

The shot-putter escorted them into another lift that took them to the eighth floor. Here they were led down a hall to a small windowless conference room with bare cream-colored walls.

"I'll just wait outside, gentlemen. Your appointment should be here shortly."

"Thank you," replied Burdick as he sat down in an uncomfortable wooden chair that was probably designed to keep meetings brief.

Faisal had no more placed his briefcase on the table and dropped his overcoat on a spare chair when the door opened and a man entered. He looked as lean and taut as a tendon, with a Gallic nose and horn-rimmed glasses. He was in shirtsleeves and tie, obviously having come from just down the hall.

"Faisal, so good to see you." He exuded warmth while extending a hand.

Faisal took the hand and replied, "Arthur, good to see you, too. You know my deputy, Jamie Burdick."

"Of course." They shook. "Always a pleasure. Well, then, shall we get on with it?" He took a seat and placed a file on the table.

Oh, Arthur, thought Faisal, *why do you waste so much time on chit-chat.*

Among his other duties, Arthur Wedley-Hooks was chief SIS liaison with GCHQ. Whenever SIS came upon a SIGINT pearl, it was routed through Arthur Wedley-Hooks to the proper division at Cheltenham. Faisal was never truly comfortable in the presence of Wedley-Hooks. The man had the nervous energy of a hawk on a perch, ready to uncurl his talons and take flight at the slightest provocation.

"Arthur," began Faisal, "I want you to know the last crib you provided on the Dragon-four machine exceeded our greatest expectations." Faisal reached into his briefcase to extract a MOST SE CRET file and passed it to Wedley-Hooks, who opened it and scanned the message. "That text about General Fong went to the PM," said Faisal, "along with our assessment that a Chinese invasion of Vietnam was imminent."

Wedley-Hooks closed the file, passed it back, and smiled. "I hope your director brought our contribution to the attention of the prime minister."

"Of course, and that's why we're here. I understand you have another 'contribution' for us?"

Wedley-Hooks lit up one of the seventy cigarettes he would torch that day and replied, "Quite." He opened his own file and extracted a stack of eight-by-ten black-and-white photographs. He passed them to Faisal and Burdick, and they inspected each one carefully. They were pictures of rectangular cards with random circles punched out. Some Chinese characters were printed along one edge, and the punch pattern on each card was different. Faisal looked up at Wedley-Hooks with the unspoken question.

The altar boy exhaled a cloud of smoke and said, "These are the keys for the Chinese Ministry of Defense Dragon-four encryption machine, for the period twenty-six November to twenty-six December."

Jamie whistled.

Even Faisal was impressed, and he handled the photos as if they were a lost Shakespearean manuscript. "Arthur, I must say, you have outdone yourself this time. How on earth did you ... "

Wedley-Hooks held up his hand in one-upmanship fashion. "Can't tell you much about that, old man. Except to say Beijing Station is running the source in the Ministry of Defense. He's a mercenary, not a freedom fighter. And he's getting scared. Wants us to pull him out soon. Poor bastard. I think he envisions a country estate in Gloucestershire with hot and cold champagne, and round-eyed girls running about. He'll be lucky to get a studio flat in South Ken. But his product has always been first-class. This may be the last of it, so enjoy."

Burdick murmured greedily, "We will, we will," as he surveyed the photographs again.

The Chinese Dragon-4 machine was electromechanical and still used punch cards to set its cryptographic key. The Americans, Russians, Western Europeans, and British government had upgraded to totally electronic encryption systems for high-level military and diplomatic traffic, and these used computer discs instead of punch cards. Though it wasn't state-of-the-art, the Dragon-4 was still one tough nut to crack. The cribs would enable Faisal's China Clippers to break the messages in almost real time.

"Superb job, Arthur. You'll let us know if anything like this comes your way again?"

"Of course, Faisal. Well, must be going. So good to visit with you."

"Good-bye, Arthur."

And with that, Wedley-Hooks rose and exited.

Jamie Burdick took no notice of their host's departure, for he was handling the photographs as if they were emeralds from the mines of King Solomon.

Faisal watched his protégé for a full minute, then smiled and said, "When you're finished salivating, Jamie, you may fetch Lolita and we'll be on our way."

The Chinese offensive into Vietnam stalled, and the operation turned into a worse sausage grinder for the Chinese than their abortive invasion of 1979. The Chinese leadership was old, decrepit, and ossified. The troops were young and untested in combat; and unlike the students in Tiananmen Square, these adversaries shot back. Oh, how they shot back. With forty years of experience in colonial warfare, the Vietnamese outmaneuvered, outguiled, and outfought the Chinese. So bad was it, that Beijing began searching for a way to extricate itself. Without losing face, of course.

With the cribs provided by MI-6, the China Clippers quickly nailed down and broke the message traffic of the Dragon-4 machine, and the deciphered messages kept senior-level ministers in Whitehall mesmerized. The Beijing defense minister railed at General Fong for not capturing the Lao Cai oil field. Fong railed back he wasn't getting enough air support. The Air Force general complained the Vietnamese SAM missiles made the battle zone too dangerous. Junior commanders and political officers were slow to carry out orders, preferring to stay in defensive positions. Fong was sacked.

Faisal decided to do some parallel analysis. He took the message traffic from the Dragon-4 machine and placed it alongside the deciphered Vietnamese traffic from the battlefront. The tone of the messages revealed as much as the texts. The Chinese epistles were shrill, accusatory, confused—the tenor of desperate men desperately seeking a way out. By contrast, the Vietnamese traffic between Hanoi and their field commanders was detached, objective, professional, businesslike.

Ah, thought Faisal, *nothing counts like experience.*

■ ■ ■

Jamie Burdick entered his superior's chambers by the private entrance. The younger man's features were drawn, the pallor of his skin a bit ashen, and his eyes encircled by fatigue from the long hours he'd pulled throughout the invasion. He found Faisal glued to the computer screen on his credenza, scrolling through an elaborate algorithm.

Burdick slapped a file down on the oversize cherrywood desk. "Just received some new traffic from the in-laws. The Vietnamese have maneuvered about three divisions of Chinese infantry into a pocket of the Song-Koi Valley and cut their lines of communication. Looks like they're about to administer the coup de grâce in a replay of Dien Bien Phu."

"Umm."

"Also—you're not going to believe this—Hanoi has issued orders to its field commander to prepare for a border crossing to capture the ten percent of the Lao Cai oil field they don't control. If the Chinese resist, they'll top the thirty thousand Chinese prisoners they've already captured, plus any more they seize in the pocket."

"Umm."

Burdick waited for his report to sink in, but apparently it didn't. Finally, he scratched his scalp and said in a brusque voice, "Faisal, what are you doing?"

His superior looked up from the screen. "Eh? What? Oh, I'm sorry, Jamie. Did you say something?"

Burdick sighed, then repeated his report—this time capturing the reaction he expected.

"Good God!" gasped Faisal. "Killing prisoners! That's appalling."

"The ways of the Orient."

Faisal grunted. "Better get this up the chain straightaway to the director, then to MoD, Foreign Office, Joint Intel Committee, and Cabinet Office. Light a fire under Beekman and tell him to get it into Sir Vivian's hands without delay."

"Right." As Burdick made a move to leave, he saw his chief turn back to the computer screen and immediately fall into his séance mode. Unable to contain his curiosity, Burdick asked,

"Faisal, what are you doing?"

"Umm? What? . . . Oh, this?"

"Yes, Faisal, *that*. What is it?"

Reaching for his onyx cigarette holder, Faisal said, "It is that Aykhal cipher we picked up a couple of weeks ago. You remember, the one with the seven-letter code groups."

"Oh, yes, I'd forgotten about that."

"Since you and the Clippers had the Chinese situation well in hand, I thought I'd give it another turn."

"So how's it coming?"

Faisal's gaze returned to the screen. "Still a brick wall at the moment." He lit up another cigarette and said, "I could use more material to work with."

"Yes, you mentioned that before. I remember now. Did you ever check with Angelfish about doing a search?"

"No. The Chinese interrupted me."

"Well, you might do that. See you later. I must be about my appointed rounds."

Burdick departed and Faisal refocused on the screen while puffing on the cigarette holder. Yes, perhaps Jamie was right. Maybe he could talk Angelfish into doing a search. He picked up the phone and punched in the extension.

"J Division," came a detached voice.

"This is Faisal Shaikh in H Division. I need you to put me through to your chief, please."

"I'm sorry, Dr. Shaikh. He's over at Block M today. Shall I take a message, or I can beep him if you like."

Faisal considered it, then replied, "No, no, that won't be necessary." And he rang off. He saved the algorithm in the computer, then rose and grabbed his coat. While passing by his secretary he flashed his pocket pager and said, "If you need me, Geneviève, I shall be at Block M."

The facilities of GCHQ in Cheltenham are divided into two campuses—Benhall on the western side of town where Faisal and his staff worked, and Oakley on the east. The two installations were

equally drab and depressing, sporting rows of hutlike structures
and dismal brick buildings that looked like abandoned textile mills.
And, of course, there were the antennae and satellite dishes sprout-
ing from the rooftops. But at the Oakley campus a new building had
recently grown from the compound floor. It was black, octagonal in
shape, three stories high, and sported several satellite dishes on top.
It might have been Darth Vader's summer home, but in reality it
housed GCHQ's inner sanctum. This was Block M.

Faisal was ushered through a heavy door into an octagonal-
shaped room that was the control center of Block M. Two rows
of control stations with recessed computer monitors painted their
operators with an eerie glow, and on the upper walls large video
screens displayed incoherent symbology. The place resembled
the bridge of a starship, and from here the Zircon eavesdropping
satellite was monitored, controlled, and kept in its proper orbit.
Also from this room the intercepted signal traffic from the Zircon
bird was sorted by type and/or transponder frequencies and
routed to the proper analyst. The symbols dancing across the
screens told the controllers what signals were coming off which
transponder, where the downlink was going, or if the downlink
had to be rerouted because a computer was down.

In the center of the darkened chamber was Angelfish, who was
conferring with the shift supervisor. They were talking in hushed
tones as Faisal approached them. The tall, enigmatic Angelfish
looked over the supervisor's shoulder at Faisal and disengaged
himself. Fully a head taller than Faisal, his narrow face appeared
crestfallen behind thick glasses. He looked like a man fighting to
hold back tears. "Yes, Shaikh," moaned the raspy voice. "What is
it?" Faisal was a bit dumbfounded. He'd never seen the nonemo-
tive Angelfish like this. Perhaps this wasn't the right juncture. "I'm
sorry, Fish, ah, is this a bad time? I can speak with you later if you
like."

Angelfish visibly stiffened, regaining his composure. "No, no,
now is fine. What can I help you with?"

Faisal cleared his throat and explained, "A rather queer signal surfaced in the hopper a couple of weeks ago. It was picked up on an HF circuit out of Aykhal, and S and T pegged the transmitter location as a Strategic Rocket Forces base."

"Hmm. A high-frequency circuit? Out of an SRF base? That's a bit odd. The SRF uses the Raduga satellites as primary and a microwave system as backup. High frequency isn't in their protocol."

"Exactly. Anyway, this signal was most curious. It wasn't scrambled or wrapped or hopped or bursted or anything. Came out straightforward in seven-letter cipher groups. I've never seen anything like it before. The Soviets have always used five-letter groups or data streams, as you know."

"Yes, I know."

"The traffic in question is a series of twelve messages. One is fairly long. My people, and I personally, have been attacking it, but so far without success."

"Have you used the Paradox on it?"

"Yes."

"And still nothing?"

"Nothing."

"Well, what do you want from me?"

"It would be helpful if we had more traffic to work with. I would appreciate it if you'd have your people do a historical search. Maybe it's cropped up before and we missed it."

Angelfish crossed his arms and looked contemplative. "How far do you want to go back?"

Faisal was quick. "I would like for you to go back a year."

Angelfish looked affronted. "A year? Well, ninety days is no problem, as you well know. Those tapes are stored on-line in the computer center, but to go back a year we'll have to pull the old tapes out of the warehouse."

"What are we storing them for if they aren't to be used? Besides, I have a feeling about this one."

Angelfish sighed in resignation and looked at the floor. "Very well. Send me the particulars and I'll authorize the search."

Faisal reached up and patted his shoulder. "Thank you, Fish. Uh, if you don't mind my saying so, you look a bit down today."

Angelfish raised his gaze to meet Faisal's and said, "Haven't you heard?"

"No. Heard what?"

Angelfish swallowed. "The MoD decided this morning. You know the second Zircon bird scheduled to go up next month?"

"Of course. You briefed us on it."

Another swallow. "The director knuckled under. He's taking that bird away from me and giving it to Toad to monitor Chinese traffic. Said we didn't need it pointed at the Bolsheviks anymore. Said there weren't any Bolsheviks anymore." His voice quavered as if there had been a death in the family, and to Angelfish it *was* a death in the family—or more precisely, a kidnapping.

Faisal was at a loss and tried to offer condolence. "I'm, uh, terribly sorry, Fish. I didn't know."

A vibration passed through Angelfish as his fists clenched, and his voice rasped like a knife on a sharpener. "Twelve years . . . *twelve* years I worked on Zircon! It was *my* idea, all my idea, you know that. I conceived it, rammed it through that damned MoD sludge pile, and got it airborne so we wouldn't have to suck up to the goddamned Americans all the bloody time. Twelve years! And Whitehall takes it away from me in an *afternoon!*" Heads around the room turned, and Faisal saw Angelfish's bottom lip quiver. Then Fish turned away, saying nothing more as he strode at a quick pace toward the loo.

Faisal hoped that in his remorse, Angelfish wouldn't forget about the search.

CHAPTER FOUR

"**F**aisal!"

Jamie Burdick's shout caused Shaikh to spill some Darjeeling tea on his tie, and nothing broke through his calm veneer like a stain on an expensive silk cravat. Wiping the spot with a handkerchief, he snapped, "Honestly, Jamie, the use of my private entrance is a privilege not to be abused."

Burdick paid no attention as he slapped a file on the desk and exclaimed, "Sod that! Look at *this!*"

Faisal wiped his fingers with the handkerchief and took the file while asking, "What is it?"

"It's a decrypt from the Dragon-four machine—a message from the Beijing Defense Ministry to the new theater commander on the border, a General Sung. The Vietnamese have crossed the border to capture the remaining part of the oil field they don't control. This cable authorizes Sung to use a 'firecracker' on the invading forces."

Faisal scanned the message in both Cantonese and English, then asked, "So, what's a 'firecracker'?"

"I just got off the secure line with Wedley-Hooks at Thames House in London. He checked his files on the code words provided by his source in the Defense Ministry—you know, the one he told us about."

"Yes, I remember. What about it?"

" 'Firecracker' is a code word commonly associated with the Chinese neutron-weapons program."

Faisal's tanned-looking features went pale. "Neutron bomb . . . you don't think . . . "

"The altar boys are pulling out the stops to try and confirm. But Wedley-Hooks says he's ninety percent certain."

Faisal hit his intercom switch and shouted, "Geneviève, get me Director Mittleditch! Wherever he is!" His hand shaking, he held the message and almost moaned, "Neutron bomb."

Any reader of spy novels can tell you the KGB was long the nemesis of Western intelligence agencies. Less well known was the Tewu, or the Department of Special Affairs, of the People's Republic of China. Headed by a bespectacled political survivor and vice prime minister named Qiao Shi, the Tewu undertook the mission in the late seventies and early eighties of penetrating the American nuclear weapons program at Lawrence Livermore Laboratory. Their success surpassed even Qiao Shi's expectations. Using visiting students and scientists to play on the sympathies of friends and professional colleagues working at Livermore, the Tewu successfully penetrated security and advanced their neutron-weapons research, to the point a neutron test bomb was detonated on the Lop Nor test range in Xinjiang Province on September 29, 1988.

Now the Chinese had their finger on another neutron trigger. And this time it was no test.

"Sorry, Dr. Shaikh," squawked the intercom. "The director is in Ulster today for a meeting with the Northern Ireland Working Group. Getting him linked up to a secure communications channel will take some time."

"Damn it all," hissed Faisal, more to himself than to Burdick. "We cannot sit on this one. I'll have to release this on my own authority. Jamie, send a copy of this message by secure fax, immediate priority, to the foreign minister, MoD, and to the cabinet secretary at Number Ten Downing." Then he hit the intercom and said, "Geneviève, find me Michael Dentwiler and tell him I need him in my office *at once* for a CRITICOM."

"Yes, Dr. Shaikh."

Faisal looked at Burdick and said, "I'll notify the SUSLO personally, as soon as he gets here."

"Should we notify SUKLO?"

Faisal shook his head. "I'm placing this in Dentwiler's hands. He can make the decision on how to pass the word to the in-laws. He may want to bypass Meade and transmit directly to State, the Pentagon, maybe even the White House. But you get on your way."

"Right," and Burdick passed out of the office as Geneviève Monson walked in, carrying a large envelope.

"Mr. Dentwiler is on his way from Oakley."

Faisal mumbled, "Umm," as his thoughts were consumed by the specter of a most wicked nuclear genie being released from the bottle.

Geneviève placed the envelope on top of his IN box pile and held out the security receipt. "You have to sign a chit for this one." Absently, Faisal scribbled his initials and Geneviève moved toward the door.

Then Shaikh caught himself and asked, "Geneviève, what is this?" while pointing to the envelope.

Imperious as ever, Geneviève Monson executed a pirouette and replied, "It just came down from J Division. The courier said it was a historical search you had requested from Angelfish."

It was truly amazing how a sleeping leviathan like the Whitehall bureaucracy could be awakened and brought to a frenetic pitch by two simple words: *neutron bomb*. By the time the sun had set over Westminster Palace, London and Washington had conferred and yoked together a plan to squelch any possible use of such an evil implement of war.

An emergency meeting of the U.N. Security Council was held where the U.S. and U.K. called for an immediate cease-fire in the China-Vietnam conflict. Then the U.S. ambassador pigeonholed the Chinese envoy and reamed his ass up one side and down the other, telling him if China popped a neutron bomb, then it was embargo time by the entire Western bloc, and the Chinese economy could die on the vine. And if the economy cratered, there would be *real* rebellion in the streets, not some student longhairs in Tiananmen Square. Meanwhile, the U.K. ambassador sequestered the Vietnam legation on the other side of the room and informed them they had best pull their troops back to the original border or their army was going to be deep-fried into crispy chips, and the Former Soviet Union wouldn't lift a finger to assist them. The president and the PM went on television that very night, emphasizing the call for a cease-fire and pullback, and warning of grave consequences if hostilities did not cease. The diplomatic message traffic between New York and Beijing, and New York and Hanoi, plus the traffic over the war front, were intercepted and deciphered by Fort Meade and Cheltenham in almost real time. It became apparent that both sides had decided to call it a day and return to a U.N.-supervised cease-fire line at their original borders.

There was a massive sigh of relief as accolades came down from No. 10 Downing and even the White House on H Division and SIS for their work in breaking the Dragon-4 encryption machine. But Faisal paid scant attention. After the cease-fire was announced, his attention had returned to the contents of the envelope sent to him by Angelfish.

"That's a week for the books, I must say," sighed Jamie Burdick, looking more haggard than usual as he stretched out on Faisal's office sofa. "It isn't often we get to nip a nuclear war in the knickers, is it? I'm going to pack Sylvia and Nigel off to her parents in Cornwall and sleep the whole bloody weekend." Burdick watched as his superior packed several files into his attaché case and placed the overflow into a larger valise. "So what are you doing this weekend?" he asked, looking at the readout on his digital watch. "It's awfully early to see you packing to leave on a Friday."

Faisal smiled, saying, "Getting out of town, Jamie. Heading off to some of my old haunts in Edinburgh."

A bit surprised, Burdick asked, "Edinburgh? At this time of year? You'll freeze your bloody duffer off. Why not try something warmer? Say like Hanover or Stockholm."

Faisal chuckled at the meteorological humor and snapped his case shut. "Thank you for the suggestion, Jamie, but I'm late for my train. My best to Sylvia and Nigel, and have a good sleep. You're entitled."

The train pulled out of Cheltenham station as Faisal struggled into the first-class compartment with his suitcase and briefcases. He had searched several compartments for one that was empty so he could enjoy some privacy on the seven-hour journey. He swung his luggage up onto the rack, pulled the shades down, and flicked on the light. Then he opened his briefcases and laid out the contents of the Angelfish envelope on the seat. Handling documents like these on public transport was against security procedures, of course, but Faisal wasn't about to toss away seven hours of a train trip when it could be put to good use. Once settled in, out came the cigarette case, the onyx holder, and the Cartier lighter, and in minutes a dense smoke cloud filled the chamber.

Angelfish had come across for Faisal, searching back through a year's worth of historical tapes for more traffic on the seven-character code group of the Aykhal cipher. And Angelfish had prevailed upon the Americans to do the same thing.

Faisal examined the TEXTA of each message carefully. The volume of traffic that GCHQ and NSA handle on a daily basis is staggering, and TEXTA is a catalog notation imprinted on each intercept. TEXTA is the acronym for Technical Abstracts of Traffic Analysis, and the notation provides the analyst with a snapshot of where the message originated, where it went, what organization or military service branch sent it, the technical means of transmission (radio, microwave, etc.), and the intercept point.

First, Faisal recapped the original intercept, which was a high-frequency radio transmission from the Strategic Rocket Forces base outside Aykhal. Then he turned his attention to the two American intercepts.

The first American intercept was snagged by a Magnum eavesdropping satellite positioned over Borneo. The Magnum picked off signals traffic aimed at a Russian Raduga satellite. On this intercept the Americans had captured a total of nine messages in the seven-letter code groups. Their origination points were pegged as Moscow and Samarkand in the Uzbekistan Republic of the new Commonwealth of Independent States. Five of the messages originated from Samarkand and four from Moscow. All of them were brief and less than a page.

The second American intercept was more recent than the Aykhal cipher. Only eight days old, in fact. It was picked up by an American RC-135 SIGINT/ELINT spyplane (dubbed Rivet Joint) flying off the Pacific coast of the Kamchatka Peninsula. The spyplane had snagged three high-frequency signals out of Petropavlovsk, which was headquarters for the Russian (née Soviet) Navy in the Pacific. There were two short signals and a longer one running for three pages.

The final signal was a short single message coming out of Tehran. It was intercepted by British listening posts on Cyprus and on Ascension Island in the South Atlantic. Faisal guessed it was transmitted from the Russian embassy, or the small Russian military advisory contingent that was still in Iran. But there was something odd about it. It was transmitted on a frequency band allocated to amateur, or ham, radio operators instead of a frequency band reserved for Russian government use. Strange. Sometimes covert operators used ham frequencies as a way to bury their transmissions. Perhaps the Russians had a covert operation under way in Tehran? Who knew.

So here they were: the results of the massive Anglo-American electronic ear that canvassed the ether for every kind of radio emission. Four intercepts of the seven-letter cipher group.

Faisal carefully reviewed the cryptanalytic "attacks" on the Aykhal cipher—first by the Red Riding Hood team, then the Purple Gang team, then by himself. The seven-letter group was proving to be the darkest of ciphers—a black cipher, one that evaded every attempt to shine a light through its impenetrable veil. And the more unrelenting it became, the more it was like a siren's song to Faisal, calling to him in a mystic voice only he could comprehend.

As the train rolled through the English countryside and daylight turned to darkness, Faisal's legal pad became filled with a puzzling array of mathematical hieroglyphics.

The taxi from Edinburgh's Waverly Station pulled up to a terrace house that was indistinguishable from the others on the snow-caked avenue of Old Town. The streetlights reflected off the white landscape with an eerie incandescence that seemed Dickensian, like something from a past century. The cabdriver hefted Faisal's luggage up the icy steps and was rewarded with a generous tip, then he departed. Overcoat held close, Faisal checked his watch, which read 10:48 P.M. Because of the late hour he avoided the bell and tapped lightly on the oaken door. It opened to reveal a short, stocky woman in the uniform of a maid.

"Faisal," came the greeting with a welcoming smile. "So good to see you. Do come in from the cold."

Lifting the luggage inside, he said, "Hello, Glenna," then gave her an embrace. "I didn't ring the bell. Afraid I would wake him."

"My, no. He's in the study waiting for you."

"Damn him. He shouldn't be up this late."

A soft laugh. "He knows that, but he wanted to see you the moment you arrived."

Faisal sighed in exasperation as the housekeeper took his camel-hair coat, then with briefcases in hand he climbed the familiar stairs to the book-lined study. A fire was burning in the ancient hearth, keeping the Scottish chill at bay and draping the room with an orange glow. Faisal glanced at the desk covered with papers, and at the study table where he'd spent so much time as a youth. He walked across the Persian rug to one of the high-backed leather chairs facing the fireplace and looked down at the frail figure—clad in slacks, sweater, and slippers—dozing in a semisleep. "Hello, Professor," he whispered gently.

The figure stirred and looked up in surprise, then delight. "Faisal," he said in a scratchy voice.

Not wanting the old man to get up, Faisal lowered himself to one knee and took a withered, liver-spotted hand between his own.

Then for a few moments their eyes locked in a mutual empathy only they could understand.

Angus Doogan was ninety years old, and the once strapping body was now frail and weathered with age. The giant bald cranium, which housed one of the most gifted minds of his generation, was fringed with white hair and set off by giant ears. Gold-framed glasses rested on a beaklike nose, and the skin on his face had the pallor of ash. But behind the spectacles his eyes still sparkled with the dynamic energy of a university don—one who was often called into "government service."

Angus Doogan had been a young mathematics professor on the ascending track at Edinburgh University when German troops stormed across the Polish border in 1939. In short order he was summoned to an obscure place called Bletchley Park in Buckinghamshire, where he met an assortment of eccentric people trying to decipher German messages generated by a machine called Enigma. Thus, Angus Doogan became one of the world's leading figures in the field of codebreaking, and helped cement the incestuous relationship between academia and Government Communications Headquarters.

From its inception, GCHQ has retained a number of talent spotters sprinkled throughout academia to identify possible recruits. One such talent spotter was a friend of Doogan's who worked in the examination bureau for A-level university admissions, and it was there a mathematics special-papers exam crossed his desk. The special papers belonged to a student of Pakistani extraction at the Reading Blue Coat School, and their content was so astounding that the spotter placed an immediate call to Edinburgh. Angus Doogan traveled to Reading the following weekend, and through the headmaster of the Blue Coat School learned more about this fascinating young man of Southwest Asian descent—a prodigy with an epic command of mathematics and languages.

Angus then found the modest dry-cleaners shop in London that was owned by his parents. Since it was a school holiday, Angus invited Faisal and his parents to dinner, where he politely probed. Had Faisal taken the Oxbridge admission test? Yes. Had he chosen a university? Yes. Which? Oxford. In the face of Oxford, Doogan knew he had to act fast. Faisal was definitely a highflier, the academic equivalent of an American bonus-baby football recruit. Would he consider a full scholarship to Edinburgh instead of Oxford? Hmm, possibly. How about a visit to Edinburgh? See how you like it? Very well.

And that was that. In the end, Oxford couldn't offer what Edinburgh could, and that was Doogan himself. The young student and the don enjoyed an empathy that cemented their relationship, one that would endure until one of them died.

"So good to see you, my boy."

Faisal patted the feeble hand and said, "Good to see you as well, Professor. I have brought you an interesting problem."

The old don's eyebrows danced. "A problem? How delightful. So hard to find a decent problem these days. Show me what you have. We'll have Glenna bring some tea."

Faisal smiled. "Not now, Professor. The hour is late. We'll start tomorrow fresh. We must get you to bed now."

The sparkle faded as Angus Doogan sighed and allowed Faisal to help him out of the chair and hand him his cane. But when Faisal tried to take his other arm to lend some support, the old don yanked it away, saying, "I'll do it myself. You must think me decrepit or something. I only turned ninety a month ago."

"My error," confessed Faisal.

In January 1913, a Cambridge mathematician named G. H. Hardy received an astonishing letter—one with a Madras, India, postmark—that would change his life. Hardy was thirty-five years of age at the time, brilliant, and already a fellow of the Royal Society. The letter he received was written by an Indian accounting clerk with no formal education who had been mired in poverty for all of his twenty-three years.

The cultural distance between the two men was not a gap. It was a chasm. Yet the letter, with its hieroglyphic contents, served as the catalyst that would bring the two men together in an exotic relationship the world of mathematics had never seen—and would probably never see again.

The letter was written by one Srinivasa Ramanujan, a poverty-stricken school dropout whose genius in the field of mathematics was nothing short of cosmic. Hardy, perhaps the leading English mathematician of his time, was dazzled by the letter; and the correspondence between the two men blossomed. Then under Hardy's patronage, Ramanujan was brought to Cambridge, where the depths of his mathematical powers were plumbed by the academics of the day.

To understand the breadth of Ramanujan's genius, it would have been as if Hardy were an accomplished literature don at Cambridge who'd received a manuscript from an unknown playwright named William Shakespeare.

Astonishing.

But the cultural and climatic shock of living in England was too much for Ramanujan. It took a toll, and he died at the age of thirty-two, his formidable genius lost forever.

In Faisal Shaikh, Angus Doogan found his Ramanujan. Although there were differences—Hardy was English, Doogan a Scot; Hardy was Cambridge, Doogan was Edinburgh; Ramanujan was a native Indian and a Hindu, Shaikh was a native Briton and a Muslim—the principle was the same. It was Doogan who grasped the depth of the mind behind the special-papers exam. It was Doogan who wooed the young lad, snatched him away from Oxford, and brought him to Edinburgh. It was Doogan and his wife, Eleanor, who let their spare room to the youthful Faisal, but treated him like a son. As Faisal moved effortlessly from undergraduate to graduate studies, Doogan began introducing him to key people at Cheltenham, while guiding him into the field of cryptanalysis. To his joy, Doogan found his protégé to be a natural. An intuitive genius whose powers, by the time he received his PhD, were eclipsing those of Doogan himself.

Upon receiving his degree, Faisal briefly entertained the possibility of a teaching career, but only briefly. It wasn't long before he took the train from Edinburgh station for Cheltenham, on a trip that seemed preordained.

After breakfast the next day, the professor and protégé sat down at the rickety old table in the study as they had years before. The fire warmed the room as they sipped the tea provided by Glenna. Doogan's wife, Eleanor, had long since died, and Glenna had taken over caring for the aging don.

Faisal laid out the materials on the Black Cipher intercepts and methodically went through them with his mentor. As he walked through his briefing, the years seemed to drop off Angus, until he was vibrating with the energy of his prime. Faisal led him through the attacks he and his people at H Division had made on the seven-character code groups, all to no avail. But like Faisal, Doogan had an intuitive feeling that the previous attacks had brought them tantalizingly close.

They broke for lunch, then Doogan took his afternoon nap while Faisal threw on his camel-hair overcoat for a brisk walk through the chilly air of Edinburgh.

Sandwiched between the North Sea and hills of northern Scotland, the University of Edinburgh still pulsed with the intellectual energy that had inspired students like James Boswell, Oliver Goldsmith, Charles Darwin, Robert Louis Stevenson, and Arthur Conan Doyle.

Ironically, the first university chair of English literature was established on Scottish soil at Edinburgh, as were the first chairs in agriculture and artificial intelligence.

Faisal paused in the plaza of the Kings Buildings, which was the confluence of the university's science and technology departments. He soaked up the remembrance of his time here and noticed how young the students looked these days. He strolled past the Maxwell building where Angus had held court in his mathematics classes, then went past the chemistry building where he nodded to the old statue of Sir David Brewster. Brewster received his MA degree in 1800 at the age of nineteen and went on to author some three hundred scientific papers. It was an achievement that intimidated even Faisal.

Just for a moment he was back in school—vibrant, full of energy and expectations. Then he returned to the here and now, twenty years later. His youthful expectations had been achieved, even surpassed, yet he longed for the days spent under Angus Doogan's wing.

His private remembrance over, he left to find his old professor and get on with the Queen's business.

Despite his Athenian skills, Faisal had come to Edinburgh because Angus Doogan was still the one man in Britain who might be able to leapfrog his own analysis of the Black Cipher. And modesty aside, Faisal knew that two geniuses working on a problem were better than one. With Angus Doogan's pedigree going all the way to Bletchley Park, no one living had more experience in code-breaking than he. Perhaps Faisal's mentor could provide the catalyst, that flash of brilliance that would turn the key and unlock the secrets of the Black Cipher.

As Glenna cleared the dinner trays from the study table, Faisal watched the energy fade from the old master as he leaned back in the leather chair. He thought Angus had fallen asleep, but then the eyes opened with a spark of electricity, causing the aged don to smile and say in his scratchy voice, "There's a super in there, mind you. I'd bet my pension on it."

"A super? You really think so?"

A superencipherment was a plaintext message that was encrypted two or more times, say if:

SCARECROW

was enciphered to read:

PSAVCBRRQ

and that was enciphered a second time to read:

GKDCBVMAL

That was a superencipherment in simple terms. But with modern encryption algorithms, a character could be superenciphered hundreds or even thousands of times.

"Yes, my boy," continued Angus, "I'm sure. There's a super at work in here. And look for a trapdoor. A way to back into the system. A frontal assault will be a hard one, even with the Americans' Paradox computer."

"Hmm. I did not think we had a super of any consequence here, but we'll look at that more carefully. And for a trapdoor."

"All right, gentlemen. That is quite enough. It is time for the Professor to retire."

Faisal and Angus looked at Glenna in the doorway, an authority not to be challenged.

"Ah," whispered Angus, "my warden, dear boy. It appears my parole has expired and I must return to my cell."

Faisal chuckled as he helped the old don to his feet, saying, "I miss Eleanor. Her memory is everywhere in this house."

Doogan emitted a distinctly bitter, "Harrumph," and snorted, "uncaring woman."

Startled, Faisal said, "Professor, what are you saying? Eleanor, uncaring? She worshiped you."

The eyes flared as the old man said, "I can't believe she would be so unfeeling as to die before me. I'll never forgive her for that."

As he shuffled off on Glenna's arm, Faisal called after him. "Perhaps a game of chess before I leave tomorrow?"

A cane was raised in reply.

Faisal watched them disappear into the bedroom, confident that Eleanor would be forgiven when they met again one day. A day not long off, he imagined.

Geneviève Monson had placed her cigarillo in the ashtray and was returning to the task of typing some correspondence when she heard, "Hello, beautiful." Geneviève was as far from beautiful as a woman could aspire, yet she instinctively felt the words were for her. The rakishly handsome man standing over her was tall with engaging features, and his sandy hair seemed a bit tousled. His smile was hypnotic, softening any defense or diffusing any attack that might come his way. Self-consciously, Geneviève reached up and tufted her white hair, asking, "What can I do for you today, Michael? Are you here to sell me a car?"

"You bet, sweetness. How about a 'fifty-seven Chevy ragtop? Chrome wheels, fire engine red. Drive it off the lot this morning, get laid tonight. Guaranteed. Nothing down with tax, title, and dealer prep thrown in." Michael Dentwiler was the senior United States liaison officer, or SUSLO. Dentwiler had put himself through Princeton by working summers as a used-car salesman. The commissions he built up during the summer saw him through the rest of the year, and despite the other accomplishments in his career he was always known as the Ivy Leaguer used-car dealer. Rather than evade the nickname, he embraced it, as a mark of distinction. As the SUSLO, Dentwiler represented American interests at GCHQ. And since he was the prime link to the awesome powers of the NSA, Dentwiler was courted assiduously, which was something Dentwiler did not object to. He pointed at the open door and said to Geneviève, "Need to see your boss."

She gestured with a hand and replied, "Go right in. He's on the computer at the moment."

"Yes," said Dentwiler while tapping on the open door, "I know."

Startled at the knock, Faisal looked up from the terminal on his credenza and mumbled, "Umm? What? Oh, why, hullo, Michael. Haven't seen you since our Chinese firecracker drill. Sit down. Can I get you some tea?"

Taking a seat, Dentwiler kept his smile in place. "No thanks, Faisal. Never cared for the stuff myself. I'm just here to play messenger boy today."

Faisal inserted a cigarette into the onyx holder. "And what's the message?"

"It's a little epistle from our crusty chief of cryptologic service, Marshall Fitzroy."

"Marshall? Crusty? You're being a bit kind, aren't you, Michael? Well, what does my dear friend Jaws wish to tell me?"

Marshall Fitzroy was Faisal Shaikh's counterpart at NSA, and due to his predatorlike persona and ghastly dental work he was called Jaws, but only behind his back.

Dentwiler brushed an imaginary speck of dust off his trouser leg. "Try and understand these are his words, not mine, but Dr.

Fitzroy told me to say, 'Tell that sonuvabitch Shaikh that the goddamn Paradox computer is not his personal toy and to quit tying up so much time or I'll kick his ass into the Irish Sea.'"

Faisal smiled. "Ah, Jaws. Subtle as ever. And I trust you gave me the sanitized version?"

"If the truth be known, yes."

Faisal put the flame to his cigarette. "Tell Jaws I've been working on a special problem. Give me two more days and things will get back to normal."

"Two days?"

Faisal sighed, knowing he had spent too much time on the Black Cipher already. That it was time to break it or move on. "Yes. Two days more. Then it's a wrap, as you Americans say."

Dentwiler rose. "I'll pass it on. Thanks for your time."

"Thank you for the time on Paradox."

After Dentwiler left, Faisal's soul felt the bitterness that surfaced when he had to grovel before the roguish Americans. They were so awesome, so powerful, and sometimes they wielded that power with all the subtlety of a hand grenade. Once the sun had never set on the British Empire. Now it was a tiny island trying to survive in a New World Order of brutal economics. He stubbed out the cigarette and returned to his algorithm on the screen.

The Black Cipher.

Where was that damned trapdoor?

CHAPTER ✛ FIVE

"**A** problem?" intoned Sir Vivian Mittleditch, director of Government Communications Headquarters. His question was cloaked with the tenor of incredulity, as if an unseen hand had dropped a mortified rat on the conference table.

"I'm afraid so, Sir Vivian," replied Dickie Bartholomew. "I'm afraid so. Marshall Fitzroy, the in-laws' chief of cryptologic service, complained to the deputy director of NSA, who called me personally. It seems the Americans want their Paradox computer back. Said that H Division had already run through their allocated time for the next two months." Dickie offered a sympathetic smile to Faisal. "Sorry, old boy, but that's the way it is."

"What's the meaning of this, Shaikh?" demanded Sir Vivian.

Faisal squirmed in his seat like a miscreant schoolboy. He cleared his throat and said, "I've been working on a particularly difficult problem that has required a great quantity of computer time. I feel I am close to cracking—"

"It appears all you are close to cracking is our relationship with the Americans," snapped Sir Vivian, and there were muffled chuckles around the table.

"But I—"

"Be done with it and call Fitzroy personally to offer your apologies. Is that clear?"

Faisal swallowed the bitter bile of defeat and replied, "Quite clear, Sir Vivian."

. . .

Faisal stormed into his office from the PM's brief and slammed his attaché case onto the cherrywood desk. His eyes were sunken from sleep deprivation, his voice raspy from an unremitting stream of latakian cigarettes, and now the bureaucratic tide had shifted against him. Faisal had become obsessed with the Black Cipher, to the exclusion of all others, and now he was paying the price. His IN box teetered with a pile of work that clamored for his attention, and his appointments were backlogged. Faisal had broken his promise to Dentwiler and gone far beyond the two-day limit on the Paradox machine because he sensed he was so close. But that did little to assuage the anger of the leviathan Mittleditch. It was time to drop the Black Cipher and move on. Being compelled to admit his H Division, and he personally, had failed was galling enough—but during the PM's brief Graeme Stoneleigh had sat there behind his tortoiseshell glasses, savoring Faisal's capitulation. Stoneleigh knew better than to dance on his grave, since Faisal had broken the lewd limerick off Stoneleigh's Tempest II machine. But in silence, Stoneleigh's smugness radiated across the table with a bitterness that was most vile. Faisal detested many things—poverty, pollution, corruption, shrinking appropriations—but the greatest revulsion came from accepting defeat.

He poured himself some coffee, having switched from tea two days ago to squeeze a few more hours of wakefulness from his exhausted body. Then he sat down at his computer terminal and called up the final permutations he'd processed through the Paradox computer. It was his last-ditch effort to hit pay dirt on the Black Cipher.

Faisal had constructed an elegant mathematical algorithm to find a trapdoor into the encryption program, one that would break through the superencipherment. Thus far he had failed, and his failure cast him into the depths of depression. He was emotionally giving up when he punched up the results of his final attempt and "The Rush" came over him.

The Rush was what all cryptanalysts yearned for. Lived for. Its effect was better than whiskey, better than cocaine, better than power, better than sex—better than any upper, downer, speedball, or Benzedrine freebasing elixir the human mind could concoct. It came when the jumbled jigsaw letters of the encryption finally leapt off the page in plaintext and the code lay prostrate before the codebreaker like the bloodied dragon at St. George's feet. They were in the Russian Cyrillic alphabet, of course, but Faisal's mind quickly transformed them into the Queen's English:

TO: **COMMANDER, STRATEGIC ROCKET FORCES, MINISTRY OF DEFENSE, MOSCOW**

FROM: **COMMANDER, START TREATY ESCORT DETAIL, NOVA STAR**

FLASH   FLASH   FLASH

HAVE BEEN ALERTED BY COMMANDER, AYKHAL STRATEGIC ROCKET FORCES BASE, OF MAJOR SILO ACCIDENT. NUCLEAR WARHEAD IS INVOLVED, REPEAT, NUCLEAR WAR- HEAD IS INVOLVED. EMERGENCY CREWS RESPONDING. LIQ- UID FUEL STORAGE DEPOT AND ADDITIONAL SILOS AT RISK. EVACUATION OF TOWNSHIP MAY BE IMPLEMENTED. U.S. TREATY VERIFICATION TEAM DUE FOR DAWN ARRIVAL . . .

Jamie Burdick was trodding down the corridor when he heard something like a growl-scream-yelp come from behind Faisal's office door. He burst in, wondering if his superior had had a seizure of some kind. "Faisal!? What is it?"

Unable to speak at once, Faisal stared at the screen for some moments, almost in disbelief. Then he turned to his deputy and spoke with a quavering voice, "We've done it, Jamie! *Masha' Allah,* we've done it! We've broken the Black Cipher!"

During the long, simmering hostility of the Cold War, the U.S. Air Force's Strategic Air Command kept a flying command post aloft twenty-four hours a day. In the event SAC headquarters in Omaha was turned into a smoking black hole during a nuclear strike, the airborne headquarters could continue prosecuting the war until every last shred of Russian humanity was vaporized. This flying command post was a specially outfitted 707, code-named Looking Glass.

During those days of brinkmanship, the Soviets also had a flying doomsday command post, which was code-named *Novaya Zvyezda,* or Nova Star.

After the Berlin Wall crumbled and the Americans grounded their Looking Glass aircraft, the Soviets followed suit by having their Nova Star stand down as well.

Then came the arms reduction treaties between the superpowers, which called for on-site inspection of ballistic missiles and silos earmarked for destruction. The Russians (née Soviets) decided to fly the American inspection team from missile base to missile base on an Ilyushin passenger jet. But the Strategic Rocket Force commander wasn't about to let the Americans snoop around without keeping tabs on the intrusive aliens. So, he sent his shadow escort team along on one of the Nova Star planes, which had been outfitted with a new, state-of-the-art encryption machine.

The U.S. inspection team was due to visit the Aykhal Strategic Rocket Force base when disaster struck. The kind of disaster the Americans call a Broken Arrow.

Broken Arrow is the American code word for an accident involving nuclear weapons. There have been thirty-three such accidents since World War II (that have been confirmed by the U.S. Defense Department)—everything from bomber crashes to silo accidents to a nuclear submarine lost at sea when a conventional torpedo exploded on board and sent the vessel to the bottom.

The Soviets, of course, were not immune to these same blunders. While the U.S. treaty inspection team was en route to Aykhal, an SS-18 missile was being removed from its silo. A chain on the hoist broke, causing the nose cone to crack against the silo wall. This triggered the reentry vehicle's solid-fuel rocket motor and caused the missile to buck off the hoist brackets and fall back into the silo. The burning solid fuel seared through the liquid-fuel line like an acetylene torch and transformed the silo into a nightmarish inferno. As fire crews bravely battled the flames, knowing they might be atomized at any moment, the Nova Star escort team used the plane's commo gear to fire off frantic encrypted messages to Moscow, apprising the Defense Ministry of the situation.

These messages now lay before Faisal Shaikh and Jamie Burdick, and the two codebreakers were mesmerized as they read the frenetic exchange. The flames threatened other silos, and fire crews worked feverishly to remove the nearby warheads that were in jeopardy. Authorization for the evacuation of Aykhal was denied, then granted, then denied again when the fire was finally brought under control. Moscow informed the Nova Star escort team the American inspectors' plane would be grounded with some faked engine trouble until the mess at Aykhal could be cleaned up or covered over. Apparently the ruse worked, because Faisal couldn't recall reading anything in the press about a Russian nuclear silo accident.

"Christ have mercy, Faisal. Do you believe this? There was almost a mushroom cloud over Aykhal and nobody knew about it."

"Until now, Jamie. Until now. Queue this transcript up on Platform to be sent to Meade on Sir Vivian's approval. Eyes only for NSA director—no, make that eyes only for the director and a copy to Jaws. I want my counterpart to know our time on the Paradox was well spent."

"Rubbing his nose in it are we?"

"With vigor. I will take this up to Mittleditch's office myself, and then I want a meeting with the Purple Gang to start attacking the keys on the remaining Black Cipher intercepts."

"Right."

Burdick left and Faisal leaned back in his leather chair, savoring the moment. Yes, there was nothing quite like reading other people's mail.

Using Faisal's intricate yet elegant algorithm into the secret trapdoor of the Black Cipher, the Purple Gang quickly found the key settings to all but one of the remaining messages.

The Black Cipher epistle decrypted from Petropavlovsk was another exchange between the Nova Star escort plane and the Defense Ministry in Moscow. The American treaty-inspection team had traveled to the Soviet naval base to witness the decommissioning of a Delta-IV class submarine, and the destruction of her SS-N-23 ballistic missiles. After a long day of witnessing duties, the inspectors retired to the local tavern. One of the Americans tossed down a tall one, made from the locally distilled vodka (which, in a pinch, could also be used as fuel for MiG-25 Foxbat interceptors). The alcohol hit the American's bloodstream and he went ballistic, attempting to rape one of the barmaids. She resisted, and her attacker broke the vodka bottle across her face.

It was a messy situation at best, for some TASS reporters were afoot, feeling their glasnostic oats and smelling a story. When the local militia arrived, the Russian escort team was at a loss as to what to do, so they radioed Moscow for instructions. The reply: claim diplomatic immunity for the inspector and pack him onto a plane to Moscow at once. Have the militia keep the inquisitive TASS people bottled up and take the barmaid into custody until it blows over, then read the riot act to the goddamned Americans. Too much was at stake with the treaty. If need be, this incident was a chit Moscow could use against Washington to help loosen up a bit more aid.

The ultimate fate of the barmaid remained unknown.

The messages between Moscow and Samarkand were chilling. The local Red Army commander was dealing with an uprising triggered by the absence of food supplies. With winter approaching and the locals facing the dark prospect of impending hunger, if not famine, they were gathering in ever-larger mobs outside the Red Army barracks, demanding food. Finally the mob reached critical mass and stormed the gates, trampling the guards in their path. Gunfire was exchanged. Some soldiers switched sides. More gunfire. Chaos was taking hold. Control of the base hung in the balance. The Red Army base commander requested authorization from Moscow to use chemical weapons against the malcontents. Permission was quickly denied and the general was relieved of command. New troops were shipped in, order was restored, and the peasants remained hungry. As it happened, the base had no food anyway.

Then there was the final message from Tehran, picked up by both the Cyprus and Ascension Island listening posts on the HAM radio band. Faisal guessed it was from the Russian embassy or the military advisory group in Iran or a covert operator of some kind. But try as they might, Faisal and his Purple Gang couldn't seem to hit upon the right key to break the Tehran epistle. It was a short message that kept coming out garbled in the Russian Cyrillic alphabet. His stubborn streak reenergized by his initial success with the Black Cipher, Faisal felt there was something about the Tehran message he couldn't quite put his finger on. Something that was within his grasp, but kept eluding him. It was doubtful anyone else in the world would have struck upon the idea, but with his extraordinary skills in languages and cryptology, a new approach came to Faisal late one night. Following an intuitive hunch, he pulled the Russian Cyrillic alphabet out of his algorithm and replaced it with a Roman alphabet. Then he reran it through a host of possible key settings, which took another chunk of Paradox time, and lo and behold a message in the Queen's English popped out.

It was brief and made little sense:

TO: **PAGEBOYS**

FROM: **SANDCASTLE**

CLOUDBURST FOR SUNDOWN HAS BEEN OBTAINED. DELIVERY IN TEN DAYS TIME. COMMENCE PREPARATIONS.

END MESSAGE

"What is a Cloudburst? Or a Sundown?"

"Code words, obviously," mused Faisal as he and Burdick confronted the nemesis of all cryptanalysts, which was: once a message was decrypted it could still contain code words, and one could speculate endlessly on their meaning. Who or what was Sandcastle? A Russian advisor in Iran? The ambassador? The Russian *rezident* in Tehran? And who were the Pageboys? Why were they commencing preparations? Preparations for what?

Burdick sighed. "It could mean bloody well anything. We may get zero from this one."

Faisal stubbed out his cigarette and reloaded the onyx holder. "Let us not admit defeat so readily, Jamie. These Black Cipher messages have revealed to us that the Russians are using a new, highly sophisticated encryption device. One that is reserved for sensitive traffic. That in itself tells us this message must be of critical importance."

That gave Burdick scant consolation, for there was still a veil drawn over the message's meaning. "I ran it through the database and found nothing on point with these code words, except that Sandcastle was the Soviet Navy's word for Cam Ranh Bay years ago. This is coming out of Tehran, so I don't think Vietnam is germane to this text. And why on earth would the Russians transmit in English? I've never seen anything like that before. Is this a new way to confound people like us? Is someone playing games with the crypto gear? Could the in-laws be playing with the Russians in Tehran and we don't know about it?"

Faisal mumbled.

"What was that?"

He cleared his throat of the nicotine phlegm and repeated, more distinctly this time, "Let's run it by Wedley-Hooks and the altar boys."

"Whatever you say. I'll send it over before I take off on my leave tomorrow."

"Leave?"

"Yes, Faisal, *leave*. Vacation. Holiday. Furlough. Amnesty. Whatever the hell you want to call it. The family and I are sodding this place for a while. Going to Cyprus to play with Nigel and get drunk on the beach."

"Well, if you must. Is there a number where I can reach you?"
"No phones where I'll be."
Faisal was unaware such a place existed.

It was late the following Friday when the messenger from
Thames House arrived at Faisal's office with a sealed dispatch case.
It must have been a sensitive letter, because Arthur Wedley-Hooks
had not entrusted it to the secure fax line or the electronic mail.
Faisal signed the chit and broke the wax seal, then unfolded the
letter, which was written in Wedley-Hooks's own hand.

Faisal—

*With regard to your query on the code words of the Tehran mes-
sage, I explored the matter with our Russian desk and came up empty-
handed, I'm afraid. But then I decided to try a different tack. I ran it
through the CIA chief of station here in London—you know him, nice
chap named Barnwood—and asked him to ask Langley to shake down
the Israelis and see if there was any intel on the Arab side of the
ledger. Damned if we didn't score.*

*The Israelis claim "Sandcastle" is a pseudonym sometimes used by
Musa Kousa. He was a confidant of Qaddafi's and held the post of deputy foreign minister in the Libyan government. Broke with Qaddafi
when the U.N. sanctions started to bite. He was rumored to have been
Qaddafi's special liaison with the likes of Abu Nidal, Hezbollah, and
every other lunatic in the Med with a pipe bomb. The Americans and
the French claim Lockerbie and UTA 772 had Musa Kousa written all
over them. By all accounts he's smooth, and deadly as a cobra. Rumored
to be in Lebanon as a "freelancer," but who knows for certain.*

*That's all we could determine at this time. The only other item we
could speculate on was "Cloudburst." One of our MoD people just
returned from attaché duties in Moscow and claims it's a Russian
nickname for a new antipersonnel munition of some type. Did not
have time to confirm. Came up with zero on "Sundown" and "Pageboys."*

*With Musa Kousa possibly involved, this sounds rather ominous
to me, but I'm leaving straightaway for Hong Kong. Remember our
friend in Beijing? Well, we're bringing him out and my presence is
required. Since I am departing, I leave it to your discretion to notify
the antiterror boys on the Joint Intelligence Committee. While ominous, this message still isn't much to go on. I have a few more feelers
out and I have left instructions with one of my staff—Fenton Slater—
to notify you if we learn anything further.*

Yours,
Arthur

A chill came over Faisal as he set the letter down. In the Western
world there was a vast inability to comprehend the Arab mind.
Influenced by Hollywood and CNN cameras panning mobs of
zealots as they massed to stone the local U.S. embassy, Westerners
had difficulty placing an Arab anywhere but on a camel in the
desert. There were Arabs who filled that stereotype, of course, but
Faisal knew that since World War Two another class of Arab had
evolved. Western educated, their careers underwritten by petrodollars, they could match any Westerner measure for measure in
intellect, sophistication, or technical prowess. And when turned to
evil enterprises, this new class of Arab was more than dangerous.
Saddam Hussein had pulled together a massive team of Arab-bred
physicists who were simply world-class and had a nuclear weapon
within their grasp when Kuwait was invaded. Musa Kousa was
an Arab of this cloth. Educated at Michigan State he was trilingual,
sophisticated, even charming, according to his dossier. And as
Wedley-Hooks said, deadly as a cobra.

Faisal rose and watched the stream of cars file out the gate. He
absolutely could not fathom why the Russians would be dealing
with the likes of Musa Kousa any longer. The Soviet Union had
cratered. They were desperate for Western aid. Old KGB hands
were falling over themselves to cooperate with Western antiterror-
ist efforts. Yet the evidence in this Tehran message was pretty well
damning. Had Wedley-Hooks considered the possibility of a rogue

operation by old KGB diehards? Had he explored the altar boys' Russian contacts about such a possibility? Curious, Faisal picked up his secure phone and placed a call to the man Slater—Wedley-Hooks's deputy—but learned he had left for the weekend. Faisal put down the phone, wondering who was defending the realm after business hours.

Frustration continued to build within him as he read the Tehran message once more. The words *Sundown* and *Cloudburst* left their imprint on his mind, but the altar boys had nothing but speculation that Cloudburst was a Soviet munition . . . Soviet munition . . . Soviet munition. A name flashed through Faisal's brain, and he began rummaging through his bottom desk drawer. Under some papers he found it—the ponderous *Ministry of Defense Directory*. Though limited in distribution, it listed anybody who was anybody in the MoD. Faisal flipped through the pages until he found the entry for RAF CHILMARK. His finger ran down the page to the name that triggered his memory: CORNWALD, ALEC, EVALUATION & ANALYSIS. Without hesitation he punched in the numbers, hoping he could collar the good Dr. Cornwald before he took his leave for the weekend.

There was a single ring before it was answered with a cryptic, "Cornwald."

"Dr. Alec Cornwald?"

"Yes, who is speaking, please?"

"Forgive me, Doctor, I don't know if you remember me or not . . ." Faisal hesitated here, for this wasn't a secure phone line, and despite the New World Order, he was confident this conversation would soon be passing through an analyst's earphones at Kuntsevo. "My name is Faisal Shaikh. I met you once—briefed you, in fact—when you were part of a senior MoD tour at, uh, Cheltenham a year or so ago."

"Umm. Vaguely. What can I do for you, Mr. Shaikh?"

"A matter has come across my desk that requires your specific expertise. I wondered if I might travel down to Chilmark and talk with you about it personally."

"Well, certainly, if you like. When?"

"I hate to impose, Dr. Cornwald, but I wonder if tomorrow might be convenient. This matter may be time sensitive."

"Of course. What is tomorrow anyway?"

"Why, it's Saturday, Doctor."

"One day is like any other for me. You're coming down from Cheltenham? Let's make it two o'clock. I'll have you met at the main gate."

"Very well, Doctor. See you then. And thank you."

"Not at all."

Faisal hung up the phone and smiled, content in the knowledge he wasn't the only workaholic in government service.

CHAPTER SIX

The Jaguar Sovereign had crossed the Wylye Valley, then headed southwest on the A303. Farther down the road it took a narrow country lane that snaked through the windswept landscape of the Dorset countryside. It was the first of December, and a wet Atlantic chill covered the brown veld like a cold, soggy blanket. It was something Faisal never got used to. The English cold. He supposed it was something in his genes that found comfort in warmer climates. And yet he'd gone to Edinburgh for his education. Absurd. Faisal's bloodlines were predominantly Pakistani, but he described himself as a mixed-breed Briton and left it at that. One grandmother was French, one grandfather Egyptian, but beyond that who really knew? His family had been in Europe and England for so long that Pakistan seemed alien to him.

The Sovereign continued on toward the village of Chilmark. After dodging a few lorries on the narrow road, he came upon a hedgerow with strands of barbed wire suspended above it. This was a sign to Faisal that he was in the right place. The road followed the hedgerow for some distance until a gap appeared, then Faisal wheeled the Jaguar past a sign that read:

MINISTRY OF DEFENSE
RAF CHILMARK

RESTRICTED ACCESS
ALL WHO ENTER SUBJECT TO SEARCH

He pulled up to the guardhouse and held out his GCHQ badge. The uniform said, "Yes, sir. You are expected." A second uniformed man climbed into the passenger seat. Smiling, the well-scrubbed youth said, "Just down the way, sir." Faisal drove past an assortment of corrugated-steel and brick buildings that seemed even more grim than Cheltenham.

RAF Chilmark was one of those rather queer establishments where science was applied to the art of war—in essence, where brainpower was transformed into firepower. Within these warehouselike buildings were an amalgam of scientists, engineers, technicians, draftsmen, clerks, and bureaucrats who designed and tested implements of war for the defense of the realm—everything from canteens to laser-guided bombs. And they tested the enemy's weaponry as well.

Faisal and his escort parked and walked quickly through the blustery wind to a steel building. They entered and went down a concrete-floored corridor to a door marked EVALUATION & ANALYSIS.

The guard opened the door to a reception area and said, "I'll just wait outside, sir."

Faisal nodded, then stood alone in the reception area for a few moments before calling, "Dr. Cornwald?"

A head poked out of the adjoining office. The skin of the face seemed tightly drawn over bone, and a lone wisp of hair was combed over a large bald head. A pair of energetic eyes peered over half-moon glasses, and a high-pitched voice asked, "Dr. Shaikh?"

"Yes."

A hand extended, along with a welcoming smile. "Alec Cornwald. Do come in. Tea?"

"Love some."

Faisal entered an utterly functional office, devoid of creature comforts or aesthetic appointments. A large metal desk and a metal table held stacks of documents and printouts, and the only item decorating the wall was an aerial photograph of Chilmark. Cornwald was wearing a long, white laboratory coat that hung loosely on his wiry body. He poured the tea and motioned Faisal to his visitor's chair. To Faisal, Cornwald seemed an energetic and focused man with intense, searching eyes.

From behind his desk, he said, "I remember you now. After your call I reviewed my notes of our tour to GCHQ. You gave us a crisp briefing on cryptanalysis."

Faisal sipped the orange pekoe tea. "And I would wager you were the only one who took notes."

Cornwald chortled and said, "Probably. What can we at RAF Chilmark do for you?"

Faisal put down his cup. "As I recall from your trip to Cheltenham, you were regarded as the leading British authority on Soviet, or perhaps I should say Russian, conventional armaments."

Cornwald shrugged, then picked up a pipe and began filling the bowl from a tobacco pouch. "My life's work, basically. Don't deal much with nuclear. There's a chap named Greyston who's the high priest on that. But conventional is my sphere. Russian weapons and aircraft that have been captured in, say, Iraq or Lebanon or Afghanistan, or procured by 'other' means, are routed through my office for evaluation by my staff. A lot of cross-fertilization with the Americans at Wright-Patterson, but then you would know about that sort of thing."

"Of course. What I have to show you is an intercepted message out of Tehran, and I want you to tell me if any of the terms ring a bell with you." Faisal reached into his coat pocket and extracted a copy of the Tehran epistle.

TO: **PAGEBOYS**

FROM: **SANDCASTLE**

CLOUDBURST FOR SUNDOWN HAS BEEN OBTAINED. DELIVERY IN TEN DAYS TIME. COMMENCE PREPARATIONS.

END MESSAGE

Cornwald scanned it thoughtfully through his half-moon glasses, then leaned back. Faisal watched Cornwald's face as it tightened, almost like a wince. Then with the stem of his pipe the scientist tapped the paper and said, "Nasty piece of work that. Wicked, really."

"What, precisely, are you referring to, Doctor?"

Cornwald ignited his pipe with a match, puffed a few times, and murmured, "Cloudburst."

Faisal felt a tremor of anxiety. "And what is Cloudburst?"

Cornwald puffed again, then softly said, "Fuel-air."

Faisal was lost. "And what is fuel-air?"

The scientist was contemplative as he continued pulling on his pipe, and during the lull Faisal took out his own cigarette case, lighter, and onyx holder. Finally Cornwald spoke. "Fuel-air bombs are probably the most lethal conventional weapons ever devised. A sad commentary on the human species, but there it is."

Curious, Faisal asked, "But what is it, exactly?"

Cornwald took a pen from his breast pocket and sketched on the legal pad in front of him. "An aircraft releases the bomb, and during its descent it deploys a parachute to slow its fall. A few hundred feet above the ground a large cloud of petrol mist is dispersed."

"Then what?"

"Then the detonator triggers an incendiary charge and the petrol mist ignites, creating a pressure shock wave which approaches that of a tactical nuclear weapon."

Faisal felt himself swallow involuntarily. "And that is what this Cloudburst is? A fuel-air bomb?"

Cornwald shook his head. "Not a bomb precisely. And I must confess my information on Cloudburst is extremely sketchy. It comes hearsay from a friend of mine, my counterpart in the French Defense Ministry. He claims that at the tail end of the Afghan War the Soviets were experimenting with a fuel-air antipersonnel landmine prototype, which they referred to as Cloudburst. The effect would be much smaller than a large, air-delivered bomb, but within its blast radius it would be devastating. My friend also claimed that Cloudburst went into limited production before the Russian economy imploded."

Faisal nervously stubbed out his cigarette. "This fuel-air land mine. What would its physical dimensions be? Its weight?"

Cornwald shrugged. "Total speculation on my part, but not too large, I wouldn't think. Small enough for a single soldier to carry. Possibly as small as, say, the size of a football, weight one to two stone."

"So we are talking about something that is man-portable, easy to conceal or smuggle, with a lethality greater than, say, Semtex plastique explosive."

"Far greater."

Faisal pondered what Cornwald had told him and said, "It's hard to believe that a small amount of petrol could be so devastating."

Cornwald put down his pipe and rummaged in the waste bin beside his desk. He extracted a small plastic bag, which he held up, saying, "From my lunch." Then he grabbed a rubber band off his desk and said, "Come along, I'll show you."

Faisal followed him through a door that opened into a large warehouselike interior. Cornwald walked past a dismantled fighter plane, laid out piece by piece on the floor. While stepping over a landing gear, Faisal asked, "What is that?"

"Oh, that? Soviet MiG-23 Flogger. Spoils from Iraq." Cornwald disappeared into a storeroom and came out carrying a small petrol can and a spent artillery-shell casing. He placed the casing on the workbench and said, "Soviet one-two-two millimeter. Afghanistan." From the workbench, he pulled off a length of dual-strand copper wire from a spool, then stripped off the insulation with a pocketknife. He opened the petrol can and said, "Let's say, an ounce?" He poured a dab of gasoline into the shell casing, which was standing upright on the workbench like a stovepipe. He took one end of the dual wire so the two exposed prongs were barely touching each other, and lowered them into the shell casing. Then he capped the shell with the plastic sandwich bag and rubber band. Once satisfied the bag was airtight, Cornwald picked up the shell casing and bobbled it several times as if it were a big martini shaker. "Helps the fumes build up." He replaced the casing on the workbench and played out the spool of wire toward the disassembled aircraft, thirty feet away. There he snipped the wire again and stripped off the insulation. "A battery," he explained, while wrapping one exposed prong to the positive terminal of a power cell that had come off the Russian MiG. Cornwald held the other strand of wire over the negative terminal and smiled while asking, "Ready?"

Faisal shrugged. "I suppose so."

"Capital." Cornwald touched the exposed wire to the terminal and the circuit was complete.

BLAM!

Faisal jumped about two feet off the ground as the shell casing executed a somersault off the workbench and fell clanging to the concrete floor. A few moments of silence passed before the guard came bounding through the door. "It's quite all right, my boy," assured Cornwald. "We were just conducting a little experiment."

The guard surveyed the scene and said, "Very well, then. I'll just wait outside."

Faisal remained dumbfounded as he stared at the shell casing. Finally he swallowed and asked, "That was a single ounce?"

"Correct."

He swallowed again. "I routinely drive around with ten imperial gallons in my Jaguar's fuel tank."

Cornwald smiled. "We all do. Motor around with a box of dynamite and don't even give it a second thought. But it's not the liquid, you see. It's the vapors. A fuel-air bomb concentrates the vapors before ignition. I think you've got the idea now."

"You've made your point most succinctly, Dr. Cornwald. Good day."

It was a gray Wednesday afternoon, and Faisal Shaikh was again at his office window, looking out at the rows of hutlike structures within the compound at Benhall. Inside those huts were rows upon rows of cubicles, lined up like sentries, where a battalion of linguists worked in a high-tech sweatshop. Each stall had a set of headphones and foot pedals, a keyboard and a computer terminal. The analysts would sit for hours at a stretch, straining to hear that key phrase in Russian, Arabic, or Mandarin that might make a difference to the defense of the realm. It was bestial work, and quite often the sound quality was poor, requiring the linguists to hit the foot pedals again and again to rewind and play the garbled tapes. Ninety-nine point nine nine percent of the intercepts were useless, but that final fraction of a percent could sometimes be compelling. Like the time Konstantin Chernenko lay dying and Mikhail Gorbachev was making his play for the post of general secretary. Those telephonic transcripts of Gorbachev wheeling and dealing made for fascinating reading, as did the transcripts of the failed Soviet coup when Gorbachev was under house arrest at his dacha on the Black Sea.

Faisal turned away from the window, and with arms folded he began to pace his office. He was waiting impatiently for the return of Arthur Wedley-Hooks from China. Faisal had bent, if not broken, the rules by sitting on the Tehran message and not forwarding it to Dickie Bartholomew's Liaison Division. He had lingered in the hope that another piece of the puzzle would materialize, but now it appeared he'd run into a stone wall. For the hundredth time he opened the MOST SECRET file and scanned the text:

TO: **PAGEBOYS**

FROM: **SANDCASTLE**

CLOUDBURST FOR SUNDOWN HAS BEEN OBTAINED. DELIV-ERY IN TEN DAYS TIME. COMMENCE PREPARATIONS.

END MESSAGE

SANDCASTLE might be Musa Kousa, the Libyan viper. CLOUDBURST might be the venomous fuel-air mine. But who or what or where was SUNDOWN? Who were the PAGEBOYS? The message was incomplete, and Faisal hated to pass on piecemeal information. There were times when partial data could foul things up worse than no information at all. But this message was potentially too grave not to pass on. If Wedley-Hooks did not appear by the end of the day, Faisal would hand it off to Dickie's division, who would pass it on to the Joint Intelligence Committee and the Iranian desk of the Foreign Office. There it would be batted around like a shuttlecock, then filed away in a folder marked INSUFFICIENT DATA, or something equally obtuse.

Faisal walked out to his secretary's office and said, "Geneviève . . ." She turned down the small radio tuned to the BBC. Geneviève Monson never had the radio on at work, causing him to ask, "What are you listening to?"

Geneviève's face betrayed a somber mood, unlike her normal defiance. "Just listening to the news about that British Airways seven-four-seven."

Faisal felt a tremor go through his body. "What seven-four-seven?"

Geneviève sniffed. "Just heard about it. It's simply terrible. Exploded in the air shortly after takeoff. Over two hundred people killed."

"Good God, this is the first I've heard about it! When did it happen?"

"About an hour ago. It was bound for London out of Hong Kong."

Faisal paused, wondering if it was possible. Then he quickly dismissed the idea. "Try and get Wedley-Hooks for me again, will you?"

Geneviève sniffed once more, then reached for the phone.

It was late that same afternoon when Geneviève stuck her head through the door and announced, "A Mr. Fenton Slater to see you, Dr. Shaikh. He's an associate of Mr. Wedley-Hooks."

"Show him in."

Faisal rose and greeted the young man, whom he guessed to be in his late twenties. He was of medium height but willowy, almost frail, and his delicate, androgynous features were acutely downcast. Faisal seated him on the coffee table couch and took the adjoining easy chair. The young gentleman extracted an envelope from his briefcase and handed it over, saying, "I've just come from London. Mr. Wedley-Hooks asked me to pass this on to you personally the moment it came in. I have no idea what it's about."

Faisal snatched the envelope and said, "Excellent. Is Arthur back in town yet?"

Fenton Slater snapped his briefcase closed and stood up, saying, "I'm afraid Mr. Wedley-Hooks won't be returning. He was on board the seven-four-seven that went down this morning in Hong Kong." With misty eyes he added, "If you'll excuse me, I really must be going."

Faisal remained seated. In shock. Beyond shock. The pit of his belly began sinking into his bowels as his mind spun into a vortex. He grabbed the arms of his chair for balance. A colleague's life had vanished with the words, "He was on board the seven-four-seven." What could he say? What could he do? As Faisal's mind continued to tumble, he stared at the envelope, whose purpose he couldn't recall. Almost numb, he broke the seal and pulled out the single sheet. It was in French, and with difficulty he shifted mental gears to translate.

TO: **ALAIN LEMIEUX, CHIEF OF STATION, LONDON**

FROM: **HEADQUARTERS, LIAISON DIVISION, DGSE, PARIS**

PER YOUR REQUEST FOR INFORMATION REGARDING LIST OF CODE WORDS SUBMITTED ON MESSAGE (TRACKING #09742): THROUGH SOURCES IN ALGERIA IT HAS BEEN DETERMINED THAT WITHIN CERTAIN EXTREMIST POLITICAL CIRCLES THE WORD "SUNDOWN" IS SOMETIMES ATTRIBUTED TO IBRAHIM AL-AZIZ AL SAUD—THE SAUDI ARABIAN FOREIGN MINISTER AND MEMBER OF THE ROYAL FAMILY OF THE HOUSE OF SAUD. NO FURTHER DATA WERE AVAILABLE.

MESSAGE FIN

Faisal leapt from his chair, covering the three meters to his desk in a single bound. He grabbed his *Times* of London and nearly ripped the newspaper apart as he searched frantically for a minor news item he'd read that morning. His shock having vanished as instantaneously as it appeared, he found the article. There. On page three. Near the bottom. Next to a shapely model wearing white panties and bra, beckoning shoppers to the pre-Christmas lingerie sale at Harrods. The three-inch story was headlined, SAUDI FOREIGN MINISTER ARRIVES FOR STATE VISIT TOMORROW.

Faisal tore the story, and part of the model's leg, from the page, then grabbed his jacket, coat, and Black Cipher file. He shot past Geneviève, saying, "Call Beekman at Oakley and tell him I need to see Sir Vivian straightaway!"

Faisal rarely ran, but he ran now. Down the hall and down the stairs because it was faster than the lift.

SANDCASTLE, the Libyan viper. CLOUDBURST, the fuel-air mine. SUNDOWN, the Saudi foreign minister. With horrifying clarity Faisal now knew who the PAGEBOYS must be. Had to be. The provisional wing of the Irish Republican Army.

Faisal shot through the door marked DIRECTOR and into the reception area. It might have been the office of a moderately successful solicitor, or an insurer, for the appointments were rather ordinary. Behind the reception desk was Anthony Beekman, Sir Vivian's eellike male secretary, guarding the door of his master.

"My secretary called ahead. I need to see Sir Vivian immediately."

Beekman scarcely looked up from his papers as he replied, "Ah, Dr. Shaikh, well, I am afraid that is quite impossible. Sir Vivian's calendar is full for the remainder of the week." He thumbed through the appointment book. "Hmm. Perhaps next Wednesday, say nine-fifteen A.M.? But then, I understand you are a late sleeper. Am I correct?"

Faisal would remember it as one of the more sublime moments of his career at GCHQ. He reached full across the desk and grabbed a fistful of Beekman's shirt, tie, and collar. Then he pulled the eel's torso across the desktop until their faces were two inches apart. In a voice with a menacing timbre, Faisal whispered, "Now you listen to me, you bloody fool. I don't have time for your gate-keeper prattle. I don't care who Sir Vivian is with, get them out of there *now!*" And he shoved Beekman back into his secretary's chair, with a force that dislodged an ear stem of the man's eye-glasses. Faisal's conduct was so alien to both men that they re-mained frozen for a moment, trying to absorb what had taken place. Faisal thought he should feel remorseful, apologetic, or em-barrassed. But he didn't. He found roughing up Beekman rather exhilarating. Beekman, however, did not. He realigned his glasses, then grabbed the intercom phone. As Beekman held his hand over the mouthpiece, Faisal could discern clips of, "Sorry to disturb . . . Shaikh insists . . . urgent . . . yes, sir." Beekman put down the phone and stared at Faisal. Then he pushed his chair back until he was comfortably out of range.

The door to the director's private office swung open and out stepped Graeme Stoneleigh, peering at Shaikh through his tortoise-shell frames. Stoneleigh paused for a moment, the smug counte-nance of his face transmitting something to Faisal, he knew not what. Neither man spoke, for the contempt between them could have been sliced like kidneys for a pie. Then Stoneleigh walked on and Faisal entered.

"Yes, Shaikh," spoke Sir Vivian Mittleditch without rising. "What is it?"

Faisal took one of the chairs across the desk. "Sir Vivian, I am here with regard to the seven-letter-cipher-group messages. The ones that revealed the nuclear accident in Aykhal, the drunk American inspector-rapist in Petropavlovsk, and the uprising in Samarkand that almost resulted in the use of chemical weap-ons."

"Yes."

"You may recall, Sir Vivian, that we also picked up a short trans-mission from Tehran, apparently from the Russian embassy or the military advisory group still stationed there."

"Yes?"

"This particular intercept was incredibly bizarre because the text was transmitted in English, not Russian. We finally deciphered it and here it is." Faisal placed the paper in front of his superior.

TO: **PAGEBOYS**

FROM: **SANDCASTLE**

CLOUDBURST FOR SUNDOWN HAS BEEN OBTAINED. DELIV-ERY IN TEN DAYS TIME. COMMENCE PREPARATIONS.

END MESSAGE

"Arthur Wedley-Hooks—the altar boy I liaised with—obtained some information through the American-Israeli intelligence link that Sandcastle is possibly Musa Kousa, a former henchman of Qaddafi's now freelancing in Lebanon or Iran. Through RAF Chilmark I learned that Cloudburst could be some type of fuel-air munition. Extremely lethal. And as for Sundown, I have just received this from the altar boys." Faisal laid the paper down. "It is a message from the headquarters of the French DGSE, speculating that Sundown could be Prince Ibrahim, the Saudi foreign minister"— he slapped down the *Times* article, along with a piece of the model's leg—"who is arriving tomorrow for a state visit. I did not think to do this before, but we can run this through the Northern Ireland Working Group. I would bet the crown jewels that Pageboys are the IRA."

Mittleditch did not react at first. Rather, he examined each document slowly, carefully, as if it were a draft of his own will. And as the director read on, Faisal shook his head and lamented, "I just cannot believe the Russians are assisting the Iranians in this. They've cooperated with us time and again on counterterrorism, but the evidence is right here in front of us. They have allowed the Iranians to use their most sophisticated encryption machine and have supplied them with this Cloudburst fuel-air device. Something is beyond the pale here. Maybe a rogue element of the old KGB is responsible."

Mittleditch placed his hands flat on the desk, then looked up at his visitor for what seemed to be the longest time. Finally a smile spread across his face—Faisal couldn't recall having seen one before—and he rose. Gesturing with a hand, he said, "Shaikh... Faisal... let's move over here, shall we?"

Somewhat surprised, Faisal did not protest as Sir Vivian took his arm and guided him toward the living area of his office. "Have a seat." Opening a cabinet, he asked, "Drink?"

"Uh, no. Thank you. Evian water would be fine if you have it."

"Oh, yes, of course," Sir Vivian said while dropping ice cubes into a tumbler. "Religious convictions preclude your partaking of demon gin, eh? Most admirable, I must say. Most admirable." While filling the tumblers, he continued, "I don't believe I ever told you, on a personal level, what a first-rate job your shop did on that Chinese machine."

I know you didn't tell me, recalled Faisal.

"Yes, a first-class job on—what was it called?"

"Dragon," said Faisal, while taking the Evian from Sir Vivian's plump hand.

"Ah, yes, the Dragon," reminisced the director while lowering his elephantine girth onto the couch. "It isn't often one gets to head off a neutron bomb before it's used. Heaps of praise came down on us from Number Ten, and even the White House."

So I heard, thought Faisal. *But not from you.*

"And now this Russian encryption machine that is putting out the seven-letter code groups. What did you call them?"

"The Black Cipher."

"Umm." The director smiled. "How sinister. Yes, I don't mind telling you the Americans were in our knickers about the computer time your boys were gobbling up." Sir Vivian actually chuckled. "But look at the rewards! We learned the Bolsheviks almost shot themselves in the groin with a nuclear bullet, plus all the rest."

"And now the Tehran message."

The smile vanished. "Quite." Sir Vivian moved forward, holding his tumbler with both hands, his knee almost touching Shaikh's. "Now then, Faisal, I want to thank you for bringing this matter to my personal attention. That was wise. Very wise, indeed. I hope you can appreciate there are times in my capacity as director that I must deal in matters which are highly sensitive. Matters that I cannot share with anyone. Not even with you."

Faisal's antennae pricked up. "Is this such a matter?"

Sir Vivian stared at his ice cubes. "Does anyone else know what you've told me? Have you mentioned this to Dickie Bartholomew?"

"No. I came here straightaway after putting it together. Only one person has . . . *had* the whole picture. But he's dead now."

The director looked up. "Dead? Who?"

"Arthur Wedley-Hooks, my altar-boy liaison. He was bringing out a Chinese source from Beijing, the one who gave us the goods on that Dragon machine. He went down on the seven-four-seven that crashed in the sea outside Hong Kong today. Presumably his spy was on board as well."

"My. How simply dreadful."

"More than dreadful. Wedley-Hooks was a good man."

Sir Vivian's gaze returned to the ice. "So no one knows the whole picture but you. Not even your deputy? Burdick?"

"No. He's been on leave. Returns on Monday."

Under heavy lids, Sir Vivian's eyes fixed on Faisal. "Then let's keep it between us, shall we?"

"Does that mean you will route this information to the proper security people?"

"As I mentioned, tell no one outside this room. Not even Burdick. But for your own information, I can assure you this matter will receive my personal attention."

"That is reassuring, Sir Vivian. Only please do not delay in acting on this. Prince Ibrahim is arriving tomorrow."

The director gave Faisal's knee a fatherly pat. "Trust me."

Jamie Burdick was slumped in the chair facing Faisal's desk, his eyes reading the communiqué. It was Friday and officially he was still on leave, but he'd sneaked back into the office to catch up on mail before reporting for work on Monday. Upon finishing the communiqué, he tossed it on the desk and muttered, "Damn them all to hell."

Faisal fingered his malachite lighter as he replied, "My sentiments exactly. Arthur's assistant, a chap named Fenton Slater, filled me in on the details of that cable. It came from the altar boys' chief of station in Hong Kong. Apparently Wedley-Hooks was much more of a cloak-and-dagger man than we realized. And this bloke they were pulling out of Beijing was, in fact, a deputy minister of defense."

"No small wonder he had access to the Dragon encryption keys."

"Quite. And somewhere along the way the whistle was blown. The Tewu were determined to stop his defection at any cost. Their agents must have been all over Kai-Tak airport looking for him."

Burdick flicked a lock of blond hair out of his violet-colored eyes. "But to shoot down a seven-four-seven full of innocent people because one defector is on board . . . " His voice faded and he shook his head.

"According to Fenton Slater, the Tewu had an agent in place with one of those shoulder-fired surface-to-air missiles—a Stinger I believe the Americans call them. He was floating on a skiff near the end of the runway. Shortly after Wedley-Hooks and his spy were airborne the agent fired, and . . . " Faisal shrugged his shoulders. "I find this New World Order rather distasteful."

Burdick emitted a grunt and said, "Think this report will ever see the light of day?"

"I doubt it. It happened at dusk, almost darkness. And what could the government do? Threaten to bomb Beijing? Impose sanctions? Refuse to surrender Hong Kong? This isn't America against Iraq. It's the tiny United Kingdom against a nuclear power with a billion people. If this report hit the papers, the government would be in a fix. There would be demands for action but little they could do."

"So the victims and their families will never know the seven-four-seven was blown out of the sky because we were trying to pull out a spy."

"That's about the size of it."

Burdick looked downcast, then changed the subject. "By the way, did you learn anything further on that Tehran message?"

Faisal took a long drag on his cigarette holder, then slowly exhaled before looking his most trusted aide in the eye and saying, "No. Not a thing."

Faisal flicked off the one P.M. BBC news on the small telly he kept in the kitchen. There was a brief mention of the Saudi foreign minister's being in town for talks, with a postscript saying he would call on the Queen at the newly restored Windsor Castle for afternoon tea. Then the commentator went on to bemoan the growing unemployment figures. Nothing about bombs, bullets, or mayhem. All was peaceful and quiet. Faisal looked out at his hibernating gardens and felt himself sinking into a trough of depression. After the frenzy of activity over the Black Cipher he was now mentally exhausted and physically spent, and it was moments like this when his loneliness caved in on him. He had no family to share his triumphs or to provide solace in defeat. When he was younger, these down moments were neither severe or prolonged; but at forty-seven, Faisal now found the specter of continued loneliness profoundly depressing.

In reaction to his funk, he stubbed out his cigarette and slid off the counter stool. *Get moving,* he told himself. It was a beautiful Saturday. Cold but clear, and the wind was still. Christmas was approaching. He'd take a brisk walk through the Cotswolds, do some Christmas shopping for Jamie's boy, Nigel, have a spicy dinner at a Pakistani restaurant in Cheltenham, then come home and curl up next to the fire with a good political novel, Trollope's *The Eustace Diamonds.* He changed into some wool trousers, a turtleneck, and threw on a tweed jacket. Grabbing his overcoat, he walked out to the garage and his Jaguar Sovereign.

The police were everywhere. London bobbies with their distinctive headgear could be found all along the route, from the Saudi embassy to Windsor Castle. On street corners, behind windows, and on rooftops they were present, keeping a watchful eye for any aberration that might breach the security of Prince Ibrahim's motorcade. It was to be the Queen's first tea at Windsor Castle since the restoration. A foul-up at this point simply would not do. So many uniforms were about that no one noticed when a constable slowly approached the edge of a terraced house rooftop. With deliberate movements, he fastened a small grappling hook to the ledge and draped a fishnet sack over the side. A sack that held an object about the size and shape of a rugby ball. The uniformed constable then turned his back and walked to the access door to the roof. He passed through the doorway and rapidly descended the darkened stairway, saying, *"Ceangail Eire,"* as he tapped the headgear of a motionless bobby slumped against the banister.

"What's that?" The thick-necked sergeant lowered his binoculars from his rooftop vantage point and stuck out his finger. "There. Along the roofline. In the middle of the block."

His companion, a thin and wiry constable, lifted his own field glasses and inspected the area in question, seeing a small baggy object. " 'Aven't a clue, Sergeant."

"Who has that sector?"

"Tommy—er, Constable Greene, Sergeant." The sergeant was new to the division. More formal in his approach than his predecessor.

"Where is he then?"

"Don't see 'im at the moment."

"Well, get him on the talkie and have him check it out quick. The motorcade is due any second."

The constable raised his hand transceiver and flicked it to the proper frequency net. "Unit Seven, this is Unit One. Do you read, over?"

The speaker squawked, then there was silence.

The sergeant's binoculars were frantically searching the rooftops now. "Where is he? Sittin' on his duffer somewhere? Why ain't he on the lookout?"

"Unit Seven, this is Unit One, respond, over. . . . Tommy, answer me."

Tommy couldn't respond. He'd been left for dead after receiving an injection of potassium cyanide from the phony bobby. When administered with a deft hand, a lethal hypodermic could be much quieter and less messy than a silenced revolver.

The sergeant lowered his binoculars. "I don't like this. Radio Central. Instruct them to reroute the motorcade away from . . . "

"Uh-oh."

At that moment, two motorcycle policemen rounded the corner, followed by a security Vauxhall. Then came the massive Daimler bearing His Royal Highness Prince Ibrahim, an honorable man who embraced peace and diplomacy.

The burly sergeant ripped the radio from the constable and screamed, "*Code nine! Code nine!* Central, tell the drivers to floor it now!"

Two miles away, in one of those glass skyscrapers the Prince of Wales was loath to see on the London skyline, stood a rough-looking specimen. The kind you might find on the docks of Liverpool or Belfast. He was standing amongst the exposed girders, cables, and insulation of the unfinished office space, bent over a high-powered telescope resting on a tripod. He watched the motorcade as it made a turn onto Vereker Road toward Baron's Court. The small parade was taking a serpentine route toward the M4 to Windsor Castle for security reasons.

Placed on a chair beside the bloke was an electronic device. One that looked like a shortwave radio with a set of rabbit ears. But it wasn't that. Not at all. Once the Daimler appeared, he licked the sweat off his upper lip and muttered, *"Ceangail Eire."*

He pressed the red button just as the motorcade picked up speed.

The rugby ball hanging in the fishnet seemed to make a *CRUMP!* sound as it disintegrated, sending out a gray, smoky-looking mist in the shape of a giant doughnut. The periphery of the doughnut cloud was just caressing the roof of the Daimler when the incendiary charge went off. The cloud of gasoline fumes fulminated in a massive airburst, and the shock wave flattened the motorcade like the foot of an angry giant squashing an insect. The constable and his sergeant saw the flash just before the pressure wave snapped their necks like a pair of matchsticks and hurled them across the rooftops—like broken crockery being tossed in the trash bin.

The terraced houses on either side of Vereker Road had their facades blown inward, where they teetered for a moment, then fell over in a kind of urban landslide. What was left of the Daimler became entombed in a pile of rubble, unlike anything on Vereker Road since a buzz bomb visited there in 1944.

The long, brisk walk through the countryside had refreshed Faisal, as had the dinner of *samosas* and curried chicken at the Pakistani restaurant. He'd heard some people at a distant table all abuzz about something during dinner, but he paid no attention. He was a weary man taking time to restore his depleted essence.

He parked the Jaguar and walked into the kitchen. Seeing it was 8:58 P.M., he flicked on the small television atop the breakfast counter. He would catch the BBC2 news before retiring to the study with his Trollope novel. The computer-graphic intro of rotating globes, spinning against a black background, was always eye-catching, and quite often more interesting than the news itself. Faisal slid onto the stool as the intro cut away to the image of a doughnut-shaped cloud exploding. Then the commentator intoned, "The death toll of the Vereker Road explosion rises to fifty-seven, including the Saudi Arabian envoy, Prince Ibrahim, who was en route to Windsor Castle. The tape you just saw was captured by BBC cameraman Lyle Jeffries just before he and his colleagues were killed by the massive blast . . . "

The words seemed to fade for Faisal as his body and senses froze, unable to accept the visions of carnage that screamed at him from the tiny screen. Over and over the explosion scene was repeated, each time sending a wrecking ball into Faisal's soul with the wail of "betrayal-betrayal-betrayal." Finally he could take no more, and his body jackknifed off the stool in a convulsion of blind rage.

He nearly ripped the door off its hinges to get to his Jaguar.

Faisal had been to Sir Vivian's house only once for a terribly dry reception to honor his appointment as director of GCHQ. It, too, was in the fashionable enclave of Battledown Estates, just one street over from Faisal's residence on Stanley Road. The Jaguar drove past the director's house before Faisal's shock-laced mind recognized he'd overshot. He turned around and wheeled into the circular drive, screeching to a halt in front of the darkened entry. Faisal exited the Jaguar and bounded up the steps to mash the doorbell. A half dozen times he punched the little button, hearing muffled chimes from within. But there was no response, so he pounded on the door with all his strength. Finally, the porch light flicked on and the heavy door swung open, revealing Sir Vivian Mittleditch. He was wearing an expensive silk dressing gown over his massive girth, and an expression of fury upon his thick features. "All right, Shaikh, what is the meaning of—"

But Sir Vivian got no further, for Faisal was upon him like an angry lioness, grabbing his lapels and shaking him. "Mittleditch! You stupid, bloody fool! I *told* you about the bomb! I told you about the IRA! It was a massacre, and all because you did *nothing!*"

Faisal was thin and wiry, and by no means could he throw someone around who was two and a half times his own weight. Stunned at first, Mittleditch quickly took the offensive and shoved Faisal against the wall, his face inches away. "Now you listen to me, Shaikh. You keep your mouth shut and just leave it alone. I told you there were things I couldn't tell you. Now just go home and be quiet. Nobody cares if a little sand wog gets topped, now do they? Just forget it. You understand? It's none of your affair."

Faisal struggled. "None of my affair? I'm going to haul you up before the JIC and blow the whistle on this, this *murder!*"

Mittleditch pressed him harder, his face coming ever closer, and for the first time Faisal became aware of the foul stench of Sir Vivian's breath. But it was his eyes that had transformed now. Instead of being moribund, thick-lidded windows to a dormant soul, they transmitted a force of such malevolence that they sapped Faisal's rage and replaced it with fear. The voice whispered with a raspy edge, "You're in over your head, Shaikh. Farther than you can imagine. If you know what's good for you, you will keep your bloody mouth shut and forget everything. Now get out of here and never come back." And with that, Mittleditch manhandled Faisal out the door and slammed it shut.

A moment later, the light over the doorway was extinguished.

During the remainder of the weekend, Faisal's rage continued to build. Time and again the fuel-air explosion was replayed on the BBC. The death toll had climbed to sixty-eight, and the television screamed with the ghastly image of children's severed limbs being pulled from the rubble. The Saudis were enraged, and the prime minister's government, already corroded by a sickly economy, would likely face a no-confidence vote after Tuesday's Question Time. After the explosion, commentators had materialized on the BBC faster than one could brew instant oatmeal, and they lobbed their questions at the government like hand grenades. Couldn't the government, at the very least, protect its own citizens and foreign diplomats from something as diabolical as a fuel-air bomb? How did such a wicked implement of war get into the country? Who provided it? How was security penetrated? Was the government asleep?

Choking on the bile of rage and humiliation, Faisal meticulously prepared the measures he would take to hang Sir Vivian Mittleditch from the highest scaffold in the realm. First, he would collect all the Black Cipher data to compose a long paper trail. Then he would seek an audience with Viscount Thornley, the chairman of the Joint Intelligence Committee. He was a crusty old barrister with the mind of a razor. Faisal didn't know Thornley well. Had only met him a few times, but knew his reputation. With evidence in hand, Thornley would get to the bottom of things and go to the foreign minister, the cabinet secretary, or even the PM.

. . .

At eight A.M. sharp on Monday morning, Faisal wheeled the Jaguar Sovereign into the security drive of Benhall, as he had done for the last two decades, and rolled down the window to flash his security card.

"Ah, yes, suh. We've been expecting you."

Faisal looked up to see the pasty-faced security guard. He was a young recruit to government service. Born to a household of meager means, he'd grown to young manhood with ideas and ambitions that far outstripped his talents or bloodlines. Indeed, he fancied himself the long-lost Duke of Landbourne, or some other extinct peerage. And with that frame of mind, he could never quite stomach the idea of a person, with skin slightly darker than his own, sitting behind the wheel of a Jaguar Sovereign. Yes, Pasty Face was going to enjoy this.

"May I have your badge, suh." It was a command, not a request, and distant alarm bells began their faint peals.

"My security badge? What for?"

No explanation. Only a smile of bad dental work was given, along with the demand, firmer this time: "Your badge, suh."

Faisal's antennae picked up the presence of two more guards. One in front of the Jaguar's bonnet and another at the passenger door. Perceiving his choice was nil, he handed over his laminated identification badge. Odd. He suddenly felt naked without it. Pasty Face retired to the guard shack and returned with an envelope, which he handed over with a smile. Then he said, "Admittance to Government Communications Headquarters is denied. Please turn around and leave the premises."

"What!?"

Pasty Face backed up two paces, a little less sure of himself. "You are denied admittance, suh. You are to leave at once."

Faisal defiantly threw open the Sovereign's door and scrambled out. "I am a divisional chief of Government Communications Headquarters! Your people will stand aside and let me pass!"

"Don't do anything foolish, sir."

Faisal turned to the guard in front of the car's bonnet. Bigger, tougher, and meaner than Pasty Face, he had his right hand resting on the grip of his sidearm. That was strange. Faisal never remembered seeing the guards with guns before. The presence of the uniform had always been adequate authority. Then the bonnet guard did something ominous. He simply unsnapped the leather strap that held the revolver in place. The sidearm remained holstered, but now uncaged.

From the chemical soup of his nervous system, a pint of the "fight or flight" hormones dumped into Faisal's bloodstream, and it took him no more than a moment to seize upon the flight option. He leapt back into the Jaguar, threw it into reverse, and squealed his tires as he backed out onto Princess Elizabeth Way. Changing gears, he sped off through the roundabout and back down Gloucester Road. His heart racing, his palms sweaty, he realized the trees along the street were whipping by at a rapid pace. He spied the speedometer, and it told him he was traveling sixty-three miles an hour down the residential street. He braked, and with shaking hands he pulled into a BP station and killed the engine. He gripped the steering wheel and labored to get his breathing under control. Dear God, he'd never been so close to the business end of a firearm before! It was frightening, and some minutes passed before his respiration and pulse dropped from their elevated levels. He looked over at the passenger seat. Sitting there was the envelope Pasty Face had given him. He picked it up, ripped it open, and read.

YOUR EMPLOYMENT WITH GOVERNMENT COMMUNI-
CATIONS HEADQUARTERS IS HEREBY TERMINATED UN-
DER THE RULES OF PERSONNEL REGULATIONS VII 6 (b)
GOVERNING SENIOR MANAGEMENT POSITIONS. REGULA-
TIONS ALLOW SAID POSITIONS TO BE TERMINATED BY THE
DIRECTOR WITHOUT CAUSE, AND WITHOUT APPEAL TO
THE PERSONNEL REVIEW BOARD.

THE PERSONAL EFFECTS OF YOUR OFFICE, ALONG WITH
TERMINATION PAY AND STATEMENT OF PENSION BENE-
FITS ACCRUED WILL BE DELIVERED TO YOUR RESIDENCE
AT NOON TOMORROW.

ALL SECURITY CLEARANCES ARE HEREBY REVOKED AND YOU ARE REMINDED—IN THE STRONGEST POSSIBLE TERMS—THAT IF YOU DIVULGE TO ANY PERSON OR PERSONS ANY INFORMATION OF ANY KIND PERTAINING TO YOUR EMPLOYMENT AT GOVERNMENT COMMUNICATIONS HEADQUARTERS . . . YOU WILL BE SUBJECT TO PROSECUTION UNDER THE OFFICIAL SECRETS ACT.

S. HEPWORTH
HEAD ADMINISTRATION & PERSONNEL

Faisal sat at the breakfast-room table, looking out on the garden, which winter had turned lifeless, brown, and cold. Overwhelmed by shock, he could not bring himself to move. And if he did move, where would he go? What would he do? With no answer he simply sat there, the letter crumpled in his hand, watching the shadow of the oak tree inch across the courtyard. In his near catatonic state, the creak of the kitchen door jolted him like the crack of a bullwhip and he turned round. The intruder was equally surprised as she stood there, silent and staring. She was late middle-aged, short, and plump. Her graying hair was in a bun and her maid's uniform properly pressed. Faisal's housekeeper was stunned to find her employer already up and dressed at this hour of the morning.

"Why, Dr. Shaikh," she stammered. "I didn't expect to find you here."

Equally shocked, Faisal mumbled, "Uh, yes, Mrs. Wheatland. I, uh, decided not to go in today. I am taking the day off from work."

Mrs. Wheatland's mouth fell open. "Day off?" An announcement that Martians had landed in the Cotswolds would've been received with less shock effect than her employer saying he was taking the day off.

"Uh, yes," stammered Faisal. "I am not going in today."

"Oh, well then, sir, I'll just fix you some muffins."

"Uh, no, no. That won't be necessary. I'm just going for a walk. A long walk." And without saying more he walked past her, out to the Jaguar.

The Cotswolds of Gloucestershire impart a feeling of tranquillity with their gently flowing landscapes of green fields, low hills, church spires, stone-roof huts, and verdant trees; where the idyllic calm is broken only by the occasional fox hunt galloping past, or the RAF Tornado streaking overhead.

To Faisal Shaikh, God had taken special care to craft a land of beauty and tranquillity in Gloucestershire, where one could feel truly at peace. In a job—well, formerly in a job—that entailed intense pressure and required meticulous skills, Faisal would sometimes seek out a footpath in the Cotswolds. There he could walk briskly, inhale deeply, and allow the curative powers of the countryside to take effect. He took such a footpath now.

He parked the Jaguar on Cold Comfort Common, which in clear weather provided a lovely panorama of the Chelt Valley. But on this particular morning a mist obscured the view and covered the grass with a slick layer of moisture. Faisal was improbably dressed as he squished along the damp footpath in his Gucci loafers, tailored suit, and camel-hair overcoat. He thought deeply about Sir Vivian Mittleditch, Graeme Stoneleigh, and the assassination of Prince Ibrahim. He tried in vain to find some connection, some logic to it all, as the scope of this monstrous crime grated against his soul. He stormed past the mound called St. Paul's Epistle and then went down to Pinchley Wood, which in the summer was alive with the songs of birds. Now it was silent, except for the wind rustling through bare branches. Then he halted, his mind made up. Come what may, he'd get to the bottom of this cancer within GCHQ. Indeed, if he was to reclaim his career and his life, he had no choice.

He turned around and headed back to the Jaguar.

Faisal had showered, changed into slacks, and was taking some lunch from Mrs. Wheatland when the doorbell rang. He opened the door to find a gorillalike figure in overalls, with the words GLOUCESTER MOVING & STORAGE stitched above the pocket. Reading from one of those metal clipboards, the gorilla intoned, "Faisal Shaikh?"

"Yes, that is correct."

"Have a delivery for you."

"Yes, of course. Come in, I'll show you where to put it."

The gorilla walked inside as Faisal glimpsed a burgundy-colored Fiat parked down the lane. That was odd. He'd seen one just like it when he'd parked on Cold Comfort Common.

Faisal built a fire in his library/study, then methodically opened the large cardboard boxes that held the trappings and memorabilia of his career at GCHQ. Personal papers, his framed membership in the KRYPTOS Society, paperweights, his Parton paintings. A note stated his personal cherrywood desk was being held in storage at the moving company's warehouse. With each article he extracted, each old paper he read, his resolve to strike back at Mittleditch grew stronger and stronger. At the bottom of one box he found three envelopes. One was an accounting and explanation of his pension benefits, one was his last paycheck, and the final envelope was blank on the outside. He ripped it open and read. It was simply a list of surnames—a kind of roll call:

WOLFENDEN

BROCKWAY

DRINKWATER

FRANKS

OAKE

WILLIAMS

Faisal involuntarily shuddered, and a foreboding chill came over him despite the crackling fire. To the uninitiated, the names meant nothing; but to a senior executive of GCHQ they represented an ominous message.

Ten days after Geoffrey Arthur Prime was arrested in 1982 for being a Soviet spy at Cheltenham, another senior GCHQ official named Jack Wolfenden was killed when his glider crashed into a Cotswolds hillside. Later that same year a GCHQ radio operator named Ernest Brockway was found hanged in his Cheltenham home. In 1983, another employee by the name of Stephen Drinkwater apparently asphyxiated himself by securing a plastic bag over his head. In 1984, George Franks, a wireless operator at GCHQ's London intercept station in the Empress State Building, died of a heart attack in his Brighton flat. He was alone at the time. Two weeks later, Stephen Oake, a traffic handler at GCHQ's Morwenstow Station in Cornwall, took his own life. Then in 1987, a retired Russian-language expert named Ronald Williams gassed himself to death with car-exhaust fumes.

Suicides? Accidental death? Natural causes? Or something more sinister? In the netherworld of intelligence-gathering, who could say? Faisal had always felt far removed from the cloak-and-dagger aspect of Her Majesty's spy machine, for his intellectual pursuits were largely done in an ivory tower. Something like Wedley-Hooks's death was an aberration for him. Yet now he had to face the fact this roll call of the dead had been intentionally placed in his personal effects. A roll call that could have but one meaning: silence, or you will join them.

So devastating was this threat that the floor seemed to collapse under him and his breathing became labored. Shaking, he went to the front window, pulled back the curtain, and peered out. The Fiat was still there, parked down the lane. And, yes, it was definitely the same one he had seen on Cold Comfort Common. He could barely make out one—no, two—figures in the front seat.

With trembling hands he replaced the curtain.

CHAPTER  SEVEN

The wind was bitterly cold and pregnant with humidity as it raced down the Thames River to Westminster Bridge. With muffler wrapped around his neck and long blond hair whipping in the wind, Jamie Burdick could not escape the river's chill. He longed for the haven of a nice, warm, smoke-filled pub; but such a respite would have to wait. Burdick's rapid pace across Westminster Bridge came to an abrupt halt as he stopped and casually inspected Big Ben at Westminster Palace. The gothic structure that housed Her Majesty's Parliament always looked so august, so noble; yet Burdick found himself freezing in Big Ben's shadow because something was very rotten within the halls of Parliament, or Whitehall, or somewhere. Something very rotten, indeed.

With overt casualness, Burdick turned and looked behind him. No pedestrians were on the bridge. Only the flow of traffic going back and forth in an unending stream. Burdick had traveled to London on the pretense of a Christmas shopping pilgrimage. He'd suffered through the crush of shoppers at Harrods, then ridden the underground aimlessly, changing trains a half dozen times before exiting for good at Westminster Station. He'd crossed, then recrossed, the bridge on foot, and no one took an interest in him as far as he could tell. Still, he couldn't quite shake a feeling. Ever since the florist had delivered those flowers for Sylvia, and ever since that Ford parked near his house had not moved.

Burdick looked up at the face of Big Ben and it read 2:28 P.M. The stream of tourist traffic was slower than in the summer, but some camera-toting Japanese were nearby as he looked down at Westminster Pier. The sight-seeing river bus was preparing for its 2:30 P.M. departure. Burdick waited until Big Ben's hands read 2:29, then he bolted down the steps to the dilapidated ticket counter. Three old seamen, filled with brine and salt water, were sitting on boxes nearby, sipping a spot of tea as Burdick bought a ticket for Greenwich and sprinted through the gangway chute to the quay below. He passed his ticket to the bored adolescent attendant, just as the vessel cast off. Then he took a seat on a flimsy plastic chair. While catching his breath, Jamie looked out the Plexiglas window and saw a slightly overweight, middle-aged man, trotting as best he could toward the boat, waving his ticket. The teenage attendant waved back, shouting, "Catch the next one in thirty minutes." For a moment, the stranded man's eyes locked with Burdick's, then he turned away.

Damn! Double damn! I am *being followed!* The codebreaker's mind was awash with questions, doubts, and fears as the boat steered into the choppy river. Fewer than a dozen people were on board, most of them German tourists, and Burdick tried without success to make himself comfortable. The vessel's tour guide came on the loudspeaker and droned on about points of interest on the river, telling Burdick more than he would ever want to know about Sir Christopher Wren's design of St. Paul's Cathedral, which could scarcely be seen due to the high-rise office buildings that poisoned the view. Mercifully, the tour guide shut up as the boat pressed on toward Greenwich.

Upon mooring at Greenwich pier, the passengers were informed that gratuities for the crew would be welcomed. Burdick dropped a fifty-pence coin into the proffered plastic bucket as he stepped off the boat. Briskly he walked past the *Cutty Sark,* the Seaman's Hospital, and up the hill of Greenwich Park toward the Royal Observatory. Huffing and puffing, he climbed the steps to the walkway apron that skirted the old observatory building, then looked back down over the park. Catching his breath, he peered at the prime meridian coming out of the antiquated observatory. It was that arbitrary line which, by an 1884 treaty, served as a departure point for the world's navigators. As some tourists sauntered past him, Burdick pretended to be interested in the telescope aperture in the tower, and it was at that moment a voice behind him said, "Charles the Second commissioned Sir Christopher Wren to build it in 1675."

Burdick jumped and spun round. Then his body almost wilted as he recognized the speaker. "Sir Christopher must have been a busy fellow," he said finally; then, "Faisal, what the hell is going on?"

Faisal Shaikh took Jamie's arm and led him away from the flow of tourists, to a more secluded area of the stone patio. He pointed at a coin-operated spyglass and said, "I watched you as you crossed the park. It appears you weren't followed. Can't say for sure, though. I've never done this sort of thing before."

"Me neither," replied Burdick, feeling like a convict on the run. "I was followed, but I think I lost him at Westminster Pier." He took a few deep breaths to get a grip on himself, then recalled, "That was a clever idea, sending your message via flower delivery."

Faisal shrugged. "We have to assume phones are tapped and mail intercepted. It was the only way I knew to get a message to you. Were you able to check the files?"

Burdick sat down on a nearby bench and sighed. "I did just as you asked in your letter. Looked through the computer for anything on the Black Cipher."

"And?"

"They were all purged. Erased. Disappeared."

"Did you check with the Purple Gang? The Red Riding Hoods? In all, more than two dozen people must have worked on the Black Cipher. Their personal computer files must have some data stored?"

Burdick shook his head. "I said *everything* was purged. I was asking some of the Purple Gang about it and they were baffled by the missing files. There are only three people who have access codes to penetrate personal library files. You, me, and . . . "

"Sir Vivian Mittleditch. But he doesn't know jerry about computers or cryptanalysis. He wouldn't know where to begin."

"No, but Stoneleigh would."

"Stoneleigh?"

"Not him personally. He's a computer illiterate. But his staff is more than competent. With the director's access code they could crash into everyone's files, then methodically purge them one by one."

Faisal pursed his lips. "Never cared for Stoneleigh much. Always thought he was out of his depth in commo security."

"Apparently Mittleditch thinks otherwise, because as of yesterday Stoneleigh replaced you as chief of H Division."

"*What!?*"

"It's true. And as of Monday I am no longer deputy chief of H Division. I have been reassigned to the Don Juans."

"The Don Juans?"

"Afraid so. I leave for Buenos Aires within a fortnight."

Faisal was stunned, and he sat down next to Jamie on the cold stone bench. After a bit of silence, he said, "So that's it then. The game is over."

"What do you mean, it's over?"

Faisal plucked out the cigarette stub from the onyx holder and tossed it on the stone ground. With his heel he ground it out with more force than was necessary. "Sir Vivian Mittleditch is involved in some way with the murder of Prince Ibrahim and an entire neighborhood in Earl's Court. He suppressed the Black Cipher information on the assassination preparations and the fuel-air bomb. The only person who has seen the entire documentation is myself, and now that documentation—that evidence—is undoubtedly destroyed. The only independent verification was Arthur Wedley-Hooks, but he is dead. And now you, my most trusted ally within GCHQ, is being shipped out to the Southern Hemisphere. All in all, a very tidy job, wouldn't you say? Why waste a bullet when you can co-opt your adversary at every turn."

"Bullet?"

"Yes, Jamie. A bullet. Whatever Mittleditch is a part of, it is a group holding the reins of power. Wicked power. They've murdered dozens of innocent people, for what purpose I cannot fathom. But after spilling that much blood they wouldn't hesitate to top someone who threatened them. Especially a mere code-breaker like me. Or you."

Burdick gulped. "Me?"

"Yes, you."

Burdick looked at his gloved hands. They were shaking. "How could this happen? My God, Faisal, this is England!"

"It could happen anywhere, Jamie. Just look at the Kennedy assassination. A professional murder—a Mafia 'hit' I believe the Americans call it—bought and paid for in Marseilles. But the fix was in from start to finish, and those in power made sure the truth never saw the light of day. If it can happen in America, it can happen here. Or anywhere."

Burdick's hands kept shaking, and some moments passed before he found his voice again. "So what do we do?"

Faisal didn't hesitate. He slapped his thighs and rose. "I will tell you exactly what to do. You pack up Sylvia and Nigel and take the first flight to Argentina. Forget about the Black Cipher. Forget about me, and forget about this whole sordid mess."

"Forget about it?"

"Yes. You carry on as if it never happened. If we had some solid evidence, we might have a thread of a chance, but now there is no evidence. Only the word of a"—Faisal paused as he surveyed the park below—"a sacked employee."

Burdick gazed at him, questioning his judgment.

Faisal could sense his subordinate's rebellion, so he put the final nail in the coffin. "You do nothing, Jamie. Do you understand me? It isn't worth getting little Nigel killed."

"Nigel?"

"They've killed a dozen children already. They wouldn't hesitate to do so again if they were in jeopardy." Faisal looked upon his trusted protégé and friend, for what he feared was the last time.

"Good-bye, Jamie. You were the best I ever saw. Except for Angus. And with time you might have surpassed even him." He turned and walked away, but before disappearing down the stone steps, Burdick whispered after him, saying, "No, Faisal. . . . You were the best you ever saw."

CHAPTER EIGHT

"Check. And after three moves, checkmate."

Faisal stared at the chessboard, the impotence of his black pieces glaring back at him. Not wishing to prolong the torment, he laid down his king like a fallen sentry and rose to offer his hand.

It was with difficulty the bald, bearded, and bespectacled botany professor contained his glee while seizing Faisal's hand. "A marvelous game, sir. It isn't often I have the opportunity to best a grand master."

Faisal perfunctorily shook the hand and growled a terse, "Congratulations."

"The chess club at Exeter will be amazed at my achievement," crowed the professor.

"No doubt," muttered Faisal as he turned and strode through the Savoy's grand ballroom. The chamber was filled with chess players hunched over their knights, rooks, and bishops in the annual United Kingdom Chess Federation Tournament. Faisal had the distinction of being picked off during the initial elimination round by a fumbling professor he should have crushed, and under a normal state of affairs he would have. But unable to concentrate, his mind elsewhere, Faisal became easy prey to a fifth-rate talent.

He exited the ballroom and made his way up the stairs to the Savoy's elegant lobby. Then he abruptly came to a stop. Where was he going? What was he doing? He had no answer, for he had nowhere to go. Nothing to do. His watch said it was half-past noon, so for lack of anything better he decided to take lunch in the Savoy's River View Restaurant. He approached the maître d', who seated him at a table overlooking the Victoria Embankment. After ordering the Dover sole, he surveyed the small vessels plying back and forth on the Thames. Down the way he could see Cleopatra's Needle, an exotic obelisk from the sands of Egypt now deteriorating in the London smog. He could relate.

The shock to Faisal's system was wearing off, only to be replaced by utter desolation. The evidence that would vindicate him was destroyed and his career lay in ruins. The institution he revered was now controlled by malevolent forces, for reasons he could not fathom. Were he to marshal his own forces, put his credibility on the line, and confront Mittleditch without evidence, he would be dismissed as a lunatic, a workaholic who'd broken under the intense secretive pressure of GCHQ. Or, even worse, simply a disgruntled employee trying to exact his revenge. And by raising a challenge, would he place his life in jeopardy? The list of the dead, discovered in his moving boxes from GCHQ, was never far from his mind.

He was a man cast utterly adrift from the anchors in his life. He'd clumsily turned to a chess tournament as a salve for his wounded soul, only to be trounced by a bumbling boffin in the first round.

The sole came. Faisal picked at it, but having no appetite, he dropped a twenty-pound note on the table and left. Returning to the lobby, he was at a loss as to what to do. He thought about going into the Savoy's American Bar for a forbidden drink, but decided no. A walk instead. He went to the cloakroom and handed the attendant a chit, not noticing the *Times* on the counter with the headline Government Narrowly Survives Confidence Vote in Wake of Saudi Slaying. He gave the attendant a tip and exited past the doorman.

He walked up the entry road, then turned right onto the Strand. He pulled up his collar against the wind as he was swept along by the tide of Christmas shoppers. Having nowhere to go, he continued on, no longer caring if he was followed, or by whom. Indeed, he might have welcomed the company. Offered the bloke tailing him a cup of tea. A scone. A pint of bitter.

His self-absorption was shattered, along with a window glass, when a mêlée erupted across the street. A group of skinhead thugs had pounced on a young Indian or Pakistani man, breaking a shop window in the process. A burglar alarm pealed as passersby backed away from the naked violence. Like everyone else, Faisal was frozen in shock by the spectacle. But as blows continued to be struck, he summoned up his courage, then started to cross the street to go to the victim's aid. How he would help, he hadn't a clue; but he had to step forward. If he'd been on the other side of the street, he might well have been the victim. He'd just stepped off the curb when the hee-haw sound of a police siren blared through the air and a car rolled around the corner. The skinheads broke and ran as the car pulled to a stop and the constables piled out. A crowd now gathered around the fallen man. Since the cavalry had arrived, Faisal decided to press on, although he couldn't help but shudder. It seemed a sickness was in the land these days. Fractures appearing along ethnic lines. It was rather frightening, actually.

To shake off the experience he kept moving up the Strand where it turned into Fleet Street, then on past the Temple and the Royal Courts of Justice to St. Paul's Cathedral. After gazing for a moment at Wren's masterpiece, he turned and wandered aimlessly until he found himself staring into the face of the Duke of Wellington's horse. Well, a statue of the duke's horse, actually, with the duke majestically astride it, on the plaza outside the Royal Exchange. Or more specifically, the London International Financial Futures Exchange, where fortunes were made and lost each business day. Faisal entered the exchange and walked up to the visitors' gallery. He stared down at the frenetic activity of the trading floor where brokers were gyrating, gesticulating, and shouting in the frenzy of buying and selling. To the world of commerce they were called brokers, but in reality they were croupiers, placing bets on the direction of currency values instead of the spin of a roulette wheel. Faisal knew. He'd placed bets here with his croupier/broker many times and come out a winner more often than not. But presently he did not feel like a winner, for he'd lost more than a fortune. He'd lost his purpose in life.

He left the gallery and staggered outside where he confronted a stone pillar flanked by two bronze soldiers. It was a monument to the young men of London who had served in the Great War, and around its base were flowers placed there by relatives of the fallen. Remarkable after all these years. From this vantage point on the Royal Exchange plaza, Faisal could see the Wellington statue, the Bank of England, and Mansion House, where the lord mayor of London lived. The intensity of these visions pressed against Faisal like a leaden weight, causing him to sag against the stone monument in the depths of despair. Before him were some of England's most hallowed monuments and institutions, yet he knew that beneath their stately veneer was a cancer so vile and so monstrous that he was powerless to stop it. Faisal was British to his marrow, had dedicated his life in service to the Crown; and now he'd discovered the maiden who possessed his devotion was a harlot. He staggered on, with depression so profound he became disoriented. His mind in a swirl, he was on the verge of tears, walking along Threadneedle Street, when it happened.

To the uneducated observer it meant nothing, but a dormant sphere of Faisal's brain—the financial sphere—screamed at him: *Pay attention, fool! This is important!*

Faisal obeyed the silent command and slowed his pace. Immediately in front of him three men had stepped out of an office building and were crossing the sidewalk to a waiting limousine parked at the curb. Rapidly, Faisal scanned their faces. One was tall and gray-haired, with the unmistakable bloodless look of an English aristocrat. Another was equally tall, but younger with distinctly Gallic features. The third was short, squat, bald, and imparted an abrasive feeling. An American perhaps? All three were smiling broadly and laughing heartily as the English aristocrat and the Frenchman climbed into the limo. The American stayed on the curb, giving a wave as he said through the open door, "It'll be a sweet deal," in a Brooklyn accent. Faisal continued past, then as the limo pulled away from the curb, he slowly turned around to catch a glimpse of the American as he disappeared back inside the building. On instinct, Faisal followed, catching up to him as he entered the lift. The squat man punched the button marked 16 and Faisal reached over and pressed 20. As they rode up in silence, Faisal's mind raced like a thoroughbred. He *knew* he'd seen all three men before. But where? And in what context? He couldn't recall. From the corner of his eye, Faisal inspected the American carefully. He was grinning ear to ear and apparently absorbed in his own thoughts, unaware Faisal was sharing the lift with him.

The lift doors opened and the American exited into an elegant reception area. On the far wall were brass letters on a marble background that spelled out:

GLASSMAN & LANGELLA, LTD.
MERCHANT BANKERS

As the lift doors closed, Faisal whispered, *Allah akbar!*

The London Library is one of those musky and dusty places that reek with history. Located on St. James Square, it was founded in 1841 by Thomas Carlyle, after he'd spent a frustrating morning in the British Museum, waiting two hours to check out a book. A century and a half later, the shelves of the London Library groaned with almost a million volumes, the result of the seed planted by Carlyle's frustration.

It would be overly kind to call the place well-worn, for the dust on the shelves seemed to date from the Edwardian era. But one contemporary item the London Library did have was an up-to-date microfilm viewer, with historical film of the *Financial Times*, the *Wall Street Journal*, and the *Times* of London. Faisal sat in front of the screen, scrolling through back issues, looking for articles on the merchant-banking firm of Glassman & Langella, Ltd.

During the decadent eighties, the Wall Street firm of Glassman & Langella became known as the shock troops of the corporate-takeover business—i.e., the art of one company gobbling up another, fueled by junk bonds. After the luster of takeovers faded in the U.S., Larry Glassman and Harvey Langella moved to London ("invaded" said the *Financial Times*) to "revitalize the EEC market for acquisitions." To a degree, Glassman & Langella succeeded by racking up a series of ever-larger deals across the continent. But the Americans were largely ostracized by the British financial community. Their garish voice, dress, and style left a sour aftertaste, and they weren't often seen in London's elitist clubs. "Whenever Harvey Langella shook hands with me," one nameless financier was quoted, "I always checked to see if my wallet was still there." To buy a little respect, the two Americans took over an ailing British merchant-banking firm. Then they sacked half the employees and hung their own shingle over the door, just to let everyone know who was boss.

It was Larry Glassman who had waved farewell to the English aristocrat and Frenchman in the back of the limousine. It was Larry Glassman who had said, "It'll be a sweet deal."

Faisal scrolled through the financial section of the *Times* and found what he was looking for. A picture of Larry Glassman shaking hands with the English aristocrat. The aristocrat was, in fact, Sir Leonard Baldwin, managing director of Gibraltar House, an industrial combine with annual revenues of £7 billion that owned fifty companies in a dozen product lines. Glassman & Langella handled the friendly takeover of a food-processing company fourteen months ago for Gibraltar House. The article on the viewscreen recapped the takeover, and Larry Glassman was quoted as saying, "It's a sweet deal for both sides."

A sweet deal. The very same words Larry Glassman had spoken on Threadneedle Street.

Faisal fell into his séance mode. There was no doubt in his mind that another takeover was in the making. Gibraltar House was the buyer, Larry Glassman was the broker, and the man with the Gallic features had to be the seller. Had to. But who *was* he? Faisal knew he'd seen the man's picture before. Racking his brain, his prodigious memory tried to retrieve the name that went with the face, but it came up empty. The tumultuous events of Faisal's recent past receded for the moment, for he recognized a potential windfall like this came along only once every three lifetimes. He had his financial security to think about. He was forty-seven. Unemployable. What was he to do? His mind massaged the problem until finally he recognized there was no choice. If he was to capitalize on this windfall, he had to act and act swiftly. He left the library and returned to the Goring Hotel, where he was staying. Using the phone booth in the lobby, he placed a few calls to some old friends back in Cheltenham. After obtaining the information he wanted, he phoned Air France and made reservations for the next flight to Paris.

He made a quick stop at his bank and left a detailed message on his stockbroker's voice mail. Then he visited a rare-book store on Charing Cross Road before checking out and leaving for Heathrow.

arnard Slickman stepped out of the metro car at Opera Station and began walking toward the exit. Alongside him was a surge of humanity in the grip of an eleventh-hour Christmas-shopping frenzy. As he jostled with the crowd, the doors to the metro train closed as some adolescents, with a glandular disorder of some kind, leapt on to the metro car's door ledge. The train pulled out of the station and gathered speed, yet the youths continued to hold on to the doorframe with their fingernails. The clearance between the train and the oncoming tunnel wall was about twelve inches, meaning the youths would smash headlong into the station's tiled wall if they remained in place. But at the last moment they dropped off the train in a stumbling run, until they braked themselves against the wall. It was a game of chicken, of sorts, seeing who could hang on the longest before dropping off. Had one of the adolescents smashed his skull, Barney Slickman wouldn't have cared a whit.

He exited the station at the Place de l'Opéra and came face-to-face with the mammoth Paris Opera House looming at him across the way. Slickman paid it no mind either as he headed down the Rue de la Paix toward the Place Vendôme. The shoppers bustled everywhere, speaking a mélange of tongues from Arabic to Greek to Japanese and everything in between. It was the noon hour and Slickman looked skyward, inspecting the weather as if he were an aviator. It was cold and overcast, but no fog, rain, or drizzle, and the clouds were high. That was good. Very good.

He entered the Place Vendôme, which was the epicenter of the world's haut monde jewelers. Here the boutiques of Cartier, Piaget, Morabito, and Van Cleef and Arpels displayed the créme de la créme of their artistry. The windows were designed to entice a moneyed clientele—like an Arab sheikh, a drug smuggler, a captain of industry, or the occasional rich Texas bitch. Slickman paid the jewels no mind, but he did take pause to examine the Armor-lite window of the Alexander Reza showroom. A glance told him the alarm was pressure sensitive, with a frequency trigger tuned to the sound of breaking glass. Nothing flashy.

Slickman was a tall man, over six foot, and sinewy. His hair was as black as the inside of a coal scuttle, and he combed it straight back with old-fashioned hair cream. His skin was tightly drawn over his angular features, and it possessed the pallor of a water lily. Like his hair, his eyes were black; and there was just the trace of a hook to his nose. The package that was Barney Slickman (and, yes, he was a slick man), taken as a whole, had a roguish handsomeness about it; but with an underlying chill. He wore a simple black raincoat over a black suit, and the suitcase he carried gave him a bit of a stoop. With his white complexion, black attire, and case in hand, he imparted the image of an undertaker on his way to a house call.

He walked past the Ritz Hotel and the Vendôme column to head down the Rue de Castiglione. He walked past Madame Jacqlene's gift shop, then turned left at Sulka's haberdashery onto Rue de Rivoli. A few more blocks and he arrived at Le Grand Plaza Hotel. He sauntered past the doorman, who could've been mistaken for a Bulgarian field marshal, and entered the marbled entryway to the lobby atrium. The Plaza's lobby was truly grand, with its Roman columns, massive atrium restaurant, ornate fountain, tapestries, chesterfield sofas, and intimate Foch Bar. Slickman lingered beside a column, waiting for an Indian couple to check out. After their bill was settled, the desk clerk busied himself with paper-shuffling until his supervisor was out of earshot. Then he gave Slickman a nod.

Slickman approached and leaned over, whispering, "Do you have it?"

The clerk continued to busy himself, then shot a quick glance at his boss before passing an envelope to Slickman.

"Seventh floor? Facing west?" asked Slickman.

"*Oui,*" whispered the clerk. "You are in seven sixteen. They will be in seven eighteen."

From his jacket pocket, Slickman took an envelope containing five one-thousand-franc notes and slid it across the marble barrier. It quickly disappeared inside the clerk's morning coat. "You best hurry," urged the clerk. "He sounded horny when he called. That means he will arrive soon."

"*Assurément,*" whispered Slickman, and he left for the elevator bank.

Riding up in the lift, he ripped open the envelope and took out the bronze key marked 716. The lift doors parted and he strode down the hallway, taking note of the location of 718 before inserting the key and entering 716. The room was like that of any other pricey Parisian hotel. Two double beds, a nightstand, a bureau, an easy chair, a small coffee table, and a slender desk that ran flush against the wall. It was as unremarkable as the lobby was spectacular. Slickman guessed the hotel management had blown its decorating budget on the ground floor and had to shortchange everywhere else.

Moving swiftly, he placed his bag on the bed, then doffed his raincoat and jacket. He opened the case and extracted a silenced cordless drill. Shoving the room-service menu, ashtray, and brochure on the Folies Bergère aside, he used the chair as a stepladder and climbed up on the desk. He chose a spot about a meter from the high ceiling. Then he pressed gently with the drill bit and squeezed the trigger. The drill emitted a low growl as the bit easily cut through the Sheetrock. Slickman felt the resistance go slack as the bit passed through one wall, then he probed farther until he felt the resistance of the wall in 718. He squeezed the trigger again, more carefully this time, and the bit cut through the second wall as easily as the first. When the resistance started to give way, he slowed the rpms to a crawl. He pulled out the drill and put his eye against the hole, detecting a pinhole of light coming from the aperture on the other side. He quickly repeated the process, giving him two tiny holes, side by side. Through the first aperture he ran what appeared to be a thick wire, but in fact it was a Reichert-7000 fiber-optic viewer. At one end of the flexible wire was a lens about the size of the mercury bulb on a medical thermometer. On the other end was an eyepiece and a small control knob. Slickman put his eye to the viewer and carefully moved the control knob, causing the tiny lens to move around, like an inchworm on the wall. Essentially, the Reichert device was a high-tech periscope. Police SWAT teams used them to peer around corners, where the business end of a Saturday-night special or a terrorist's bazooka might be lurking.

The lighting in room 718 was dim, but as Slickman moved the lens around, he could see the bed, and that was all that mattered. Using electrical tape he secured the eyepiece to the wall and retrieved another wire from the suitcase. This one went into the second hole. It was a microphone that could pick up an ant farting at a hundred paces. From the black valise he pulled out a Sanyo VDC-3850 handheld video camera, a Sony 8mm VCR, a tripod, and a device that looked like a small telescope. From the VIDEO OUT jack of the VCR he ran a cable into the small telescope device and mounted it on the tripod by the window. From the VIDEO IN jack he ran a cable to the Sanyo camera, then he opened the window. The air was brisk outside, so he put on his jacket and turned the heat up to the max. He checked the video and audio feed into the VCR, and once satisfied the camera/microphone feed was coming in clearly, he aimed the tripod-mounted laser to a position he'd previously calibrated. Then he dialed a number. It rang once and was answered. Slickman asked, "Do you have the feed?"

"Not yet," came the reply.

Holding the receiver to his ear, Slickman traversed the laser beam ever so slowly until the voice on the other end said, "Stop. . . . No, you went past. Back up . . . there, we have it."

Slickman locked the tripod in place and punched the VCR RECORD button, then he climbed back up on the desk with the Sanyo camera where he unscrewed the viewer's eyepiece and screwed in the video camera. Now the feed from the fiber-optic lens was going into the camera, through the VCR, and out through the laser. Slickman put his eye to the video camera's eyepiece and waited.

He did not have to wait long. Light from an opened door stabbed through the room. Then the interior lights flicked on. A man walked into Slickman's field of vision, oblivious to the tiny holes near the ceiling. He was of medium height, heavily muscled, and wearing a vicuña overcoat. His broad face had a look of intensity; and his thinning brown hair, touched by a spot of gray at the temples, was combed with precision. He paced up and down several times, with the energy of a caged panther, while smoking a Gauloise cigarette. Here was a man of authority, perhaps in his midfifties, at the peak of his powers—and obviously accustomed to getting his way. Yet he was a shade uncomfortable. He tossed the vicuña overcoat onto the chair as if it were a used wash towel, then he turned at a knock on the door.

Slickman turned the manipulator knob and followed him as he walked to the door and opened it. His guest entered. She was blond, beautiful, and cloaked in a luxuriant lynx jacket that opened to a chiffon minidress. In the blink of an eye the door was closed, the lock was turned, the chain was hung, and he turned to face her. Slickman noticed she was a bit taller than he—but then, she was wearing spike heels. They paused for a moment, like two gladiators poised to join in combat. Then he grabbed her and savagely tore her clothes away. She matched him, savagery for savagery, as layer upon layer of clothing fell to the floor; and they tumbled onto the bed in a catfight of lustful flesh. Groping, grabbing, heaving, sweating—the tempo was a bit disjointed, until at last they found a mutual rhythm and he began to heave and thrust, heave and thrust, heave and thrust. Slickman had the image of her ankles locked around the man's bare ass as the pace grew faster and faster, until his back arched in a final, sexual spasm and he emptied his lungs with a primeval *"Arrrggghhhh!"*

"Arrrggghhhh!"

Madame Pascale Laurent shuddered at the sight and sound of her husband emptying himself into another woman, and it was at that moment Monsieur Boutin turned off the live video feed. From a liquor tray in his opulent office, Monsieur Boutin poured a generous Courvoisier and held it in front of the shocked woman, saying, "A cognac, Madame?"

She grabbed the snifter and tossed the burning liquid down as if it were lemonade on a hot Bastille Day picnic. "Another," she commanded.

"Of course, Madame." Being the premier private detective in Paris, Monsieur Boutin had replayed this scene more times than he could count. A wealthy, aging wife watching her husband empty his loins into the wetness of a younger woman . . . on television . . . Live. It was a shock to the system like no other. Monsieur Boutin had found cognac to be the best tonic for times such as these.

After downing her fourth Courvoisier, Madame Laurent regained a semblance of composure. She was an attractive aristocrat to be sure, from her Mikimoto pearls to her Ferragamo pumps. Just past sixty, Monsieur Boutin guessed. Her gray coiffure complemented her Ungaro suit, but her face had lost the luster of youth and was overdue for another lift. From a wealthy family, she'd married an ambitious government bureaucrat six years her junior and had nurtured his political career like a sow her sucklings, to the point that the post of interior minister was within his grasp. But after twenty-seven years of stroking, nurturing, and underwriting his ambitions, enduring countless insufferable parties, and bearing his children, *this* was her reward.

"You have this taped? Recorded?"

"Of course, Madame."

"You will send copies to me and my lawyer." She took a linen hanky from her Gucci handbag and dabbed her running mascara. Then with the venom of a spitfire she screamed, *"How dare he do this to me! . . . To me! With that little strumpet!"* More tears. More venom. "I will destroy him with this!" She pointed at the empty screen. "His career. Everything. I will cut him off without a *sou!"* Another cognac was placed in her hand and it followed the others. "He has no money of his own, you know. My father told me never to marry him. He was correct, of course. My father was always correct."

"Certainly, Madame," comforted Monsieur Boutin. He had played out this scene so many times he could almost set his watch by it. First came the shock, then the painful remorse, the tears, then the anger; and the anger was what Monsieur Boutin valued most. Blinded by revenge, they didn't think rationally at this moment.

Madame Laurent rose and wobbled. "You will send me the tapes?"

Monsieur Boutin held the floor-length Barguzin sable for her and said, "Certainly, Madame."

"And to my lawyer?"

"By the end of the day."

"Very well." Trying to salvage a shred of dignity, Madame Laurent fumbled with her kid-leather gloves as she staggered toward the door. Now was the moment.

"Madame, there is one matter."

Still in the grips of rage, she stopped and turned. "What?"

Deferentially, Monsieur Boutin said, "The matter of the bill."

Madame Laurent whipped out her checkbook and pen. She held the Mont Blanc over the bank draft as if it were a dagger over her husband's heart. "How much?"

Using his considerable experience, Monsieur Boutin gauged her income, position, grief, rage, and state of inebriation like a sailor sticking a moist finger into the air. Finally he replied, "A hundred and thirty thousand francs."

Without hesitation, Madame Laurent scribbled the figures and her signature and handed the draft over, with the words, "The tapes to my lawyer."

"Before the sun sets, Madame."

Once she had departed, Monsieur Boutin rang for his secretary, and handing her the draft, he ordered, "To the bank. Before the sun sets."

Monsieur Jean-Phillipe Boutin had started his professional life as a generic flatfoot gendarme with the Paris Prefecture of Police. He was seven years into his career when a friend asked him to get the goods on his cheating bitch of a wife. So, employing a camera borrowed from the prefecture station, Monsieur Boutin snapped the pictures and discovered a gold mine. He found cuckolded spouses would pay handsomely for the goods; and the dirtier the evidence, the higher the price. While extramarital affairs were as common in Paris as dead mackerel in Les Halles, there is a misperception in the non-Gallic world that French cuckolds do not give a damn about their cheating spouses. In fact, they often do give a damn; and the higher the social strata, the more lucrative the damnation becomes. To the point that Monsieur Boutin—fifty-three, cherubic, dressed in a Cellini suit and silk bow tie—could afford this opulent office in the La Défense complex. Not bad for an old gendarme.

Carefully, Monsieur Boutin counted out the notes. "Twenty thousand francs. Not a bad afternoon's work, wouldn't you say, *mon cher* Barney?"

Slickman picked up the notes and counted them before saying, "Plus five for the concierge. Expenses."

Monsieur Boutin raised his hands in mock surprise at his oversight. "But of course, *mon ami*." And he counted out five more bills. "I must say, Barney, you are an absolute wizard. Such an innovative mind. It was a stroke of genius to have a client watch her husband screw another woman in—what did you call it?"

"Real time," replied Slickman as he pocketed the cash. "How much did you stiff m'lady for on this caper anyway?"

Monsieur Boutin looked affronted.

"Just curious."

Monsieur Boutin studied his manicured fingernails as if they held the secrets of the universe, then he looked up at Barney with a sad pair of eyes. Finally, in a voice reserved for the confessional, he whispered, "Ninety thousand francs."

CHAPTER TEN

F aisal pushed the BMW 535i through the Col des Mosses toward Château d'Oex. He'd picked up the car at Lausanne airport, after ensuring there was no trailing vestige of his former life. Then he drove along the dual N9 carriageway as the clouds parted and the day became pristinely clear. At Montreux he'd crossed over to the trunk road that hugged the coastline of Lake Geneva and watched the frosty whitecaps dance on the dark water. At Villeneuve he'd bidden farewell to the lake and taken another trunk road through Aisle and Le Sepey as he climbed toward the Col des Mosses. He'd visited the Alps a few times before, but never had he seen them blanketed with snow. The craggy, white-capped bergs were spectacular, and they seemed to caress the turquoise sky. The driving was demanding, forcing Faisal to turn away from the alpine scene and focus on the black strip of asphalt. Fortunately the road was clear, save for the occasional patch of ice lingering in the shade.

Faisal made it through the Col des Mosses, then on through La Lecherette and L'Evitaz, before arriving at the resort village of Château d'Oex. He'd booked a room sight unseen at the Hotel Ermitage and was pleased to find it a quintessential Swiss inn. As he walked from the BMW, he spied skiers schussing down the slopes of Les Monts-Chevreuils in the new equipment and couture they'd found under the tree on Christmas morning. Faisal climbed the steps leading to the inn and paused halfway up to catch his breath, unaccustomed to the altitude.

He registered and was received graciously by the *direction*, M. Fabio Piazza, who showed him to a comfortable suite. Since it was late in the day and he'd taken no food since breakfast in Paris, Faisal showered, changed into wool slacks, turtleneck, and a cashmere jacket and went downstairs for an early dinner.

Again, M. Fabio Piazza was the gracious host, suggesting the lamb, which was superb, and understanding at once why Faisal did not order from the wine list. As more diners filed into the dining room, Faisal requested a map of the village, which was instantly provided.

It was early evening when he walked out onto the snow-encrusted streets of the village. Château d'Oex was still decorated for Christmas, and the lights reflected off the snow with a cheery luminescence that uplifted Faisal's spirits. With a spring in his step he walked through the village, passing shops and aprés-ski partygoers. Faisal had never set foot on skis and decided he should try it sometime. But first, to business. He took out the map and oriented himself, then took a path to the Hotel Edelweiss. He found the hotel a bit more spartan than the Ermitage, and inquired at the concierge desk if a certain gentleman was registered.

"*Oui, monsieur,*" replied the concierge. "I believe he is in the dining room at the moment."

"*Merci.*"

Faisal entered the rustic-looking restaurant and surveyed the scene. It was a wood-paneled chamber with red-and-white checkered tablecloths, accented by Chianti bottles with candles. He found his quarry sitting alone in a corner booth, a half-emptied bottle of port on the table in front of him. Faisal walked up and said, "Hello, Barney."

Slickman lifted his gaze to the intruder. Faisal waited for a flicker of recognition, but the black eyes stared through him as if he weren't there. So blank was the expression, and so ashen was the face, that Faisal feared he'd made an error in tracking down Slickman. He decided to prompt him. "Surely it hasn't been that long since Delhi, has it, Barney?"

The eyes remained blank. "Delhi?"

"Yes, Delhi. The Bulgarian embassy. Eleven years ago. Remember?"

There was a glimmer now. "Bulgar embassy ... wait ... oh, yes ... yes, I seem to remember now. Lawd, it's been years! You were that Paki everyone was raving about. From H Division. Called you the new crypto-wizard, or some such thing."

"Actually, I'm a third-generation British subject, but, yes, some of my bloodlines do go back to Pakistan. May I join you?"

Slickman gestured to the empty bench. Like Faisal, he was wearing a turtleneck, but with a ski jacket. "Care for a drink?"

"Tea, please."

The waiter came and took the order.

Slickman reminisced. "That was a nice caper, that one. It's coming back to me now. One of my better black-bag jobs, if I do say so myself."

During the Cold War the superpowers made unrelenting quests to pry open and read each other's mail. Acting in secret, neither side left a stone unturned to unlock the enemy's classified epistles. When the West lost one of those battles, the results were catastrophic. Doubly so when they were splashed onto headlines—as with Geoffrey Arthur Prime, Ronald Pelton, and John Walker. But when the West won a round, rarely did that victory see the light of day.

Such an event had occurred eleven years ago. Faisal had been plucked from his post at Cheltenham and sent off to Delhi in search of a crib. The Soviets had begun deployment of a new-generation field-encryption device. Earmarked for embassy use, it was called the YB-88 and it replaced the older model YB-42 machine. As they had done previously, instead of destroying the old YB-42 machine, the Soviets farmed them out to Eastern-bloc surrogates. This relieved the satellite countries of the expense of developing their own encryption devices and also allowed the KGB's Sixteenth Directorate to read Eastern-bloc messages at will.

Faisal had received the urgent summons to Delhi for two quix-
otic reasons—one, the Soviets inexplicably did not exchange older
encryption machines for new ones overnight. Instead, they phased
them in over a period of many months. Also, the Soviet embassy
in Delhi was the second diplomatic post (after Bonn) to receive the
new YB-88 machine. Through covert means, SIS learned the Soviet
delegation had been instructed to pass their old YB-42 machine to
the Bulgarian embassy in Delhi, along with the machine's technical
manuals. If one could obtain those technical manuals, it would
mean *all* the Soviet YB-42 traffic could be broken until they were
phased out of Soviet embassies worldwide. And after the phase
out, Eastern-bloc traffic could still be read.

It was a potential windfall.

Faisal was dispatched to Delhi where GCHQ and SIS station
chiefs briefed him on the plan. The Soviet embassy was impregnable, but security surrounding the Bulgarian embassy was slip-
shod, and the building was cleaned every night by host-country
nationals. The janitorial crew's supervisor had been bribed. Faisal
would enter disguised as one of the untouchable cleaning crew.
After the embassy had been cleansed, Faisal would stay behind
and let the black-bag team in through an alley window. At the end
of the briefing, Faisal gulped, then agreed. The potential fruit was
simply too tempting.

That night he entered the Bulgarian embassy with the foul-
smelling crew, somewhat aghast that people lived in such squalor.
The guard waved them in without counting their number. Faisal
blended in with the crew, and they eyed him curiously as he
moved through the building with them, emptying ashtrays and
wastebaskets, and wiping off desktops. When Faisal reached the
office of the trade ministry attaché, he stayed behind. Then he
turned out the light and curled up in the well of the attaché's metal
desk, where he waited for three hours. His pulse pounded the
entire time and nearly stopped when the door opened and the
lights were flicked on for a moment. But then they were doused
and the door closed. Faisal guessed the guard was making a routine check. He hoped the bribed supervisor of the cleaning crew
hadn't sought a higher bid from the Bulgars.

At the appointed moment, Faisal crawled out of the desk well, stretched to get his circulation going, then stepped to the burglar-bar windows. They were heavily latched, and he prayed the creaking sound wouldn't raise the guard. He opened the window, expecting to hear an alarm, but there was none, and immediately three men dressed in black entered: the first was the safecracker who doubled as a photographer, the second was Barney Slickman with his small black bag, and the third was a shadowy gentleman who in the dim light appeared to be holding a rodlike object. Faisal had been told he was on loan from the Special Air Service.

Together the four men entered the lighted hallway of the ground floor, and wearing rubber-soled shoes, they made their way up the stairwell.

The Bulgarian embassy was a small two-story structure. The secure area for the crypto gear was on the upper floor. At the top of the stairs was another hallway. Down one wing was a string of offices, while at the other end was a gray steel door. Slickman, the safecracker, and Faisal made their way down the hall. Meanwhile, the SAS man remained in the shadows of the stairwell, holding the silenced 9mm Browning High Power pistol in his left hand (he was a southpaw).

Beside the gray steel door was a keypad panel with several multicolored lights. Slickman opened his bag and set to work. He unscrewed the face of the panel and pried it back. Then he rummaged around in the innards and snapped on a few alligator clips. Finally, he said, "Here we go." Faisal heard a series of beeps, then a distinct *clung* that reverberated down the hall.

Footsteps.

Slickman rapidly replaced the panel facing.

The SAS man stepped out of the shadows at the head of the stairs, Browning at the ready.

The safecracker opened the gray steel door.

No alarm.

Faisal waved urgently at the SAS man.

Footsteps coming up the stairs.

As the SAS man trotted silently down the hall, Slickman pulled something out of his bag that looked like a furball and laid it on the floor. They all entered the secure area, and quietly the safe-cracker eased the door closed. Faisal put his ear to it and could faintly hear footsteps approach, then pause. There was silence, then a muffled exclamation in Bulgar about the bizarre critters one found in India. Then the footsteps retreated.

Barney Slickman had deposited a sedated mongoose on the floor outside the steel door, in the hope it would satisfy the guard's curiosity.

The safecracker reached into his black bag and handed out head-lamps—the kind that miners use. Once in place, the four beams danced around the room until they all came to rest on a wall safe the size of a doorway. A large combination lock was in the center, with another keypad panel just above the circular dial.

"Time lock," whispered Slickman. The safecracker's headlamp nodded, and the two of them opened their black bags and set to work. There wasn't anything Faisal could do at this point, so he went from desk to desk looking for something, anything, that might be of value. All nine desks were bare, which told him this was the chamber that housed the Durzharna Sigurnost, the Bul-garian counterpart of the KGB. The papers of each desk were in locked filing cabinets against the wall. Faisal didn't dare touch anything, for fear of revealing an intruder had been present.

It was nearing two A.M. The time-lock panel on the safe was removed, revealing a hairnet of wires that Slickman played like a concert pianist. Finally, he stuck his hand deep inside the panel and whispered, "Override complete."

The safecracker took out a stethoscope, and like a doctor min-istering to a patient, he placed it next to the dial and slowly began turning.

The SAS man remained by the door. Silent.

It took twenty minutes before all the tumblers fell into place, allowing the safecracker to ease the lever over and retract the bolt. Like the Dutch boy with his finger in the dike, Slickman kept a pincer on two wires that held the time-lock override steady as the door slowly swung back. Faisal and the safecracker then entered the heart of the beast, the communications room of the embassy.

The narrow chamber had a long table and a bank of transceivers along one wall. Against the other wall were three Teletype machines, a small table, and a small safe. On top of the small table was something that looked like a portable-typewriter case, with two coaxial cables attached to one of the Teletype machines. The case was secured with a small padlock, and Faisal knew it to be the Soviet YB-42 encryption machine. The desire to grab it and run was almost overwhelming, but to do so was the worst action he could take. The Bulgars and the Russians must never know their communications security had been breached. Faisal pointed at the safe and whispered, "It has to be in there."

Apparently the small safe wasn't wired with an alarm, because the cracker immediately set to work with his stethoscope, and within minutes the door swung open. Greedily, Faisal reached inside, but the safecracker grabbed his wrist and murmured, "Not yet."

Out of the black bag came a Polaroid camera. The cracker took a shot of the contents and ripped out the print. "This is so we can replace everything just as it was," he explained calmly.

Faisal's headlamp bobbed in reply.

The cracker peeled off the print and, when satisfied all was in order, said, "It's all yours."

There were several three-ring binders in the safe, which were manuals for the radios and Teletypes, but Faisal quickly found the one with Cyrillic lettering. It was the technical manual for the YB-42. "This is it," he gasped.

The cracker pulled out a small Minox camera while Faisal placed the binder on the long table. For the next hour, while Slickman held the time-lock override wires in place, Faisal illuminated the pages with his headlamp as the cracker snapped off frame after frame. Once that was done, Faisal rummaged through the small safe and found the punch-card key settings for the YB-42 for the entire month. He could barely suppress a yowl and had the cracker photograph them, too.

"It's time," said Slickman finally.

Faisal rapidly replaced the safe contents according to the Polaroid print. The cracker double-checked him and said, "Let's close it up." He swung the door shut and reset the dial on its original position.

Resetting the time-lock took Slickman another twenty-five minutes. That done, they carefully exited the room and entered the hallway. Slickman took off the electronic panel again and started to reset the alarm. Faisal was afraid the bolt would cause another *clung* to sound, but this time the SAS man contributed something. From his pocket he extracted some tissue paper and stuffed it into the female receptacle for the lock bolt. The door was closed, Slickman reset the alarm, and the bolt struck the tissue with a *thhtt* instead of a *clung!*

The four men listened but there were no footsteps, nor any sign of the mongoose. They tiptoed down the hall, down the stairs, and into the office where Faisal had hidden. Carefully, they exited through the window and into the alley, just as the first hint of dawn began filtering over the Delhi sky.

Two telltale clues to the break-in had to be left behind. The tissue paper in the lock receptacle, and the unlatched window to their alley getaway. But hopefully the security people would be preoccupied with the discovery of a mongoose on the premises and would overlook the clues.

The ruse must have worked, because for the next several months, until the machines were phased out, GCHQ and NSA read YB-42 message traffic in real time, as senior Soviet diplomats exchanged loquacious epistles on strategic arms negotiations, the disaster in Afghanistan, shipments of armaments to the Iran-Iraq bloodfest, Andropov's health, and some up-and-coming star in the Politburo named Gorbachev.

Slickman poured another glass of port. "Yes, that was a nice piece of work. One of my best capers I would say."

Faisal sipped his tea, then said, "I often wondered whatever happened to the mongoose."

Slickman shrugged. "Should have given him the Victoria Cross, poor beast."

Faisal nodded. "At the very least. Tell me, Barney, what did you do after Delhi? Fill me in."

Slickman stared. "Why do you ask?"

"I'm recruiting."

A spark seemed to flare in the black eyes. "Recruiting?"

"Yes."

"For Cheltenham?"

Faisal shook his head. "No. For a freelance operation. I've been given my papers by GCHQ, and like you I'm on the street. You interested?"

"Maybe."

"Then fill me in. What happened after Delhi?"

Slickman shrugged again. "Went on to a number of black-bag jobs from there. Cairo, Lisbon, Ottawa, even Washington. Mostly embassies, or the odd tap on a telephone exchange—that sort of thing. For some reason Whitehall seemed keen on Arab embassies at the time."

Faisal took out his cigarette case and offered one, while asking, "Ever get caught?"

"No. There was only one thing you had to worry about when you broke into an Arab embassy."

"What was that?"

"You had to take care not to trip over the Israelis."

Faisal chuckled and proffered a light. "Then what?"

"Tapped phones for Tinkerbell for a while. Didn't care for it much. Then went to Cyprus. Spent a year as station electronics chief. Not a bad post. Charming, really. But got a bit boring towards the end."

"Umm. And then?"

"Off to Moscow, squire. Eyewitness to history and all that. Got to see the rise of Gorby and watch the bloody Bolsheviks take a powder."

"What was your assignment?"

"You know the foreign-posting routine. Jack-of-all-trades. Pulled maintenance on the embassy intercept machines and commo center. Ran a few hogs from time to time."

Faisal was impressed. "You were a hog carrier? I had no idea."

A "hog" was a microwave scanner/recorder that was disguised as an attaché case, suitcase, or large radio. There was a bench in Moscow's Sokolniki Park that was directly in line with the microwave path from the Kremlin to the main Moscow telephone exchange. Barney Slickman would sit on the park bench, for hours on end, innocuously feeding the pigeons while the "hog" attaché case rested beside his knee.

Slickman exhaled a puff of smoke and reminisced. "Those tapes were buggers. Really they were. We would play them back and hear Gorbachev talk out of both sides of his mouth a dozen times before lunch. He was a bloody high-wire act all the time, balancing one side against the other."

Faisal nodded. "From Moscow where did you go?"

"Back to London for a stint at Empress State."

The Empress State Building near Earl's Court housed one of GCHQ's most sensitive listening posts, for it was here that transmissions to and from foreign embassies were intercepted.

Faisal refilled his teacup. The restaurant was growing noisier as the après-ski crowd began to filter in. "And what did you do at Empress State?"

"Same old thing. Pulled maintenance. Made sure all the traps and bugs were working. Run-of-the-mill stuff until . . . "

"Until what?"

Slickman didn't answer at once. Instead he took a long pull on the cigarette, as if gathering his thoughts. "That's when GCHQ began those random drug tests. You know, where you pee in the cup and they run it through some sort of analyzer?"

"Yes, I know."

"Well, my name was called, I peed in the cup, they poured it into the analyzer, and . . . "

"And?"

Slickman looked a trifle uncomfortable. "Blew up the bloody machine, basically." He stubbed out the remnants of the cigarette.

"They said go into some rehab program or get cashiered out. I told them I was the best in the business and they could take their rehab crock and put it in a very dark place."

"So you were sacked?"

Slickman's head gave the trace of a nod, and when he spoke, the bitterness welled up. "That same day. Seventeen years in, and tossed out on the street in an afternoon. Fucking vermin."

"So what happened then?"

"Decided to put Dover in the rearview mirror and never set foot in that swill pit called England again. Went to Paris and never looked back."

"Became a contractor for a private investigator, I understand. That's how I found you. Monsieur Boutin would not divulge your whereabouts . . . until I mentioned a hefty fee might be involved."

"Umm. A mercenary. But he pays in cash."

Faisal raised an eyebrow. "You here on a job for Monsieur Boutin?"

Slickman's clammy white face broke into a wicked grin. "That swine Boutin has an old fart of a client. You know, one of those with a fossilized dick. Rich as—no, *richer*—than the Bank of England. Married this little trollop half his age who's your basic sex machine. Just waiting for the old bugger to go toes up and cash in."

"And you are at Château d'Oex to capture her infidelity on film?"

"Video, old boy. Video. Nobody uses film anymore."

"Forgive me. Have your efforts borne any fruit?"

Slickman's smile turned roguish. "As we speak. I have the room wired and the VCR on programmed record. Care to go watch? The little trollop is humping Sven the ski instructor this evening."

"Ah, no, thank you. As I said, I'm here to recruit, but I need your answer in a hurry. Time may be of the essence."

"So fill me in."

Over the next half hour, Faisal filled him in.

Barney's appetite was whetted. "So what's in it for me, old man? I mean, we'd be breaking the law, wouldn't we?"

"Yes, but what are a couple of misfits like us going to do with our unique skills? We have to make a living, don't we? This would secure a lucrative retirement for us."

Barney nodded.

"You get twenty-five percent of the take. That's a whacking pile of sterling you'll never see peeping for Monsieur Boutin."

It was an easy sell, and Barney said, "I'm in."

"Excellent. Let us call it a night and turn in. We must leave for Liechtenstein first thing in the morning."

CHAPTER ELEVEN

Herr Anton Grobert stood at the leaded-glass window of his baronial office and surveyed the vista before him. In this panorama he could see the church spire in the town of Vaduz, and the prince's castle perched on the hillside above. Quite often, after spending hours at his Louis XIV desk reading printout after printout of banking figures, Herr Grobert would rise and spend a few moments at the giant bay window. He took solace from the permanency of the scene, just as his father, grandfather, great-grandfather, and great-great-grandfather had done before him. Imbued with a refreshed sense of purpose, Herr Grobert would return to his desk with vigor. As managing director of the two century-old Grobert und Dortmünder Bank, Anton saw himself as the rock for which the stream parted, the keeper of the flame in a world gone mad. Simply mad.

Anton Grobert was born to banking in the Old World tradition, and to him banking and tradition were inseparable. Tradition meant knowing your depositors and customers from cradle to grave. It meant security on a loan two and three times over the amount extended. But above all, to Herr Anton Grobert, scion of this Old World financial dynasty, tradition and banking meant *privacy*. What a man did with his money was *his* business, and privacy was sacrosanct. Anton learned on his grandfather's knee that a priest might betray a confessional, a doctor his patient, a lawyer his charge, but a banker never, ever disclosed the business of his clients. Never even disclosed who they were, let alone what they did. Privacy was a banker's credo. His talisman. His heart of hearts. Yet everywhere around him, Anton Grobert found his sacred profession raped by intrusive politicians, journalists, and bureaucrats—probing here and there for private information on bank balances and letters of credit. It was appalling, really. Everywhere you turned, the institution of banking was falling asunder. The French were corrupt from top to bottom, of course; the Japanese had more money than sense; and the Americans were impossible. Absolutely impossible. Why, a U.S. citizen couldn't withdraw more than $10,000 in cash from his account without a report being filed with some nameless bureaucrat somewhere. Simply appalling.

But what had rocked Anton Grobert's belief system more than anything else was that the Swiss, the *Swiss*, had succumbed to American pressure and opened their files to probing policemen. Anton found it unconscionable what the Swiss had done to Ferdinand and Imelda. Frozen their accounts after that untidy business in their homeland. It was cruel, really, and they were such lovely people. Imelda especially. Anton had served them tea in this very room on several occasions. Imelda had been shattered by her treatment at the hands of the Swiss. Then there was Ferdinand's death and that circus of a trial. Humph. Well, hell could freeze over, there could be an angry mob at the gates with pitchforks and torches, but the banking house of Grobert und Dortmünder would not cough up one scintilla of information on any client's account. Anton Grobert would see to that. And he didn't care if the client's surname was Sicilian or Colombian or Malay or whatever—or where the money came from. In fact, Anton's devotion to his credo was why new clients flocked to him in increasing numbers. At Grobert und Dortmünder secrecy was still sacrosanct.

His resolve strengthened, Anton Grobert squared his round shoulders and returned to his desk. He took out a linen handkerchief and cleaned his gold-framed spectacles, then checked his desk calendar. Yes, they all flocked to him now. Indeed, he had an appointment within the hour. A gentleman—Indian or Arab, he guessed—had called him personally from London, wanting to discuss "a sensitive matter."

The Mercedes limousine cruised along the N3 motorway at a pace befitting the idle rich, while Porsches and BMWs, with ski racks on top, whizzed by on their way to Davos or Kitzbühel. At Sargans, the Mercedes turned north, following the Rhine River as it snaked through the spectacular alpine vista.

Who was in the rear cabin of the limousine, which was polished to an enamel gloss? Who lurked behind the tinted windows? An Arab sheikh? A foreign potentate? A diplomat? A mafioso perhaps?

At Vaduz the limousine took the turnoff, weaved through the town, and pulled into the oval driveway in front of an old Romanesque structure. The hired chauffeur popped out and opened the passenger door. Barney emerged first, then Faisal, wearing one of his Gieves & Hawkes suits and wraparound sunglasses. He handed his briefcase to Barney, who opened the heavy oaken door to the Grobert und Dortmünder Bank. They stepped into a marbled foyer where paintings by Rubens adorned the walls. An elderly gentleman in morning coat was sitting behind an antique desk; and nowhere did Barney see a teller window or a line of wage earners making a weekly deposit.

It wasn't that kind of bank.

The elderly gentleman stood and bowed as Barney walked up and said, "Mr. Katami Mousef to see Herr Grobert." The gatekeeper picked up the gaudy French phone on the desk and muttered into it, then hung up and gestured, saying, "This way, *meine Herren.*" They followed him down a hallway punctuated by Goyas, El Grecos, and a Pissarro; then they entered the baronial office of the managing director.

Faisal's sunglassed eyes adjusted to the dim light as a beach ball of a man, wearing a tailored silk suit and bow tie, floated toward him with a Cheshire-cat smile. "Mr. Mousef, what a pleasure to meet you." Herr Grobert had the softest, pudgiest hand Faisal had ever shaken. The banker motioned toward the massive fireplace and said, "May I offer you some tea?"

"Tea would be lovely. Darjeeling if you have it." Faisal turned to Barney. "My briefcase, Henderson. You may wait outside." Barney handed over the attaché case and replied, "Very good, suh." When the door was closed, Faisal smiled and said, "My bodyguard."

Herr Grobert nodded knowingly. "A nuisance, but what can you do?"

"Exactly."

As tea was served, Faisal inspected the office from behind his wraparound glasses. It was dark, dank, vaulted, and reminded him of the Nibelheim cavern from *Das Rheingold*. After the butler served and withdrew, Herr Grobert made pleasant small talk, then said, "Now then, my dear Mr. Mousef, what can we at the Grobert und Dortmünder Bank do for you?"

Faisal reached into his attaché case and extracted a sheet of paper, which he handed to Herr Grobert. As Anton pulled out his gold-framed reading glasses, Faisal—aka Mousef—explained, "I would like for Grobert und Dortmünder to open stock-trading accounts at the brokerage houses listed on that paper."

Herr Grobert inspected the list. They were branches of major brokerage firms scattered around the globe. Four in Britain, seven in the United States, three in Paris, three in Tokyo, and one each in Frankfurt, Hong Kong, Milan, and Singapore.

"I wish these to be margin-trading accounts under the name of a Liechtenstein corporation, Investment Research, G.m.b.H."

Herr Grobert nodded. "*Ja*. That can be done."

Faisal continued, "Sometime in the weeks to come I shall telex you with specific instructions for the purchase of equity options through these accounts. When these instructions reach you, they are to be executed without delay, for time will be of the essence."

Herr Grobert got the drift and muttered, "*Verstehe Sie*." But then he eyed Faisal cautiously. Tradition demanded caution, of course. His banker's antennae sensed something about this man Mousef.

He had a presence about him, to be sure. No rug merchant here. Nothing of the kind. The man spoke flawless German with a Westphalian accent. Was he an intellectual of some type? Perhaps a gifted artist turned financier? He had to probe further. "I must confess, Mr. Mousef, I know nothing about you."

Faisal remained inscrutable behind the sunglasses. "That is as it should be. All you need know is that my information is valuable and, shall we say, timely." Faisal could see that Anton was wavering between greed and caution. He decided to give the banker a gentle push toward greed. "Of course, I would have no objection if you utilized my information to trade on your personal account."

That was sufficient. Herr Grobert smiled and said, "We at the Grobert und Dortmünder Bank would be delighted to serve you, sir. We shall, of course, require capital to open the accounts."

Faisal reached into his attaché case and pulled out an envelope. "This is a cashier's check from Swiss Bank Corporation in Zürich for a hundred thousand francs, payable to bearer. You are to divide the amount equally among the trading accounts."

Herr Grobert nodded. "That will be sufficient to open the accounts, but margin accounts require fifty percent minimum capital with each order."

"A wire transfer of funds from Barclay's in London will accompany trading instructions by telex."

The banker nodded again. "And what about profits, should there be any?"

"Upon instructions by telex you are to liquidate each trading account, transfer the proceeds here, and convert the funds into British pounds. Cash withdrawals will be made periodically."

"I see. And what, may I ask, is the source of your valuable information?"

Faisal remained impassive behind the sunglasses. "Innovative research."

Herr Grobert pondered the reply, then said, "I understand."

Faisal extracted another sheet of paper from his briefcase and slid it across the coffee table. "Any telex from me must include this code name and code number and be dated on the fourteenth of the month. A telex may arrive at any time, on any day, but must always be dated the fourteenth. And remember, upon receipt of instructions, time is of the essence."

The banker pulled out a business card from his breast pocket and handed it to Faisal, who checked to see if the bank's telex number was embossed upon it. It was.

Herr Grobert smiled. "Is there anything else I can do for you, Mr. Mousef?"

"Yes, there is one more thing." Faisal reached into the briefcase and extracted a book and another envelope. The book was a copy of Mark Twain's *The Adventures of Huckleberry Finn*, purchased from the rare-editions store on Charing Cross Road. He slid the two items across. The banker picked up the book and shot Faisal a quizzical glance. "Timeliness and security are paramount in these transactions," explained Faisal. "Therefore, telex instructions shall reach you in encrypted form. The envelope contains instructions on how to decipher the telexes using this edition of *Huckleberry Finn*. You are fluent in English, I presume?"

"Harvard Business School."

Well, we all have our faults, thought Faisal.

"But I must confess, Mr. Mousef, this method seems a bit crude for encryption purposes. I'm sure you realize our bank must deal in secure communications frequently." The beach ball inflated a bit. "That is why we at the Grobert und Dortmünder Bank have a Stortmann encryption machine in our communications center that—"

"Can be broken by a schoolboy with a decoder ring. I regret to tell you this, Herr Grobert, but if you are using a Stortmann device, your telexes are being routinely broken and read by all the major governments in Western Europe . . . and the Americans, too, of course."

Anton went pale.

"Using *Huckleberry Finn* with the enclosed instructions will provide absolute security. The method is unbreakable, you see."

Herr Grobert gulped and clutched the Twain novel as if it were a life jacket. Who *was* this man?

Faisal snapped his Hermès case shut and stood. "I believe that covers everything, Anton. *Auf Wiedersehen.*"

The firm of Glassman & Langella was housed in one of those semifilled, fashionable structures along Threadneedle Street in The City—London's financial district. The firm occupied the fourteenth through eighteenth floors, and it clocked in every morning at nine A.M. to search vigorously for ways to fleece another million from an unsuspecting client, or wring still another million from the point spread on the trades of the day. The trading floor was a hive of frenetic activity. Computer screens flashed stock and bond quotes from Japan and Hong Kong. Traders held phones to each ear and screamed at each other. Secretaries bustled back and forth with papers, messages, and orders. Phones rang, fax machines purred, and telexes clattered; and while coffee was consumed, pile upon pile of money was made. So dependent was this whirlwind on modern communications that no one paid attention to the two British Telecom technicians as they stepped off the lift and onto the trading floor. They walked through the trading pit toward a door with a plastic plate that read FIRE EXIT.

Barney and Faisal entered the stairwell and went down half a flight to another door marked UTILITY. It was locked, so while Faisal kept a lookout, Barney inserted a wirelike feeler into the keyhole and jiggled it around. There was a click and the knob gave way. They entered a small, darkened room where Faisal flicked a switch that provided a harsh light from a naked bulb. The chamber was slightly bigger than a large closet. Several pipes came up from the concrete floor and passed into the false ceiling. One conduit was for water, one was for sewer, and two others were for electrical and telephone cables. There was also a telephone junction box.

The gray junction box was dusty, had a faded decal that proclaimed BRITISH TELECOM, and was secured by a small padlock. Again, Slickman's wirelike device was inserted into the lock, and in short order the junction box swung back, allowing Barney to make a quick appraisal. The conduit fed into the top of the box where a bundle of multicolored wires dropped down. They, in turn, fed into parallel rows of connecting terminals that poked out of a plastic board like dragon's teeth.

"Torch," said Barney, and Faisal dutifully reached into the black bag for a penlight. Slickman trained the torch on the wires and methodically examined the color-coded strands. Once he found the pairs he wanted, he pulled the handheld telephone off his belt—the kind that telephone linemen use. With alligator clips he connected it to the wires and handed the set to Faisal, saying, "Make the call." As Faisal dialed the main number for Glassman & Langella, Barney used another set of alligator clips wired into some headphones to work the dragon's teeth.

"Glassman and Langella."

"Mr. Glassman's office, please," said Faisal.

"A moment."

Pause.

"Mr. Glassman's office." The voice was abrasive.

"Yes, this is Derrick Lonsdale at Gibraltar House calling. I work in Sir Leonard Baldwin's office."

The voice became supplicant. "Oh, yes, sir. What can I do for you? Do you wish to speak with Mr. Glassman? I'm afraid he's out of town."

Barney worked the alligator clips at a feverish pace.

Faisal spoke slowly. "No, no, that's not necessary. It's something you could help me with. A trifle, really, but when Sir Leonard last met with Mr. Glassman at your offices, it seems he may have left his reading glasses behind. They're black frames in a brown leather case. Have you seen them?"

Barney gave him a thumbs-up.

"A moment."

Pause.

"No, Mr.—ah . . . ?"

"Lonsdale. Derrick Lonsdale."

"No, I'm afraid they don't seem to be here."

"A pity. Well, thank you for your help. Please give us a call should they turn up."

"I will. Good-bye."

"Good-bye."

Barney smiled and said, "Good actin', squire. Now do it again."

After they repeated the subterfuge on Harvey Langella's secretary, Barney yanked off the alligator clips and said, "Tape. Six pieces." Faisal quickly pulled off six small pieces of electrician's tape, which Barney affixed to the cluster of wires that went to Larry Glassman's and Harvey Langella's office phones.

"Drill," ordered Barney. The cordless tool quickly appeared, and the master tapper bored a tiny hole in the top of the junction box, immediately behind the larger opening for the conduit. He handed the drill back and said, "Wire." Faisal pulled out a spool of copper wire that was jacketed in green plastic. With expert hands, Slickman pulled off six lengths about six feet long and snipped them with a wire-cutting tool. Then with the same tool he shaved off two inches of the green plastic jacket from each end.

"Transmitter." From the black bag Faisal pulled a small rectangular metal box with a telescoping antenna on top. On the bottom of the transmitter were twelve spring-loaded input receptacles, the kind you might find on the back of your stereo speaker at home. Into each of these receptacles Barney inserted an exposed end of a green-jacketed wire, then he handed the transmitter to Faisal. Next, he plucked the wires marked with tape from the terminal connections and twisted them with the other ends of the green wire, then he replaced them in the terminal board. If anyone was talking on those lines, the connection would be broken. But then, people got cut off every day. It was common.

Faisal was impressed with the rapidity and precision of Slickman's movements, like a surgeon's hands restoring life to a dying patient.

"Batteries," said Barney, and Faisal pulled out two objects that looked like small black ingots with cables attached. These were nickel-cadmium batteries that would give the voice-activated transmitter a week of life. Slickman plugged the batteries into the transmitter, turned it on, and extended the antenna. Then he looked up at the false ceiling, which was a network of corkboard panels laid out on a metallic grid. "Up you go, squire." Barney knelt down and Faisal climbed onto his sinewy shoulders like a schoolboy going for a ride on Daddy's back. Straining under the weight, Barney hefted Faisal up, where he deftly pushed back the cork panel with the indentation for the telephone conduit. Then he placed the transmitter on top of the neighboring panel and replaced the one he'd pushed aside. With the leftover pieces of electrical tape he fastened the green-jacketed tapping wires to the back side of the telephone conduit, then Barney lowered him down. They admired their handiwork. Unless you looked carefully, you wouldn't know the tapping wires were there. And after all, how often was this junction box visited by a BT technician?

Just then the door opened, causing Barney and Faisal to jump and spin round. They were confronted by another man standing in the doorway, wearing the same blue coveralls as they, with the yellow BRITISH TELECOM stitched over the breast. The intruder was a short, barrel-chested bloke, with a creased face and a cigarette dangling from his mouth. "'Ello?" he said, a bit stunned himself. "Who are you? I never seen you in my section before. And what might you be doin' 'ere?"

Faisal was frozen as Barney leaned over and whispered, "Close the box." Then he turned to the intruder with a smile. "There, there, nothing to worry yourself about, boy-o. We're from Tinkerbell, you see."

The intruder's mouth gaped open. "Tinkerbell?"

As Faisal closed the junction box and relocked it, Barney pulled a small plastic-laminated ID from his pocket. He thrust it in front of the intruder's face.

The man from British Telecom studied it for a moment, then cocked an eyebrow. "Government Communications Headquarters?"

Barney plucked the ID back before the technician could read the card's expiration date. "That's right, boy-o," he said with a wink. "Assigned to the Tinkerbell tapping center. National security and all that." Slickman prayed the man was a Tory.

A look of understanding came over the intruder's face, then a conspiratorial smile. "Of course. I got you now. I know 'bout Tinkerbell. Everybody do. Seen some of your handiwork from time to time. First place I stumbled onto you in the flesh."

"Life's full of little surprises. Just leave our piece of work undisturbed if you will, boy-o. We're after some nasty money launderers in this building."

The intruder was stunned. "You don't say?"

"Oh, my, yes," lamented Barney. "Money laundering, drugs, orgies, bank fraud, the lot. Thieves everywhere, and they all wear Savile Row suits these days. We could tell stories that would curl your hair."

The man from British Telecom looked profoundly indignant. "Well, blimey. I hope you nail the buggers."

"Don't worry, boy-o. We intend to. The Home Office has given this job top priority. Just make sure nobody disturbs our little setup here."

The technician winked and said, "Don't you worry, laddie. I'll keep it safe and sound."

"Right. So good to find a man you can trust these days."

Once they were back in the hired van, Faisal took a few deep breaths to ease his pounding chest, then he turned to his partner in crime. "Barney, I've just decided to up your percentage to thirty percent."

CHAPTER THIRTEEN

A female voice. "What do you mean you can't tonight?"
Pause.
"A bridge party?"
Pause.
"Since when does a rubber with your wife mean more to you than me?"
Pause.
"But what about Thursday . . . ?"
Pause.
A bit shrill now. "What do you mean it's *inconvenient?*"
Short pause.
"Are . . . are you telling me it's over? Is that what you're saying?"
Long pause.
Tears. "But you said you were going to divorce that bitch and marry me!"
Final pause.
"You beast! You brute! You cad! You can go to hell!"
Receiver slammed down.
Barney struck a match and torched a cigarette while saying, "That was some one-way bleedover from the PBX trunk line. It's the next one." He and Faisal were hunched over a tape recorder in their suite at the Goring Hotel, playing back the conversations picked up by the bugs. They had spent Thursday

and Friday in the suite, wearing headphones and listening in on various phone calls from the tapped lines. After a break for the weekend, they'd resumed on Monday when Barney's rig captured the vital call.

"Mr. Langella's office."

"Yeah, Fiona, it's Harv."

"Oh, yes, sir. How are things going in New York?"

"Great. Super in fact."

"You have quite a number of calls—"

"Screw 'em. I'll get to 'em when I get back. Listen, I've been trying to get ahold of Larry—"

"He's still in France."

"You think I don't know that? Listen, I left my damn Rubidium phone on the plane. Get word to Larry I gotta talk to him, private like. Not with the other froggies around. Where's he staying?"

"At the Crillon."

"Okay, when he calls in, tell him to stay put at the hotel until I ring him there. But if he has to leave, tell him to take his Rubidium phone along. I'll call him from the Gulfstream tonight. Gotta talk to him about this Gibraltar House gig. It's—what's the code word we're using on this tender offer? I forget."

"Mincemeat."

"Oh, yeah. Mincemeat. Did Larry say if the old fart at Mincemeat had croaked yet?"

"Still among the living, as far as I know."

"Okay. Just tell him to nail his ass to the phone until I call. Gotta run."

"Yes, sir. Good-bye."

Barney clicked off the tape recorder as Faisal mumbled, "Mincemeat, indeed. My, my, these Americans can be so vulgar at times."

The Rubidium satellite communications system was a marvel to behold. A network of seventy-one low-orbit satellites swarmed above the earth like a hairnet, acting as relay stations for the pocket phones of the rich and famous. And at £5 per minute of airtime, only the rich could afford a call. But what a marvelous toy! At its extreme, it enabled a caller to stand on the South Pole and dial up her broker in New York, her banker in Geneva, or her studly lifeguard in Miami. The caller would punch in a number and hit the SEND button on the pocket phone. The signal would be transmitted to the nearest overhead satellite, where a computer chip would interrogate the system and find the best "route" to the addressee. The signal would then be "hopped" through a critical path of satellites, then downlinked by the Rubidium bird soaring over the addressee's head. If a Rubidium caller was dialing up a conventional terrestrial phone, then the system would downlink into the telephone grid of, say, Rome or Hong Kong. But if another Rubidium phone was being rung up, and this was the beauty of it, the system could totally bypass the terrestrial networks. Essentially it was a worldwide, spaceborne, cellular phone system.

But, of course, Larry Glassman knew nothing about the technical aspects of the Rubidium phone. He was simply an investment banker with an electronic toy, climbing into a cab on the Place de la Concorde. It was great fun to whip out the pocket-size phone on business trips, flip open the microphone panel, and say, "Beam me up, Scotty!" Clients were always impressed, and Larry often bragged he could ring up his partner "in the can" if he wanted to. Yes, a great toy, one that showed clients what the score was.

Larry was on his way to meet a potential client now. A producer looking for a banker to underwrite a private placement on a movie venture. Sounded like a long shot, but since he was in Paris, what the hell? The French producer promised to bring the starlet along. Larry exited the cab at the Place Vendôme and entered the Ritz. He strode through the blue-carpeted lobby and down the hallway of boutique displays toward the Hemingway Bar. Ernest Hemingway had personally liberated the Ritz Hotel in 1944 as he accompanied Allied troops into the city. The bar, which was a delightful, wood-paneled alcove, had a bust of "Papa" resting on the counter.

Larry Glassman knew nothing about Hemingway either. Nor did he notice the tall, dark-haired man in the black raincoat following him with a briefcase in hand. Glassman found the frog producer, bald and rotund like himself, ensconced at the corner table with a tall, leggy, red-haired starlet. Larry shook hands with the mogul, then leaned over to catch a better view of the cleavage. Jesus, what a set of headlights! After drinks were ordered, the mogul droned on about distribution and video licensing agreements. Larry ogled the starlet and began plotting a way to get her upstairs. As she tossed her long hair back and leaned forward to take a cashew from the bowl on the table, Larry was transfixed. He certainly paid no mind to the tall, dark-haired stranger who took a seat in the opposite corner.

The waiter greeted the man in the raincoat and took his order for Vichy water. While filling the glass, the barkeep noticed something in Barney Slickman's ear. A hearing aid, perhaps?

Larry Glassman felt the starlet's foot press his own under the table. He figured this was de rigueur for a movie deal. He liked it and was about to press back when his Rubidium phone jingled. He plucked it from his inside pocket and flipped open the microphone panel, saying, "Beam me up, Scotty!"

The mogul and starlet stared at him with blank expressions.

Larry was crestfallen. Didn't these frogs watch "Star Trek"? He thought Paris was supposed to have a little class. Irked, he pressed the RECEIVE button and said, "Yeah?"

"Larry, it's Harv."

"Hang on a minute." Larry turned to the starlet and said, "Be back in a minute, sweetness. Have another cashew." The producer might not have been there. Larry rose and stepped into the foyer for some privacy. Holding the phone to his ear he said, "Harv?"

"Yeah, Larry, you old shit face! You're beautiful! This Mincemeat gig is the sweetest deal we've had in years! I'm gonna kiss your ass when I hit Gatwick!"

"Never mind that, lover boy. You got the dinero lined up?"

"No problem. I got Solomon—"

"Speak up, this connection is fuzzy."

"I said, no problem. Solomon's gonna eat the whole banana.

Gibraltar gets a bridger loan for one point one billion pounds and makes a tender for Mincemeat's shares at five hundred ten francs per share. Simple as that. Once the deal is done, Solomon will handle a bond issue and knock down the bridge. We get the transaction fee from Gibraltar and don't have to hang our nuts out on the underwriting. It's a win-win all the way. By the way, has the geezer croaked yet?"

"Nah, but that's no problem. Andre wants to preempt the old man from changing his mind about selling out. He says he and Sir Leonard should make an announcement on Gibraltar's tender for Lucerne on Friday."

"Say that again. You're breaking up."

"I said, they want to announce on Friday. Did you get that?"

Barney Slickman flicked off the cassette recorder of his receiver unit, which was tuned to the Rubidium downlink frequency, and whispered, "Got it."

"Lucerne Pharmaceutique!" Faisal slapped his forehead. "Of *course!* The third man, the Frenchman I saw getting into the limousine, was Andre . . . DuMont I think his name is. Heir to the family business. Evidently he and his relatives want to cash the business out from under their grandfather. As I recall, the old man founded the company."

"How'd you know about that?" asked Barney.

"I recently made a share play in the pharmaceutical industry. I came across Lucerne in my research." Faisal tore through the latest issue of the *Financial Times* and found the share quotation. "Here they are. Traded on the Paris Bourse at three hundred sixty-eight francs per share." Just then a chilling thought struck Faisal. "Play the tape again, Barney."

Barney did so.

"Blast! They're going to announce on Friday!"

Barney shrugged. "So?"

"Today is Monday." Faisal checked his watch. "Early Tuesday morning, actually."

Barney shrugged again. "I caught the first plane back from Paris. But what's the big deal? That gives you plenty of time to place the share orders with that bloke in Liechtenstein. . . . Doesn't it?"

Faisal cleared his throat. "Not exactly."

"What do you mean by 'not exactly'?" Barney obviously was not pleased.

Faisal paced a bit, then said, "I must have my housekeeper bring my dinner jacket down from Cheltenham."

CHAPTER FOURTEEN

A converted mansion, it was located on a small side avenue in Mayfair. The only declaration that it was a commercial address was a small, polished brass plate on the Grecian column that read PARTHENON. As Faisal mounted the steps, the ebony door was opened from within. He was greeted by a liveried servant wearing a red-tailed jacket, powdered wig, white stockings, and brass-buckle shoes. Faisal guessed his approach had been seen by a surveillance camera hidden in the hedge somewhere. The doorman bowed from the waist, and Faisal graced him with a slight nod in reply.

He entered a high-ceilinged foyer with a sparkling chandelier that illuminated the white marble floor. Off to his left was a posh dining room, where gamblers put on a few pounds before losing hundreds at the roulette table. Off to his right, in an alcove sequestered from the gaming room, was the bar. The British Gaming Board forbade alcohol at the tables. Better a man be sober as he was separated from his inheritance. Dead ahead of him was the casino.

Faisal's stock portfolio, which he kept on account with his broker, had a market value of some £173,000. He was proud of that achievement, having built up the value over a period of years.

He'd intended to use it as a nice retirement nest egg. But then came the opportunity, out of the blue, to partake in a little insider trading and explode that number ten- to twentyfold. He'd used his immediate cash reserves to open the stock-trading accounts through the Liechtenstein bank, and the balance in his bank account was down to £3,427. He'd intended to use the £173,000 as working capital to purchase options in Lucerne, but the short fuse on the tender announcement had pulled the rug from under that idea, due to a quirk in the London Stock Exchange rules.

Settlement on stock exchange transactions takes place at the end of each "account settlement period," which are twenty-six two-week terms during the year. A customer can buy and sell any number of shares during each period, but at the end of the fortnight period the customer's net buy/sell balance is tabulated. Another week passes to allow the back-office paperwork to be done, then on the following Monday the customer must pay a check to his broker or receive a check from his broker for the net buy/sell balance.

At the outset of his adventure, Faisal had instructed his broker to liquidate his portfolio into cash. At this moment it was Thursday of the paperwork week, and his check for £173,000 would not be in hand until the upcoming Monday. Gibraltar and Lucerne were announcing the tender offer on *Friday*, which was tomorrow. The Liechtenstein Bank required a wire transfer of cash if it was to execute the share-option purchase orders before the announcement. In short, the train was fixing to leave the station, and Faisal's £173,000 nest egg might as well be on the moon. He needed cold hard sterling, in hand, before the sun came up.

Faisal took a deep breath, set his compass, and strode across the foyer toward the gaming room, trying to project the image of a gentleman with petrodollars dripping from his pockets.

As he stepped off the marble and onto the wine-colored carpet, he paused to examine the scene. The gaming room wasn't particularly large, but it was imposing. Gold-encrusted marble pillars rose up to a grand trompe l'oeil ceiling, where another massive chandelier was suspended. Against the far wall was a giant flower arrangement resting upon a Louis XIII table. On either side of the table were mirrored doors. The gaming tables were arranged in a horseshoe pattern, offering roulette, punto banco (baccarat), black-jack, chemin de fer, and, rare for a London gaming house, craps. Green-shaded lights hung from the ceiling to illuminate each table, and the smoke curling upward gave the room a conspiratorial air. Faisal had chosen the Parthenon because it catered to a clientele that was wealthy. Seriously wealthy. The kind of people who pre-ferred to part with their riches in an elegant atmosphere. The Par-thenon achieved this exclusivity by simple means. Although London gaming houses were nominally "clubs," in fact they were open to the public. There was no blackballing. No social register. No confidential membership list. Such was the case with the Par-thenon. It was open to the public. Any public who could afford a minimum bet of £25. That kind of seine tended to filter out the tourist trade. The tables were populated by elegantly dressed men and women on the downside of seventy. The kind of people who owned Suffolk or Southampton, or some such thing. There was the quintessential Arab, replete with robes and *kaddifayeh* headdress, who sprinkled five-hundred-pound plaques over the roulette table like black rain from an oil gusher. And he uttered no protest as the croupier raked them in, like a farmhand bringing in the sheaves.

Faisal walked to the usher at the lectern, who greeted him with, "Good evening, sir, and welcome to the Parthenon. Are you reg-istered with us?"

"Yes."

"And the name?"

"Shaikh. Faisal Shaikh."

The usher tapped a keyboard at a small computer screen. "Ah, yes, Mr. Shaikh. You registered over forty-eight hours ago. Just under the wire, what? Ha, ha. Enjoy the club."

"Thank you."

British gaming rules required potential gamblers to register forty-eight hours before they began losing their money. To the authorities it was considered a "cooling-off" period, but to Faisal and Barney it was a nettlesome hurdle that eroded their window of opportunity down to the nub.

Faisal entered and slowly strolled by the tables, soaking up a feel for the action and the venue. There was an undercurrent of tension and electricity that could only be found in such a place: the roulette wheel spinning, the cards turning, the dice rolling. Its effect was intoxicating. At the blackjack table he paused. An aged baroness was sitting astride the nearest stool. Apparently she suffered from poor circulation, for she clutched her mink stole for warmth. Next to her was a Malayan gentleman in a white dinner jacket, looking poker-faced as only Orientals can. Beside him was an overweight Texan wearing three garish gold rings on his stubby fingers. The pit boss was also in a dinner jacket, a cadaverous man who looked as if he'd been exhumed for the evening's play. The croupier was just completing a shuffle of six new decks when Faisal approached and watched him load up the shoe. Perfect, thought Faisal, as he stood off at a distance to kibitz the game. He remained there for the better part of half an hour, eliciting curious glances from the pit boss. There was an ebb and flow to the game, but more ebb than flow as the players swam against the inexorable tide of the casino. When the American's pile of plaques evaporated to a final hundred pounds, he uttered a low, guttural sound. Then he pocketed the chip for cab fare back to his hotel and slid off the stool in the "third base" position. Better and better, thought Faisal as he climbed onto the American's warm seat. He reached inside his tuxedo pocket for his black alligator wallet and extracted twenty fifty-pound notes. Tossing them in front of the robotic croupier, he said, "Twenty-five-pound plaques, if you please." The money disappeared into a cash slot, and while the croupier counted out the red plaques, Faisal pulled out his gold cigarette case, the onyx holder, and his malachite lighter. It was going to be a long night.

As a gifted undergraduate at Edinburgh, Faisal was on full scholarship, which meant tuition, books, and a standard of living one step removed from a church mouse. Living rent free with the

Doogans helped, the occasional grant from his parents helped; but as he moved into graduate studies, the constant state of penury became a source of lament for him and his fellow students. Since they were bright, young, and mathematically inclined, Faisal and two of his colleagues struck upon the idea of applying probability theory, Bayes' theorem, and mathematical-statistical tools to the art of gambling. Faisal and his friends broke the games down and studied them—baccarat, roulette, and blackjack—and decided to have a go. Brimming with expectation and youthful enthusiasm, they scraped their meager resources together and took a holiday train to London, confident they would break the back of some poor unsuspecting gaming house.

The trip back to Edinburgh was different. The student with the "system" for roulette left everything but his Skivvies at the table. The baccarat player broke a little less than even. But Faisal returned with pockets bulging. He'd applied his intellectual powers in mathematics and statistics to the art of card counting, and he became so adept that he was turned away by two gaming clubs.

Casino holidays then became a regular with Faisal. And as his skill progressed, he became befuddled as to why casinos allowed blackjack in the first place. Unlike other games of chance, the odds actually favored the player, not the house. By keeping a running tab on whether the deck was "ten rich" or "ten shy," a skillful player could beat the dealer more often than not. The casinos don't worry much about this problem, however, because 98 percent of the gamblers play a blundering game and have difficulty remembering their own telephone numbers. It was rare they ran into a customer with a photographic memory and a mastery of probability theory.

By the time of his graduation, Faisal had developed expensive tastes and become persona non grata on the London gaming scene, but by then he'd found an alternative income stream from the stock market.

He hadn't set foot in a casino in twenty years, but the skills he'd possessed as a student were still there. Perhaps even better.

■   ■   ■

A hundred twenty-six playing cards had been dealt from the six-deck shoe, and each one, its suit and sequence played, was imprinted on Faisal's mind, where it would stay until he chose to erase it. Faisal was up to thirty-five hundred pounds as the croupier raked in the cards and chips from the last hand. His old skill and confidence returned, Faisal ratcheted up the wager and slid five one-hundred-pound blue plaques into the betting rectangle. This raised the eyebrow of the pit boss, who followed the cards as the croupier laid out the deal, faceup. The baroness received a seven and five, the Malayan an eight and six, Faisal a three and jack, and the croupier—with the single faceup card of the London deal—showed a four. From the cards imprinted on Faisal's mind, he knew the deck was now ten rich in the extreme. The baroness, with twelve showing, called for a card and was rewarded with a queen, breaking her hand and sending her two hundred quid south. The Malayan with fourteen said, "Card," and received a four, pushing him to eighteen, where he stood. Faisal took a puff from his cigarette holder and said, "Stand," knowing what the next card had to be. The croupier flipped over a king. House rules required the dealer to stand on sixteen or draw on anything below, so he took another card, which was another king, which pushed him to twenty-four.

Faisal received a black £500 plaque in return, but did not rake it in. He let it stand by his original wager as the croupier dealt the baroness a queen-nine, the Malayan a queen-jack, Faisal a pair of aces, and the house a ten. Faisal split the aces and pushed out another thousand pounds to cover the second hand. He received a king on the first and an eight on the next, giving him twenty-one and nineteen. The dealer turned over a deuce for a hard twelve total. Beautiful, thought Faisal, for the next card had to be a . . . ten. The house paid off, and Faisal raked in the winnings, letting two thousand of the split bet stand.

"A thousand-pound limit per hand at this table, sir," said the croupier in a barely audible voice.

Faisal flicked the ash from his cigarette and replied, "My apologies." He pulled back the yellow plaque imprinted with £1,000 on its face.

As the minutes passed into hours, Faisal pressed his hand, and at one point he was £32,300 ahead, with the eyes of the pit boss boring in on every card. As the hour approached midnight the baroness left for her beauty sleep and the Malayan for his round-eyed mistress, leaving Faisal and the croupier to slug it out alone. It was at this point Faisal had to show he could lose. The pit boss was hovering like a hungry vulture, and Faisal knew he was within a hair's breadth of being told, "Your membership is no longer active"—the euphemism casinos use to expel a winning player. The pit boss knew Faisal's play was extraordinary, but he'd never met anyone who could count through six decks of cards. Before the croupier reshuffled the shoe, Faisal dropped the next five hands (four by intent), then won the next two, lost two, won two, lost two, putting him at £29,300. A big stake, but one he had to leverage further. The pit boss looked a bit relieved at Faisal's falling stock. That was more like it. So he was amenable when Faisal asked, almost casually, "Could we raise the stakes a bit?"

The pit boss eyed the stack of plaques in front of the Arab—or was he Persian? The cadaver didn't want him to walk out with almost thirty thousand quid, so he inquired, "You wish a private game, sir?"

"A private game would do nicely, yes."

"A moment." The cadaver left to confer with the casino manager in hushed tones, then returned and said, "This way, sir. I'll see to your chips." Faisal slid off the stool and followed the pit boss through one of the mirrored doors, into a small chamber that possessed a single blackjack table and a single roulette wheel. The lighting was subdued except for the green-visored bulbs illuminating the green felt. Oil paintings of equestrian scenes adorned the walls, and the only other feature was a second door at the back of the room. Faisal guessed this was where high rollers were relieved of their rolls. Private baccarat and chemin de fer tables were probably in the neighboring room.

Standing in the doorway, the cadaver said, "Have a seat, sir. A croupier will be with you in a moment. Would you care for a drink?"

Faisal climbed onto his perch at the table and said, "An Evian water would be fine."

The pit boss snapped his fingers and uttered the order to a waiter. Meanwhile, the croupier carried in the stack of plaques and placed them on the table. Then he withdrew. The Evian water arrived and the cadaver closed the door. "It will just be a moment, sir." He spoke with the warmth of a jailer.

Faisal checked his Bertolucci watch, which read 12:38 A.M. Still adequate time, he told himself. He occupied the lull by arranging his plaques on the felt-top table. Then the back door opened . . . and Faisal nearly fell off his stool.

She had that alluring femininity that petite women seem to possess. Her figure was shapely but symmetrical, and clothed in the uniform of a female croupier—a low-cut, black silk bodice that flared out to a petticoat bubble of a miniskirt. As she stepped up to the table, Faisal glanced at her legs, which he rated two notches above dead solid perfect. Yet shapely though they were, even her legs could not compete with her eyes. They were almond shaped and black as the night, and when she smiled in greeting, they sparkled like a pair of stars from Orion's belt. Her skin was silken and her voice velvet as she nodded slightly and said, "Good evening, sir." Faisal mumbled something incoherent as he watched her shuffle the cards and drop them into the shoe. He cleared his throat, sipped his Evian, and inquired, "Is it permissible to ask your name?" She looked demurely at the green felt on the table, then up to his eyes, and replied, "Razia."

Razia feared she might fumble the cards as the shuffle progressed. Never had she been so unnerved by the mere sight of a player across the table. Who was this Adonis in black tie? Was he in oil? Finance perhaps? She felt an electric presence about him, an aura of sorts, that transmitted across the green baize. Then he'd looked at her with those soft brown eyes and asked her name. She'd nearly wilted. *Get ahold of yourself, Razia,* she told herself. *Focus on the game. This is business.* "Your bet, sir."

"Umm? Sorry?"

Faisal was bordering on the paralytic. At this moment he was transfixed by her hair. It was dark as a raven's feather and caught the dim light with a lustrous reflection. Where was he? Why was he here? What was this place?

"Your bet, sir. Do you wish to place a bet?"

Oh, yes. Cards or something. "Of course. Forgive me." And he shoved out a five-hundred-pound plaque.

"Thousand-pound minimum at this table, sir."

Faisal looked behind Razia and saw the casino manager. How did he get there? Had he been there all along? A burly man, he was. Looked like a Siberian bear in dinner jacket. Faisal shoved out another plaque to reach the minimum, and Razia dealt him a nine-seven and herself an eight. Silence ensued until she asked, "Do you wish a card, sir?"

"Umm? Card? Why, uh, no . . . I will, uh, stand."

"Yes, sir." She dealt herself a jack for a total of eighteen and expertly raked in Faisal's plaques and cards. The cadaver and the Siberian bear looked a bit relieved, and Razia dealt the second hand.

Faisal silently screamed to himself, *Get a grip on yourself, man! This isn't the time to get distracted. You have business to attend to.* With difficulty he focused on the cards, but his mind was still fogged by the woman only inches away. Her perfume was jasmine, and the scent of it nearly pushed him over the edge. He pulled out his cigarette case, but then saw her nose wrinkle at the sight of it. Immediately he shoved it back into his pocket. He was planning to quit anyway. Yes, absolutely. He was going to quit. He gulped the Evian instead and said, "Card." He busted without remembering how.

All right, Faisal, enough! Concentrate!

The bet was placed, the cards were turned, and with all the self-discipline he could muster, Faisal went into his séance mode, imprinting each card into his memory. At the start, Faisal's play followed a trend of one step forward, three steps back, and at one point his stake fell under seven thousand pounds. This elicited a gloating look from the manager and pit boss. But as the shoe wore down and the trend of the cards became more predictable, Faisal began raising his wager and doubling down when the hand was right. Then it became three steps forward, one step back. Then five forward and one back. His stack grew to over forty-six thousand pounds, and the casino men looked positively grim. Even Razia appeared apprehensive.

Now Faisal faced several factors. The hour was approaching three A.M. The casino closed at four A.M. The deal was approaching the cut card inserted two-thirds deep in the stack of the shoe. When the deal reached the cut card, Razia would reshuffle. That would send Faisal back to square one, with little time to reestablish the trend. And besides, the cadaver and the bear could cut him off at any time. He had to make his major play now, if ever. Faisal shoved out ten thousand pounds into the betting rectangle, eliciting some heavy breathing from the cadaver and bear. Razia deftly dealt out the hand—a three-three to Faisal and a queen to herself. Faisal knew the ten-value cards had been largely expended as he split the threes and pushed out another ten thousand to cover the second hand. A grumbling sound was audible in the room. Razia flipped the first card—a four for a hard seven total.

"Again," said Faisal.

A deuce for a nine total.

"Again."

An eight for a seventeen.

"Again."

Was this man for real?

Another deuce for a nineteen.

"Stand," said Faisal as he tapped the three of clubs of the second hand.

He received an ace for a hard four or a soft fourteen.

"Again."

A five for a hard nine or a soft nineteen. The manager and pit boss figured he would stand, but Faisal fell deeper into his séance mode. They were perhaps a dozen turns from reaching the cut card in the shoe. Silently he recalled all the cards played. Statistically he ran through the possible permutations and combinations of what he could hit, or Razia could hit, and he knew what he had to do. "Card," he commanded.

"Sir?"

"Card, please."

"But you have nineteen showing, sir," said Razia. "Are you certain?"

"It's a soft nineteen, and, yes, I'm certain. Thank you."

Razia sighed and flipped over a jack, giving him an absolute nineteen.

Faisal sighed, relieved the final spoiler was out of the deck and said, "Stand." Had he not taken the jack it would've been Razia's.

Now in quick succession she dealt herself a four and a four to stand at eighteen, giving the hands to Faisal. With a look of apprehension she pushed £20,000 in winnings across the table, bringing the mysterious man's total to £66,300. Not bad for an initial investment of a thousand quid.

The cadaver and the bear mumbled to each other, then the casino manager came round the table and whispered in a low, menacing voice, "I'm afraid your membership is no longer active, sir. I must ask you to leave."

Razia could hardly bear the tension, but the player remained unruffled and casually sipped his Evian. "I suppose you're a trifle upset with the trend of the game. Very well, give me the opportunity to make it up to you." He smiled at the bear, then set down his Evian and shoved £66,300 across the table. "One last hand and we'll call it an evening. Winner take all."

The bear involuntarily took a step to the rear. The idea of taking a 132,000 quid hickey from this Arab was frightening to him. The thought of sending him home empty-handed was much more appealing. It was greed against fear, and Faisal hoped greed would win out.

He was not disappointed.

The bear nodded at Razia. She shoved the pile of plaques out of the way and nervously began the deal. Faisal received an ace-six and she an eight. She looked up and said, "Your play, sir?"

"Card, please."

Razia started to deal but noticed something. The gentleman wasn't even looking at the cards. His eyes were locked onto the stare of the Siberian bear. "You said you wished a card, sir?"

"Yes, if you please." His gaze did not waver.

Razia turned another six for an absolute thirteen. She looked up.

He didn't even glance at the table. And was there the trace of—what?—a smile on his face?

"Card."

Razia turned a four for seventeen.

Not a glance. "Card."

A three for a twenty.

"Stand."

Razia dealt herself a nine and said, "House stands on seventeen. Player wins."

The bear emitted the kind of sound a grouse makes when its neck is wrung. The cadaver looked ready for reinterment.

Faisal walked out of the Parthenon with a check payable on Barclay's Bank for £127,600—his winnings less a five-thousand-pound tip for Razia. He didn't take time to savor his victory or recount the extraordinary woman he'd met that night. There wasn't time. It was nearly four A.M. when he finally flagged a taxi to take him to the Goring Hotel.

Faisal stunned the cabbie by flipping him a hundred-pound note for the fare, then he hustled up to his suite where he opened the volume of *Huckleberry Finn* on the coffee table. He began enciphering detailed instructions for Herr Grobert at the Liechtenstein bank. Growing weary from strain and the lateness of the hour, Faisal ordered up tea from room service and chain-smoked as the sun came up. Meticulously he rechecked his instructions to Herr Grobert, for to put a foot wrong at this point would invite disaster.

When Barclay's opened, a startled teller found his first customer of the day to be a tired-looking Middle Eastern gentleman in black tie. He was equally startled when presented a bearer check for £127,600. The gentleman gave the teller a typed sheet with precise instructions for the wire transfer of the money to the Grobert und Dortmünder Bank in Vaduz. The teller told the assistant manager, who told the branch manager, who said a check from the Parthenon Club was as good as gold. The transfer went through.

Faisal then went to a private post office that offered a telex transmission service. He paid cash for sending a telex of jumbled letters to a Liechtenstein number. That done, he took a cab back to the hotel. He returned to his room, dropped his jacket, loosened his tie, fell on the bed, and was instantly asleep with his patent leather shoes still on.

Herr Anton Grobert sat in shirtsleeves, the volume of *Huckleberry Finn* lying open on his Louis XIV desk. He smiled in delight as he rechecked his decryption of the telex from Mr. Mousef. Anton Grobert had dealt with encrypted letters before, of course. But that was always via an impersonal machine. And unsafe, as Mr. Mousef had pointed out. Doing it this way was so clever. Deciphering the message and watching the words take form was, for lack of a better word, fun.

Let's see now, he told himself. The wire transfer had arrived with instructions to buy as many call options as possible of Lucerne Pharmaceutique, SA, traded on the Paris Bourse. Without delay. The £127,600 transfer was to be divided equally among the margin accounts opened at the various brokerage houses. Anton checked his morning edition of *Le Monde* and saw the shares in Lucerne were trading at 371 francs. He compiled an instruction telex for the list of brokerage houses, then rang his male secretary. "Telex this immediately to all addressees on the list and execute the wire transfers accordingly."

Wordlessly, the young man took the sheet and disappeared. Once the door was closed, Herr Grobert picked up his phone and speed-dialed his broker across town. After a single ring it was answered.

"*Guten Morgen,* Franz. Anton here. I wish to place an order on my personal trading account for options in Lucerne Pharmaceutique . . ."

Barney and Faisal paced the suite incessantly, seeing who could build the highest pile in his respective ashtray. It was late Friday afternoon and their eyes were riveted to the Reuters business newswire carried on a cable TV channel in their suite. So far, nothing. After a brief deep slumber, Faisal had called Herr Grobert for confirmation that his instructions had been executed. They had. Now there was nothing to do but wait. And pray.

Barney ran through the numbers on his pocket calculator again. One hundred twenty-seven thousand pounds, less conversion charges, would convert to 1,134,000 French francs at the prevailing rate of exchange. Less brokerage commissions, that would buy 177,188 call options of Lucerne, which could be exercised at 364 francs per share. Those 177,188 call units in a 50 percent margin account could be leveraged up to options in 354,376 shares. If the sale of Lucerne went through, they would cash out the difference between the option price and the tender offer price. If the sale *didn't* go through and the stock dipped below the option price, they would face a margin call for the difference. A margin call for money Barney did not have. Then the only price he'd have to worry about was the price on his head.

Faisal couldn't bear the tension any longer. He grabbed his coat and said to Barney, "I'm going for a walk." He was halfway out the door when he heard Barney's voice emit something like a laugh-scream-yowl, followed by, "Yes! Yes! *Yeeeaaaaassss!*" Faisal nearly jumped over Barney to get a look at the newswire as it typed out the epistle of their salvation:

(REUTERS) PARIS—THE BOARD OF DIRECTORS OF LUCERNE PHARMACEUTIQUE, SA, ANNOUNCED TODAY THEY HAVE ACCEPTED A TENDER OFFER FOR ALL OUTSTANDING SHARES IN THE COMPANY AT 510 FRANCS PER SHARE FROM GIBRALTAR HOUSE.

LUCERNE IS AN OLD-LINE PHARMACEUTICAL FIRM WITH PRODUCT DISTRIBUTION THROUGHOUT EUROPE AND NORTH AMERICA. SIR LEONARD BALDWIN, MANAGING DIRECTOR OF GIBRALTAR HOUSE, SAID THE £1.1 BILLION ACQUISITION WOULD COMPLEMENT THEIR RECENT ACQUISITION OF APOTHECARY CHAINS IN SPAIN AND THE BENELUX...

Barney whipped out his calculator and began tapping out the numbers. The option share price of Lucerne was 364 francs per share. The tender offer was 510 francs per share. He was so nervous his fingers would hardly obey as he stroked the keys. That meant a 146-franc profit per share—or sixteen pounds twenty-two pence at the current exchange rate. Sixteen twenty-two multiplied by 354,376 optioned shares came to a total profit of *five million, seven hundred forty-seven thousand, nine hundred seventy-eight pounds!* And seventy-two pence.

With no intrusion from Inland Revenue.

A housekeeping maid was passing by the suite when she paused for a moment, then walked on. She could've sworn she heard the voices of grown men inside chanting ring-around-the-roses.

ieves & Hawkes. No. 1 Savile Row. London. The epitome of England's bespoke tailors, Gieves & Hawkes had cut and fitted uniforms for the likes of Adm. Horatio Nelson and the Duke of Wellington (not to mention the stage regalia for Michael Jackson). It was a firm that served up a rich history to a rich clientele. Housed in a building that was once the map room and library of the Royal Geographical Society, Gieves & Hawkes boasted its own museum on the second floor. Here one could find the Royal Navy shaving-kit footlocker of Robert Falcon Scott (a deceased client), plus photographs of the royal family, and mannequins wearing dress uniforms of the British military.

But that was history. The here and now of Gieves & Hawkes (along with the bread and butter) was just down the hall in the fitting rooms.

Faisal Shaikh inspected his reflection in the full-length mirror, admiring the bolt of fine woolen broadcloth draped over his shoulder.

"Just in from the mills, Doctah Shaikh," said Wilton the tailor. "Goes right with your coloring, if I do say so myself, suh."

"Umm. I believe you're right, Wilton. Let's add this one to the others."

"Very good, suh." Looking cherubic as ever, Wilton pulled the fabric off Faisal's shoulder and placed the bolt on the mahogany table.

Wearing a waistcoat with shirtsleeves rolled up, Wilton looked as if he'd stepped off the pages of a Dickens novel. He peered through a pair of granny glasses and made a notation in his order book. "Let me see now, that makes eleven all together—seven double-breasted and four single-breasted with waistcoat."

"Correct."

"Very good, suh. We'll bill you as we go along."

"That will be fine."

Wilton helped his client on with his jacket and said, "Good to 'ave you about again, suh. 'Aven't seen you in quite some time."

Faisal buttoned his jacket and replied, "Been terribly busy, Wilton. But now I have some time to catch up on things. Enjoy life a bit, you might say."

"Glad to hear it, suh. Eleven suits. That's quite an order, even for you. Shall we say the first fitting in five weeks' time?"

"That would be fine, Wilton." Faisal draped his raincoat over his arm. "Have a good day."

"You as well, suh."

It was a brisk winter's day as Faisal found himself strolling along the Strand with energy in his step. He felt light-years removed from the depression he'd experienced just weeks ago. Amazing what a few million pounds could do to raise one's spirits. The money was safely tucked away in the Liechtenstein bank, hidden from the prying eyes of Inland Revenue. He and Barney now had the means to enjoy life, and Faisal meant to do just that. It would help heal the scar of his former life.

He walked past the Ritz and turned down a side street, finding himself face-to-face with a BMW dealership. Following an impulse, he entered. On the showroom floor was a two-seat roadster of some kind, in British racing green with tan leather interior. Faisal approached it and a voice from behind purred, "A real beauty, this one. Wind in the hair on the open road. The throb of the engine. Sweep a little lassie off her feet in one of these, I dare say."

Faisal glanced at the salesman and mumbled, "I'm sure," then refocused his attention on the vehicle. The salesman's prattle aside, it truly was a smart little machine, with its sloping bonnet and spokelike wheels.

"Naught to sixty in under seven seconds, she'll top out around one forty, and—have a look at this . . . " The salesman punched the button of the door handle, but instead of swinging out on hinges, the door dropped down into the side panel.

Faisal was genuinely impressed. "My goodness, how fiendishly clever. Never saw anything like that before."

"Our Teutonic friends across the Channel can do wonders. Hop in. See how it feels."

"Hmm. Don't mind if I do." Faisal handed his overcoat to the salesman as he climbed over the doorsill and slid into the driver's seat. The luxurious leather enveloped him as he caressed the steering wheel and ran his fingers over the instrumentation. He adored his Jaguar Sovereign. It was so stately, so majestic. But this little roadster seemed to have FUN written all over it. And Faisal was ready for a spot of fun. "How much?" he asked.

The salesman girded his loins for the ensuing haggle. "Thirty-three thousand seven hundred pounds, including papers and dealer preparation."

"I'll take it."

"Only thirty-one meters? I was hoping for something bigger. Say, thirty-five or forty. . . . Already booked for the season, eh? Oh, how disappointing." Sigh. "I suppose it will have to do. Fully crewed and all that? . . . Jolly good. Have it pick me up at Southampton the first of May. Be going to the Med. . . . What? . . . Of course. Check's in the mail." Barney hung up the phone. "Blast it."

"Got some trouble?" asked Faisal as he slipped into his dinner jacket.

Barney scowled as he put his feet up on the coffee table. "Never knew it was so hard to charter a bloody yacht. All the big ones are already booked for the spring and summer. Had to settle for some thirty-one-meter skiff called the *Sea Crest*. I suppose it will have to do."

"Bad luck, old man."

Barney eyeballed his coconspirator. "I say, squire. You gettin' all dressed up again?"

"Yes," replied Faisal. "You might say I have to repay a loan."

As Faisal entered the Parthenon, he walked past the liveried doorman and straight into the bar. He ordered a martini but let it sit untouched as he watched the chief usher at the entrance to the gaming room. As patrons appeared, they were checked against the membership list and allowed inside. Faisal knew his membership "was no longer active." So from his vantage point on the barstool he watched and waited for the better part of an hour. Finally, the usher had to answer a call of nature. When he disappeared down the hallway to the loo, Faisal tossed a twenty-pound note on the bar and walked briskly into the casino. Without hesitation he went directly to the blackjack table and climbed onto an empty seat. Razia looked up and almost fumbled the deal. He waited until the hand finished out, then he reached inside his tuxedo pocket for a clutch of bills. "Good evening," he said casually. "Ten thousand in chips, if you please."

The pit boss standing behind Razia was not the exhumed cadaver from the previous evening. This one was a bald, clerkish fellow wearing pince-nez glasses, unaware of Faisal's history at the club. By all rights, Razia should have sounded the alarm. But she didn't. Expertly, she counted out the fifty-pound notes and shoved them through the cash slot. Then she peeled off the correct number of plaques and shoved them across the baize. Faisal placed five hundred quid in the betting rectangle, then watched Razia as she pensively dealt the hands around the table. He drew an eighteen and said, "Card."

Bewildered, Razia flipped over a seven and pulled in the plaque, then moved on to the next player.

No longer having a need to follow the cards, Faisal devoted his total concentration to Razia, and the view surpassed a million winning hands. She was more exquisite than he'd remembered. Without her high heels she might clear five feet, if that. The almond-shaped eyes set into her high-cheekboned face were hypnotic as ever, and the scent of jasmine quickened his pulse just as before.

"Your play, sir?"

"Card, please."

Another broken hand.

As Razia pulled in his cards and plaque, she had to consciously avoid his gaze, lest she become lost. She sensed his presence as before, only stronger this time. What was he doing here? Why had he returned? How did he get in? And why was he losing on purpose? Showing a nineteen, he said, "Card," and Razia flipped him an eight.

Methodically, Faisal went through the first ten thousand at five hundred pounds a turn. Then another ten thousand. Then another—all under the approving eye of the clerkish pit boss. At the end of his stake he put two thousand pounds on the betting rectangle and Razia said, "A thousand-pound limit at this table, sir."

"My apologies," replied Faisal, and he pulled one of the plaques back.

The hovering pit boss said, "Would you care for a private table, sir?"

Eyeing Razia, Faisal said, "Yes, I would."

"Very good, sir. Right this way."

Faisal slid off the stool and fell in behind the pit boss as he strode toward the private gaming room, just as the casino manager stepped out of his office. At first stunned to see Faisal, he quickly garnered his composure and cut them off before they reached the mirrored door. "I told you never to show your face in here again," growled the Siberian bear. Faisal said nothing, waiting for the pit boss to intercede, which he did. Whispering rapidly into the manager's ear, the pit boss recounted Faisal's losing trend. Again poised between greed and fear, Faisal felt the bear would make the right choice. And he did.

"All right," he grumbled, "but you try any of that stuff from last time, I'll take care of you personally, you understand?"

Faisal shrugged. "I have no idea what you mean. I'm simply here to play a wagering game. A shame my luck's been running bad lately."

The bear grumbled again and said, "Be on with you."

"Very good of you. By the way"—Faisal nodded his head toward Razia—"I rather fancy that dealer over there."

"She's busy."

Faisal stood firm. "I'm afraid she deals or it's no deal."

The bear remained stubbornly silent until the pit boss chimed in with, "C'mon, Jerry. What difference does it make?"

The bear relented, allowing Faisal and the pit boss to enter the chamber. Faisal took a seat at the table and waited. Everything was just as he'd left it. All that was missing was Razia and the bear, and shortly they came through the door. Razia looked apprehensive, so delicate and feminine beside the burly manager. Faisal wanted to say, *Let me take you away from all this.* But that would have to wait. For now.

Again she shuffled the six decks of cards and asked, "Chips, sir?"

Faisal pulled out a £100,000 cashier's check from Barclay's, made out to bearer, and handed it over. Razia raised an eyebrow, then passed it back to the manager, who gave the nod. She then counted out a hundred £1,000 plaques and pushed them across the table.

Wagering in three-thousand-pound increments, Faisal dropped hand after hand as the pile wilted away. He won twice by accident, but doubled the bet each time to insure he kept up the losing pace. When the pile had evaporated to a single plaque, he pushed it over to Razia and said, "Something for your trouble. Appears my luck has taken a turn for the worse." He nodded. "Good evening, gentlemen."

Razia watched him walk out the door, more bemused and entranced than ever. Then she picked up the £1,000 plaque and felt something underneath. She palmed it and said to her bewildered superiors, "Excuse me, I must go powder my nose." In the sanctity of the ladies' room she inspected the card. It provided a name, a telephone number, and a suite number at the Goring Hotel.

"You almost got me sacked," recalled Razia over her hearts-of-palm salad. "The manager is a toad if there ever was one, and because you and I are Pakistani, he felt we must be conspirators of some kind." They were in the River View Restaurant of the Savoy, and the lights were dancing on the Thames as gentle music wafted through the air. She was wearing a black silk designer dress by Iva Braovac that clung to her shapely figure. Gold earrings and a gold necklace topped off the package, imparting an aristocratic image. Here was a woman of refinement and education, yet she seemed quite at home dealing cards. "Fortunately, I know the managing director of the casino," she said, "and he interceded for me."

Faisal sipped his tea. "So how did a lady like you wind up as a croupier?"

Razia spiked her salad and answered, "I only work there part-time. I'm pursuing my doctorate in economic history at the London School of Economics."

"A doctorate? How many PhD candidates work in casinos?"

"Not many, I wouldn't imagine."

"Neither would I. Don't you get a stipend to underwrite your education?"

"Yes, but . . . "

"But?"

She shrugged and fingered the necklace. "I have expensive tastes."

Faisal nodded. "I quite understand. But still, you leave some gaps. Where do you come from? And how did you wind up at the School of Economics?"

Razia put her fork aside and looked out toward the Thames. "My father was in the foreign service of Pakistan. I was raised abroad for most of my life—Commonwealth countries for the most part. My father was posted to London as trade attaché when I was eighteen. We spent three glorious years here. It was so exciting to be so young and in London." She seemed to sparkle as she recounted the memories of her youth, transmitting a happiness that must have been hers. "My parents and I were quite close. I was an only child. I was in my third year as an undergraduate at the University of London. I became betrothed to a man of my parents' liking. A junior diplomat. My life seemed mapped out before me, but then . . . "

"Then?"

She shrugged again. "Then disaster struck. My parents flew home with my fiancé to meet his family. I was to follow them after I finished my exams. Their plane went down outside Karachi. No survivors."

"Good Lord! It must have been devastating for you."

She nodded. "'Twas. Hardly functional for almost two years. Returned home to Pakistan and lived with relatives for a time, but having been raised abroad, I felt alien in my own country. My uncle—my mother's brother—is now a British subject and has a small import-export firm. He brought me back to London, got me back into school, and into some therapy. It helped. I still live with my aunt and uncle, but plan to get my own flat when I graduate. Then I'll leave the casino as well."

"When will that be?"

"As soon as I finish my dissertation, in six months' time."

"Then what? Teaching?"

"Perhaps later. I've been offered a consulting position with McKinsey and Company which I plan to accept."

"Impressive."

After the waiter served up their tournedos of beef, Razia smiled and focused her black eyes upon her mysterious escort. "So, enough about me? Where did you learn to count cards like that? I've never seen anything like it."

Faisal swallowed, then replied, "I was a graduate student at Edinburgh and . . . "

He'd hired a Daimler and a driver for the evening, and the chauffeur took them on a slow, languid ride around Hyde Park. Then he drove them across the Thames to see Westminster Palace majestically illuminated on the far side of the river. As the Daimler motored along, they talked in the passenger cabin. Faisal was captivated by the way her hands animated her speech. And she was equally entranced by his elegant presence, his intellect, his mystery, and the way he danced around her questions about what he'd done in "government service." On and on they talked, until the driver lowered the privacy partition and said, "'Scuse me, guvnah, but we're running a bit low on petrol. Should I stop and fill 'er up, or will you and the lady be calling it a night?"

Faisal looked at his watch and exclaimed, "Good heavens! It's half-past one. I confess I lost all track of time."

"Yes, I really must go home. I have to teach a nine-o'clock class tomorrow."

"Of course." Faisal turned to the driver. "Ah, excuse me, your name again?"

"Sydney, guv."

"Of course, Sydney. To Fulham Road."

"Right away, guv."

As they mounted the steps to the Fulham Road house, Faisal said, "It appears your uncle's trading firm does rather well."

"Yes. He works hard. But he and my aunt have raised seven children on their own. I was their eighth, you might say. They've been wonderful to me, but I think we'll all be glad when I graduate and move to a flat of my own."

Faisal nodded and said, "When may I see you again?"

Razia held his gaze. "I teach and study tomorrow, then work tomorrow night. I'm free this weekend, though."

"Marvelous. Dinner again?"

"No. Let's do something different. How about lunch in the country? In Leicestershire."

"A luncheon in the country it is. In Leicestershire."

CHAPTER SIXTEEN

Faisal pushed the BMW Spyder through a back lane of hedge-
rows in Leicestershire, trying to impress Razia with his ersatz
Formula One skills. It was a glorious winter day in the country, and Razia's raven locks were wrapped in a Chanel scarf
against the wind. It wasn't too cold, so he'd put the top down on
the Spyder and turned up the heater and defroster full blast to
keep them comfortable.

"Turn left here!" She had to shout over the engine and wind.

Faisal whipped the Spyder into the turn a bit harshly, causing
Razia to press against him. As he whiffed her perfume, he made
a mental note to always take left turns with vigor.

The Spyder weaved along a gravel road that led to a baronial
estate on a hilltop, surrounded by giant oaks and a few peacocks
walking about. As Faisal pulled to a stop in the driveway, he
asked, "Now will you tell me where we are?"

Razia pulled off her scarf and shook her raven hair back into
place, then smiled at him. She was wearing a cream-colored silk
blouse under her jacket and black stretch pants, while a single gold
chain adorned her neck. Faisal searched mightily for a flaw, but
could find none. "This is the ancestral home of the baron Colin
Drakeson," she said. "He's master of the Boar's Head Hunt."

Just then the front door—which had the size and mass of a
drawbridge—swung open, and a short, white-haired, rotund gentleman emerged. He waved and called, "Razia! So good to see you.

Come in, come in." A second white-haired butterball emerged, this one wearing a dress, and Faisal presumed this was the baroness.

Introductions were made and the baron led them into the foyer of the magnificent Gothic structure. Razia and the baroness peeled off toward the kitchen, while the lord of the manor gave Faisal a tour of the sitting room, billiard room, gun room, and his study, which essentially functioned as headquarters of the Boar's Head Hunt (the baron was a sportsman). The paneled chamber held painting after painting of hunt scenes, a bronzed horseshoe over the door, and a table with a cluster of faded photographs. One showed the baron's grandfather with Lord Salisbury, another his father with Churchill and Lloyd George, and still another showed the young baron himself in the cockpit of a Supermarine Spitfire. Faisal's host patiently narrated each photograph, but only said of his own picture, "Did a spot of flying during the war." Then he asked, "So how did you meet Razia?"

"On the other side of a blackjack table."

The baron laughed. "Hope you escaped with your shirt."

"Win some, lose some. How did you and the baroness come to know her?"

"Met her father at a fund-raising soirée for a hospital. That seems to be my lot in life. Fund-raising. And the hunt, of course. Gave up flying after the war. Khalid Musavvir was his name. In the Paki embassy. Mind like a razor, he had. Spoke seven languages. And what a horseman! The man was a magician. Rode like the wind, he did. Became a regular on the hunt. Met Razia. Delightful. Absolute tragedy about her family. She spent some time with us afterward. By the way, do you ride?"

"Never been on a horse in my life."

The baron chuckled. "If you get to know Razia, that will change, I assure you."

The butler, who looked like a retired prime minister, appeared at the doorway and announced, "Luncheon is served in the solarium, m'lord."

After finishing their crème brûlée, the luncheon party fell silent and enjoyed the pastoral scene that stretched out through the solarium windows. The rolling hills, the checkerboard fields, and the blue sky was a beauty only England could bestow. Finally, the baroness broke the silence and said to Razia, "Why don't you take Mr. Shaikh on a tour of the stables?"

"I believe he would like that," chimed in the baron. "Told me he was an avid horseman."

Razia turned to Faisal in surprise. "You never told me you rode."

"Born in the saddle."

"Well, come on then." She took his hand and pulled him up from the table. As they departed, Faisal received a baronial wink.

The stable was a stone structure downhill and (thankfully) downwind from the manor. Faisal was reveling in the warm electric touch of Razia's hand when they rounded the corner of the stable and he stopped dead in his tracks. "What in heaven's name is *that?*" He was looking at the rusted, charred remains of a wing, a landing gear, and a tail section sticking out of the ground, all cordoned off by a short, iron picket fence.

"A Messerschmitt," replied Razia casually. "Shot down during the Battle of Britain. The pilot parachuted and the baron's father captured him with a pitchfork. The baron was actually second in line for the title. His brother was killed at Normandy, and their father ordered the plane to remain untouched as a reminder of how tenuous their way of life is."

"Rather effective, I would say."

"Come along," said Razia, and she tugged on his hand.

They entered the stable and walked along the cobblestone floor. The light was dimmer inside, and it took a minute for Faisal's eyes to adjust.

Razia paused at the first stall and said, "This is Maple Leaf and her foal Shamrock." Faisal watched, entranced, as the gray foal walked across the straw and nuzzled Razia's outstretched hand, where he found a carrot stolen from the lunch table. She scratched the foal between the ears, then led Faisal down to the next stall. "This is my favorite, Charlemagne. They let me ride him whenever I come down." The head of a magnificent Arabian poked through the opening to nuzzle against Razia, and she took the animal's neck into her embrace and cooed to him.

Faisal found himself envious. "The Drakesons may have title to him, but he's obviously your horse."

Razia drew back and patted his neck, then slowly she turned to Faisal, her face upturned in the dim light, her eyes imparting surrender. His heart racing beyond measure, he slid his arm under her jacket and took her into his embrace. As he felt her supple body under the silkened blouse and smelled the jasmine in her hair, there was a moment of hesitation—then he brought his lips down on hers, with a passion and a savagery that surprised them both.

Charlemagne neighed to protest.

CHAPTER SEVENTEEN

The estate agent from Hoffmann Properties sighed as she caught her reflection in the foyer window. At fifty-six she should have been looking toward retirement, but that seemed farther off than ever now. The lines in her face grew deeper by the fortnight, and her breasts sagged under the prim wool suit. You had to have the strength of a horse to make it in this business: keeping a smile laminated to your face, your suits pressed, and kowtowing to the venal customers trying to wring a few extra pence from your commission. And the market! It was dead as yesterday's news. Oh, to return to the decadent eighties! You could convert a flophouse into flats overnight, then sell out the next day. Sigh.

Faisal paused to look out the window near the upstairs landing, and a smile of remembrance danced across his face. He'd been a lad of—what? thirteen? fourteen?—when he'd delivered the dry cleaning from his parents' shop to this very house. He'd been an only child, working in the shop after classes, until he went off to board at the Reading Blue Coat School. His parents had operated the prosperous dry-cleaning shop, serving the carriage trade in Mayfair and Belgravia, where they instilled in their son the importance of proper dress and deportment. Their clientele expected such things. Faisal wondered what his parents' reaction would be if they knew he was going to live in the house of an old client, and it was a moment of great poignancy for him. His parents knew they had given birth to an extraordinary child and spared no expense on his education. Yet even they would've been surprised at this achievement.

The agent dumped her cigarette butt into a planter that resembled a giant bullfrog. Then she put the laminate smile back into place and straightened her wool suit. Faisal stepped onto the Italian-marble foyer and approached her.

"Moving to London are you?"

Faisal inspected the chandelier. "Let's say I've found a reason to relocate in London for the time being."

She wondered who this man was. What was he? Egyptian? Persian? Indian? Hard to say exactly, but somewhere east of Suez, surely. Ordinarily she didn't fancy the sandy kind, but this one, well, there was something about him, wasn't there? Could give one a flutter with a look.

"So precisely how much are we talking here?"

The agent had to clear a bit of phlegm before answering. "Ahem, for this luxurious three-bedroom, three-and-a-half-bath, fully furnished Belgravian mansion with two-car underground garage, study, gourmet kitchen, billiard room, and Jacuzzi spa, the lessor will require a year's lease, a ten-thousand-pound security deposit, and eleven thousand five hundred pounds a month, first and last month payable in advance. The house staff includes cook, maid, and valet, but you must employ them separately at your own expense for the duration of the lease."

Faisal nodded and said, "You've got a deal."

The estate agent held on to the bullfrog for balance.

"Perhaps the most prestigious address in the whole of The City," cooed the manager in his ersatz Cambridge accent. "Being a stone's throw from the Royal Exchange, we at the Kahn Centre have access to every facility you could possibly desire." He droned on as Faisal walked down the carpeted hallway of offices. Some were full, some were empty, yet the manager continued his soliloquy as if he were a guide showing off Longleat. "On the arcade we have a variety of restaurants, a travel agent, shoeshine, hairstylist, bookstore, and an athletic club. A brisk swim to start off the morning always puts a new spin on the day."

"Not my sort of thing, I'm afraid."

"Oh, well, mine neither, I must confess," confessed the manager as he changed the subject. "We provide a receptionist, mail drop, phone lines, fax machine, and copier, plus common-area kitchenette and conference room. This is a turnkey service that allows you to open for business the first day."

Faisal had suffered enough of the sales pitch and pointed. "I'll take that corner office there."

"Our largest suite. Excellent."

"The furniture will be delivered tomorrow. However, there is one thing."

"Yes?"

"I would like to install a satellite receiver on the roof in order to pull in real time stock-market quotations from various wire services. Is that a problem?"

The agent smiled, revealing two rows of perfectly capped teeth. "No problem whatsoever. I shall draw up the lease papers immediately. What is the name of your firm by the way?"

"Investment Research, Limited."

Barney Slickman screwed in the terminals on the last wire, then flipped a switch that brought the computer to life. Faisal keystroked the commands, and quotations from the Hong Kong and Tokyo exchanges danced across the screen.

"Excellent, Barney. Thanks to your handiwork we can track any stock worldwide in real time."

"Piece of cake, squire. Since you're gracious enough to manage my money, I can at least get you wired up."

"There are two investment philosophies I can pursue. Short-term transactional plays, riding the near-term ups and downs of the markets, or longer-term plays. For us, I think the transactional plays are the best. It cuts our downside in case we want to get our money out."

"Whatever you say, squire."

Faisal stretched and looked out the window, and when his gaze fell upon the roof antenna of a neighboring building, it gave him an idea. "Say, Barney, do you suppose you could rig a scanner on the roof to snare some diplomatic traffic?"

"Diplomatic traffic?"

"Yes. Pick off some of the embassy cables sent into and out of London."

Barney shrugged. "Well, I suppose so. They would be on the high-freq bands. That's easy enough to rig. But why?"

"What's an unemployed cryptanalyst to do? Playing the investment game all day long can cause one to become weary. Since we have the means, and some leisure time, why not have a spot of fun and read someone else's mail?"

"Whatever you say, squire. You've done right by me so far."

"And I guess we'd need a direction finder to peg the incoming traffic. Could you rig that up as well?"

"An omnidirectional or directional set?"

"Omni."

"Hmm. Well, yes, but it would be a bit crude." Barney thought for a moment. "And we'd have to keep it small so no one would get curious."

"Of course. Just so we could figure out the general direction of the incoming traffic. That helps enormously, you know."

"You've got it, squire. . . . Well, I best be off. Got to do some house hunting."

"House hunting?"

"Yeah. Decided I had enough of the hotel, although room service was grand. Think I'll get a flat in London and rejuvenate my English ties before heading out for the Med on the *Sea Crest*."

"Hmm. Since you're such a nomad, why not stay at my Belgravian house when you're in town?"

"Well, I wouldn't want to impose."

Faisal pulled a spare key off his key ring and tossed it to his coconspirator. "I've taken a year's let on it. Cook, maid, and valet included. Plenty of room. Make it your base when you're in town."

Barney pocketed the key. "Mighty decent of you, squire. I'll get on to that scanner of yours straightaway."

CHAPTER EIGHTEEN

Faisal checked his watch for the twenty-eighth time that day and decided it was time to ring the concierge at the Connaught. Had the package arrived from Cartier? Yes, sir. Just came in and placed it in the safe. Excellent. He rose from his office chair and worked off some nervous energy by pacing around the desk. It had been a glorious spring and summer. Razia had captured his heart, and his efforts at Investment Research had pushed up the value of his and Barney's combined portfolio by 17 percent, after expenses.

Barney had alternated between London and the *Sea Crest*. He was toying with the idea of buying the yacht and running her as a charter; but to do so would mean cashing out his share of the portfolio. Faisal was sympathetic.

Razia had quit the casino to concentrate full-time on teaching her classes and completing her dissertation. That way, her evenings were free, allowing her and Faisal to concentrate on each other.

Faisal checked his watch again. The hands seemed to have stopped. How maddening. Might as well do the daily chore. He took out a key and unlocked the file-room door. Inside, the Teletype clattered away as it generated a long stream of paper bearing the intercepted radio-Teletype traffic of London's embassy row.

The intercepts had been a source of great satisfaction for Faisal. He'd written some codebreaking algorithms and leased time on a powerful Convex super-minicomputer to attack the encrypted intercepts. He'd broken a number of them, a few of them juicy. There was the cable from Rome, recalling the Italian ambassador to testify in a burgeoning corruption trial. Shortly after that intercept, Roman newspapers exploded with stories of the recall, and the ambassador disappeared. Faisal guessed the Mafia's hand was involved. Then there was the cable from Oslo, outlining negotiation terms for the new North Sea oil treaty for the Norwegian ambassador. Then came the (almost identical) epistles from Warsaw-Prague-Budapest-Sofia-Bucharest, instructing their ambassadors to request additional aid from the British Foreign Office. And from Bern, the Swiss ambassador was told to probe his contacts in Whitehall about the possible entry of Switzerland into the European Community. Faisal chuckled at that last one. The Swiss would always follow the money, even if it meant flushing their cherished neutrality down the loo.

Although playing with the diplomatic traffic had been a source of great fun for Faisal, the Russian, American, and British traffic remained closed to him. He no longer had access to the massive computing power and memory that was required to break them. But no matter. He felt it was time to shut his hobby down. If someone stumbled onto this lot, they might start asking uncomfortable questions, and who knew where that would lead? He'd have Barney dismantle the frequency scanner next time he was in town. Yes, it was time to develop other interests. Perhaps fox hunting. Razia had coaxed him onto the mare named Maple Leaf. He took a ride around the paddock and actually enjoyed it. Maybe it was the Arab in his blood. Yes, time to move on with a new life. He bundled up the telex paper and began feeding the roll into the shredder. Just like old times, he told himself. As the machine reeled in the stream of paper, Faisal scanned the messages and saw that, as usual, some were encrypted and some were not. Not that he really cared any longer. It was time to get out the door. He had a pressing engagement, in a very real sense.

Like a ravenous goat, the shredder gobbled up the roll and turned it into unreadable chaff. The long sheet was nearly consumed when something caught Faisal's eye. Something that made him rip the remaining paper from the shredder, as if he were snatching a lamb from the jaws of a wolf. Once saved, he held the slightly crumpled paper at arm's length and focused his keen eyes on the characters before him. They were only symbols on a page, but as he continued to stare, they silently screamed with the resonance of a derailing freight train, for they were arrayed in a unique fashion:

BREAK BREAK

QRAZS9P	ES6DL4T	FF35ANR
NCD11RB	5NOSR8D	PQV7G9J
YALE5TO	C2H8EKN	IKNIAM4
HA3G2NE	XTLCPMA	DNII1HN
REDNUHT	SUBERED	IPERTNI
JEF82DN	DJUU03M	QP44MFF
TBVPFPP	XX5PTMD	YSAZZX9
HGFKSL7	KSJWU4U	SLSL6BW

DF: 103 DEGREES

"No," Faisal whispered to himself. "It can't be." He remained there, in shock, as the characters engraved themselves upon his mind, refusing to be ignored. "It can't be," he whispered again, his throat dry as parchment.

With shaking hands he returned to his office and placed the paper gingerly on his chair. Then he unrolled a large map of Europe and the Middle East.

Barney Slickman had rigged the frequency scanner and direction finder so that each time a new frequency was queued up, the Teletype would initialize it with a BREAK BREAK notation. Then it would print out the azimuth of the transmission at the tail end of the "trapped" message. Barney had lamented his omnidirectional finder was crude, but Faisal had found it to be remarkably precise. Particularly if the signal strength was high. The map on the desk already had pencil lines drawn on it, radiating from London to intersect points with Rome, Madrid, Prague, Budapest, Bern, and the like. It was how Faisal identified the sender. The message said DF: 103 DEGREES. Using a drawing compass, he plotted a hundred-three-degree azimuth from London. Then using a ruler he drew a long pencil line from City center outward across the Channel. The line passed through Calais, clipped Belgium, and intersected Luxembourg before entering Germany. Faisal kept the pencil true as it crossed over the Alps and the Balkans, then splashed into the Black Sea at the Bulgarian seaport of Varna. The pencil came ashore on the Turkish coast, crossed Turkey, then entered Iran well south of Mount Ararat. It cut across Lake Urmia, then remained south of the Caspian Sea before intersecting—like a lance through a ring—the lost home of the Shah's peacock throne, Tehran.

Faisal held fast to the desk as his knees gave way and his blood pressure dropped a score of points. Dizziness seized him as the evidence sucked him into a vortex of fear and loathing. His soul was free-falling, plummeting, and there was no rip cord to pull.

He plucked the sheet from his chair and lowered himself into the seat. With wet, trembling hands he held the foolscap tightly and examined the jumbled characters, counting them like a schoolboy his marbles. Then he double-checked the azimuth he'd drawn on the map. There was no mistake.

It was a Tehran transmit point.

With seven-letter code groups.

The Black Cipher had returned.

Faisal had chosen the Connaught for this singular occasion because he wanted to dazzle Razia. But it turned out he was the one to be dazzled, for Razia had worn a traditional sari of stunning blue silk. It wrapped around her petite body like a second skin, turning heads and evoking ungentlemanly thoughts from the English gentlemen in the lobby. Faisal was dressed in black tie and looked rakish as ever; but from the moment he arrived in the hired Daimler, Razia sensed something was amiss. He seemed remote, uncommunicative, tense. She had always commanded his complete attention, but now it was focused elsewhere and she found she missed it. Terribly.

"You seem preoccupied this evening."

Faisal looked up. "Umm? I beg your pardon?"

"I said, you seem preoccupied this evening."

"Oh, yes. You must excuse me. I've been thinking."

"Is something bothering you? You hardly touched your sole."

Faisal pinched the bridge of his nose and said, "Forgive me, darling. I have been a slothful escort. It's something at work."

"Oh, did the market take a downturn? I didn't check the closings this evening. I was busy getting dressed."

"And you are stunning beyond words. It has to do with something outside the financial realm. But I refuse to let it intrude further. Not on this evening, especially."

Razia demurely sipped from her crystal goblet. "What's so special about this evening?"

"It is your birthday, is it not?"

She smiled over the goblet. "I thought you'd forgotten."

"I believe you're twenty-nine, if my memory serves me correctly."

Her laugh was soft as rose petals. "A man who can count through six decks of cards cannot recall my date of birth? Am I to believe that? Let's just say it is my third twenty-ninth birthday."

"As you wish, my darling. And in celebration of this moment I have something especially for you." He motioned to the waiter, who nodded and left to fetch the concierge. Razia was fluttery as a schoolgirl, trying to guess what was coming. Then the package was placed before her on a silver tray. For a blissful time the Black Cipher was purged from Faisal's mind as Razia oohed and aahed over the present. It was wrapped in glossy green paper and a broad white ribbon. Meticulously, she unwrapped it—part of her not wanting to tear the paper, another part wanting to rip it away and seize the prize. But her reserved instincts prevailed until she finally freed the white box underneath. She pulled open the top, then lifted the cotton buffer and gasped, "Oh, Faisal! It's beautiful!" She held it up so he could see it. It was a custom-made Judith Leiber evening bag, fashioned into a replica of a Fabergé egg. It was made of green enamel, bejeweled with crisscrossing gold strands that were studded with small diamonds.

Faisal delighted in the way she held it up to watch the light play off the diamonds. "It is *magnificent*, darling. Thank you so much. I shall treasure it always."

Faisal had forgotten the Black Cipher completely now as he said, "Open it."

A bit puzzled and surprised, Razia lowered the egg to the table and unsnapped the small clasp. The clutch came open like a clam-shell, revealing a small red velvet box inside. Razia gazed up at him with a Is-this-what-I-think-it-is? look. But Faisal revealed nothing except a gentle smile. With hands that slightly trembled, she pulled out the small box, gulped, and opened it. 'Twas the first time in her life she'd come face-to-face with an eleven-carat round diamond, purchased at Cartier for £178,000. The multifaceted stone radiated light like a small star in the palm of her hand. She tried to speak, but her voice failed her. She raised her gaze to Faisal's, and he simply said, "My darling, you are my diamond, and I love you beyond measure. You have captured my heart, and it is with this token I ask for your hand in marriage."

Archibald was the tall, thin, esthetic maître d' who embodied the Connaught's reputation for service, and for snobbery. He wore a monocle that gave his face an extra measure of scowl, and he guarded the entry to the dining room as if the crown jewels lay beyond. Anyone who entered his domain without a reservation was made to feel like an unwelcome relative. He held himself aloof from the customers, the staff, and even the management. So it was with discomfort he received Rudolph the waiter as he clambered up and gasped, "Do we have a first-aid kit?"

Archibald's left eyebrow shot up, allowing the monocle to fall free and dangle at the end of its tether. "First-aid kit?" He'd never been asked that before.

"Yes," replied Rudolph breathlessly. "Quickly."

Archibald was not to be moved. "And what do you require a first-aid kit for?"

"Smelling salts."

"Smelling salts?"

"Yes." Rudolph jerked his thumb backward. "The lady at table nine just fainted."

• ∎ ∎

Once resuscitated, Razia was escorted by Faisal to the powder room to regain her composure. While she was gone, Faisal settled the dinner bill (which cost only slightly less than Razia's eleven-carat diamond). When she emerged, she took her fiancé's arm. Together they exited the hotel and climbed into their carriage for the trip home. Razia was filled with anticipation and couldn't wait to announce her engagement to Uncle Qasim and Aunt Anazir. In their excitement, they walked past the newsstand, which held the late edition of the *Evening Standard*. Buried in the obituaries was a small story with the headline: EDINBURGH DON SUCCUMBS.

"Ashes to ashes, dust to dust, with these prayers, O Father, we commit the earthly body of Angus Arthur MacKenzie Doogan to the ground. May his soul rest with you in eternal peace. In the name of Christ our Lord we pray, amen." The Anglican vicar seemed older and more frail than Angus had been in his final days, yet his voice resonated with authority over the hillside cemetery outside Edinburgh.

They had *just* made the funeral. Angus's housekeeper, Glenna, had notified Mrs. Wheatland, who was still keeping watch over Faisal's Cheltenham home. She, in turn, broke the news to Faisal that Angus Doogan was to be buried the next day. Faisal and Razia had flown to Edinburgh where they were met by Glenna, and together they drove straightaway to the graveside service. Absently, Faisal scanned the small assembly gathered round the coffin. There were some old friends from the university, and a few very old retired hands from Cheltenham. Faisal knew one or two well enough to nod an acknowledgment, but basically he was appalled at the meager turnout. Angus Doogan had contributed mightily to the defense of Britain in her darkest hours. He felt his mentor deserved a flyover by the Royal Air Force, at the very least, and perhaps interment in Westminster Abbey.

Now Faisal's final link with his past was laid to rest, almost anonymously, in the Scottish soil. He took solace knowing that Angus was now with his beloved wife, Eleanor.

Faisal was standing between Razia and Glenna as the vicar said the benediction. Then the small gathering began to break up. Faisal said in a quavering voice, "Excuse me a moment." He then turned away and walked up the slope of the small hill. Razia watched the back of her fiancé as he slowly climbed the gentle incline. She'd never seen him like this. On the journey to Edinburgh he'd hardly uttered a word, and Razia left him alone to sort things out. "They must have been very close," she said finally.

"Cut from the same cloth, those two," remarked Glenna. "Faisal was the son Angus never had. They loved each other dearly."

"I see." Razia contemplated Faisal's figure for a few moments, then said, "What's the expression? You're never truly a man until your father dies."

Faisal crested the hill and felt the cool sea breeze wash over him. In the distance was the foreboding presence of the North Sea, and Faisal could recall feeling its cold sting on many occasions. He looked behind him and saw the ending and the beginning, the omega and the alpha, from this watershed event in his life. The remains of Angus were being lowered into the ground, and only a few feet away was Razia. Such a clear demarcation, except for the pall of the Black Cipher. Faisal reached inside his jacket pocket and withdrew the slip of paper imprinted with the seven-letter code groups. Just a jumble of characters they were. So simple, yet so sinister. Their appearance from out of the blue had rocked Faisal off the foundation of his new life and forced him to confront the past. And it all had to happen on the day the soul of Angus Doogan departed for Paradise.

What was he to do? What could this Black Cipher signal mean? What dark forces were at work? The same forces that had expelled him from GCHQ and set him adrift? The damned Black Cipher. What was he to do? What could he do? Although wealthy now, he was but one man arrayed against forces so powerful and so malevolent that he could impale himself in an effort to find the truth. He looked down the hill and saw Razia climbing toward him. And what of her? He had her future, *their* future, in his hands. He had to give weight to that. He looked at the paper again. He'd labored his entire life for the good of Britain, and if Britain cared not a whit that her government was rotten from within, then why the hell should he? He shoved the paper back in his pocket, his mind made up. Yes, the whole lot of them could be damned. He'd marry this fantastic woman and retire to a villa on a Grecian isle. Blast it, they could buy their own island! Have children. It wasn't too late. Yes, that is what he would do. Marry Razia, retire to the Aegean, sire his children, and let Britain and her invisible government go to hell.

Razia took his arm and leaned against his shoulder. "We must be going if we're to drop Glenna off and catch our plane."

Faisal nodded, and slowly they began their descent from the hilltop.

"I forgot to tell you. Just before I left home Uncle Qasim and Aunt Anazir invited you to dinner tomorrow night. They want to introduce you to the rest of the family."

At that moment, Faisal saw the coffin of his mentor disappear into the grave, and his soul tremored with an unspoken message— a message that caused him to stop in his tracks. Softly he said, "No . . . no, I'm afraid I can't make it."

Razia squeezed his arm. "I understand, darling. You're upset about Angus. We'll make dinner another time. Qasim and Anazir will understand."

"No, it's not that." His gaze remained fixed on the grave. "I must leave for Tokyo tomorrow."

CHAPTER NINETEEN

The *shinkansen* bullet train roared across the rice paddies of northern Honshu like a fighter plane on a low-level pass. The long, swift chain of forged steel looked like a menacing eel, seeking to devour some unsuspecting prey on the tracks ahead.

As the landscape whipped by the window at 130 miles per hour, Faisal found himself a white-knuckled rider. The *shinkansen* was so massive and so heavy, yet it traveled so *fast!* There was no *clickety-clack* sound as it moved along. Rather, it was a swaying motion, with a loud undertone that sounded like running water. It wasn't a particularly smooth ride, and Faisal marveled at how the two gentlemen in the neighboring chairs adroitly ate noodles with their chopsticks.

In the next car a group of Japanese schoolgirls were evidently holding a pep rally of some kind, because whenever the door opened a chorus of cheers roared out. One of the young ladies walked by Faisal and he noticed she wore a Dallas Cowboys emblem on her backpack. He didn't understand the fashion statement.

Somewhat fidgety, Faisal rose and went to the club car for a spot of tea. He was dying for a cigarette, having kicked them for Razia, and tea was a weak substitute.

On the long, over-the-pole flight from Heathrow to Narita, Faisal had used the sequestered time to reflect upon what he was about to do. The odds of success were remote, and pursuing such an elusive grail bordered on madness. The thought of a comfortable retirement with Razia was compelling; but as he'd watched Angus Doogan's coffin lowered into the ground, the spirit of his old mentor lay heavy upon him. Angus always rang true, his courage never wavered; and in his own gentle way, the don demanded the same from Faisal.

Angus had spoken.

The Black Cipher beckoned.

And Faisal had departed for Tokyo on a quest to break the encryption to hell and gone. Where the trail would end, he hadn't a clue; but to crack the seven-letter code groups he required more grist for his cryptanalytic mill, and *that* meant he had to obtain some of the old Black Cipher message traffic. Since the door at Government Communications Headquarters was welded tightly shut, Faisal knew he must procure the old messages by other means. And that was why he'd journeyed to the land of *asahi*—the rising sun.

Upon arrival he'd checked into the Hotel Seiyo in the bustling Ginza district of Tokyo. There he found the level of service, along with the prices, nothing less than staggering. The hotel's credo: never use a single bellhop or waiter when three will do. Since he'd arrived on a Friday, he took the weekend to decompress from the jet lag and reacquaint himself with the capital of Nippon. He ventured out into the Ginza on Saturday afternoon, which was a time when the police blocked off the streets and turned the district into a giant shopping mall. Faisal strolled along, soaking up the feel of the place and refurbishing his *Nihon-go* (Japanese) skills. He walked past a municipal worker polishing a brass fire hydrant to a mirror finish. A seedy-looking American, with a bass drum strapped to his back and a guitar in his hand, belted out a rock song to a curious and bemused audience. A high-end gift shop displayed a boxed melon for sale at ¥22,000—roughly £95. Faisal shook his head, trying to figure out what could be done to a melon to make it worth £95.

He took a subway to the Meiji Shrine and was impressed by the immaculate grounds, the magnificent temple, and the Shinto priests in their vestments. He observed the Japanese as they washed their hands at the fountain, tossed in their offering coins, clapped their hands, and offered a prayer to their *kami*. Out of respect, Faisal washed his hands and tossed in an offering for the temple.

The following Monday, Faisal made a few discreet inquiries at the headquarters of the Nippon Self-Defense Forces. He was informed the party he sought was not available. Was there a message? In his broken Japanese, Faisal left his name and room number at the Hotel Seiyo. The next day he received a call, from a voice he did not know, instructing him to come to Misawa.

The *shinkansen* slowed to a creep as it pulled into its northern terminus at Morioka station. There Faisal grabbed his suitcase and followed the group of schoolgirls down the station steps to another train. He took a seat at a window where he could view the station clock. As the minute hand clicked over from 1:42 to 1:43, Faisal felt the 1:43 train for Misawa get under way. This was a conventional train that moved along at a mere 60 mph. The flat terrain of central Honshu gave way to rolling hills that possessed surprising forestation.

Across the aisle from Faisal was a woman with the size, girth, and disposition of a sumo wrestler. She eyed Faisal warily. Then a man wearing a resplendent white uniform entered the car, and Faisal thought he must be an admiral in the Japanese Navy. When he started punching tickets, Faisal realized he was the conductor.

At the coastal town of Misawa, Faisal took a cab to the Park Hotel and placed a call to the number given him in Tokyo. A voice—American—answered with the cryptic response, "Extension seven four nine."

"Mr. Watanabe, please."

"I'm afraid Mr. Watanabe is in a meeting and can't be interrupted. May I take a message?"

Faisal left his name, hotel, and room number and said he would wait. While waiting for the return call, he showered and changed into a polo shirt, slacks, and jacket. Evening was nigh, so he ventured outside and walked through the unremarkable streets. He found a small restaurant and ordered a dinner of tempura that was better than he expected. He stopped at a newsstand and picked up a *kanji* newsmagazine, then returned to his room to read and to wait.

The call came at half-past eight. A Japanese voice speaking broken English asked if Mr. Shaikh would be kind enough to take a taxi to the main gate of Misawa air base. He would be met there.

Faisal picked up a cab outside the hotel for the short drive to the main entrance of the Misawa installation. As they approached, the cab drove down a lane called "green pole" street. It was here the local merchants catered to the American and Japanese military who populated the base, and the sidewalks were covered with awnings held up by a string of poles painted green.

The cab emerged from the lane, drove past the Red Dragon saloon and up to the guardhouse of the main gate. There Faisal paid off the cab and was met by a lieutenant in the Japanese Air Self-Defense Forces. He bowed vigorously to Faisal several times, then opened the passenger door of the staff car. Faisal climbed in and they were off, pulling out past a rapierlike statue of an American F-16 fighter plane. They drove slowly down a street of banal, low-rise buildings, the kind often found on military bases. A few people could be seen under the streetlights wearing their camouflage fatigues, and an occasional jogger was running hither and yon. As the car turned left beside some large hangar buildings, Faisal heard the roar of jet engines. He figured this was the airfield.

Misawa air base was an odd piece of real estate, for it was here the victor and vanquished of World War II jointly housed their engines of war—a half century after the fact. For the Americans it was home to the 432nd Fighter Wing, flying state-of-the-art F-16s that bristled with a dazzling array of weaponry and electronics. For the Japanese it was home to their 3rd Air Wing, flying the older but still formidable Mitsubishi F-1 fighters. What brought the former enemies together in an enduring relationship was that the old Soviet empire lay within spitting distance of Hokkaido. Had shooting broken out during the Cold War, Soviet doctrine called for the Sea of Okhotsk to be used as a staging area. Once the ships of the Red Banner Pacific Fleet had assembled, they would've attempted a breakout into the open sea through the Kurile Island chain. That was why the Soviets tenaciously held on to the Kuriles, and why Misawa air base was honed to a razor's edge.

But now the Soviet ships were Russian, and they lay rusting in the harbors of Vladivostok and Petropavlovsk, stripped of anything worth selling and manned by skeleton crews on the brink of despair. Yet Misawa remained at a razor's edge. An anachronism perhaps?

As the staff car descended a hill, Faisal noticed some bunkerlike earthen mounds cordoned off with high barbed-wire fences. He had no idea what they were.

The Japanese Air Self-Defense Forces (known as Jazzdaf by the Americans) are organized into four major geographic commands, each under a three-star general who commands the aircraft and missiles in his sector. The Southwestern sector is based on Okinawa; the Western sector on Kyushu; the Central sector in Iruma near Tokyo; and the Northern sector in Misawa, which resides on the northern fringe of Honshu.

Since they'd been eyeball-to-eyeball with the Soviets for several decades, the Japanese had developed elegant and precise protocols to deal with their air defense. Around Hokkaido and northern Honshu, the airspace was cordoned off into an inner defense zone and an outer defense zone. When a bogey penetrated the outer defense zone—which happened a couple of hundred times a year—two F-15 Eagle fighters would scramble from the Chitose Jazzdaf base on Hokkaido to intercept and identify. During the Cold War these bogeys were almost always Soviet aircraft on training missions, probing the Japanese air defenses and appraising their response. Once they were acquired by the Japanese fighters, the Soviet aircraft would sometimes play a spot of tag and then head for home. But if a bogey continued on and crossed the inner defense zone, then the commander on the scene was authorized to engage with the interceptors or surface-to-air missiles. But during the Cold War this never happened. The Soviets knew better. However, even though the era of confrontation was in the past, the presence of the Russian aircraft was still considered a thorny problem. And of course, one always had to keep an eye on the North Koreans.

To maintain the required vigilance, the Japanese air defense system possessed a comprehensive radar grid, plus an elegant command and control network that was a central nervous system, so to speak. The nexus of this system was sequestered in the underground bunker Faisal had just driven past. In this subterranean redoubt was a large chamber filled with Japanese radar operators. Here they worked in semidarkness to control and defend their airspace. Americans were here, too, but their role was to control their aircraft operating in Jazzdaf airspace. The Japanese bunker was known by the rather bizarre call sign of Headwork, and at the very time Faisal's car drove past, the Jazzdaf duty commander was closely following a group of Russian bogeys that had left Sakhalin Island. This group of eight radar blips had ventured over the Sea of Okhotsk, crossed the Kurile Island chain, and continued east over the Pacific. Then they turned south and loitered outside the Jazzdaf outer defense zone, in a pattern that told the radar operator they were refueling. When the biggest blip turned north and headed for home, the operator figured it was a Mainstay refueling tanker. Then the other blips turned en masse and headed due west, tripping the wire of the outer defense zone. Following standard procedure, the duty commander scrambled two F-15s from Chitose to intercept. And because there were seven bogeys in this flight, which was rather unusual, the duty commander of Headwork ordered two more F-15s brought to superalert status.

As the staff car took a long curve, Faisal looked out the window to see a long, lighted runway stretched out before him. He instinctively ducked as a lumbering winged craft seemed to spin its wheels on the roof of the car. Faisal only got a glimpse, but recognized it as the VQ variant of the P-3 Orion subhunter aircraft. Instead of subhunting, the VQ's mission during the Cold War was to fly "Beggar Flights." These Beggar Flights would probe Soviet coastal defenses and shadow Soviet warships to record their radio transmissions and radar signatures. It was all part of the invisible warfare practiced on both sides of the Iron Curtain for almost half a century. An invisible war in which Misawa had long played a pivotal role. And since Russia seemed one step removed from anarchy these days, the Beggar Flights kept on flying, monitoring the Siberian coast and shadowing the occasional Russian warship that still put to sea.

At the next intersection the staff car took a left where a sign pointed to Security Hill. The road descended to an isthmus across Lake Ogarwa, then it rose up the incline to Security Hill, and that's when Faisal saw it. It loomed through the trees in a stark and ghostly light. This was the giant Flare-9 Wullenweber antenna, known as the Elephant Cage by the locals. And it did, indeed, look as if elephantine beasts should be roaming within it. The massive Wullenweber was circular in shape, consisting of four concentric rings of antennae, the outermost having a diameter that could hold three rugby fields end to end. The Elephant Cage identified the direction of a radio source and also scooped up a basket of emissions—from fighter-pilot chatter to low-frequency submarine traffic.

Faisal's driver said nothing as the car crested the hill and approached another cluster of banal, military-style buildings. The driver pulled into a parking lot; then he opened the door for Faisal and led him toward a pillboxlike structure, which was set into a barbed-wire fence. To Faisal's left, illuminated by garish klieg lights, were gigantic white spheres that dotted the landscape. They gave the impression that the Jolly Green Giant often played golf here. These giant golf balls were actually geodesic radomes that covered massive antenna dishes that uplinked Misawa, via satellite, with NSA's headquarters at Fort Meade, downlinked data from eavesdropping "ferret" satellites, and listened in passively on a variety of frequency bands.

Faisal entered the guard hut and stepped up to a counter where he was eyeballed by a dour-looking U.S. Air Force security guard. He signed in and was issued a visitor's pass "to be worn at all times." Here his Japanese escort handed him off to a black sergeant, whose forearm was about the diameter of Faisal's thigh. The sergeant ushered Faisal through a turnstile with overlapping metal bars. It looked like some sort of slicing machine, and Faisal hoped that wasn't prophetic.

They walked across a tarmac to a long, low, beige-colored building that looked like the rear of a large supermarket. The escort opened the entry doors and Faisal stepped into the SCIF, or the Security Communications Intelligence Facility of the 6920th Electronic Security Group.

In the netherworld of signals intelligence, of which most of the planet is scarcely aware, the practitioners of this esoteric art have their own superstars. Just as medicine has Denton Cooley and the movies Tom Cruise, signals intelligence has its own breed of celebrities. Although they practice their craft in prisonlike conditions and occasionally have personality disorders, SIGINT superstars do emerge. They sit in semidarkness for hour upon hour, tuning their receivers to and fro, straining to hear a staticy voice or the *ditteybop* signal of a Morse code operator. They not only listen for a familiar voice, but for its inflection as well, for sometimes the timbre of a voice can tell a superstar more than the words. Was there an exercise under way? Did a fighter pilot sound strained? Tired? Upset? Drunk? (Happens often.) Was there fuel for the aircraft? Was his ground crew hungry? Or rebellious? Was he scared? The superstars listen for these things. In banks of stalls (called squirrel nests) they sit in near darkness, for low light seems to improve one's auditory powers. They sit and sit and strain and strain, until their ears ache and their butts go to sleep. This is the life of a SIGINT superstar, slogging through days of boredom and seconds of terror.

The 6920th Electronic Security Group is a U.S. Air Force unit and the dominant force at Misawa, but it operates closely with the Naval Security Group and the Army's Intelligence and Security Command. The squirrel nests of the unit are manned twenty-four hours a day by "flights" of linguists, cryptanalysts, and technicians with quirky nicknames like Cujo Pups and Able Assassins.

For decades, the Far Eastern Military District of the Soviet Union was the 6920th's primary concern. A heavy Soviet air and naval presence along the east coast of Siberia, as well as impact areas on the Kamchatka Peninsula for test ICBMs, required a large electronic ear tuned toward the *Rodina*. Just as the Soviets placed their superstars in their Cuban listening post of San Cristóbal, the Americans placed a host of their celebrities at Misawa.

When Korean Air Lines Flight 007 was shot down over Sakhalin Island in 1983, the world was appalled. Then astounded when the actual recording of the Soviet fighter pilot's dialogue was played at the United Nations. It was a dialogue with his ground controller that ended with the cryptic statement, "The target is destroyed." It was an inadequate epitaph for the 269 innocent people who died on board.

The pilot–ground controller dialogue had been captured by a joint Japanese-American operation called Project CLEF. It was a remote listening post on the northern coast of Hokkaido. Automated equipment picked up and recorded the fatal transmission, which was brought back to Misawa for analysis by the superstars. (Surprisingly, it was the Japanese equipment that provided the better-quality recording.)

Faisal was led down a hallway of identical doors by his American escort. They walked past one door just as it was opened from within. Faisal glanced inside and saw a darkened chamber, with rows of glowing dials shining back at him. He knew he'd just seen a squirrel nest.

The escort led him to another door, indistinguishable from the others, and ushered him inside. It was a small, empty conference room, and the escort said, "Have a seat. Mr. Watanabe will be with you shortly." The door closed and Faisal sat down, wishing he had a cigarette.

The door opened.

He was late middle-aged and indistinguishable from the thousands of business-suited men Faisal had passed on the Ginza. His head was almond shaped, with thinning hair combed over its dome. He stood perhaps five feet two, and there was gray at the temples. Faisal rose and bowed deeply at the waist, then Soichiro Watanabe bowed in reply. That piece of etiquette behind them, the two men fell into an embrace of comrades too long parted.

"Shaikh-*san*," said Watanabe softly. "Too rong . . . too rong."

Faisal replied, "Yes, old friend. Much too long." He held the little man at arm's length and inspected the face. The lines were deeper, and gray had encroached on the temples, but he still looked the same. How long had it been since they'd chased over the Pacific in that wild adventure? Had a decade truly gone by?

The signals intelligence arm of the Japanese government is contained within the uniformed ranks of the Army, Navy, and Air Force branches of the Self-Defense Forces. Their capability is much smaller than the Americans or the British, but certainly potent, as demonstrated by the intercepts of KAL 007's final moments. While each service branch has its own uniformed chief of signals, the SDF minister was advised on such matters by a civilian deputy. That deputy was Soichiro Watanabe.

The demure Japanese gentleman shook his head and said fretfully, "So sorry about delay, Shaikh-*san*, but strange things happening on Sakhalin. Bad things."

"Bad things?"

Even the inscrutable Watanabe betrayed some frustration. "Strange, strange. Do not understand. Russian radio traffic unprecedented. . . . But that not why you here. Sit! Sit! Tell me everything since you leave."

"Soichiro, it's been almost ten years."

Watanabe thought for a moment, then said, "Impossible."

"I wish it were, Soichiro. But time has passed us by."

Watanabe shook his head, then said, "Why you come to Japan?" He paused. "This not holiday for you?"

Faisal contemplated this little man and thought carefully about the favor he was about to ask. It was not a gentlemanly thing to put a friend at risk, but Faisal knew he had no choice. "I have come here, Soichiro-*san*, because I must ask a favor of you."

The eyes remained passive, but the voice said, "Anything for you, Shaikh-*san*. You know that."

Relieved, Faisal replied, "That is reassuring, old friend. Lean back and make yourself comfortable, for I have an incredible story to tell you. . . . "

The Jazzdaf F-15 visually acquired the flight of seven Russian aircraft and closed in on the lead MiG-29 Fulcrum. As he approached, the other Fulcrums and the single Fencer fighter-bomber began to spread out. The Japanese pilot signaled the Russian with his handtorch to tune his radio to an international flight com frequency. They were seventeen miles from the inner defense zone and the Russians showed no sign of breaking off. The Japanese pilot continued signaling, not seeing the Fulcrum on the far starboard side fall back and come around on his "six" position. The Russian pilot punched a sequence of buttons on his armament panel and activated the Atoll missile slung under his fighter's wing. The glowing tailpipes of the Japanese F-15 were bright against the cold night sky and made perfect targets for the heat-seeking weapon. The young Russian aviator was sweating. What he was about to do made no sense, but what choice was left to him? He hadn't eaten in three days. Better a quick death than to waste away like some sallow-eyed African in the desert. He executed the final arming sequence on the Atoll missile and received a growling noise in his headphones, telling him the weapon was locked on. This was it. He swallowed, then toggled his radio microphone and said, "Leader break." The lead Fulcrum's tailpipes rolled inverted, then shot straight down for the sea, taking him out of danger as the young Russian pulled the trigger to let the missile fly. In almost the blink of an eye, the Atoll shot off the rail and raced into the starboard tailpipe of the F-15, creating a giant fulmination against the night sky.

As planned, the remaining Fulcrums bolted in different directions, like a covey of quail flushed from a cornfield. The surviving Japanese pilot pulled his craft abruptly skyward, consumed by the confluence of fear and revenge. As his targets scattered, he jabbered excitedly to his ground controllers back at Headwork, failing to notice that the Fencer bomber had gone into a powered descent toward the Tsugaru Strait.

■ ■ ■

" . . . so to reconstruct the algorithm that will break the Black Cipher, I must have additional traffic to work with."

Watanabe nodded. "Understand."

"There were three messages in addition to the Tehran intercepts. One was a silo accident at a Strategic Rocket Force base in Aykhal, one was a civilian uprising in Samarkand, and one was a diplomatic incident in Petropavlovsk involving the American treaty-inspection team."

"Diplomatic incident?"

Faisal reached into his jacket pocket and withdrew a slip of paper. "It was a barroom brawl, actually. Seems an American couldn't quite stomach the high-octane vodka and went round the bend. Smashed up some barmaid as I recall. I've put all the particulars on this paper, including what I remember of the TEXTA data."

Watanabe took the paper and asked, "How intercept made?"

"It was picked off by an RC one-three-five Rivet Joint flight out of Shemya. But if I had to wager, I would bet it was also snagged here at Misawa. That would mean it is still in the tape depot on base."

Watanabe nodded. "Quite possible. Often happens. But signal strength probably not as good."

"I'll take what I can get."

Watanabe studied the paper, then said, "I see what I can find. Under agreement with Americans, they must provide access to historical tapes of signals. This frequency and time frame precise?"

"Fairly precise. Not far off, surely. The seven-letter code groups are distinctive."

Watanabe continued to stare at the paper and thought about the monstrous story Faisal had told him. "This unbelievable. Unbelievable. Someone in government murder Saudi foreign minister?"

Faisal nodded.

That his friend had been the victim of such an injustice stirred Watanabe's samurai blood. "You—Shaikh-*san*. Dismissed? Unbelievable. You legend at Cheltenham. *Legend*." He shook his head and repeated, "Unbelievable. I help you, Shaikh-*san*. Whatever I can."

"Arigatō, Soichiro-*san."*

Watanabe contemplated the paper again. "I wonder if—"

The door slammed open and a lanky airman almost shouted, "Mr. Watanabe, Colonel Oliver wants you in the ops center *now!*"

Startled, Faisal and his friend sat silent for a moment, then Watanabe rose and said, "You come with me, Shaikh-*san."* In a reflex, Faisal followed him as they walked down the antiseptic hallway to another door with a keypad. The lanky sergeant punched in a number and the door clicked open. Faisal's muscular escort had disappeared, he knew not where.

They entered a large chamber similar in many respects to the Zircon control room in Block M at Cheltenham. Rows of consoles were manned by technicians in Air Force fatigues, and some elevated screens were on the forewall. One screen depicted a map of northeastern Asia with graphic displays of the intercept traffic. Another screen displayed the ebb and flow of data streams, to and from Fort Meade and the Joint Sobe Processing Center. The Sobe operation was a triservice facility on Okinawa, where massive banks of computers handled traffic analysis and cryptologic number-crunching for listening posts all over the Pacific.

The staff of the operations center took the data flow from the squirrel nests scattered throughout the compound, then brought it together to form a coherent SIGINT picture for the operations officer. Faisal and Watanabe entered from a side door, and the lanky sergeant took them to the op officer's station at the rear of the chamber. They approached a man in fatigues whose back was turned to them. He was talking urgently on the phone and flailing his free hand as he spoke. Watanabe leaned over and whispered to Faisal, "Colonel Oliver. Commander here. Americans carr him 'Hard Ass.' "

Faisal nodded as Hard Ass said, "Stay on the goddamned line." Then he turned around. He had the face of an overly ripe persimmon, and his gray crew cut seemed to spark with static electricity. "Watanabe!" he said in a strident voice. "We damn well got us a real furball here! A flight of Russian MiGs just splashed a Jazzdaf F-fifteen inside the ODZ and . . . " He stopped and drilled Faisal with two laser-beam eyes. Then he pointed. "Who the hell is he?"

Watanabe remained unperturbed, standing as if he were waiting for a bus. "He with me," came the soft reply. "GCHQ."

Hard Ass's face turned a bit riper, and he was about to have Faisal bounced out of the place; but then Watanabe interceded by simply saying, "I vouch for him."

Hard Ass was obviously unhappy with the intruder, but it was a testament to Watanabe's stature that the American finally grumbled, "Okay, okay, he can stay. Can't deal with him now anyway. We got one F-fifteen down. His wingman splashed two MiGs, but the rest have scattered. The backup F-fifteens at Chitose have scrambled and the Jazzdaf Hawkeye has been alerted to get airborne ASAP. Headwork says some of the MiGs have dropped down under their shore-based radar. I don't know what the hell they're doing, but they're using live ammunition. You've been monitoring the situation with us, and I wanted you here as a witness for your government . . ."

Just then the side door opened and another full colonel entered, but this one had matinee-idol looks and was wearing a flight suit. He strode up to Hard Ass and thundered, "What the hell is going on, Phil!? We got Russkies shooting the Jazzdaf out of the sky and not a lick of warning! Why didn't we get some kind of tip-off about this?"

Watanabe leaned over to Faisal to whisper again. "Colonel Wade. In charge of American fighter wing here. They carr him Horrywood."

Faisal nodded and noticed that even Hard Ass looked a little intimidated by the flight-suited colonel.

"We don't know the score on this one, Jim," lamented Hard Ass. "But here's the situation. The garrison commander at the Dolinsk-Sokol air base on Sakhalin Island has been screaming at his headquarters in Vladivostok for months. Claims they've been shortstopping food earmarked for his unit and selling it on the black market. Eating it is more likely, but there it is. You were briefed on that."

"Yeah, some time ago."

"Well, about six hours ago a Rivet Joint picks up some tactical radio stuff that sounds like a live-fire infantry exercise. Small-unit tactics. That sort of thing. After that it's lights out at Dolinsk-Sokol. Every circuit dead as a frozen turkey. Zero emissions until a couple of hours ago when we pick up Dolinsk-Sokol tower giving clearance for takeoff. Two things here. The tower controller says 'good luck' to the flight leader, and the squirrel monitoring the freq swears the ground controller was crying."

"Crying?"

"That's a rog. Anyway, Headwork monitors a flight of seven fighters and one heavy out of Sakhalin. They fly east over the Kuriles, then turn south. The heavy is apparently a Mainstay because we pick up in-flight chatter that indicates refueling. They stay just outside the outer defense zone as they fill up. Then the Mainstay heads for home and the MiGs turn due west. They trip the ODZ and the Jazzdaf scrambles two F-fifteens. Next thing we know it's a real shootin' match."

Hollywood looked grim. "But why the commo blackout—"

"*Colonel!*"

Faisal turned and saw a plump female sergeant standing by her console, holding a headphone to one ear.

Startled, Hard Ass said, "Yeah?"

"I've got a Cujo Pup on the wire! You better hear what he's got to say! He's on channel nine!"

Hard Ass grabbed a headset and motioned for Watanabe to pick up a spare set plugged into a console jack. On impulse, Watanabe nodded to Faisal to pick up a neighboring set as he switched the intercom dial to channel nine. The voice of Hard Ass came through clearly.

"This is Colonel Oliver. Who am I talking to?"

"Sergeant Zyrwinski on Cujo Pup Flight, sir."

"Talk to me."

"Well, sir, after we heard the firefight chatter about six hours ago, I began monitoring the Molniya satellite link used by the KGB—er, excuse me, by the Interior Ministry troops—based on Dolinsk-Sokol."

"And?"

"Picked up a voice transmission, sir. Really frantic. Said he was a lieutenant in C Company, Third Battalion. That checks out. They're a resident unit at Dolinsk-Sokol."

"Get on with it."

"Yes, sir. Sorry, sir. This L-T opens a clear voice channel straight to the Interior Ministry in Moscow. He says the Air Force troops and some factions of the Interior Ministry garrison overpowered the guards at the nuclear depot at Dolinsk-Sokol. He said the mutineers were going to fry the Air Force HQ at Vladivostok for stealing their food."

"WHAT!?"

"That's all I got, sir. Like I said, the guy was frantic. He was cut off in midsentence. Sounds to me like there was definitely some kinda mutiny, and maybe some nukes are on their way to Vladivostok—as we speak."

Hollywood ripped the phone off the cradle and mashed one of the buttons. "Get me the OIC of Headwork! *Now!* . . . Major Yishiri? This is Colonel Wade! Your F-fifteen that survived the furball with the Russians! What was his ident on the aircraft?" There was a pause, then Hollywood turned to Hard Ass. "The Jazzdaf pilot said there were six Fulcrums and one Fencer. Sounds like an escort. The Fencer is capable of hauling nukes."

"And that's probably all the serviceable aircraft they had in Dolinsk-Sokol," said Hard Ass. "They must be desperate."

"Colonel!" shouted the plump sergeant. "It's Zyrwinski again!"

Hard Ass yelled, "Talk to me!"

Faisal winced from the volume.

"Zyrwinski here, sir. We just picked up a snap-on transmission from Moscow on a Molniya circuit reserved for Russian Air Force HQ in Vladivostok."

A "snap-on" referred to an encryption device being connected to a communications channel that was previously a clear transmission.

"A snap-on?"

"Roger, sir. My bet is they're sounding an alarm."

"Colonel Oliver," another voice—female this time—broke in on the intercom. "This is Lieutenant Cernack. We just copied a live relay link with a VQ Beggar Flight off the Russian coastal buffer zone near Nakhodka. It's a high-freq radio circuit reserved for air-defense units. They're scrambling everything that flies along the Russian east coast."

Hard Ass pulled off his headset and looked at Hollywood. "It's the real thing. That Fencer's got to be carrying a nuke and he means to use it." Hollywood started screaming into his phone again while Hard Ass turned to his operations officer. "CRITICOM to Meade and copy to CINCPAC in Hawaii. 'Russian-to-Russian nuclear strike possible—no, make that *probable*—in Vladivostok area. Nuclear-armed Russian aircraft violating Japanese airspace en route."

Faisal had never felt his testicles go numb before.

They did so now.

"Scoop" hit the pickle on his control stick and the dummy bombs dropped off the racks of his F-16, sailing down until they impacted on the sands of Ripsaw target range. He flew on through his low-level exit pattern, then pulled straight up and peered out the Perspex canopy, looking for the other F-16s in his flight. Scoop was a flight leader and basically addicted to the rakish single-seat fighter. He was waiting for the night bombing exercise to end so he could radio "Clear," then break away to dance with his fighter in the moonlit clouds. He was still ascending when his headphones crackled with, "Pelican Leader, this is Lightsword."

Scoop toggled his mike switch. "Lightsword, Pelican Lead, over."

"We have a DEFCON one situation, Pelican. This is no drill."

The American pulled his Falcon level and shook his head. "Say again, Lightsword?"

"Listen up! This is *no* drill! We have a Russian bandit inbound. A Fencer with probable nukes. It crossed the ODZ and splashed a Jazzdaf Eagle out of Chitose."

"*What!?*"

"Shut up! There's not much time! Jazzdaf is scrambling every-thing they've got, but the Fencer has dropped under coastal radar. Form up your flight and go to lane defense. I say again, lane defense. Hit your burners and vector three-five-five at angels two one. You'll be covering the entry to Tsugaru Strait. Look for a fast-moving skimmer on the water."

"But Lightsword, we have no weapons—"

"*Just find it!* The Jazzdaf will splash him and we've got ICTs under way. Now hit your burners!"

"Roger, Lightsword. Pelican Flight, form up on Lead. We're goin' huntin'. This is no shit."

"Bronco" pulled his F-16 into a hardened aircraft hangar at Misawa Air Base and killed the engine in preparation for an integrated combat turn, or ICT, which was, in essence, a pit stop to arm the Falcon with live ammunition. Once the fighter's engine spooled down, the ground crew would swarm over it like a hive of angry bees to make it combat ready.

Bronco's American Falcon had been at the end of the runway about to start its takeoff roll for a night exercise over Ripsaw range. Then the "General Recall" order came down from Lightsword, telling him to return to the hangar for an ICT, DEFCON one. No drill. No shit.

The "jammer" driver wheeled the hydraulic lift around like a ballet master, then engaged the elevator arm to raise the AM-RAAM missile up to wing level. The weapons crew cradled the missile on their shoulders as they guided it off the jammer and onto the wing rail. Once it was in place, the crew chief twisted a socket wrench to lock down the dual anchor bolts and engage the umbilical to the plane's electronics. Then the American crew scurried out of the way and Bronco cranked the engine. They'd only had time to load a single missile.

Scoop was at twenty-one thousand feet, the APG-66 radar in the Falcon's nose trained in a downlook mode toward the entrance of Tsugaru Strait. The strait separated the islands of Honshu and Hokkaido and connected the Pacific Ocean to the Sea of Japan. Scoop's flight of four F-16s were spread out on a line abreast, ten miles apart. Their radars were aimed down and overlapped like four flashlights merging into one wide beam. This was the "lane defense" maneuver that massed the radar capabilities of the F-16s and turned them into a jerry-rigged AWACs platform.

Scoop was oblivious to the full moon as he concentrated on his cockpit display. He'd picked up small boats on the surface, but that was all.

"Pelican Lead, this is Three."

"Go, Three."

"I got something. Coming across my beam on the deck. This sucker is moving, I'd say, four hundred knots."

"Lead, this is two. I've got him now. He's on a beeline for the mouth of the bay. Christ, that baby is *low*."

A blip popped up on Scoop's display and he toggled his mike switch. "Lightsword, Pelican Lead."

"Go, Pelican."

"Got a fast mover on the deck, heading for the entry point of the Strait."

"Roger, Pelican! Stay with him. We've got you tagged and will vector an intercept. Whatever you do, don't lose him!"

"Roger, Lightsword. Pelican Flight, this is Lead. Alaman left on my mark, boys. Three, two, one, mark!" And like a gate swinging around on a hinge, the line of Falcons executed a turning maneuver that kept them abreast—and kept the Fencer in the spotlight.

Faisal watched Hollywood as he put the phone down and turned to Hard Ass. "Two more MiGs have been splashed. One by a Jazzdaf Eagle and one by a Patriot shore battery."

"That means three are still at large, including the Fencer."

Hollywood put the phone back to his ear. "What's that?. . . Yeah. . . . Yeah. . . . *Awright!* Stay with him! Lose him and it's your ass! How many birds have been turned on ICT? . . . Good. Vector them out north in a spoke pattern and tag Bronco to intercept the one we're tracking." He turned to Hard Ass. "We're tracking a bogey flying low and fast through the Strait. Looks like it might be the Fencer. I've got a sixteen with an AMRAAM on his way to intercept. The Jazzdaf is still looking for the others, but they're concentrating east of the Strait."

Hard Ass nodded, then scratched his head. "Why are they doing this? If they're trying to hit Vladivostok, why didn't they take a direct shot over the Sea of Japan?"

"This way they avoid the shore radars on the Siberian east coast. By taking this route they can even loop under and come in from the southwest. The Russians will be searching north and east. It's like when the Israelis blindsided the Egyptians in the Six Day War."

"Colonel!" It was the plump female sergeant again.

"What?"

"One of the guys on the Assassins Flight has trapped something real time. You better listen to this on channel seven."

Watanabe turned the knob to the seventh channel and Faisal listened.

"Colonel, this is Captain Lydell on Assassins Flight. One of my people is picking up an *en clair* high-freq transmission out of the Russian Far East Military District HQ in Khabarovsk. They're repeating the transmission as we speak. The transcription reads"—paper shuffling—" 'Attention Japanese and American military commanders, northern Japan. This is Major General Valery Patkin, senior air-defense commander in Vladivostok. Renegade force, nuclear capable, has escaped Sakhalin Island. May be in your vicinity. Request assistance to locate and shoot down criminal aircraft. Know you are monitoring this channel.' . . . Then it repeats, sir."

Hard Ass looked at Hollywood and said, "You better nail this son of a bitch."

Hollywood growled into his phone, then said, "I've got a sixteen on the way."

Col. Piotr Letsov saw the giant power lines approaching on his infrared screen at 450 knots. The hawserlike cables spanned the Tsugaru Strait from Honshu to Hokkaido, carrying electricity north to Sapporo and beyond. His swingwing Su-24 Sukhoi "Fencer" fighter-bomber was skimming so low he thought about flying under the lines. But years of training exerted their influence and he eased back slightly on the control stick. The sleek aircraft responded and rose, then Letsov rolled inverted to watch the lighted tower whip by his canopy. Then he pulled the Fencer back down on the deck to hide under the sweep of Japanese coastal radar.

Letsov's motions were numb, almost robotic, and his flight suit hung on his emaciated frame like a deflated spinnaker. His once-strapping body had withered away over the last months due to lack of food. He'd watched his once-cocky unit decline from pride to anger, then from anger to despair. He scanned the cockpit and didn't know whether to laugh or cry at the tragic irony. How could the Motherland build such a sleek engine of war but have no food for her pilots! It was as monstrous as it was pathetic. Letsov had not eaten for four days and was running on nothing but adrenaline. Sakhalin Island was starving, but Vladivostok did nothing! Moscow did nothing! His men had taken to scavenging from the local fishermen at gunpoint, and hunting deer in the forests.

There was food, he knew, earmarked for his unit. It was being diverted in Vladivostok and sold on the black market by those pigs in their gold braid. Letsov knew not what his final mission would bring. Perhaps the opening salvo in some kind of civil war? He couldn't say and no longer cared. He simply wanted to kill the pigs. Letsov had no family, save his men; and he couldn't sit idly by and watch them starve.

Hunger and nuclear weapons made a dangerous marriage.

Now past the strait, he jettisoned his fuel drop tanks, then hit the afterburners on the Fencer to climb to cruise altitude. He was clear of the Japanese shore batteries.

Bronco leveled off at twenty-nine thousand feet and came out of afterburner as his earphones crackled with, "Bronco, this is Lightsword."

"Go, Lightsword."

"Handing you off to Pelican Flight for target acquisition. You are cleared to arm and fire. Down the bandit."

"Roger. Pelican, this is Bronco."

"Roger, Bronc, this is Scoop. Where you at?"

"Feet wet off Kodomari. Angels two-niner, on vector three-one-one. You got a bandit?"

"Roger. He's just south of Ko-jima Island, climbing through angels ten and picking up speed fast, headed due west. You better put the spurs to it if you're gonna catch him."

Bronco switched on his nose radar and began sweeping the inky sky. He received no return and was about to call Scoop again when a small blip appeared, then disappeared, in the upper-left-hand corner of the screen. He pointed the nose of the fighter toward the fleeting echo and cut in the Falcon's afterburner again, then he toggled his mike switch. "Lightsword, this is Bronco."

"Go, Bronco."

"I got a return off Ko-jima, but this bandit is hauling ass. Must be a Fencer. I'm in burner trying to close. Fuel dropping rapidly. Have we got a tanker somewhere?"

"One is on the way up from Kadena, but it's thirty minutes out."

"Aw, shit." Bronco focused on the radar blip as it faded in and out, then he looked at the fuel gauge, which was dropping precipitously. "Lightsword, I can't close for a tailshot and have enough fuel to make it back. The bandit has too much of a lead."

"Wait one, Bronco."

Bronco waited for what seemed an interminable time as his fuel supply continued to hemorrhage.

"Listen up, Bronco. Maintain afterburner and close for your shot. This Fencer is carrying a nuke."

"A *nuke?*"

"That's a roger. And it looks like he means to use it. You are authorized to eject if you have to."

Bronco swallowed. Punching out at night over water wasn't what he'd enlisted for. "You're sure about this?"

"Straight from Hollywood, Bronco."

He swallowed again. "Okay. Just get a fix on me."

"Roger, Bronco. The Jazzdaf Hawkeye is up now and we're getting the feed. We've got you pegged, and the search-and-rescue boys are on the way."

Under his mask Bronco grimaced, then said, "Roger, Lightsword. Bronco will comply."

■ ■ ■

As Bronco's Falcon raced through the night sky in pursuit, a Black-hawk helicopter at Misawa spooled up to full power as two para-rescue airmen scrambled on board. Once the door slid shut, the pilot flipped down his night-vision goggles and pulled up on the cyclic for the long ride over the Sea of Japan. As it became airborne, the Black-hawk of the 39th Air Rescue Squadron looked like something akin to flying narwhal, for its air-refueling boom resembled a tusk sticking out of its jaw. The pilot did not relish the idea of a dicey nighttime midair refueling operation over water, but there it was.

Bronco was cursing a red, white, and blue streak as his fuel drained down to vapors and the Fencer remained at the fringe of his radar envelope. The bandit was about forty miles out, and obviously in afterburner, too. The American hoped the Russian would power down to cruise speed in time for the F-16 to close within range. But that prospect was looking remote. He was fingering the zipper of his survival suit and wondering about the water temperature when the blip started falling back. Relief washed over Bronco, but only for a moment as he eyeballed the fuel gauge. It was gonna be close.

The advanced medium-range air-to-air missile, or AMRAAM, on Bronco's wing had a twenty-mile range, but on a high-speed tailshot that range was cut by half. He called up the AMRAAM on the multifunction display, then flipped the DOG FIGHT switch on his throttle to the long-range mode. He slaved the AMRAAM's electronics to the F-16's radar and overlayed the cursor on the Fencer's blip. Then he hit the ARM switch and got the LOCK ON prompt from the multifunction display, just as the Falcon shimmied and the engine flamed out from fuel starvation. Bronco needlessly pulled his throttle back as he watched his airspeed bleed off. When it fell below supersonic, he hit his pickle button and the AMRAAM roared off the wing rail.

"Mayday! Mayday! Bronco is going down!" As his magnificent machine began its downward arc toward the black waters of the Sea of Japan, Bronco saw the pinpoint of light that was the AMRAAM's tail plume race into the night sky.

. . .

Hollywood pressed the phone to his ear, then turned to Hard Ass. "My pilot took the shot just before he ran out of fuel. The missile's away and he's going down."

Hard Ass scratched his bristly crew cut. "But what about—?"

Hollywood held up a hand to cut him off. He listened a bit more, then his body sagged. "Bronco splashed the Fencer. The AM-RAAM got him."

"You sure?" pressed Hard Ass.

"Jazzdaf Hawkeye had the shot on-screen. Says it was a definite kill. They got it on tape."

Now Hard Ass sagged as he turned to Watanabe. "You were a witness, Watanabe. Remember."

Watanabe gave him a solicitous bow, then said, "Excuse, please." He took Faisal by the arm and led him out of the operations center and back to the small conference room. With a shaking hand he offered a cigarette to Faisal, who joyfully jumped off the wagon and grabbed it. After three attempts, Watanabe was able to strike a match and offer the light to Faisal. But both men were shaking so hard that the cigarette and the match looked like two boxers sparring. Finally, Faisal clutched Watanabe's hand between his own and brought the flame to the tip. After ignition, he inhaled deeply several times. Watanabe lit up and followed suit. After smoke filled the chamber, the oriental gentleman sat down and looked up at Faisal. "Forgive me, Shaikh-*san*, but tell me again. What was it you needed? It escapes me at the moment."

Two days later, Faisal boarded the train for the return journey to Tokyo. In his grip was a spool of magnetic tape.

As he waited for the train's departure, he scanned the *kanji* newspaper for any word on a nuclear-armed Russian aircraft shot down over the Sea of Japan. There was none. Just a brief news story lamenting the loss of a Japanese F-15 fighter pilot who died when his plane went down on a routine night-training exercise.

CHAPTER ✠ TWENTY

The swirling column of the iron-red dust devil danced along the black asphalt highway as if it were following the stripe in the road. Faisal thought the taxi driver might slow down or give way to the whirlwind, but the cabby seemed indifferent as his ancient vehicle plunged into the vortex. Faisal tried to roll up the passenger window, only to have the handle come off in his hand. Covering his face for protection, the backs of his hands were sandblasted with red grit. Once they'd passed through the whirlwind, the cabby pulled out his toothpick and murmured, "Get a lot of those round here."

Faisal brushed the dust off his shoulders and replied, "I'm sure," as he glanced at the odometer of the clatter-trap Dodge. The numbers had stopped turning at 187,442 miles, and he guessed the only thing that worked on the dashboard was the fare meter.

The driver was as grizzled as a strip of tanned crocodile hide. His round, bald head was brown from the unrelenting sun, and Faisal suspected he was permanently bolted to the front seat.

Faisal surveyed the landscape through the half-open window. He'd never been to Mars before, but decided it must be quite like this. The low, rolling, unbroken sweep of red sand and rock gave the place an aura of desolation unlike anything Faisal had experienced.

"You be one of those spookers?" asked the cabby over the wind.

"Pardon?"

"I said, you be one those spookers? I mean, you got to be now, don't you? Nobody else heads out this way—'cept the water authority to check on the wells. And if you don't mind my sayin' so, you don't look like no water authority type."

"You must be a detective."

"So you be one of those spookers?"

"Retired spooker, actually."

"Uh-huh. Well, I guess what you want is just up ahead there."

Faisal looked through the smudged windshield and saw the low silhouette of the Macdonnell Ranges mountains. In the foreground was a tall Hurricane fence with the telltale strands of barbed wire on top.

"Pull up outside the guard hut and wait for me."

"Right, mate." And the cabby obeyed.

Faisal exited the cab and walked toward the small, stucco structure that was the only sign of habitation in a 360-degree sweep. Faisal's eyes peered down the road, looking for some sign of what was beyond; but it was hidden away in the foothills, in a valley called Pine Gap.

He glanced at the sign on the fence that read JOINT DEFENSE SPACE RESEARCH FACILITY—NO ADMITTANCE. A guard stuck his head out of the hut and asked, in a distinctly American accent, "Can I help you?"

Faisal withdrew an envelope from his hip pocket and handed it over, saying, "Would you please see to it that Mr. Mattea receives this as soon as possible?"

Taking the envelope, the guard asked, "And whom shall I say it's from?"

Since there might be some people at Pine Gap who might recognize his name, Faisal replied, "Tell him it's from Mr. Ivy. He'll understand."

"I'll see to it, sir."

"Thank you." Faisal climbed into the cab and said, "Back to town."

"To the Alice it is."

And the clatter-trap Dodge squeaked away.

■ ■ ■

The world changed on December 7, 1941; but few things changed as profoundly as the island nation of Australia. A vast influx of American and British troops poured into the southern continent, and within that teeming wartime cauldron a multinational SIGINT community was born.

After the war, this Anglo-American-Australian SIGINT community formalized their relationship in a secret 1947 treaty called the UK-USA Agreement. This document called for the U.S., Great Britain, Australia, Canada, and New Zealand to cooperate and share in the collection and dissemination of certain flavors of signals intelligence. They would also operate certain installations on Australian soil, and the crown jewel of these installations was Pine Gap.

Seven miles beyond the guard shack where Faisal exited the cab was a small colony that looked like a space outpost on Martian soil. Nestled in the foothills of the Macdonnell Ranges, Pine Gap (code-named Merino) consisted of eighteen concrete buildings and eight geodesic radomes. Here a community of six hundred Anglo-American-Australian technicians and eavesdroppers worked together, pointing their electronic ears into the air and toward outer space.

Hovering 22,300 miles above Borneo was a satellite that looked like a huge unfolded umbrella. This was the MAGNUM SIGINT satellite, and it was essentially a spaceborne electronic vacuum cleaner, sucking up signals over the Asian land mass. With its 140-foot antenna that had unfolded when it reached orbit, the MAGNUM could pull in microwave phone calls, uplinks to Russian commo satellites in neighboring orbits, radio Teletype, radio car phones, and even walkie-talkie chatter by Russian and Chinese Army infantrymen. MAGNUM was not the Mercedes of the SIGINT world. It was the Rolls-Royce. A vehicle that could almost do it all. Built at a cost of $300 million, its frequency scanner possessed a massive capacity that could canvass the entire radio spectrum. The first MAGNUM lifted off on the space shuttle *Discovery* on January 25, 1985, and its harvest of signals was downloaded to a large dish antenna at Pine Gap. The antenna is covered by a white geodesic radome to protect it from the blowing dust, and once the

MAGNUM signals are captured, they are fed into a massive bank of one-inch reel-to-reel tape recorders. So sensitive is the MAGNUM harvest that the intercepts are seldom relayed in real time via satellite to Fort Meade. Instead, sealed containers of tapes are airlifted out of Alice Springs twice a week and physically transported to Fort Meade, where they are picked apart and examined by a small army of analysts.

Duplicate tapes are, of course, retained in a depot at Pine Gap should they be needed.

Faisal sat in the rickety booth of the Billabong Saloon, nursing his third Coca-Cola. The bartender eyed him warily, not trusting anyone who didn't order beer. The Billabong looked like a cross between a dusty East End pub and the saloon from a B-grade western. A single fan lazily stirred the air as a dingo slept in the corner. Cigarette butts dotted the wooden floor. There was a spindly piano but no piano player, and even a set of Wild West swinging doors hung in the doorframe.

For two hours Faisal had been the only patron. He sat quietly, sipping his Coke and reading the local *Centralian Advocate* newspaper. But as the clock moved toward late afternoon, the place began to fill up with an influx of regulars, ready to toss down a brew to celebrate the end of the day. Faisal was reading the paper for the fourth time when all of a sudden the light in the saloon dimmed. He instinctively knew his appointment had arrived.

The imposing figure stood in the doorway, holding the swinging doors open as he surveyed the saloon like a western marshal. So massive was he that his form blocked most of the afternoon sun. To Faisal, the backlit silhouette was unmistakable—with its Stetson hat, bull-like shoulders, jeans, and Tony Llama boots. All that was missing were the spurs.

The intruder approached the booth and Faisal rose to greet him, bracing himself for what was to come. A hand with the size and mass of a rump roast made a wide sweeping arc until it impacted between Faisal's shoulder blades with a *thwack!*

"Faisal!" boomed the voice. "Hot damn! It's good to see you, boy!"

Faisal staggered under the blow, certain that three of his verte-brae had been crushed. With the trace of air that remained in his lungs, he managed to whisper, "Hullo, Tex." An attempt to inhale was curtailed by a suffocating bear hug, then Faisal was held up at arm's length, his feet dangling six inches above the ground.

"I can't believe it!" Tex continued to boom. "Musta been six years. And here you drop in out of nowhere!"

"Tex, put me down, please."

"Oh, sorry, little buddy. Got carried away. Just ain't seen you in so long."

Faisal's feet mercifully touched down, and he motioned Tex into the booth. His guest was barely able to squeeze in, but made it. The barkeep wandered over and asked, "What'll it be, mate?"

Tex ordered, "Sarsaparilla." The barkeep grunted and walked away. Apparently no one at this booth was to be trusted.

"Still on the wagon, are we?" asked Faisal.

Tex took off his Stetson and laid it on the seat. "For eight years, three months, two weeks, and four days—but who's counting?"

"Glad to hear it. By the way, Watanabe sends his regards."

"Watanabe!? You been to see him, too? What you got goin' here? Some kinda Ivy Bells reunion?"

Faisal remained silent as the barkeep dropped off the sarsapa-rilla. Tex drank greedily, and after he set the glass down, Faisal examined him carefully.

Mason "Tex" Mattea (no relation to Kathy) had played defensive tackle for Texas A&M. He was chosen in the first round of the pro football draft by the Houston Oilers, but a separated shoulder in training camp derailed a promising career on the gridiron. How-ever, unlike many of his peers in the locker room, Tex had a brain that went beyond the goal posts. Indeed, he was a kind of a cow-boy intellectual. With his broken shoulder he returned to A&M and tackled a PhD program in mathematics. He was then recruited by the NSA, where he flexed his natural people skills and technical abilities. Few in the ranks of NSA possessed that rare hybrid of human and technical talents that could manage an engineering project and make it hum like a dynamo. Tex was just such a rarity and had been appointed deputy director of the Pine Gap station.

Tex had a massive head that sat on top of an oxlike neck, yet his complexion was fair and complemented by clear blue eyes that always seemed curious. He wore an open-collared western shirt, jeans, and a cowboy buckle with a turquoise plug in the center. Incessantly, he twisted his A&M class ring. He was in totality a Texan, and it wasn't an act.

"I suppose you're running Merino now?"

Tex shrugged. "Never figured out why, but a CIA guy is always the chief on paper. Some guy named Glomski. Politics, I guess. He's off in Melbourne or Canberra most of the time. I'm deputy director, but run the place in a hands-on sense. Got three months to go, then I'm outta here."

"Where to?"

"Who cares? As long as it ain't here. This place makes El Paso look like Maui."

Faisal smiled. "I'm sure."

Tex took another gulp, then wiped his mouth. "So you saw Watanabe, huh? Something tells me this ain't no reunion on our gig back in Hong Kong."

"You always were a quick study, Tex. Did you know I was cashiered out of GCHQ? The better part of a year ago?"

Tex was genuinely stunned. "What!? You?"

Faisal nodded.

"What the hell happened?"

Faisal sighed and said, "Get comfortable, my friend. I have much to tell you."

The sun was down and the desert cloaked in its evening chill, but Tex Mattea remained riveted to his seat as Faisal recounted his quest to crack the Black Cipher. Tex was alternately stunned, aghast, transfixed, angry, and in the end, perhaps a little frightened. When Faisal had finished, Tex stared at his empty sarsaparilla glass. Finally, he said, "So why are you here?"

"In order to attack the Black Cipher I must re-create, from scratch, my cryptanalysis algorithm. To do that I require additional message traffic to work with. Watanabe provided me with the tape containing the message of the American barroom brawl in Petropavlovsk. Another Black Cipher message dealt with an uprising in Samarkand. The Russian Army commander telexed Moscow on a Raduga satellite circuit, using a Black Cipher encryption. The Raduga circuit was trapped by MAGNUM, and you would have it in your tape archives at Pine Gap."

Tex continued staring at his empty glass. "And you want me to get it for you."

"I do."

Tex didn't answer for a while as he thought through all that Faisal had told him. At last, he said, "You and I go way back, little buddy. Way back. But this is a long limb you're asking me to climb out on."

"I realize that."

"If this thing cracks back on you, the tape would lead straight back to me."

"Yes, it would."

"Watanabe has more clout and less exposure than I do. He could survive. But I'd be on the street. Maybe even prosecuted."

"Highly possible."

"I got nineteen years in. Marge and I were thinking about early retirement."

"That would all be lost if I fail."

Tex locked his blue eyes on Faisal. "Aw, hell, I hate it when I sound like a bureaucrat. It's fourth and ten, and Faisal Shaikh wants to throw the long bomb. How can I say no? We raised a submarine together. Been shot at together. If that don't count for somethin' in this world, then why are we here? Right?"

"Right."

Tex ran a hand through his crew cut, then said, "To do a search, it would help to have some specs on the intercept you want."

Faisal pulled out a folded piece of paper from his shirt pocket and handed it over. "These are the TEXTA particulars, as close as I can recall them. Just look for seven-letter code groups. They're unmistakable."

Tex took the paper and scanned it, then put it in his pocket and buttoned it up. He gave his friend a wry smile and asked, "Anything else I can do?"

"Forget that I was here."

"Forget you were where?"

"Exactly."

Tex put on his Stetson and said, "Faisal, you be one loco sumbitch."

Two days later, Faisal's plane was wheels up from the Alice Springs airport, the second tape tucked away in his grip.

CHAPTER ✛ TWENTY·ONE

Water.

In every direction, as far as the eye could see, there was nothing but the unending, unyielding vista of Neptune's domain. It stretched out before him like a deep blue carpet, from horizon to horizon. Impenetrable. Overwhelming. So overpowering was this watery vision that the iron-red dirt of Alice Springs began to look attractive.

The engine coughed and Faisal immediately reached back for his emergency flotation suit.

A hand patted his shoulder. "No worry, *senhor*. Just changing tanks. Happen sometimes."

Faisal kept a death grip on the flotation suit. "You're certain?"

More comforting pats. "Sure, sure, *senhor*. I tol' you. No *problema*. Jorge get you there good shape."

Faisal sighed, and as he shoved the rubbery suit into the rear compartment, he became bound and determined to bring his quest for the Black Cipher to an abrupt halt. *If* he ever got his feet back on dry land. But as the single-engined plane sputtered over the vast expanse of the South Atlantic, that possibility seemed painfully remote.

Faisal had flown (commercial) from Sydney to Johannesburg, and from Johannesburg to Rio de Janeiro. He'd taken a few days to decompress from the travel, and to carefully chart the course he intended to follow. In dealing with Watanabe and Tex, Faisal could rely on old and trusted friendships. Now he was headed for no-man's-land, where anything could happen.

While in Rio he'd taken a taxi to the crest of Corcovado, where the majestic figure of Christ overlooked the magnificent city. Or what had been a magnificent city. Crime was everywhere now. Accustomed to long walks, Faisal stayed close to the Copacabana Hotel. He only ventured out to find a stationery print shop and to visit the Galeão *aeropôrto*.

Fortunately, his spoken Portuguese was better than his *Nihon-go*, so his discreet questions at the aerodrome bore some fruit. He went from charter service to charter service, making oblique inquiries about who could handle an "unconventional transport job."

"What sort of job?"

"I need someone who can fly thirty-five hundred miles over water—nonstop."

His audience invariably rolled their eyes, convinced he was a Mideast drug runner, and said, "Go see Crazy Jorge."

Faisal found Crazy Jorge. He operated from a rusty, ramshackle hangar beside an overgrown, potholed airstrip west of the city. Jorge was a short, wiry man with a wild, perennial grin and curly, black hair. He wore grease on his face like war paint, and the faded sign over the hangar said ANJO ASA—Angel Wings. He greeted Faisal enthusiastically, speaking in rapid-fire Portuguese that was indecipherable. But Faisal caught the drift that Crazy Jorge could do anything with an airplane. No runway was too short. No payload too heavy. No cargo too hot for Jorge to handle. It was only a question of cruzeiros. Faisal probed with a few questions, and each one was answered with a bobbing head, a grin, and a response of, "No *problema*." Faisal became utterly convinced that Jorge was, indeed, crazy as a March hare; and he was about to leave when he popped the final question: What about a nonstop, unrefueled, thirty-five-hundred-mile flight? Over water?

Jorge jumped up with glee and cried, "My specialty!" He led Faisal out of the dusty office and into the hangar proper. The change was astonishing. The concrete floor was spotless, and parked upon it was a single-engine Beechcraft Sierra that gleamed under the klieg lights. Like a child showing off a new train set, Jorge took Faisal by the arm and led him around the aircraft. Jorge jabbered away, explaining how he'd turned the baggage compartment into an auxiliary fuel tank. The rear seats had been ripped out, and the floorboards cut out and replaced with panels. The panels could be opened and closed by a servomotor, like a set of bomb-bay doors. There was no question in Faisal's mind what kind of payloads were carried inside the plane. Jorge proudly showed off the specially fabricated wing tanks, which looked like bombs slung underneath. "For extra range," he explained. Then he popped off the engine cowling to show Faisal the power plant. "My pride and joy," he said robustly. "I make modification. Two modes. Turbocharged for takeoff. Need more power because extra fuel weigh more. *Compreender?*"

"*Compreendida,*" replied Faisal. Well, sort of.

"Once we make altitude, switch to economy cruise. Burn off fuel, better distance as we go along. *Compreender?*"

"*Compreendida.*" Faisal didn't know squash about aeronautics, but he could see the plane's engine shone like a sterling silver pin. Whatever personality disorders Jorge might suffer, Faisal instinctively knew he'd found his pilot.

They returned to the dirty office, where Faisal explained in precise detail what he wanted to do. Jorge's grin never wavered. He simply unrolled a map of the South Atlantic on a drafting table. With a pair of dividers he ticked off the distance over water, then punched some numbers into a handheld navigational computer. After a few seconds the readout flashed up, and Jorge exclaimed, "No *problema!*"

Faisal dearly hoped it was "No *problema.*" He sighed and asked, "How much?"

Jorge thought for a few moments, then said, "Two hundred and fifty million cruzeiros," fully expecting to haggle.

"Done," replied Faisal. "I have to make arrangements for the transfer of the money. I suspect you shall want cash?"

"*Sim.*"

"Very well. Two hundred fifty million cruzeiros. That's about eight thousand pounds. Let's plan on departure in three days' time."

"*Excelentíssimo!*"

Faisal was preparing to depart when he noticed a framed photograph hanging on the wall. Faisal did not play golf, but to him the grainy photograph resembled an aerial shot of a golfing fairway—one with a dogleg in the middle. He pointed and asked, "What's that?"

The amperage of Jorge's grin increased about 200 percent. "*Sim!* That my best takeoff and landing ever! Absolute. That why I take peecture."

It finally dawned on Faisal. "You mean, that was some sort of runway?"

"*Sim.*"

"Uh, where was that, exactly?"

"Colombia."

Faisal continued to stare at the photograph. "But, Jorge, I mean, this runway is *bent* in the middle."

The pilot's head bobbed vigorously. "*Sim!* My best ever! Absolute!"

Faisal looked at the ceiling, now utterly convinced that Jorge had gone round the bend without a return ticket.

They had flown from Rio to the city of Salvador on the east coast of Brazil, and from Salvador to their jump-off point at Recife. After spending a short night at a rather spartan hotel, they'd gone wheels up several hours before dawn, headed east over the South Atlantic. Faisal's fears about Jorge were not allayed when they reached cruising altitude. The Brazilian put the airplane on autopilot and promptly took a nap.

Now they were eight hours out from Recife, and Faisal began squirming in his seat, wanting to stretch his legs. The unending expanse of the South Atlantic weighed heavily upon him now, and his apprehension grew with each spin of the propeller. But why should he worry? He was only crossing the deep blue sea in a single-engine airplane the size of a gnat, with a certifiable wacko at the controls. Piece of cake.

Jorge reached behind the seat and pulled out a jar half-filled with a clear, yellowy fluid. "You need take peece?"

Faisal raised his hand. "No, no thank you. I will wait until we land."

Jorge shoved the jar in back and said, "No *problema*. Time to start descent anyway." He pointed. "See?"

Faisal squinted as he looked through the windshield. Even his remarkable eyesight was taxed, but yes, there was a tiny bump on the horizon.

Jorge unfolded a chart and studied it for a few moments, then reset the frequency on his radio. He brought the plane out of autopilot and took the controls as he keyed the microphone. "Ah-seen-si-ohn tower, Ah-seen-si-ohn tower, this is Sierra Tango one seven Foxtrot, do you read, over? . . . Ah-seen-si-ohn tower, this is Sierra Tango one seven Foxtrot, do you read, over?"

Faisal heard the radio crackle as a staticy voice replied, "Sierra Tango one seven Foxtrot, this is Ascension tower. Go ahead."

"Roger, Ah-seen-si-ohn. This one seven Foxtrot. I am private aircraft en route from Recife to Kinshasa. My engine overheating. Request permission to land and make repairs."

Pause.

"We are not a civil airfield, one seven Foxtrot. Are you certain you can't make it through?"

"Negative, Ah-seen-si-ohn. My temperature gauge rising. Must put down immediate. I declare emergency. One seven Foxtrot approximately twenty miles out, due west at thirteen thousand."

"Very well, one seven Foxtrot. If you must. Approach from the southeast. Winds are out of the northwest at ten knots. Do you require a fire team?"

"Negative, Ah-seen-si-ohn, but must get down. Quickly."

"Roger. We'll be waiting."

As the Sierra made a slow descent, the silhouette of Ascension Island came into better focus.

Discovered by Portuguese navigator João da Nova on Ascension Day in 1501, Ascension Island is the tip of an extinct seafloor volcano sticking out of the South Atlantic. Since 1922 it has been administratively governed by the British colony of St. Helena Island (where Napoleon spent his final days). With a rocky land mass nine miles long and six miles wide, Ascension registered zero on the aesthetic meter. But its geographic location made it an attractive petrol station. During World War II, American engineers built an airfield and used it as a refueling stop for aircraft en route to the Mediterranean theater.

Ascension received a spot of notoriety during the Falkland Islands War when it became a staging area for Operation Corporate. Vulcan bombers fired the opening salvos when they sortied 4,500 miles from Ascension to drop their payloads on Argentine positions.

After the Falklands War, however, Ascension quickly faded from the public's consciousness. Much to GCHQ's relief. Because the spotlight of publicity might have unveiled more about Ascension's past and present than the powers at Cheltenham would have liked.

Jorge brought the Beechcraft out of a long, sweeping bank, then trimmed it up for final approach. To Faisal, the island looked like a spit of moonscape sticking out of the water.

"Hokay!" gushed Jorge. "Here we go, *senhor*."

"You sure this is going to work?"

"No *problema!* You say you want it look good."

"Yes. I want it to look good."

"Hokay! Here we go." From a tiny hole drilled in the instrument panel, Jorge grabbed a thin cable and yanked hard. The cable was attached to a plug in a hot-water bottle that was mounted under the engine cowling. When Jorge yanked the cable, the top popped off and two liters of water spilled out on the hot engine. As the Beechcraft touched down, a cloud of white steam billowed out from under the cowling. To an observer on the runway, it was obvious the bloke made it down just in the nick of time.

"Good, no?"

"Good, yes," replied Faisal, as Jorge taxied over to the small terminal building. Playing it to the hilt, Jorge pumped the throttle as they came to a stop, making the Beechcraft go chug-chug-chug before he killed the engine. Faisal unlatched the door and struggled to pull his semiconscious arse out of the cockpit. He staggered down the wing and gratefully stepped down on terra firma. Jorge followed, shouting a stream of off-color Portuguese as he popped open the engine cowling. A white cloud went up like an Apache's smoke signal, and another stream of amplified Portuguese was heard. The man should have been an actor, thought Faisal as he stretched his legs and got blood going to his toes.

From the terminal building, a uniformed man emerged and sauntered over to them. He had an ethereal look in his eyes, as if he'd spent a chunk of time in the Twilight Zone. He walked up to Faisal and said in a bored American voice, "Dexter. Airfield security. What's your problem?" Mr. Dexter was obviously "rock happy," a malady suffered by many island dwellers after too much time on Ascension. They didn't handle human contact very well. As Faisal fished in the breast pocket of his safari suit for his passport, he said, "Engine trouble of some kind. Damned lucky this rock appeared out of nowhere, otherwise we'd be in the drink." Faisal handed over his passport. "Where the hell is this place, anyway?"

The security man showed a flicker of interest as he examined the British passport. "You're on Ascension Island. This is a joint British-American government facility not usually open to civilians. But since you've got an emergency . . . "

"Ascension Island? Never heard of it. Quite nice of you to give us a hand."

Dexter shrugged and pointed to Jorge, who was still jabbering. "How bad is your engine problem?"

"Can't say, really. Not a mechanic myself. I'll ask. . . . Excuse me, Mr. Velasquez? What seems to be the problem?"

Jorge shifted into stilted English. "Gasket broken. I can feex. I have spare. Tools, too."

"How long will it take?"

Jorge threw up his hands—as called for in the script—and said, "Two . . . three days, maybe."

"Hmm," mumbled Faisal. "Sorry to be such an imposition, but

it looks like we're marooned. Is there some type of accommodation on the island?"

Dexter gave him a bored shrug. "There's the visitors' quarters in the barracks on base. If they got room."

"That will be fine."

Dexter shook off his rock-happy persona for a moment and asked, "What were you doin' over the Atlantic in a little puddle jumper like this?"

Faisal chuckled and replied in a voice that was almost apologetic, "I guess you could say I'm a bit of a sportsman. I was on a fishing trip up the Amazon when I received a cable from a friend of mine. Said to join him in Nairobi for a safari. Ran into this chap here who said he could fly me direct. Sounded like an adventure. We were headed for Kinshasa when the engine went south. Like I said, we were lucky to have stumbled onto you."

This seemed to satisfy Dexter. "Some adventure. Come on, then. Sun's going down. I'll give you a lift in the jeep. Your pilot can start repairs tomorrow."

"That's very good of you."

There was a vacancy at the government-issued billet on the American base, but only one room was available. The barracks manager set up a cot so Faisal could share the room with Jorge. (The things one did for queen and country.)

The barracks manager said to Faisal as he was getting settled, "Since you're British, I figured you might like to stay on their RAF base. I checked with the RAF people about putting you up over there, but they were all full."

"A pity," lamented Faisal. "Very kind of you to put us up."

"That's all right. I don't mind as long as we got room. Don't get many drop-ins here."

"I shouldn't imagine. By the way, what do you Americans do here? I was told the island is British."

"Yeah, it is. We built an airstrip during the war. Now we operate a tracking station for space shots out of Canaveral. Also, we run the airfield on a ninety-nine-year lease from you Brits."

"I never knew that."

The manager went on to explain where the mess hall was located, then added, "If you boys want a drink, you can hitch a ride or walk down to Georgetown, that's our little settlement here. Drinks at the Exile Club. No barkeep. It's on an honor system. There's a snooker table there if you play."

"Afraid I don't."

The manager seemed disappointed. "Well, if you get bored, we got a movie every night at the amphitheater on post. Free admission. Everybody welcome."

Faisal's ears pricked up at that. "Do your British colleagues attend the movie?"

"Oh, sure. Most every night. Best show in town. Only show in town, as a matter of fact."

"Sounds intriguing. What's the film tonight?"

"I think it's *Robin Hood.*"

"Excellent. I wouldn't miss it."

As the Red Menace spread over the globe, and the unseen SIGINT war between East and West became colossal in scale, the charms of Ascension Island were not lost on Cheltenham and Fort Meade. First and foremost, it was supremely isolated—its nearest neighbor was St. Helena, an island seven hundred miles to the southeast. In this part of the world there were no prying eyes about, and virtually zero radio interference. Secondly, like Pine Gap, it was a beautiful "window" in SIGINT terms, where bouncing radio signals from Moscow often landed with surprising clarity. And finally, as the Americans began lobbing their spy satellites into orbit, Ascension found a new role as a spy-satellite downlink station.

Most of the British contingent on Ascension were RAF personnel, or support workers hired from St. Helena. But about twenty people were assigned to the Composite Signals Organization (CSO). The CSO was the division of GCHQ that staffed overseas listening posts in places like the Seychelles, Hong Kong, Cyprus, and Ascension. The intercept operation on the island was largely automated now, so the CSO staff were mostly technicians who maintained the equipment. The raw SIGINT feed was analyzed after it was retransmitted to Cheltenham or Fort Meade.

Ascension station, however, maintained a backup tape depot of the raw SIGINT feed.

Faisal walked out of the visitors' quarters and looked up at the highest landmark in view. It was dusk, but he could see the extinct volcano Mount Green, which rose 2,817 feet out of the sea. His eyes traveled down the slope to the compound of featureless buildings and white geodesic domes. This was the installation of the Composite Signals Organization, and the reason he was here. He was apprehensive, knowing that a minefield with a thousand trip wires lay before him. His longing for Razia went beyond description, and the thought of losing her was more than he could bear. Yet he was about to put it all at risk. He sighed, then walked down the lane toward the mess hall. No sense entering a minefield on an empty stomach.

Kevin Costner was standing on the riverbank, a quiver of arrows strapped over his shoulder. Mary Elizabeth Mastrantonio was in a rowboat, heading into the fog. Gad! Had the Empire come to this! An American actor, and an American actress of Italian extraction, playing the English icons of Robin Hood and Maid Marian. Faisal went to the cinema about once every seven years or so. He'd no idea the British film industry was so far in the tank. What could be next? Sylvester Stallone as Henry VIII? Well, at least the Sheriff of Nottingham was a Brit. And he was the bad guy. An allegory, perhaps?

Faisal surveyed the audience at the amphitheater. He guessed approximately three hundred people were in attendance. Some were American civilians who operated the radar station. Some were RAF. Some were British support workers. All were held in rapt attention by the cinematic spectacle on the screen. It *was* the only show in town.

Faisal stood off to the side and carefully inspected each row of upturned faces. They were illuminated by the screen's reflective light. Although there might be someone who knew him, thus far Faisal hadn't seen a familiar face. Slowly he moved toward the rear, and that's when he saw him. Sitting on a seat one shy of row's end. He was of medium height and slender, and like everyone else he wore casual, comfortable clothes. He was in his early thirties, with kindly features that seemed to say, "I'm your friend." His name was Evan Sears, and Faisal had chosen him carefully.

Evan had entered GCHQ with a class of cryptologic trainees. A graduate of Exeter in mathematics, he'd demonstrated mediocre skills in his entry-level position. But two things about Evan compensated for his lack of technical prowess: people instinctively liked him, and he possessed unbridled ambition. Sort of a younger version of Dickie Batholomew on the make. So rather than set him adrift, Faisal decided to farm him out. He would become a cryptologic liaison officer to the CSO field stations, where the tasks were more administrative than technical. Evan blossomed in this environment, and he garnered glowing fitness reports during his tours at Little Sai Wan in Hong Kong, and in the Seychelles. He'd since transferred to CSO full-time and was now the supervisor at Ascension station.

On the screen, the sheriff held Maid Marian in the tower, and Faisal's blood began to pump. It was now or never. He whispered a prayer to Allah, then slipped onto the neighboring chair and said in a low voice, "Good evening, Evan."

Evan Sears's attention was torn from the screen, and it took a moment for him to recognize the stranger. "What the . . . ? No, it can't be. Faisal Shaikh? Here? I don't believe it!"

"Keep it down, will ya, buddy?"

"Of course, sorry," whispered Evan. Then he stuck out his hand. "This is incredible! I heard you had left Cheltenham . . ."

Faisal shook the hand perfunctorily, then replied in a low but firm voice, "Keep your voice down, Evan. I need to speak with you—away from here."

Evan hesitated, not wanting to leave Maid Marian stranded.

Faisal motioned with his hand. "Come with me, Evan. Now." It wasn't a request. It was an order, and Evan Sears soon found himself walking out the main gate. Maid Marian was on her own.

After they passed a space-shuttle statue at the main entrance, Faisal marched them down the narrow lane. The temperature was comfortable, but a shade on the chilly side; and the stars were brilliant against the inky sky. Once they'd gone a few hundred yards, Faisal stepped off the road and marched across the moon-like terrain until he came to a large volcanic boulder. Here he paused and leaned against the rock, then asked in a friendly voice, "So how have you been, Evan?"

Evan Sears spoke cautiously, his bureaucrat's radar up and tracking. "Well enough . . . What's this all about, anyway? I'd heard you left GCHQ. The rumor was you left under a cloud."

"A cloud of rather vague improprieties? A whiff of scandal, perhaps?"

"Something like that. And then you pop up on this rock out of nowhere. What, exactly, is all this about?"

With dramatic flare, Faisal pulled out a package of Player's and lit one up, inhaling deeply. God it tasted good. Then he exhaled and began to explain. "My departure from Cheltenham—'under a cloud,' as you said—was a rather well-done cover story."

Beneath the canopy of stars, Faisal sensed Evan's tension.

"Cover story?"

"Precisely."

"Cover story about what?"

Faisal took another long drag, then said in a low voice, "It seems, Evan, that we have another Geoffrey Prime afoot at Cheltenham."

The whites of Evan's eyes became discernible in the moonlight. "Another Prime?"

"Someone just like him, I'm afraid."

Evan Sears gulped, then leaned against the boulder. "Good God, no."

Geoffrey Arthur Prime was an intelligence agency's worst nightmare, for the damage he'd inflicted upon Her Majesty's government rivaled that of Kim Philby. But at least Philby brought a measure of style and élan to his treachery. Prime was a wretch.

He'd joined the RAF in 1956 at age eighteen and underwent training to become a Russian linguist. He was posted to signals intelligence at RAF Gatow in West Berlin, where he developed an affection for things Soviet. He turned spy in 1968, then went on to join the Joint Technical Language Service at Cheltenham.

Prime was proficient at his duties. Indeed, his prowess at GCHQ earned him a promotion to the Soviet section of the "Special SIG-INT" J Division, the inner sanctum of intercept worlds. And irony of ironies, he was made a personnel security supervisor, responsible for annual security reports on his colleagues. But apparently Prime's double life took a toll, for he left GCHQ in 1978 to become a taxi driver.

The damage done by Prime's decade-long treachery was simply beyond measure, for he dropped a trainload of secrets on the steps of the Kremlin. Through Prime, the KGB learned of GCHQ's internal structure, its operating procedures, its SIGINT targets, its technical means, commercial and diplomatic covers of clandestine intercept operators, and the spy satellites of Big Bird and RHYO-LITE. In short, the KGB knew quantumly more about GCHQ than did your loyal British subject.

But beyond his treachery, Prime had an even darker side, in that he was a pedophile. His obsession for pubescent girls was simply off the meter. He would telephone young girls and try to extract information from them, such as their age, where they attended school, and when their parents were at home. He kept meticulous records of his calls on index cards, compiling an incredible stack of 2,287.

From 1980 to 1982, however, Prime could no longer control his sexual urgings. He hung up the phone and went on the prowl, physically assaulting three girls in Gloucestershire. The police tracked him down, whereupon he confessed about his secret lives of pedophilia and spying.

"So why are you here?" asked a tremulous Evan Sears. "I mean, what does this have to do with me?"

Faisal didn't answer at first. He wanted Evan more than a little scared, so he let him dangle a bit longer while he enjoyed a few puffs off the cigarette. When he felt Evan's angst level was sufficient, Faisal began. "Someone at Cheltenham, we don't know who, has been systematically compromising our clandestine skin grafts, only days after they've been implanted."

Evan Sears swallowed and stammered, "I, I didn't know skin

grafts actually existed. We all hear rumors of course, but I didn't know they were for real."

Faisal was the soul of sympathy as he patted Evan's shoulder. "Of course you didn't. Only a select group at GCHQ know the details. Plus some altar boys, and a few special-ops people in the SAS and Royal Marines."

In GCHQ parlance, a "skin graft" was a means to defy that nemesis of all electronic eavesdroppers: the secure landline cable. Although it is technically feasible to probe a coaxial cable from a distance of a few feet or so, it remains largely impervious to eavesdroppers. Especially if it is buried. During the Cold War the Soviets were well aware of this, and that is why they invested billions to link Moscow with key military installations via a dedicated cable system. The underground cables radiated from Moscow, like spokes on a wheel, to such places as the Red Banner Northern Fleet Submarine Headquarters in Polyarny, the Soviet Aerospace Defense Warning Center in Magnitogorsk, the Strategic Rocket Forces Battle Center in Chelyabinsk, and the Red Banner Black Sea Fleet Headquarters in Sevastopol.

So inviting were these SIGINT targets that GCHQ's technical wizards developed some ingenious methods to tap into the secure cables—clandestinely on Russian soil.

There were more skin grafts in place than you might imagine, and so successful was the concept that the Americans mounted a similar effort in a program called Ivy Bells.

But that was another story.

Evan paused to digest the incredible story Faisal had told him. "You said skin grafts are being compromised as they're implanted?"

"Exactly," replied Faisal.

Evan was genuinely surprised. "You mean, that sort of thing is still going on? I thought everything was pretty much *en clair* these days. I mean, the Russians have taken a powder, haven't they? The Iron Curtain rusted away and all that. You mean to say we're still doing the skin-graft thing?"

"Now more than ever, Evan."

Evan didn't reply at once. He scratched his chin a few times and said, "That's hard to believe."

Faisal sighed, like a headmaster dealing with a not-so-bright pupil. "Evan, did you know that just two weeks ago there was nearly a Russian-to-Russian nuclear exchange in the Far East Military District?"

Evan shook his head.

"Had an American aircraft not intervened, we might be dealing with a nuclear civil war in the Far East?"

Evan shook his head again. Did he appear a little frightened now?

"Had we not been listening, the Americans could not have intervened. There might have been mushroom clouds all over eastern Siberia. And who knows where that might have led. If you don't believe me, check it out. Discreetly. . . . So, yes, Evan, we still have the bloody skin grafts under way. Now do you understand why?"

Evan swallowed, then nodded his head like a repentant child. "But what does all this traitor business have to do with Ascension? With me?"

Faisal flicked off an ash. "Because, Evan, you are in a singular position to help us discover who this mole is."

"Me?"

"You."

"How . . . how can that be?"

"Because something very curious happened when our skin grafts were compromised. Messages in a special encryption format were transmitted to and from Moscow. It was in an unusual seven-letter code group. We intercepted three—between Petropavlovsk and Moscow, Samarkand and Moscow, and Aykhal and Moscow."

"So?"

"Petropavlovsk, Samarkand, and Aykhal. Those were the locations of three skin-graft pods. The seven-letter code groups were transmitted immediately before and after the pods uplinked their SIGINT harvest to one of our commo satellites. In each case, the eavesdropping pod went stone dead shortly thereafter. Suspicious, wouldn't you say?"

Evan cleared his throat. "Well, yes, very. What do you think it was?"

Faisal sighed wearily, as if he were approaching the confessional. "I think the seven-letter code groups were sent by a special field team of the GRU's Radio-Technical Directorate to their HQ in Moscow. I think they were coordinating their search efforts for the skin-graft pod with the overflight of our commo satellite. It's my guess our traitor told the Russians where to look."

Evan gave a low whistle, then was silent for a moment. "But how does that figure in with you? I mean, why were you sacked?"

Faisal put an edge on his voice. "I wasn't sacked, you fool. I'm trying to track down a damned traitor."

Evan cleared his throat. "Sorry, Faisal."

"Sir Vivian and I worked closely together on this. We studied this seven-letter cipher carefully, and we decided I should work on it personally to see if I could break it. I was making progress. Getting close. Then . . . "

"Then what?"

"A curious thing. All of my computer files on the seven-letter cipher were purged."

"Purged?"

"Erased. Dumped. Cleansed. Gone."

"You mean . . . ?"

"Exactly. Our mole is someone very high up at GCHQ. Technically competent. Knew about the skin grafts. Knew how to break into my personal files, search them, and purge them. That tells me these seven-letter ciphers might shed some light on his identity. And that is why it's crucial to recover the messages and have another go."

"Recover?"

"That is why I am here, Evan. The Aykhal message was trapped here at Ascension and should be in your tape depot. I want you to do a search and give me the recording."

Evan paused. "But why come here? Why not search the Oakley depot back at Cheltenham?"

"Because, Evan, whoever this mole is, he knows the drill. If I pulled up the tapes and had them reloaded into the system, he might fear the game was up. Bolt and run. We don't dare touch them at Oakley. That's why Sir Vivian and I faked my dismissal. With me out of the way, the mole probably feels safe. I'm visiting the field stations to collect the tapes. Once I have the raw copy, I'll go to work on the encryption."

"How can you do that if you're expelled from Cheltenham?"

Faisal dropped the butt on the hard ground and snuffed it out with his shoe. "Good question, Evan. I always said you were bright. That's why I kept you on. How I deal with the raw copy is none of your concern. What I need from you is the tape."

Evan eyed him warily. "I'll need a reference point to do a search."

Faisal pulled out a folded slip of paper from the breast pocket of his safari suit. "Here are the TEXTA particulars. Or as close as I could come from memory. Just look for the seven-letter code group. You can't miss it."

Evan took the paper and unfolded it, trying to make out the characters in the starlight. He remained silent for a time, then said in his best bureaucratic manner, "I . . . I don't know about this, Faisal. You show up out of nowhere, asking for a tape search. Claiming there's another Prime loose in Cheltenham. It all sounds rather queer."

"Doesn't it?"

"I, would, uh, need some kind of verification."

"I quite understand, Evan. I would want the same if I were in your position." Faisal unbuttoned the other breast pocket and retrieved another piece of paper, which he handed over. As Evan held it, Faisal struck a match to illuminate the text—which was written on GCHQ letterhead:

TO WHOM IT MAY CONCERN:

FAISAL SHAIKH IS A DIVISION CHIEF OF GOVERNMENT COMMUNICATIONS HEADQUARTERS. HE HAS UNDERTAKEN A MISSION OF GREAT URGENCY FOR THE DEFENSE OF THE REALM. ALL GCHQ PERSONNEL ARE TO PROVIDE HIM WITH UNQUALIFIED ASSISTANCE, AND TO OBEY HIS

INSTRUTIONS WITHOUT QUESTION. SECRECY AND SECU-
RITY ARE TO BE ABSOLUTE.

SIR VIVIAN MITTLEDITCH
DIRECTOR

The match went out. "Sir Vivian typed that himself." Faisal chuckled. "Notice he misspelled *instructions.*"

Evan still seemed to be wavering, poised between ambition and anxiety. Faisal decided an appeal to ambition was in order. "You know, Evan, the person who helps Sir Vivian and me nail this mole can write his own ticket. Station chief in Paris. Deputy SUKLO in Washington. Parliamentary liaison. It would be the gold ring for one's career. But should you upset the applecart, I'm afraid it could harm your advancement."

Faced with a carrot or stick, Evan seized the carrot. "Very well, Faisal. I'll do the search. Just remember who helped you."

"Till the end of time, Evan."

He held up the forgery. "May I keep this?"

Faisal plucked it back. "Afraid not, Evan. I have some other stations to visit yet."

Under the moonlight, Evan looked trapped. "Where do I send the tape?"

"I have a private plane and pilot at the airfield. His name is Velasquez. Have it delivered to him. There must be no further contact between us. Be discreet. You understand?"

"I understand." Evan paused for a moment, thinking things over. Then he asked, "What happens if you find the mole?"

Faisal sighed, as if already in mourning. "I'm afraid he may have a serious accident."

Evan swallowed hard. "Accident?"

Faisal nodded wearily. "We aren't going to have a damned public relations fiasco like we did with Geoffrey Arthur Prime, Evan. Our funding, the relationship with the Americans, the very survival of GCHQ, would be at risk if Fleet Street got ahold of it. It will be dealt with quietly."

Evan was trembling now. It was like Faisal had become a viper coiled up on the rock beside him. "So that's what it's all about, is it? You have to nail the mole, all quietlike. Keep everything under wraps. Otherwise the budget cutters will carve Cheltenham up like a roast. Westminster has wanted to pull our funding for years. This would give them the stick."

Faisal's voice took on a prickly sternness. "No, it is not just about budgets, Evan. It's about the Crown having its ear to the ground in an uncertain world. It's about not having security compromised. It's about cutting the cancer out of an institution to which we have given our lives. Is that *clear?*"

A chastened Evan shuffled his feet. "You're quite right, Faisal. Sorry . . . I, I best be off."

"Yes, you best be off."

As Evan disappeared into the night, Faisal wondered if, perhaps, he should have pursued a career in the theater.

Two days later the Beechcraft Sierra was wheels up, on a vector for Kinshasa, with the third and final tape tucked inside Faisal's grip.

As the deep blue Atlantic passed under them, Crazy Jorge flashed his perennial grin at Faisal. "You get what you need?"

Faisal did not answer. Instead, he pulled a roll of five thousand pounds from his grip and shoved it into Jorge's hand. "A small bonus. Just forget you ever landed at Ascension Island."

CHAPTER ✠ TWENTY·TWO

The hired Ford Taurus cruised through the township of Bowie, Maryland, like a slow-moving ice cream vendor. The terrain was rolling hills with beautiful trees in what had been horse-farm country. Now it was broken up by the occasional subdivision. Faisal found the street for which he was looking and turned onto it. Creeping along, he watched the address numbers on the curb as they grew closer to his destination. A pair of boys raced by on their bicycles, while a nearby group of adolescents indulged in a game of touch football. The calendar was nearing the end of September and the first leaves had fallen, signaling that winter would arrive early this year. The dwellings were slightly upscale with a Federal motif, the kind favored by upper midlevel government bureaucrats with two-income families.

Faisal pulled to the curb and killed the engine under the shade of a tree. The man he had come to see was just three houses away on the front lawn, raking leaves into a large pile. He was middle-aged, overweight, balding, and wore a REDSKINS windbreaker to keep the late-afternoon chill at bay.

Faisal gripped the steering wheel tightly, for like a cancer the fear had grown within him. Once he stepped out of the car, there was absolutely no turning back. If what he'd done on Ascension Island was equivalent to shoplifting, what he was about to do now was armed robbery in broad daylight in Piccadilly Circus. But he was so close now, he could almost touch the Black Cipher.

He now possessed the historical tapes that would enable him to reconstruct the algorithm to break the Black Cipher. But to execute the algorithm, he required access to the National Security Agency's formidable Paradox computer. To gain access, he would quite simply have to bluff his way in. To bluff his way in, he would have to con someone to help him. Preferably someone who was gullible and not too bright, which presented a problem, because persons gullible and not too bright were in rather short supply at Fort Meade. The middle-aged man down the way, however, met those criteria.

Faisal whispered a prayer to Allah, then exited the Taurus, zipped up his jacket, and walked down the sidewalk. He stepped onto the lawn and approached the leaf raker from behind, saying, "Hello, Gerard."

The man wielding the rake stopped and turned round. It took him a few moments to recognize the stranger because he appeared out of nowhere and out of context. Also, Gerard wasn't especially quick on the uptake.

"Faisal Shaikh," he said finally, while pushing his thick glasses back up on his nose.

"Yes, Gerard," replied Faisal, while extending his hand. "I guess it's been two years since we saw each other last, at the BRUSA conference in Ottawa, I believe."

Gerard shook the hand warily, obviously uncomfortable with the intruder's presence. "What . . . what are you doing here?"

"We have much to talk about, Gerard. Is there a place we can chat? Privately?"

Gerard twisted the rake handle in his hands, his pudgy face betraying his confused state.

"It's important, Gerard. To your career especially."

Faisal spoke with such authority that Gerard ceased to waver and said, "Let's go inside."

They went round back and entered a door to a small study. There was a desk with household bills neatly stacked upon it, a television tuned to the Redskins game, and a sofa with an overweight adolescent stretched out on the cushions. A crumpled potato chip bag lay on the floor.

"You'll have to leave, Junior. I have to talk with this man."

Faisal wondered why Junior wasn't out raking the leaves.

A whiny voice said, "Awww, do I have to? It's the Cowboys."

"Move it, Junior!" Gerard looked embarrassed at having raised his voice.

"Aww, okay." Junior rolled off the couch with the grace of a sea elephant lumbering up the beach. Once he left, Gerard closed the door and locked it, then looked at Faisal and shrugged. "Kids. Whaddya gonna do?"

"I quite understand," replied Faisal, while taking a seat on the warm sofa where Junior had lain.

Gerard plucked the potato chip bag off the floor and tossed it in the wastebasket. Gerard was a tidy man. Then he took a seat on the chair across from the sofa and pushed up the glasses that always seemed to be slipping. "Okay, Faisal, what's this all about? I'd heard you were fired from Cheltenham."

Gerard Fogelson's presence at NSA was a mistake. Someone, somewhere, at some time, had made a grievous error when that crop of recruits arrived at Fort Meade twenty-two years ago. Yet Gerard Fogelson was still there—for two reasons. Although not impossible, it was difficult to fire a bureaucrat, and secondly, Fogelson did have one saving grace. He was a master paper shuffler. A man who could track and file memos, count paper clips, expedite correspondence, and crunch budget numbers with the best of them. With sixty thousand employees, NSA's administrative load was immense, so Gerard wasn't a total loss. However, his asset ledger was truncated at paper shuffling, for his people skills were on par with a barnacle, and his technical skills nonexistent.

Somehow, Fogelson's career path led him into the cryptologic service branch of the NSA, where he now served as head paper shuffler to Dr. Marshall Fitzroy, chief of the branch. Theirs was an overseer-slave relationship, with Gerard being the downtrodden, browbeaten, humiliated, spirit-broken serf. Beyond paper-clip counting and a rote knowledge of NSA's ponderous procedures manual, Gerard was utterly out of his depth in cryptology.

Faisal had chosen carefully.

The visitor leaned back on the sofa and smiled. "I'm so glad you heard I was sacked, Gerard. That means our cover story is holding up nicely."

Fogelson stared at Faisal with a look devoid of comprehension. "Cover story?"

"Yes, Gerard. It seems we have another Geoffrey Arthur Prime afoot in Cheltenham . . . "

Faisal fed Gerard the same cock-and-bull story he'd given Evan Sears at Ascension Island, but with a few variations to make it plausible to the American. And so far, it seemed to be working.

" . . . so you see, Gerard, I could not tap into the Paradox computer from Cheltenham for fear of alerting our mole. He is technically bright, for he broke into and erased my personal computer files on the Black Cipher. Sir Vivian decided we must make the traitor feel secure, so that is why we faked my sacking."

Gerard's blank gaze froze in place for a time, until at last he shifted his girth and said, "I never heard about skin grafts before. Never seen anything for them in our division's budget."

Faisal shrugged. "They must be paid for by another division's budget."

Blank stare. "But I don't understand. Why have skin grafts anymore? The old Soviet Union's pretty much an open book these days. That's what Marshall says. They don't even bother to encrypt a lot of their traffic now."

Once more, Faisal assumed his exasperated-headmaster role and sighed. "Gerard, the Soviet giant has fallen, but that giant is still having death spasms. We have no idea when one of those spasms will lash out in ways we can't predict. Maybe a renegade Rocket Forces commander will threaten to launch his missiles. Maybe a submarine commander will try to sell his vessel to Qaddafi. Who knows? We can't predict. We have to keep our ear to the ground."

Blank stare.

Faisal pressed his case. "Did you know, Gerard, that only a few weeks ago a Russian-to-Russian nuclear exchange almost took place in the Far East Military District?"

Now the blank face showed genuine surprise.

"A CRITICOM was filed out of Misawa. Check it out. Discreetly, of course, but check it out and you'll understand why the 'special relationship' of America and Britain still plants skin grafts on Russian soil."

Gerard cleared his throat and shifted again. "Uh, no. I didn't know that. . . . But why tell me all this? Why not go to Marshall?"

Faisal didn't answer at once. He took time to light up a cigarette and let Gerard dangle a bit. "Because, Gerard, the last compromised skin graft was located outside Petropavlovsk. It was ninety percent an American operation. As well as Sir Vivian could determine, only a half dozen senior-level NSA officials knew about it. One of them was Marshall Fitzroy."

Gerard grasped the arms of his chair, seized by a spasm. In a voice that was barely audible, he whispered, "What are you saying?"

"What I am saying, Gerard, is that there is a real chance an American mole is working in concert with our traitor at Cheltenham. A very real possibility. And the evidence suggests that person could be Marshall Fitzroy."

The room was spinning for Gerard as his belief system imploded upon his shoulders. He held the chair tighter and whimpered, "Not . . . not Marshall. He . . . he's my boss. You—you're lying."

"I wish I were, Gerard, I truly wish I were. I've known Marshall for a dozen years. But the evidence says he may be a traitor. And that is why I came to you."

Fogelson swallowed. "Me?"

"Yes, you, Gerard. Sir Vivian and I faced a dilemma. We needed access to the Paradox computer to break the Black Cipher, but with Jaws—er, I mean, Marshall—being a suspect we couldn't go through him, now could we?"

No response.

"Of course we couldn't. So Sir Vivian suggested that since I was deputy SUKLO at Meade some years back, could I put forward the name of someone who could help us. Someone who was above reproach. Someone who could provide us with discreet access to the Paradox computer, but whose loyalties were beyond question. Well, of course, Gerard, I thought of you immediately."

Gerard blinked, a bit dumbfounded. Was that flattery? Gerard had never encountered flattery before, so he wasn't quite sure. "Uh ... you mean, you want me to let you into the compound to use the Paradox?"

"Discreetly."

Gerard licked his lips. "Gee, Faisal, I don't know if I can do that. I would need some kind of authorization." The man was a bureaucrat to his loins.

Faisal pulled the forgery from his pocket and passed it to Gerard, who read it slowly.

TO: **GERARD FOGELSON**

DEPUTY CHIEF/ADMINISTRATION

CRYPTOLOGIC SERVICE DIVISION

NATIONAL SECURITY AGENCY

FORT MEADE, MARYLAND

FAISAL SHAIKH IS A DIVISION CHIEF OF GOVERNMENT COMMUNICATIONS HEADQUARTERS. HE HAS UNDERTAKEN A MISSION OF GREAT URGENCY FOR THE DEFENSE OF THE REALM. I ENTREAT YOU TO ASSIST HIM IN ANY WAY YOU CAN, WITH ABSLUTE SECRECY AND SECURITY.

SIR VIVIAN MITTLEDITCH

DIRECTOR

"*Absolute* is misspelled."

"You simply don't miss a trick, do you, Gerard? Sir Vivian typed that himself and he isn't much of a typist."

Gerard puffed up a bit. Yes, this must be flattery. He found he rather enjoyed it. "Well, if Marshall is under suspicion, I would have to verify this through the chief of P Group. Maybe even the director."

Faisal sighed his headmaster's sigh. "Gerard, I said Marshall is a suspect, not *the* suspect. You bump this up the chain, the mole might get wind of it. Absolute security must be maintained, otherwise he could slip through our fingers."

Gerard squirmed. He was loath to climb out on that limb.

"As of this moment, the only people who know about my mission are Sir Vivian, myself, and you, Gerard. Were you to compromise my mission, Sir Vivian would be most displeased. He would raise the issue with the Prime Minister, who would undoubtedly raise it with your President."

Gerard gasped. "The *President?*"

"Yes, Gerard. And you would be called on the carpet to explain why you raised the alarm and flushed the quarry. We *have* to find him, Gerard. He may have been in place for years. Perhaps *decades.* If he gets away and word gets out, it could mean disaster for Fort Meade's budget."

Another gasp. "Budget?" Faisal was treading on sacred ground now.

"Yes, Gerard. The NSA's budget. Your budget. It could all collapse with just one single mole getting away and living to tell the tale. You know those blaggards in Congress. They would castrate the lot of you, given the chance. Close up Fort Meade, then take the money and run. All they need is one little excuse. One little mole."

Gerard wheezed. "We've *got* to find him. We can't let him do this."

"Exactly. I'll ride in with you tomorrow."

CHAPTER ✜ TWENTY·THREE

very time Faisal made the journey from Cheltenham to the National Security Agency campus at Fort Meade, he felt like a sailor stepping from a destroyer escort onto a dreadnought battleship. The scope and the scale of NSA's operations, capabilities, and budget were simply overwhelming, even for veterans who worked there. The NSA was the center of an electronic web that covered the globe and extended into outer space. It directly employed some 60,000 people, mostly civilians, and when the Army, Navy, Air Force, and Marine Corps SIGINT branches were thrown in, that number ballooned to 110,000. When the minions congregated at Fort Meade each working day, the military post turned into a not-so-small city. It possessed its own police force, medical staff, power station, food service, library, convenience store, barbershop, TV station, movie studio, post office, bank, and travel agency. However, rote numbers and support services do not convey the sheer firepower Fort Meade has at its command.

In the mid-1930s, the payroll of the U.S. SIGINT community numbered exactly six people. Pearl Harbor changed all that, and World War II turned out to be the SIGINT equivalent of an anabolic steroid, fueling growth that could only be called explosive. Growth that was driven by a single credo: Never again would the American giant be caught with its pants down as it was that Sunday morning in Hawaii. Fifty years later, the glass-and-steel buildings that sprouted from the Fort Meade campus were a testament to that resolve.

As Gerard Fogelson drove his Chevrolet Caprice along the Fort Meade road, Faisal glanced at the Special Processing Laboratory. It was a massive, low, windowless structure that possessed *the* state-of-the-state-of-the-art facility for the fabrication of semiconductors. You see, the NSA did not entrust the manufacture of semiconductors to outside contractors. Oh, no. They built their own factory where the entire production process could be controlled by white-suited technicians in magnificent clean rooms. The silicon chips that came out of SPL's ovens went into COMSEC equipment aboard Navy ships, Air Force planes, Army tanks, in U.S. embassies, the Pentagon, and even the White House. The Japanese (could they have gained entry) would have been envious of the SPL's technical elegance.

The Caprice continued on, driving past the new Research and Engineering building that sparkled with its bronze reflective glass. Within the confines of this gleaming intellectual juggernaut was a brigade of PhDs, or "fuzzy heads" as they were known at Meade. Some worked in the upper theoretical realms of mathematics and cryptanalysis, while others designed new equipment for secure communications, or explored new ways to "unwrap" an adversary's signal that was electronically scrambled. Faisal had visited the new R&E building a few times before he'd been cashiered out of GCHQ. Each time he came away convinced that the Americans had a printing press in the basement where they rolled out stacks of money to pay for the never-ending construction at Fort Meade.

The Caprice turned and cruised past something that looked like a giant papermill, and that's exactly what it was. The NSA generated fifty *tons* of classified material a *day*, and the recycling plant was built to slice, dice, shred, and repulp the mountain of used paper that rolled out of Fort Meade's printers, presses, copiers, Teletypes, and fax machines.

As always, upon his arrival at Fort Meade, Faisal was reminded what the brass-knuckled term *superpower* really meant. Whatever failings the Americans had on the automobile production line, they did not bring their foibles to signals intelligence. At Fort Meade the in-laws were, quite simply, in a class by themselves.

The car turned again and cruised by the stately wrought-iron fence along the perimeter of the campuslike lawn. Beyond the pretty iron fence, out of sight, were additional barriers that weren't so pretty and hummed with electricity.

The Caprice followed a stream of cars off the exit ramp to the employee parking lot. (Faisal mused to himself that this single parking lot was as big as the Benhall campus at Cheltenham.) Gerard Fogelson remained silent as he pulled up to a guard hut that was set into the barbed-wire Hurricane fence. A guard looked at the bumper sticker and waved them past. Gerard pulled into an empty space and they exited the Caprice. From the trunk of the car Faisal retrieved the three computer tapes he'd obtained from Misawa, Pine Gap, and Ascension Island; and along with Gerard he joined the stream of employees headed for the gatehouse entrance to the OPS complex. Although Faisal knew quite a number of people at Meade, the number of employees was so vast that his chance of discovery was remote, as long as he stayed away from the cryptologic division and the OPS common areas. Even so, he wore a fedora hat and sunglasses as they approached the entrance of the OPS complex.

"You have the forms prepared?" queried Faisal.

"Yeah," replied Gerard.

"How did you do that? I only contacted you late yesterday afternoon."

Gerard shrugged. "I always keep spares at the house. I like having them around."

"I see."

Before them loomed two obelisks of blue-mirrored glass. They weren't as new as the Research and Engineering building, but nearly so. These were the eight-story OPS 2-A and 2-B buildings. As they mounted the steps to the entrance, Faisal got a sinking feeling in the pit of his stomach. A typical symptom of raw fear. "I hope Marshall is nowhere about," he whispered to Gerard.

Gerard opened the heavy glass door and mumbled, "He's out of town. Visiting field stations."

Faisal sighed. Well, at least that was something.

They entered the reception foyer of the OPS complex and Gerard immediately took Faisal to a doorway on the right marked VISITORS' CENTER. Faisal walked into a chamber that looked like a Holiday Inn reception area. There was a raised counter, with clerks on the far side signing in three queues of visitors. Faisal scanned the room behind his sunglasses and saw no one he recognized. Their turn came and Gerard flashed his NSA identification and shoved a form in front of the clerk while saying, "I need a level-seven visitor pass. Here's the DD Form four seven nine for contractor access." The clerk checked the documents, shuffled her papers, and retrieved a plastic badge colored purple. "Sign in please," she said in a monotone. Faisal stepped to the counter and signed in as Khalid Mousef, a contractor from IBM headquarters in Armonk, New York. He was given a purple badge, which gave him extraordinary unescorted access.

They exited the visitors' center and stepped to the security gates manned by guards of the Federal Protective Service. Gerard and Faisal presented themselves to the bored guard, who asked, "Do you have any film or recording materials in your possession?" Faisal placed his satchel on the inspection table as Gerard whipped out another prepared form and flashed his ID. "NSA Form nine three two, transmittal of recording tape to depot. My authorization." The guard inspected the three tapes carefully and insured they matched the serial numbers on the form. Satisfied, he waved the contraband through.

Now they came to the badge reader, which kept track of all the people—or rather, all the badges—into and out of the building. NSA employees wore green tags, while most visitors wore red badges. Faisal had routinely worn a purple badge when he was deputy senior UK liaison officer (SUKLO) at Meade, so he knew the ropes. He inserted the purple card into the reader and Gerard said, "Punch in four sevens." Faisal inserted his hand into a hooded keypad with an LED readout and punched in the numbers.

That done, they passed under an electronic bulletin board of red lights that urged sign-ups for the upcoming basketball league, then walked straight toward a wall emblazoned with NATIONAL SECURITY AGENCY. To the left of the sign was the seal of the NSA, which was a tile mosaic of a cantankerous eagle clutching a key in its talons. A key to unlock secrets. In front of the seal was a small pedestal with a piece of the Berlin Wall on display. (Presumably for those who failed to notice who won and who lost the Cold War.)

They turned right, then left, and went through a short hallway where a row of portraits enshrined past deputy directors of the NSA (the ones who really ran the place). Portraits of Louis Tordella, Benson Buffham, Robert Drake, and Ann Caracristi. Faisal paid them no mind. He was busy scanning from behind his dark glasses as they went past a wall full of awards, a bank of elevators, then continued down the passageway and outside to a courtyard. They walked along a covered walkway and entered the Operations Building (not to be confused with the OPS 2-A and 2-B buildings). Gerard led him down the longest unobstructed corridor in the world (980 feet) to a bank of elevators where they got on the lift and went down. The doors opened to another secure area where they signed in before a guard, then passed through a door that was electronically locked. Now they were inside a secure subterranean corridor. They walked down a few doors and entered one of Fort Meade's computer centers.

The NSA possesses the greatest concentration of computing power in the world. To comprehend just how much, they don't measure their computers by number, gigabytes, or megaflops. Instead, the NSA measures its computers by the *acre*. Faisal and Gerard had entered one of three subterranean labyrinths beneath the Operations Building that housed some of the fifteen acres of computers at Fort Meade.

There was a small reception area, a counter, and behind that was a small forest of tape drives spinning their reels incessantly. A bespectacled clerk rose from behind a desk and stepped to the counter. Gerard slapped another piece of paper on the counter. "NSA Form four four seven six. I need a TEXTA search of these tapes and a job number assigned." Gerard was in his paperwork element.

The clerk said nothing. He tapped into his computer for a job order number, stamped the date/time of receipt on the duplicate form, scribbled in the job order number, gave the duplicate to Gerard, and whisked the tapes off the counter.

Now they were in the system.

Faisal and Gerard exited the computer center and found themselves back in the corridor. Without a form to cling to, Gerard's angst level began to rise. He seemed to be freezing up, like a fish too long ashore. Faisal said, "Come on, man. Let's get on with it." Gerard began perspiring as he led Faisal down the passageway. They went about a hundred feet and made a turn that brought them to what was essentially a miniature subway. Gerard and Faisal stepped on board a vehicle that looked like a carnival bumper car on rails. Gerard hit the button and they were off, traveling under Fort Meade from the Headquarters-Operations Complex to a separate facility known as DEFSMAC (pronounced "deaf-smack"). A couple of bumper cars passed them going in the opposite direction on the three-quarters of a mile journey.

At the terminus on the far end they exited the bumper car and started walking along the corridor toward another bank of elevators down the way. Just then the lift opened and a rather dumpy-looking chap in shirtsleeves and tie emerged—his nose buried in a clipboard. Faisal froze, then spun round and whispered to Gerard, "That's Jamieson!"

Gerard froze, too, as he recognized his colleague from the cryptologic division. "Wha . . . what is he doing here?"

"Never mind that, you fool! He knows me! We can't let him see me—or you." Faisal stared at the double steel doors on his immediate left. On the wall beside the doors was an electronic keypad. "Can you get us in here?"

Gerard remained paralytic as Jamieson approached with his nose still buried in the clipboard.

"Get a grip on yourself, man! Can you get us in here?"

Gerard stared at the keypad. "I . . . I don't know the access code."

Faisal feared the game was up, then the steel door swung open, blocking their view of Jamieson. A young Army lieutenant courteously held the door open for them. Faisal nodded his thanks while gently shoving Gerard inside. The door swung closed as Jamieson walked by. Faisal breathed a sigh of relief, then turned around and realized they had sought refuge in the heart of the beast.

The Defense Special Missile and Astronautics Center (DEFSMAC) was the cerebral cortex of the American SIGINT nervous system that stretched around the globe and into outer space. From Misawa to Pine Gap to Diego Garcia in the Indian Ocean to Arecibo in Puerto Rico to the Magnum satellites in orbit—all the remote sensors fed their critical pulses into DEFSMAC, where Faisal and Gerard now found themselves.

Faisal had been here before, of course, and then just as now he was bowled over by the scene. It was like an indoor amphitheater, similar to Block M at Cheltenham, or the operations room at Misawa, only much bigger. The screens on the forewall pictured different regions of the world—Southeast Asia, the Middle East—and graphically showed the evolving SIGINT picture. Other screens tracked the data flow into and out of the computer centers for processing. Below the screens were rows of consoles manned by technicians and experts in traffic analysis, satellite communications, and telemetry analysis; and by regional specialists, who evaluated the incoming product. They chatted with their counterparts in the field over the SPINTCOM satellite network, taking pulses minute by minute to constantly update the global SIGINT picture.

Meanwhile, another console bank handled the *outflow* of data from DEFSMAC to America's early-warning network. One officer had a SPINTCOM linkup with the North American Aerospace Defense Command in Cheyenne Mountain, Colorado. Others were linked to the National Military Command Center in the Pentagon, the National Operational Intelligence Watch Officers Network, and the White House Situation Room.

When Faisal witnessed the near Russian-to-Russian nuclear exchange from the U.S. listening post in Misawa, Japan, the Americans had fired off a message over the Critical Intelligence Communications Network, or as it was known in the trade, a CRITICOM. The CRITICOM protocols require a message of that ilk to be in the president's hands within ten minutes of transmission. This was a far cry from the ponderous SIGINT procedures used prior to Pearl Harbor, when minutes could have made a real difference.

Understandably, the Americans jealously guarded everything about DEFSMAC. In fact, the NSA and DIA only grudgingly acknowledged its existence. So when two unexpected visitors walked in, they were not greeted with warmth. At the rear of the dimly lit DEFSMAC chamber was a console where the shift supervisor and two deputies monitored the global SIGINT picture. When Gerard and Faisal appeared unannounced, the supervisor dispatched a deputy to find out who the hell they were. The deputy approached and scrutinized Gerard carefully, then said, "You're Fogelson from the crypto branch, aren't you?"

Gerard remained apoplectic, unable to speak, so Faisal thrust himself into the breech. Extending a hand, he put the best possible spin on his Urdu accent and said, "Yes, he is indeed Mr. Fogelson of the cryptologic division. He is escorting me."

The hand was shook mechanically. "And you are?"

"I am Khalid Mousef of the Pakistan Intelligence Service. I will be borrowing some office space upstairs while we negotiate a new SIGINT-sharing treaty between our two governments. I see our joint listening post at Peshawar is displayed on your screen up there."

The deputy was not impressed. "Be that as it may, Mr. . . . ?"

"Mousef."

"Mousef. You are not supposed to enter the Operations Center unless escorted by a DEFSMAC officer." The deputy glared at Gerard. "Mr. Fogelson should know that."

By this point, Gerard appeared embalmed.

"I fear we have intruded. Please forgive our negligence. We will be going." Faisal discreetly took Gerard's arm and led him out into the corridor. Then he hustled Gerard to the nearest men's room and shoved him inside. He checked the stalls to ensure they were alone, then turned and slapped Gerard with all the strength he could muster. The thick spectacles went flying as Gerard reeled back against the lavatory. Faisal seized him by the lapels and shook him violently. "Now listen, you bloody fool! Get a grip on yourself! Whether you like it or not you are in this mole hunt up to your *neck*. Another stupid-fool mistake like that and this operation is blown. Now pick up your glasses and let's get out of here."

A hyperventilating Gerard fumbled on the floor to retrieve his spectacles, then they left and took a lift to the third floor of the DEFSMAC building, where a number of administrative offices were housed. Gerard led Faisal down the corridor to a reception office where a middle-aged secretary (indistinguishable from the others at Meade) was primly typing a document. Gerard paused at the door. "Uh, Mrs. Gregg, this is Mr. . . . Mousef. He will be, uh, using Mr. Penwane's office down the hall while he—Mr. Penwane, I mean—is on medical leave."

Mrs. Gregg nodded. "Pleased to meet you Mr. . . . ah?"

"Mousef."

"Yes, Mr. Mousef. Please let me know if I can be of any assistance."

"Thank you, I will."

A trembling Gerard led Faisal down the hall to a small cubicle office with a metal desk and a computer terminal. They closed the door as Gerard looked near the point of a stroke. "You didn't have to do that," he said finally.

"Do what?"

"Hit me."

"We don't have time for the luxury of remorse, Gerard. Now what's the drill here?"

Gerard swallowed. "This is the office of Henry Penwane. He is the crypto division's liaison with DEFSMAC. He doesn't do much, though. He's only here because Marshall doesn't like him very much."

"Marshall doesn't like anybody very much."

Gerard swallowed again. "Penwane is on medical leave. Gallbladder. You can log on to the Paradox computer on this terminal." With a shaking hand, Gerard pulled out a sheet of paper from his pocket. "I've written out the log on procedures and given you an access code for the Paradox."

Faisal took the sheet and scanned it. "I will need a lot of time on the Paradox."

"I know. That's why I gave you Marshall's access code."

Faisal's face betrayed the trace of a smile. "Why, Gerard. I didn't know you had such—what's the Yiddish term?—*chutzpah*?"

That did nothing to relieve Gerard's angst level. "No one from the crypto division ever comes over here, so you should be able to work undisturbed. Just the same, stay out of sight."

"Jamieson was over here."

"I . . . I forgot. He's due for a clearance upgrade. He must have been getting an endorsement from someone here at DEFSMAC."

"Make sure that's the case."

"Okay."

"Discreetly."

"Yeah. Okay. The canteen is on the first floor. Avoid the lunch rush."

"Certainly." Faisal inspected the paper. "Remember to inform me when Marshall returns from his inspection tour. Come collect me at half-past six. The rush hour will be past by then and fewer people will be about."

Gerard hesitated. "But my daughter has a ballet lesson at six. I have to drive her."

"Half-past six, Gerard. I will see you then."

In the relentless progression of computer science there have been a number of watershed events that have propelled the technology to a higher plane: Alan Turing's paper on the *Entscheidungsproblem*, which outlined the conceptual framework for the computer; the transistors of Bardeen, Brattain, and Shockley; the first genuine computer, called ENIAC; the integrated circuit; Seymour Cray's supercomputer; and Steve Wozniak's Apple. The pace of these events was nothing short of breathtaking, and unbeknownst to the taxpayer on the street, the NSA underwrote a healthy portion of this advancement.

Yet the greatest leap forward in computer science took place only recently, when a machine at Fort Meade crashed through a barrier known as the teraflop, which was a *trillion* floating-point operations per *second*.

To understand how the Paradox computer achieved such a breakthrough, think of a corral full of cattle in Wyoming earmarked for shipment to Omaha. The wrangler has to herd them through a single cattle chute and ramp them up to the railway cars. It is a slow and laborious process because there is only one chute for the cattle to pass through. This same "cattle chute" principle can be applied to conventional computers, in that data can only be crunched through a single microchip processor. In short, like a cattle chute, the data can only flow through a single path. Even supercomputers were hobbled by this fundamental limitation. So what to do?

Enter parallel processing. Think of that same corral, but this time with a dozen cattle chutes leading into the rail cars. The corral is emptied twelve times as fast, and this same principle applies to parallel computers.

Fort Meade had long been on the cutting edge of computer technology, so it was a natural home for the first teraflop computer. Built by Thinking Machines Corporation of Cambridge, Massachusetts, the Paradox computer occupied a gymnasium-sized chamber under the new Research and Engineering building. Its sleek, modular design of black boxes with flashing red lights was imposing, but that was just the veneer. Inside the boxes was a system that cobbled together not a dozen "cattle chute" processors, or even a hundred. No, the Paradox computer used sixteen *thousand* processors that could crunch numbers at a speed approaching two teraflops, or 2 trillion floating-point operations per second.

That's a lot.

Yet processors alone do not a system make. What coaxed the Paradox to sing was its extraordinary software and a linkup with a state-of-the-art, high-speed memory bank.

It went without saying that a cryptanalyst would sell his wife, sell his children, take a lien on his soul, to possess time on the Paradox machine. It could attack the most impregnable ciphers with massive computing power that was often described as "brute force."

Faisal had been hammering away at the Black Cipher with the brute force of the Paradox computer for seven days, and his stay at DEFSMAC had evolved into a routine. With his purple pass he no longer needed Fogelson to escort him about, so he parked his car in the DEFSMAC lot, arriving early and leaving late. He'd been working nonstop, inhaling coffee and cigarette smoke, as he slowly and painstakingly reconstructed his elegant algorithm to break the elusive encryption. Bit by bit it came back to him, like a sculptor's masterpiece emerging from a block of marble. When he finally had it reconstituted, he began using the Paradox for an attack against the keys. The messages from Petropavlovsk, Samarkand, and Aykhal that he'd obtained from Misawa, Pine Gap, and Ascension Island were being probed more than a trillion times a second now. Surely they must yield to the awesome confluence of his skills and the Paradox machine. It was just a matter of time. Fortunately his presence had remained undiscovered. He leaned back in his chair, fired up another Marlboro, and puffed away. The screen flashed but one word: WORKING. All he could do now was wait.

"Damn those sons-a-bitches to hell! Fogelson! Get in here!"
Gerard Fogelson's palms went clammy as the voice of Marshall Fitzroy seared through him like a jolt of lightning. Trembling, he rose from his chair and ventured into the hallway of the OPS 2-A building. As deputy for administration of the cryptologic division, Gerard's office was adjacent to Marshall Fitzroy's, and Marshall had obviously returned from his tour of the field stations. Having worked under Fitzroy for seventeen years, Gerard knew when his superior had stepped onto the warpath. Now was such a time. With trepidation he entered Fitzroy's domain.

The screen flashed up with the Cyrillic letters of the Petropavlovsk message, and Faisal almost howled with excitement. On the desk he had a printout of the 417 lines of programming code that comprised his algorithm. He flipped through it and examined the source code relating to the key search for the Black Cipher. He scribbled some corrections, then called up the algorithm on the screen and made some adjustments. Then he keystroked in the new coding and hit RUN.

Marshall Fitzroy was fifty-eight years old, and his wiry torso seemed melded to his chrome-plated wheelchair. His face bore a striking resemblance to that of a leopard shark's, but without the charm—and a mouthful of ghastly dental work had earned him the sobriquet of Jaws.

Jaws was probably the only person on planet Earth who could give Faisal Shaikh a run for his money in the field of cryptanalysis. And while some geniuses wore their brilliance on their sleeve, Jaws swung his around like an electric cattle prod, unmercifully zapping anyone who came within reach. From sunup to sundown his staff cowered under this brutal treatment, and they learned quickly his temper had three settings: cantankerous, blind rage, and warpath.

Gerard Fogelson knew this was the warpath as Jaws railed, "Goddamned Limeys! Goddamned Limeys! God*damned* Limeys! If I've said it once I've said it a thousand times, we should have let Hitler bury the stuck-up bastards when he had the chance!"

As Jaws pounded the desk, Gerard swallowed. "Some, ah, something wrong, Chief?"

"Sit down!"

Gerard obeyed as Jaws bared two rows of hideously serrated teeth. "Get a message off to all field stations right away!"

"Sure, sure, Chief," Gerard stammered as he pushed his glasses back up on his nose. "What kind of message, Chief?"

Jaws wheeled around from behind his desk and started rolling back and forth over the open area of his office. It was his way of pacing. He stopped abruptly and wheeled to face Gerard. "Goddamned Limeys! You can't trust them farther than you can throw a grand piano!" His body vibrated as his fists flailed the arms of his wheelchair.

During his Cold War career, Jaws liked the Soviets only slightly less than he liked the British; and he was convinced throughout his professional life that if you ever sent a message to that fag-pinko-infested swill pit called London, you might as well send a copy to Moscow so it wouldn't be garbled in transmission. (Jaws, of course, turned a blind eye to America's failures in these areas.)

"Goddamned Limeys!"

"Uh, what seems to be the trouble, Chief?"

Jaws began wheeling again. "The Limeys got a loose cannon rolling around and want us to help them. We shouldn't give them the time of day; but if we don't, those baboons upstairs will come downstairs and piss all over our legs."

"Exactly what is the problem, Chief?"

Jaws snorted. "I was at Menwith Hill showing the flag when I get a message from that tuba Mittleditch to drop everything and come to Cheltenham. Has to see me at once. I go into his office, and Mittleditch—what a lard ass—is sitting there with some idiot named Stoneleak."

"Stoneleigh. Graeme Stoneleigh. He was named deputy director of GCHQ last month."

Jaws waved his hand. "Who gives a crap! The man's an idiot. Anyway, this tuba Mittleditch has a corncob shoved straight up his ass like all the Limeys do, and he tells me that Faisal Shaikh— *Faisal Shaikh* mind you—has gone off his rocker. Or gone into business for himself, or some such crap. Says he showed up on Ascension Island and fed some cockamamy story to the Brit in charge there about some mole being on the loose in Chelten-ham . . ."

For Gerard Fogelson, the room took on a surreal dimension as the words from Jaws' mouth slammed into him like one haymaker after another. His body seemed suspended in the air as the room began to spin round and round in a vortex that consumed his senses. The floor opened up like the jaws of a sinister shark seeking to devour his body, his career, his life. His balance gone, the cham-ber a blur, Gerard slid off the chair and onto the floor, lying there in the fetal position as he whimpered like a sobbing child.

" . . . I never trusted that Shaikh anyway. That son-of-a-bitch was always too damned smooth for . . . " Jaws heard the whimper and wheeled around, finding his aide prostrate on the floor. "Fogelson! What the hell's the matter with you! You need a doctor?"

There was another whimper. Indecipherable.

"What!? Speak up, man! I can't hear you."

A whisper. "I said, he's here."

"He's here? Whaddya mean he's here? Who's here?"

A sob. "Shaikh."

"Shaikh!?"

The original Aykhal messages recounting the missile-silo accident flashed up on the screen and rekindled the euphoria within Faisal. He called up the algorithm again to identify which key setting broke the encryption, then he noted the setting and compared it to the key setting of the Petropavlovsk messages. He readjusted the algorithm to narrow the search parameters and keystroked the RUN button again to attack the remaining ciphers.

It was all downhill now.

Nobody knew how Marshall Fitzroy came to be in a wheelchair. Nobody had nerve enough to ask. But while his legs hung lifeless off the chair, his torso possessed the steely strength of a gymnast.

Gerard Fogelson was on his knees, as if in fealty, as Jaws clutched the lapels of his jacket with sinewy fingers. Jaws brought his menacing face to within two and a quarter inches of Fogelson's and spoke with the low, molten breath of a primeval dragon. "You worthless tub of slime, what have you *done*!? Tell me everything. *Now!*"

Gerard began hyperventilating and couldn't speak, so Jaws shook him violently. "Spit it out!"

A stem of Gerard's spectacles was shaken askew as he stammered. "Shaikh . . . he . . . he came to my house."

Jaws shook him again. "And then what?"

"He . . . he said there was another mole at GCHQ. Like Prime.

But to catch him he . . . he needed to use the Paradox computer. Away from Cheltenham."

"And you let him *waltz* in here? Just like that?"

Gerard swallowed. "He, he gave me a letter. From Mittleditch. It was an authorization. I have it in my files."

Jaws pulled him even closer. "You think just because it's on paper it's okay? You stupid, stupid oaf! You'd bury your own grandmother alive if somebody handed you a death certificate. Why didn't you call me immediately?"

Gerard had cotton mouth and couldn't speak.

Jaws shook him again.

"Shaikh said that . . . that . . . "

"*What!?*"

"He said you were a mole suspect, too."

"*Me!?*"

Jaws released Gerard and he fell to the floor like a sack of doorknobs. "And I bet you wait beside the chimney every Christmas Eve!" He wheeled his chair forward and rammed into Gerard's supine form, eliciting a howl; but Jaws paid no mind to his subordinate's scream. "Now listen to me, you stupid schmuck! I don't know what Shaikh is up to, but we can't let him get away! Where is he now?"

Gerard nursed his side and moaned, "He's at DEFSMAC."

"DEFSMAC!?" Jaws seethed fire through his hideous teeth and once more rammed his wheelchair into Gerard's flabby torso. "Why didn't you just give him the goddamned keys to the place!?"

Gerard rolled over and struggled to his knees while holding his side. "He's using Penwane's office. He's on medical."

"How did Shaikh plug into the Paradox?"

Gerard sucked in his breath. "I gave him your access number."

"*My* access number!?"

That was too much. Too personal. Jaws went ballistic and seized Gerard by the throat to close off the air supply—but then reason exerted its influence upon his rapier mind. Forget Fogelson. He could be hanged later. Jaws had to apprehend Shaikh. Otherwise, Marshall Fitzroy would be the one dropping through that trapdoor at the end of a rope. He released Gerard, who went down for the mandatory eight-count. Jaws wheeled to his desk and ripped the phone off the cradle. He mashed a red button and growled, "Get me security. We have an intruder."

The Samarkand messages acquired from the Pine Gap tape appeared on the screen. Faisal's heart was racing now, like a hound on the scent. He made the final finetuning adjustments to the algorithm and shifted the search format from the Cyrillic alphabet to the Queen's English. He called up the final Black Cipher epistle from Tehran, set the parameters for the key search, and hit the button marked RUN. The screen flashed again with the terse notation: WORKING . . . WORKING . . . WORKING . . .

Faisal leaned back, both relieved and energized. Success was within his grasp now. He could feel it. He could also feel a call of nature. So as the computer worked on, he got up and crossed the hall to the men's room. After washing up, he exited and happened to see Mrs. Gregg, the secretary from down the hall, standing outside her office door. She looked at him oddly for only a moment, then turned and went back inside. In the recesses of Faisal's mind distant alarm bells began their faint peal, like the barely audible rush of an approaching waterfall. Something told Faisal to paddle his canoe toward shore or he would plunge over the precipice. Obeying his instincts, Faisal walked swiftly down the carpeted passageway, halting just outside Mrs. Gregg's door. The words were hushed, but audible and distinct. "Yes . . . yes, he's still here. . . . Yes, I'll wait for the guards. . . . Do you think he's dangerous? I don't want to stay here if you think he's dangerous."

The alarm bells were clanging now, and Faisal was seized by the onrush of fear. He knew he had to move—move without hesitation. He raced back to his office, his heart pounding like a locomotive. The waterfall was rushing toward him now, and he had no paddle. He had to leap from the canoe and swim for shore. He looked at the screen and it continued to flash its interminable: WORKING . . . WORKING . . . WORKING. So close. But it might as well be on the moon. Faisal sucked in air. He had but minutes, perhaps only seconds, to flee. He grabbed the algorithm printout, folded it up, and stuck it in his belt behind his back. Then he pulled on his jacket and grabbed the Black Cipher hard copy. He looked at the computer screen one last time, but all it would say was WORKING . . . WORKING . . . WORKING. It was with overwhelming anguish that Faisal tore his eyes away and raced to the bank of elevators—just as the plaintext flashed on the screen.

Standing impotently at the lift, he hammered the button, pleading, "Come on, come on." Finally a lift arrived and he leapt inside. He hit the lobby button and the doors slid closed, just as a neighboring elevator opened and two muscular guards of the Federal Protective Service emerged.

Faisal's lift arrived on the ground floor of the DEFSMAC building and he went directly to the gatehouse entry station. The guard smiled as Faisal pretended to enter his plastic card into the hooded reader for the exit procedure.

"How 'bout those Skins?"

Faisal didn't comprehend. "I beg your pardon?"

"I said, how about those Redskins?"

"Oh, yes . . . uh, what about them?" asked Faisal as he sauntered casually past.

"They really put it to the Vikings, didn't they? Forty-three to seven."

"An outstanding achievement, I must say. Well, I'm off for a spot of lunch."

"Have a good one."

Faisal walked down the steps and strode quickly across the parking lot to his hired Taurus. He climbed in, started the engine, and pulled out toward the guard-hut exit. As he approached the gate, he heard the *woooo! woooo! woooo!* of a siren coming from the DEFS-MAC gatehouse. Faisal whizzed through the gate, catching a glimpse of the guard talking on the phone behind the bulletproof glass. He drove down the access lane to the main thoroughfare, and as he wheeled onto the main road, he saw the guard in the rearview mirror, standing in the roadway and staring intently at the back end of the Taurus.

For Faisal, in the grips of distilled fear, the pastoral scene of Fort Meade looked unearthly as he floored the Taurus. Then he remembered the military police were manic about speeders, so he throttled down. It was maddeningly slow as he glided through the post and then onto the Baltimore-Washington Parkway toward Baltimore. He floored it again, but reined himself in at 65 mph as he quivered like a loose fan belt. He'd blown it. He'd been so close, but now he was a man on the run. A fugitive. And he had to run fast—very fast. He knew at this moment police forces were being alerted. The guard had seen the Taurus. Gotten the plate number, surely. He had to ditch the car. Quickly.

He thought about the airport, but figured that would be the first place they'd look, so he drove toward downtown Baltimore, bucking against the noon-hour traffic. Get rid of the car. That was the absolute priority. Two blocks back in the rearview mirror he spotted a bus coming up from behind. He wheeled into an empty parking space curbside to the Baltimore Inner Harbor. The historic trimasted warship *Constellation* was anchored nearby, reeling in tourists, but Faisal failed to notice. He was fixated on the damned bus, which seemed to take forever getting there. At last it pulled up and the doors slapped open. He was behind an elderly lady with a cane, and although he was on the lam, Faisal couldn't shake his inbred tendencies as an English gentleman. He helped the woman struggle up the steps, and as she fumbled for her change, Faisal saw a police car go past the bus in the opposite direction. Then it wheeled around in a U-turn. Faisal dropped a handful of coins in the slot, then walked rapidly to the back of the bus and peered out the rear window. The police car halted behind the Taurus. One officer got out and approached it as his partner jabbered on the police radio.

Faisal quickly turned and sat down as the bus pulled away, his every cell limp with fear.

CHAPTER ✛ TWENTY·FOUR

Faisal entered the Belgravian mansion with the coiled tension of a cat burglar on a desperate heist. He was exhausted, brittle, afraid, and had nowhere else to hide. His home back in Cheltenham was certainly crawling with security people by now. He walked into the living room, half-expecting to find a Special Branch detective with sidearm drawn. But the parlor, like the rest of the house, was empty. Even the servants were away. Faisal fitfully went from chair to sofa to piano, touching each piece of furniture to assure himself he'd arrived at a safe harbor.

Back in Baltimore, Faisal had ridden the bus into downtown, then found a public phone and looked in the yellow pages under AUTOMOBILE RENTAL. He hailed a cab and rode to a Hertz office where he plunked down his international driver's license and Diners Club card. After a few tense moments the card was electronically approved, but Faisal couldn't imagine the dragnet was yet wide enough to flag a credit card imprint. He was given a Thunderbird, which he drove straightaway to the rather downmarket Holiday Inn where he'd been staying. He collected his things and checked out, paying cash so his credit card would not be used.

From there he drove nonstop across Maryland and Pennsylvania, then over the tail end of New York State and into Toronto.

The Canadian border guard only glanced at his British passport before waving him through. He parked the car in the airport lot, leaving the keys in the visor. It would find its way back to Hertz eventually, he reckoned. At the airport he exchanged American dollars for Canadian at the currency kiosk, then went immediately to the ticket counters to check schedules. Using his Eurocard he bought tickets from Toronto to Dallas on American Airlines, to Los Angeles on Air Canada, and to Tokyo on Japan Airlines. Then he walked up to the Aer Lingus counter and paid cash for a first-class seat to Dublin. He had to show his passport to obtain the ticket, but he hoped the credit-card charges would throw up a smoke-screen to divert the Royal Canadian Mounties long enough for him to make an escape.

The trip across the Atlantic was horrendous. At least it seemed so. The plane was buffeted by storms much of the way. Faisal could only sleep in snatches, and a snoring Irishman in the next seat made matters worse. He arrived in Dublin exhausted, but forced himself to press on. Every minute counted now. He knew about the long reach of the security services—knew what they were capable of. Passport control in Dublin was no problem and he whizzed through, but the minefield lay in front of him. He hired another car, a Renault this time, and struck out north. He reached the border crossing at Pettigo and faced his moment of truth. He'd selected this venue to cross into the U.K. in the hope that this remote outpost on the Irish frontier had not yet been alerted that a manhunt was under way.

Two Scots Guards soldiers with SA-80s at the ready approached his car at the crossing. His British passport was inspected, and since he did not look like an Irish rogue, his passport number was merely recorded and the Guards waved him through. The number would eventually percolate up to Special Branch, but that would take some time.

He bore ahead for the ferry terminal at Larne where he ditched the car and climbed on board the vessel for the trip to Stranraer, sighing with relief that all the passport checks were behind him.

At Stranraer he boarded a train and slept in fits between changes for London. When the train finally put in at Waterloo station, Faisal was near the end of his tether. The cab ride to Belgravia seemed to take forever before the cabbie finally dropped him off outside the empty mansion.

Exhaustion, nerves, and fear made him jumpy as a frog on a hot rock. He stank and was in need of a shower. Thinking the hot rush of water might be a salve for his skittishness, he was starting for the stairs when the front door opened. Faisal's heart ceased beating for a moment, then it restarted with breakneck rapidity. Soft footsteps came down the foyer until Barney Slickman appeared at the parlor entry, wearing a warm-up suit and toweling off his sweaty forehead.

"Why, hullo, squire! Haven't seen you since you left for the funeral of that old don of yours." His tanned features creased in a smile. "Just got back myself only two days ago from my charter on the *Sea Crest*. Had an absolute sweet time. Sun, swimming, sex—the lot. Those rich tarts are beyond the fringe, I must say. Yacht swapping, they call it. Decided to take a cure and transformed myself into a health nut. Pumped iron by day and tarts at night. Turned myself into a lean, mean sex machine. Became the rage along the Côte d'Azur, I'm told. Snagged the *Sea Crest* for another month and head out tomorrow for another go. Who knows, I may buy the bugger. Go into business for myself . . . " Barney took a closer look at Faisal's unshaven face and rumpled clothes, then ceased his babble. Cocking an eyebrow, he said, "If you don't mind my saying so, squire, you look a sight." Barney stepped to the wet bar that was built into the parlor wall. "What say you join me in a spot of refreshment? How about a glass of Evian? Perrier? Vichy water? I know, why not walk on the wild side and have a lemon squash?"

Faisal inhaled deeply, then said, "A Scotch, and make it a bloody double."

Barney froze for a moment, not sure he'd heard correctly, then Faisal prompted him by saying, "Pour it, man, pour it."

Still in shock, Barney mumbled, "Whatever you say, squire." He slopped two jiggers of Glenfiddich into a tumbler and handed it to Faisal, who clutched it between his hands and tossed it down in three gulps. As the forbidden liquid burned down to his stomach, he passed the empty glass back to Barney and said, "Another."

Barney stared at the empty tumbler, not comprehending. "I, uh, thought you didn't partake of the, ah, firewater?"

"Allah is forgiving beyond our comprehension, Barney. Now pour."

Barney shrugged, then poured a second round. Faisal drank greedily again, then wiped his mouth with the back of his hand.

"All right, squire. What's the score here? We be in trouble or something?"

Faisal clutched the tumbler. "Not we. . . . Me."

"You? The Duke of Caution. How so?"

Faisal didn't answer at once. Instead he began pacing, going back and forth across the room until he stopped abruptly and fixed his stare on Barney. "From your contacts in Paris, do you know someone who can whip up a fake passport? Say, Egyptian or Pakistani? One that would fool any border guard?"

Barney blinked a few times. "You mean, a forger?"

"Exactly."

"Well, sure, squire. That's no problem. Maximillian on the Left Bank does the best work on the Continent. Canadian immigration papers, Swiss stock certificates, the Magna Carta, you name it. Old Max can do it all."

"And a visa?"

Barney shrugged. "Like I said, no problem. For the money Max can handle it. Say you want a visa? I take it you're going on another voyage. Where to this time?"

Again, Faisal didn't answer at once. His mind was racing through a maze—twisting, turning, searching desperately for a way out. With the long tentacles of the state reaching for him, Faisal knew he had but one avenue left open. One bullet left in the chamber. One card left to play.

To escape the dark hole of Brixton Prison, or perhaps a nameless assassin, Faisal knew he must break the Black Cipher to hell and gone. To do that he required massive computing power. It was that simple—and that difficult. Since the doors of Cheltenham and Fort Meade were welded tightly shut, there was only one place left on earth where that kind of computing power could be had.

And that was in Moscow.

CHAPTER TWENTY FIVE

T he black Chaika sedan mushed along Moscow's outer ring road, squishing through puddles left by the early snowfall. Faisal looked to his right and saw flashes of incandescent light stabbing through the veil of birch trees; and when a large gap in the woods appeared, the Chaika wheeled off the main motorway and onto an access road. The vehicle pulled up to an electronically-controlled gate and stopped, where it was scrutinized by unseen men in a guardhouse off the road. Then the gate opened and the Chaika pulled into the three-hundred-acre, campuslike compound of Yasenevo, home of the Russian Foreign Intelligence Service— or, as it was formerly known, the First Chief Directorate of the KGB.

Barney Slickman had ferried Faisal across the Channel in the *Sea Crest*, and under cover of darkness they rowed the yacht's skiff onto the beach near Arromanches. Faisal bade Barney farewell and walked into the village where he caught a morning bus to Bayeux. There he boarded the train to Paris.

Using Barney as a reference, he'd found Maximillian the forger on the Left Bank, and for an exorbitant fee Max had prepared a superb Egyptian passport and a Russian entry visa. With the new documents, Faisal became Fouad Tajouri and boarded an Aeroflot plane for Moscow.

Once ensconced in the Metropol Hotel, he wrote a brief note on the hotel stationery, then made some discreet inquiries through the bell captain. A short time later a well-muscled "contractor" body-guard knocked on his door. The thug might as well have carried a neon sign that read: FORMER KGB AND UNEMPLOYED, but he was just what the doctor ordered. Faisal asked him if he could deliver a letter to the reception desk at the old KGB headquarters at 2 Dzerzhinsky Square.

"*Nyet* problem," came the reply.

Faisal gave him the letter and a hundred-dollar bill.

It wasn't long before a message was slipped under Faisal's door, saying a car would call for him at nineteen hundred hours.

The architecture of the Yasenevo compound was of modern design, dominated by a twenty-one-story structure and a sepa-rate low building that was shaped like a boomerang. The Chaika pulled up to the floodlit entrance in the crook of the boomerang where a muscle-bound gentleman—a hammer thrower, Faisal guessed—opened the door and said, in English, "Follow me, please." Faisal did so and they walked through the marble foyer and into the lift. They exited on the fourth floor where he was led down a carpeted hallway. Since it was eve-ning, only one or two offices had lights on, and a cleaning crew was at work. The hammer thrower took him into a reception room where he was greeted by a baby-faced aide wearing a ci-vilian suit and a half-smile. "Dr. Shaikh, welcome to Yasenevo. Let me take your coat. That will be all, Illyanov." The coat was placed on a rack and the hammer thrower retired. The aide picked up one of three white telephones on his desk and mut-tered into it, then he hung up and opened the inner door, say-ing, "The general will see you now."

Faisal self-consciously straightened his tie, offered a silent prayer to Allah, and entered.

He was a tall man, undoubtedly an athlete in his youth, for he moved with graceful precision as he rose from behind the mahog-any desk and buttoned his double-breasted suit. The hair that framed his classic Slav face was dark and flecked with gray. Faisal was rarely intimidated by taller men, but he was by this one. Not because of the Russian's height, but by his measure; for this was a man accustomed to command.

"Dr. Shaikh, I am honored to meet you." A hand was extended as he spoke in perfect English. "It isn't often I have the opportunity to visit with the chief cryptanalyst of Government Communications Headquarters."

Faisal shook the offered hand and replied, in perfect Russian, *"Former* chief cryptanalyst. It was good of you to see me, General, but I must confess I was surprised you brought me to Yasenevo. It was my understanding the KGB's Sixteenth Directorate still maintained its headquarters at Dzerzhinsky Square."

The general pursed his lips. "We are now the Federal Agency for Government Communications and Information, and, yes, our headquarters are still in Moscow, but I maintain an office here. For a meeting such as this, it is more private. The Centre is a rather grim place these days, with all kinds of people in and out. But please, sit down. I understand you prefer tea."

"Tea would be fine."

The general sat back down in his leather chair and picked up one of six phones on his desk—apparently a status symbol instead of a single phone with multiple lines. As tea was served by the baby-faced aide, Faisal inspected the general more closely. The lines in the face were deep and the eyes a bit puffy from too many cigarettes, and Faisal noticed two packs of American Chesterfields on the desk. The suit was tailored, probably Italian, and the tie definitely an Armani. After the aide withdrew, the general offered a Chesterfield to Faisal, then fired up his own.

After a long, deep drag the general exhaled and said, "So, Faisal Shaikh. Doctorate in mathematics from the University of Edinburgh. Onetime 'cultural attaché' to the British embassy in Moscow. Deputy liaison officer to the American National Security Agency. Chief cryptanalyst and head of H Division at Cheltenham, as well as a grand master of chess with a penchant for American tobacco."

"Actually, my preference is for a Turkish tobacco blended in Latakia, Syria."

The general smiled. "Forgive me. I must have your dossier revised. We pride ourselves on being precise."

"Under the circumstances, however, an American cigarette is most welcome." Faisal lit up the Chesterfield with a matchbook from the Metropol Hotel and said, in Russian, "Lieutenant General Piotr Aleksandrovich Romanenko. Born April thirtieth, 1952, in Volgograd. Doctorate in technical sciences from Moscow University. Joined the KGB out of university and vetted to the Sixteenth Directorate. Son of a KGB colonel, progressed rapidly through the signals-intelligence ranks. Politically helped by father but own abilities carried you further. Youngest KGB lieutenant general on record. Deputy KGB *rezident* for SIGINT at Ottawa embassy, then Washington. Second-in-command of the Sixteenth Directorate during the coup against Gorbachev. Threw your support to Yeltsin during the coup and rewarded with top post when Yeltsin became Russian president."

Romanenko shrugged. "My father was disappointed in my backing Yeltsin, but there it is. He does not understand all the changes taking place in his country . . . not that I do."

"I can empathize."

It was a strange verbal exchange. The Russian speaking in English, the Englishman in Russian. Both men were polite to a fault, but neither was willing to show weakness by crossing over to his native language.

"So what can I do for the former chief cryptanalyst of Her Majesty's Government Communications Headquarters? Unfortunately, your dossier sheds no light on your departure from Cheltenham. Do you wish to defect? Defections are becoming an anachronism, but for the chief cryptanalyst of GCHQ I might be able to arrange something. Perhaps even lucrative."

"Defection is not my motive. I am here to make an unusual request."

Romanenko shrugged. "Be my guest."

Now it was Faisal's turn to take a long, deep drag on a Chesterfield. He puffed, then said, "I would like for you to make the computer facilities at your research center in Kuntsevo available to me, along with the required technical staff, in order that I may attack a cryptologic problem."

Romanenko's Slavic features hardened rather quickly, causing Faisal's palms to become damp. "And why should I do that?"

"Because I can prove that someone in the Russian Ministry of Defense was a conspirator in the assassination of Prince Ibrahim last December in London."

The Slavic face froze. "Prince Ibrahim? The Saudi foreign minister?"

"Yes."

"Killed by that terrible bomb?"

Faisal nodded. "Killed by that terrible fuel-air land mine of Russian manufacture, code-named Cloudburst."

Romanenko's mouth went dry and he gulped some tea. Had anyone else brought him this outlandish story he would have dismissed it as the ravings of a lunatic. But the source, this man Faisal Shaikh, carried extraordinary credibility. Romanenko knew that in Western crypto circles Shaikh's reputation was nothing short of legend. He could not be ignored. "Please continue."

Faisal sighed and said, in English, "You had best open another pack of Chesterfields, General. I have quite a story to tell you."

Faisal was betting that the Russian (née Soviet) spy machine was as byzantine as it was massive. It was a safe bet, for the channels of authority for the old KGB and the GRU (military intelligence) were so jumbled and cross-referenced that they resembled a tangled fisherman's line, and signals intelligence was not immune. Just as the American FBI was separate and distinct from the CIA, under the old Soviet regime SIGINT resources were split into two camps, each one serving different masters and pursuing different agenda. One was the Sixteenth Directorate of the KGB, which served the political hierarchy within the Communist Party and the Politburo. The other was the Radio-Technical Intelligence Directorate of the GRU, which was (and still is) the SIGINT arm of the Russian military machine. These two organizations were (and are) so huge and so ponderous that duplication of effort was the order of the day, and quite often the right hand did not know what the left hand was doing. As the new Russia limped along the path of reform, this messy state of SIGINT affairs had grown even more ill-defined, and Faisal was banking on this trend. Indeed, he was betting the lot.

General Romanenko stubbed out his Chesterfield as he contemplated the incredible story Faisal had told him. "So the messages concerning the silo accident at the rocket base in Aykhal, the bar fight at the Petropavlovsk naval base, and the near use of chemical weapons at the Samarkand Army base—they were all transmitted on this Black Cipher encryption machine? As were the responses by the Ministry of Defense in Moscow?"

"That is correct," said Faisal. "And since the Radio-Technical Directorate of the GRU supplies the military with encryption equipment, I can only conclude that someone within the Russian military worked hand in glove with Musa Kousa and the Irish Republican Army. They were provided with the Cloudburst bomb and the Black Cipher encryption machine to keep their communications secret. The original message from Tehran confirms it."

Romanenko flipped through the pages of Faisal's algorithm printout. "And you managed to obtain this from Fort Meade through *maskirovka?*"

"By deception? Yes."

Romanenko shook his head and muttered, "Unbelievable."

Faisal felt a pang of fear. Did Romanenko mean Faisal was not to be believed? Or just that the situation was beyond belief? The difference in nuance was only slight, but critical. Faisal cleared his throat and asked, "So then, General, will you help me?"

Romanenko didn't answer at first. He dropped the printout on the desk, then rose and stepped to the window. Absently, he contemplated the darkened woods of the Yasenevo compound, and he seemed so detached that Faisal tried to prod him. "I take it you had no knowledge of the GRU's new Black Cipher encryption machine?"

Romanenko replied with a grunt. "The only time I talk with my 'colleagues' in the GRU nowadays is when we are fighting each other for budget funds. Even in the old days we didn't care for each other much. Now the funds are drying up, and my contact with the GRU has grown increasingly acrimonious."

"So they could have deployed this Black Cipher machine without your knowledge?"

"In the old days, certainly not. Now, they certainly could . . . and apparently they did." Romanenko's shoulders sagged, as if he were in mourning. "My country has gone through so much upheaval these past few years. Enough for ten lifetimes. The military, the economy, the KGB, everything has fallen asunder. Crime everywhere. Seems the church and the Mafia are all that's holding the Motherland together these days. Anything is for sale, and I mean *anything*. Two weeks ago we barely stopped a nuclear warhead before it crossed the border into Iran. The commander of a nuclear depot outside Kharkov had gone into business for himself. So I would have to say, yes, a little thing like an encryption machine could certainly make its way to Tehran without my knowledge." Romanenko sighed. "And now this. The murder of a Saudi diplomat and innocent civilians with a Russian bomb. It appears my 'colleagues' at the GRU have blood on their hands." He turned to Faisal. "And for what reason? Why on earth would elements of the GRU, Musa Kousa, and the IRA conspire with the director of GCHQ—this Vivian Mittleditch—to murder a Saudi diplomat?"

Now it was Faisal's turn to sigh. "I simply do not know, General. All I can hope is that this second message from Tehran will shed some light on the assassination of Prince Ibrahim—and the conspiracy behind it. Will you help me decipher it?"

Romanenko returned his gaze to the window. A few moments passed, then he said, almost offhand, "What, exactly, would you require?"

Faisal felt the rush of relief and was quick to respond. "I would need access to the computer facilities at your research center at Kuntsevo, plus assistance from your technical staff to convert my algorithm into compatible programming language that will run on your computers."

"Umm, that could take some time."

"Exactly. That is why I will need a message and travel documents hand-delivered by diplomatic courier to a colleague of mine.

A British subject whom I wish to bring to Moscow. He can work with your people to expedite the conversion process."

Romanenko raised an eyebrow. "And where will this person be coming from?"

Faisal extinguished the Chesterfield. "From Buenos Aires, Argentina."

The Chaika sedan pulled up to the guard hut and the uniformed man inspected the two visitors in the backseat. That done, he waved them through.

"Crikey," whispered Jamie Burdick. "Never, *ever*, did I think I'd wind up inside this place."

"Nor I," said Faisal.

The Chaika cruised through the campus of the Kuntsevo research center, passing a number of low-rise office buildings along the way. Kuntsevo was analogous to the Americans' Research and Engineering facility at Fort Meade, and it was here some of the finest technical minds on Russian soil explored the upper reaches of computer science, cryptanalysis, and the nature of radio waves. Kuntsevo was under the jurisdiction of the Russian Federal Agency for Government Communications and Information, while the GRU maintained a separate facility in Moscow known as the Central Scientific Research Institute.

The Chaika pulled up to the entrance of one of the buildings, and the driver led them through what seemed a labyrinth until they entered a small conference room. There they found a small table, chairs, a computer monitor, and a lean, spidery-looking man wearing a white laboratory coat. The spider bowed slightly, then stuck out his hand to Burdick.

"Jamie Burdick, may I present Dr. Boris Armatov, director of computing sciences for the Russian Federal Agency for Government Communications and Information."

"Nice to meet you, Dr. Armatov." Jamie shook the hand, then turned to Faisal. "Now that I'm here, what exactly do you want me to do?"

Faisal opened his briefcase and took out the precious algorithm printout. "Our problem is this, Jamie: here we have my algorithm for the Black Cipher. As I explained to you, it is written in the standard format compatible with our GCHQ/NSA cryptanalytic software—we call it Folklore, Dr. Armatov."

The scientist nodded. "I know."

Although startled by the Russian's response, Faisal continued. "Since you were on the Cheltenham team that developed Folklore, Jamie, I need you to work with Dr. Armatov to convert this algorithm into a format that is compatible with the Russian cryptanalytic hardware and software."

Jamie seemed to brighten up. "Hmm. Now that sounds like a bit of fun. Always wanted to see what kind of toys the other side had."

"I anticipated you'd think so. Dr. Armatov is fluent in English, so you two should get along famously. Now get to work."

"You're not staying?"

Faisal shrugged. "I would only be in the way. I'll meet you for dinner at the hotel."

The waiter cleared away the remnants of the grilled sturgeon as the balalaika orchestra played vigorously from the balcony. It was an incongruous scene, for Faisal and Jamie were alone in the grill room of the massive hotel, save for the orchestra and the dining room staff. Yet the musicians played as if it were a command performance at Covent Garden.

When the music finally faded away and the orchestra took a break, Faisal nursed his Russian tea and examined his onetime protégé. The boyishness had faded, and although it had been less than a year, Jamie had aged, the stress and the unknown having taken their toll.

"So how did you slip out of Buenos Aires?"

"Told the station chief we were taking a holiday. Took the family to Santiago, then caught a plane out from there. Sylvia and Nigel will stay on the beach until I get back. When I return, I'll drop dead from jet lag, no doubt."

"No doubt."

Jamie sipped his Russian beer. "Your letter blew me away, but I should have suspected you'd not allow things to lie fallow."

"More of an accident than anything else. Now I'm a wanted man. Can't say where it will all end. But let's get on with it, shall we?"

Jamie pulled some papers from his briefcase and sketched as he explained. "This is the score. The Russkies have a different slant on parallel processing. Instead of thousands of microchips in one housing to process the data, their KOSMOS computer breaks up the processing and farms it out to a network of computers. Think of it as spokes radiating out of a central hub."

"What is your assessment of their KOSMOS computer?"

Jamie shrugged like an art critic sizing up a painting. "A bit crude, but not bad. Nothing near what the Americans have, of course."

"Of course."

Then Jamie became animated. "But what really drives their system is the software. That Armatov is one shrewd fellow. His software design breaks the task into batches, farms it out to the computer network, then reassembles the end product at the hub. You might say his software for the KOSMOS computer is like putting a jet engine on a carriage."

"I see. So how long will it take you to write the conversion program?"

"Since I'm not reinventing the wheel, just changing a tire, so to speak, I'd say a day. Two at the most. All I have to do is reformat your algorithm. But keep in mind that the Russkies' computer, even with the hyperdrive software, can only attain a tenth of the speed of the Paradox computer."

Faisal shrugged. "As long as General Romanenko gives us his blessing, we should have all the computer time we require."

As the orchestra began filtering back in, Jamie closed up his briefcase and looked at Faisal with troubled eyes. Sensing his protégé had more to say, Faisal asked, "Something else on your mind?"

Jamie nodded. "This is some kind of expedition you're on, Faisal. You've got the whole of England trying to run you to ground. You're a wanted man."

"I'm aware of that."

Jamie swallowed, then continued, "If this long shot of yours doesn't work, you're in a box."

"You think I don't know that?"

"You set foot outside Russia, it's only a matter of time before the security services catch up to you."

"I'm well aware of Her Majesty's very long arm, Jamie."

"Well, what I'm trying to say is that I took a risk in coming here. If you do get caught in the net, I must ask you to leave my name out of it. I've got Sylvia and Nigel to think of."

Faisal stared at his colleague for a few moments, then nodded. "I give you my word, Jamie. If I have to, I'll fall on my sword, but I'll keep your name out of it."

Jamie remained silent for a while, then seemed satisfied and snapped his briefcase closed. "Okay, Faisal. Your word."

"My word."

"Well, then, I best get to work on the conversion program. I'll be up in my room." And he left.

As Faisal watched his colleague's receding figure, he pondered his situation. If caught, he had no doubt it was only a matter of time before the invisible government lurking behind the staid veneer of Whitehall could make him sing like a nightingale. By methods he couldn't begin to guess. He was just grateful his trusted friend had bought the lie.

The musicians struck up for an audience of one.

It was the fourth day since Jamie's arrival and the KOSMOS computer was running nonstop. In the small conference room, the spidery Dr. Armatov, Jamie, and Faisal seemed to be having a contest as to who could fill his ashtray the fastest. The smoke became so dense that Jamie found the little room suffocating, so he left to go outside and pace the snow-covered grounds. Faisal followed.

Once outside on the campus setting, Faisal stopped to watch a deer as she foraged through a thin layer of snow for a few blades of grass.

"I have to leave tomorrow at the very latest," said a tense Jamie. "I hope this journey wasn't for naught."

Faisal cleared his throat. "Me, too."

"You're in the tank if this doesn't work, Faisal."

Faisal tried to keep his shaky voice steady. "We've been over that ground before, haven't we?"

"Faisal! Jamie!"

The Englishmen looked up to see the white-coated Armatov leaning out the third-floor window.

"Da?" yelled Faisal.

"I tink we haff something!"

Lt. Gen. Piotr Aleksandrovich Romanenko, director of the Russian Federal Agency for Government Communications and Information, rubbed his brow as he read the brief message for the eighth time.

TO: **PAGEBOYS**

FROM: **SANDCASTLE**

SEVRUGA FOR MAIDENHEAD WILL ARRIVE LONDON SAFE HOUSE OCTOBER EIGHTEENTH.

MAY THE GHOST OF GUY FAWKES BE WITH YOU ON HIS GLORIOUS DAY.

END MESSAGE

"So you suspect this 'Sandcastle' and the 'Pageboys' are Musa Kousa and the IRA, like in the previous message?"

"It has to be them," replied Faisal. "No question."

Romanenko pulled on his chin. " 'Sevruga' is caviar, of course, but it must be a code word of some kind. And this 'Maidenhead,' do you have any idea what it means?"

Faisal shrugged. "Maidenhead is a town west of London. In Berkshire, I believe. It can also be a reference to the, ah, virginal integrity of a maiden. Beyond that, I haven't a clue. I thought perhaps you could shed some light on it."

Romanenko leaned back in his leather chair and stroked the lapel of his Cellini suit. "I have no idea, offhand. I will run it through our archives and see what I can come up with." He examined the message again. "October eighteenth—that was seven days ago. And Guy Fawkes—wasn't he the man who tried to blow up Parliament?"

"In 1605, yes."

Romanenko studied the ceiling. "Oh, yes, of course. It is coming back to me now. Fawkes and some conspirators tried to blow up James the First, his family, and Parliament. Planted gunpowder under Westminster Palace. The plot failed, though."

"Yes. He and some religious militants wanted to take over the country."

Romanenko pondered the message once again, then pursed his lips and said, "It seems things have not changed much in four centuries."

"Quite."

"When, precisely, is Guy Fawkes Day?"

"November fifth."

"That is only eleven days from now."

"Yes."

Romanenko drummed his fingers on the mahogany desk. "Is Guy Fawkes an allegory? Do you think the IRA intends to blow up Westminster Palace? And Parliament along with it?"

"I'm sure they would like nothing more. But security around Westminster is extraordinary. And the palace is a massive structure. It would require tons upon tons of explosives to inflict significant damage."

Romanenko rose and stepped to the window, obviously brooding. When he spoke, it was like a lamentation. "When you first walked into this office, I thought you must be a plant. Some final attempt by the West of subversion. But everything you told me, I verified, including the fact that Cloudburst is a Russian Army fuelair mine. Based on those verifications I ordered my archival division to conduct a historical search of intercept recordings, and do you know what?"

"No, no, I don't."

"We also intercepted two messages out of Tehran, encrypted in seven-letter code groups. They matched the Black Cipher raw copy you brought with you."

Faisal nodded. "It is reassuring to be believed."

Romanenko's features turned hard, and now he spoke with a vile bitterness. "So I can only embrace your premise that my brethren in the GRU have, in fact, deployed a new encryption device. Further, because of its use in Tehran, I can only agree that elements of the GRU are working in concert with the terrorist Musa Kousa and the Irish Republican Army, and that those elements within the GRU obtained and delivered a Cloudburst fuel-air bomb to the IRA—the one used to assassinate Prince Ibrahim."

"I find no flaw in your analysis," said Faisal as he leaned over and tapped the message. "We know that 'Sandcastle' is Musa Kousa. We know that 'Pageboys' are the IRA. We know that the 'Sevruga' is now in London and will likely be employed on Guy Fawkes Day, November fifth, which is eleven days from now. We don't know what 'Sevruga' means. I would wager it is some sort of munition—a bomb, land mine, what have you—but we don't know for sure. And as for 'Maidenhead,' I am simply at a loss."

The young general pulled on his chin once more. "Perhaps it means Sevruga will be employed at the town of Maidenhead on Guy Fawkes Day?"

"I don't think so. The message says 'for' Maidenhead, not 'at' Maidenhead."

Romanenko sighed. "Well, time is of the essence. I am taking this up with our President. I will have him contact your Prime Minister. She can alert her police forces on Guy Fawkes Day and—"

"You do that, General, and you will win the battle but lose the war."

"I beg your pardon?"

"We are dealing with an unknown dark force in Britain. We know that Sir Vivian Mittleditch and Graeme Stoneleigh of GCHQ are involved, but who else? Surely they are not alone. Who are the other conspirators? Where are they placed within Whitehall? Perhaps they are near the Prime Minister. Perhaps they are within the security services themselves. If your President contacts the Prime Minister and she raises the alarm, you may stop a tragedy on Guy Fawkes Day, but the quarry will go to ground. They'll remain invisible and wait for another time and another place to employ this 'Sevruga,' whatever it is. So, no, raising the alarm will do little good."

Romanenko seemed befuddled. "Well, then, what would you suggest?"

Faisal fell into his séance mode for a few moments, then replied, "We must find out what 'Sevruga' and 'Maidenhead' mean. We can do nothing to flush the quarry until then. Use all of your resources to find out their meaning, and do it quickly."

"But I must bring this to the attention of our President so we can track down the rogue elements within the GRU."

"Very well, but *after* Guy Fawkes Day. Word of your investigation in Russia might get back to the GRU, then back to England, and again, the quarry would go to ground. Your priority should be the code words."

Romanenko grumbled, knowing this mystic of an Englishman was right. "Very well, I will do as you ask." He opened his desk drawer and tossed a small black object to Faisal, who caught it on the fly.

"What's this?"

"A beeper. I will let you know when I have something."

Faisal turned the device over in his hand. "Impressive, General."

"In the Sixteenth Directorate we made our own for years. We plan to market them commercially soon."

The snow crunched under the soles of Faisal's Gucci loafers as he sauntered along the bank of the Moscow River. The wind was sharp with a prickly feeling. Somehow the Russian cold had a sharper sting than England's, and Faisal knew not why. He turned up the collar of his overcoat as pedestrians passed him going the other way, looking uniformly cold, grim, and on the brink of despair. He gazed at the Kremlin across the river and contemplated the absurdity of his situation. Here he was, in the epicenter of his former enemy, trying to unscramble the puzzle of some words on a page. And even if he did solve the puzzle, what then? Would the solution be his ticket back to a safe harbor? A passage back to his homeland? To Razia?

And what of her? How unfeeling and insolent of him to have embarked on this perilous quest without taking her concerns and fears to heart. He'd been a fool. An uncaring fool. He'd put their future in jeopardy and now he was paying the price. All he could hope for was that General Romanenko could pull it off.

The black object in his breast pocket emitted a *beep-beep*. He checked the readout display, then stepped to the curb and waved a ten-dollar bill in the air to hail a cab for Dzerzhinsky Square.

Faisal exited the cab and dodged the Zhiguli sedans as he crossed the street to the roundabout island in front of the old KGB headquarters building at 2 Dzerzhinsky Square. In the middle of the island was an empty pedestal where an imposing statue of Feliks Dzerzhinsky once stood. Dzerzhinsky was the founding father of the Cheka secret police and was held in high regard by Lenin and his Soviet heirs. Now his statue was consigned to a junkyard and Western tourists posed on the empty pedestal to have their pictures snapped in front of the ocher building. Faisal crossed to the sidewalk and entered the structure that had been a locus point for fear and terror for so many years. Once its basement had contained prison cells where the tongues of political prisoners were loosened by ghoulish means. Now it housed a cafeteria. It was an eerie feeling for Faisal as he pushed opened the heavy wooden doors and walked up the steps to the reception area. Two surly uniformed guards eyed him suspiciously as he approached another uniformed man sitting at a desk.

"*Da?*" inquired the guard.

Faisal replied in Russian, "Faisal Shaikh to see General Romanenko. I am expected."

The guard checked a list, then picked up the phone and muttered into it, saying, "A moment."

In no time General Romanenko's baby-faced aide appeared. He was not in civilian clothes as before, but in a retread uniform of the KGB bearing the rank of major. Faisal guessed the new Russian SIGINT agency was making do with what they had.

They exited the lift on the third floor and walked to the end of the corridor where they entered an anteroom. Baby Face motioned him to an easy chair and said, "Please have a seat. The general will be with you in a moment." Then he took his place behind the secretary's desk and began sifting through paperwork. Faisal sat down and was lighting up a Chesterfield when he heard something like a low growl come from behind the closed door of the general's office. Measure by measure, the growl increased in intensity, until muffled shouts could be heard and the door seemed to vibrate like a tympanic membrane. Faisal was befuddled, for there was obviously a bloody row under way, yet Baby Face continued to smile as he shuffled paper. Finally the row reached a crescendo and Faisal feared the door might become unhinged. Were blows about to be struck? Perhaps shots fired? Slowly the noise level tapered off to silence, and the phone on the aide's desk jingled. Baby Face listened, then smiled at Faisal and motioned to the inner office. "You may go in. The general will see you now."

Faisal went to the door and gingerly opened it. Behind a massive desk sat Romanenko—stern, sullen, and in the uniform of a lieutenant general. His face was still flushed red from the shouting match. Faisal glanced over at the living area of the office and saw another man. This one was short, squat, and wearing the uniform of a Russian Army general. While Romanenko carried himself like an aristocrat, Faisal sensed this other general was of peasant stock and mean as a junkyard dog. He was balding, wore spectacles and a mustache, and his face was a deep hue of crimson.

"Dr. Shaikh," said Romanenko, "may I present Colonel General Valery Buskin."

Faisal recognized the name at once. "Valery Buskin? Chief of the GRU's Radio-Technical Directorate?"

"One and the same," replied Romanenko.

Faisal felt off-balance. He had not a clue what was going on. "And why, may I ask, is General Buskin here?"

Romanenko cleared his throat. "Let me explain. The story that you told me was so incredible that it was difficult to believe. Yet from my sphere of contacts within the government, I was able to verify the key points of your testimony. The silo accident in Aykhal, the bar fight in Petropavlovsk, and the food riot in Samarkand—all were confirmed. But the two Black Cipher messages coming out of Tehran—the first portending Prince Ibrahim's assassination, and the second which you deciphered here about Guy Fawkes Day—it was difficult to believe they were part of a conspiracy involving the GRU."

"But they had to be," protested Faisal. "All the Black Cipher messages *had* to come from the same encryption machine."

"My thoughts exactly," replied Romanenko. "But General Buskin and I have known each other for many years. And while there is no love lost between us, I have developed a grudging respect for my counterpart in the GRU." He glanced at the squat man. "I would emphasize the word *grudging.*"

Buskin remained on a low boil.

"I know Valery Buskin is a cantankerous and stubborn man, but above all he is a soldier. He expressed to me on many occasions how he despised terrorists and terrorism. He said they had no honor."

Faisal was still confused.

"Therefore," continued Romanenko, "I decided to confront General Buskin with your evidence and submit your thesis to him. He confirmed that his Radio-Technical Directorate had, indeed, developed a new encryption machine. It is the device which generated the Black Cipher messages from Aykhal, Petropavlovsk, and Samarkand; and it was deployed without my knowledge. As I told you, relations between our two agencies are strained, and quite often the right hand does not know what the left hand is doing."

Faisal nodded.

Romanenko became even more grim. "But as to the Tehran messages . . ."

Here the general hesitated, so Faisal prompted him. "What about them?"

It was General Buskin who nearly spat as he said, "They did not come from our machine!"

"What?"

Buskin fumed. "I said, the messages from Tehran were definitely *not* generated on the new GRU encryption machine."

Faisal almost laughed. "Not your machine? But they *had* to come from the same machine. Any other explanation is statistically impossible."

Romanenko shot Buskin a glance, then sighed. It was time to come clean. "In this case, it is not impossible."

Faisal's mind was racing. "I do not understand. How could identical encryption patterns come from two separate sources?"

Romanenko cleared his throat. "The Black Cipher has a unique format, in that the encryption is expressed in seven-letter code groups. Is that not correct?"

"Yes, that is correct."

"Think, Dr. Shaikh, think. Have you ever seen a seven-letter code format before?"

Faisal was becoming irritated. "I've worked on Soviet encryption systems for twenty years and I've never encountered a seven-letter format before."

"Yes," said Romanenko mournfully. "But I did not necessarily mean a Soviet encryption format. Think. Have you *ever* seen the seven-letter format before? Anywhere?"

Faisal searched through his memory banks. "No, I have never seen a seven-letter format before . . . except for the Swedes, they had a seven-letter format some years ago, as did the Italians . . . and of course there is the . . . " His voice trailed off as the realization imploded on his shoulders like a derailed express train. His knees went slack and he sat down, unable to speak for the dryness in his mouth. Finally he swallowed, then whispered, "Dear God . . . the Bloodstone."

"*Da*. The Bloodstone."

The room was swirling, spinning, throwing Faisal off-balance as his mind raced back to that meeting at Cheltenham—the PM's brief where he'd nailed Graeme Stoneleigh's hide to the wall. He'd broken Stoneleigh's Tempest II encryption machine by deciphering the lewd limerick. Stoneleigh had wanted to deploy the retrofitted Tempest to reap a huge cost saving instead of manufacturing a new-generation encryption machine—the one code-named Bloodstone. The Bloodstone seemed to be impregnable, and it used a format of *seven-letter code groups!* Faisal was almost in physical pain as he whimpered, "How?"

A morose Romanenko replied, "As I said, sometimes the right hand does not know what the left hand is doing. Although the world has changed dramatically over the past few years, General Buskin's GRU still operates a number of, ah, intelligence 'assets' in Britain."

"You mean spies?"

Romanenko shrugged. "Yes, spies. We call them 'illegals.' "

Buskin wheezed.

"General Buskin and I had a heated discussion about this situation just prior to your arrival, but I insisted that you be told. The GRU has an illegal—a spy—in a position that gives him access to technical matters within the British government. That is all I can tell you about him. However, I can tell you in plain language that General Buskin's agent in London was able to obtain the circuit design for your Bloodstone machine, and the GRU used that design for its new generation of encryption machines."

Faisal felt as if the earth had opened up and he was falling into the abyss.

"Further, we know that the Bloodstone machine was prototyped by GCHQ at Cheltenham. Since the GRU's equipment was not used to encrypt the Tehran messages, I can only conclude they were encrypted on one of the Bloodstone prototypes."

Faisal whispered, "I find no flaw in your thinking, General."

"So these people at GCHQ, the director, Mittleditch, and his deputy, Stoneleigh, they must have given Musa Kousa and the IRA some of the Bloodstone prototypes to keep their communications secret, but they did not anticipate two things—that the GRU had deployed a machine with the same circuit design as the Bloodstone, and that Faisal Shaikh could break their Black Ciphers."

Faisal turned on Buskin. "Why, may I ask, did you use the circuit design of the Bloodstone for your own machine?"

Buskin's mustache twitched as he replied, "I concluded that the English would only deploy an encryption machine they themselves found impregnable. Why should I reinvent the wheel? I could save time and money by using your own design and enjoy making fools of you English."

Faisal found himself nodding in agreement. "You are quite right, General Buskin. We and the Americans labored mightily to break the Bloodstone but found it impregnable. It is most ironic that when I was attacking the Black Cipher, I was really attacking the Bloodstone. I only broke the Black Cipher by the narrowest of margins."

There was silence as Faisal absorbed the outlandish situation he found himself in. "So where does that leave us?"

Romanenko lit up another Chesterfield. "That leaves us with the final Tehran message. I shook the tree within our intelligence community and learned that the code-word Sevruga is the nomenclature used for a new generation of plastique explosive."

"New generation?"

"Yes. I am told it was specially designed for use by Spetznaz troops. Reputedly, this Sevruga is equal in force to a half volume of pure nitroglycerine. That is to say, the explosive power of a liter of Sevruga is equal to a half-liter of nitro. But, of course, the Sevruga is stable."

Faisal swallowed. "And what about 'Maidenhead'?"

Romanenko shook his head. "Alas, of that I could learn nothing."

Faisal pondered what he was told, then he fixed Romanenko with his brown eyes. "You have taken great pains to demonstrate the Russian government had no complicity with Musa Kousa and the IRA in the assassination of Prince Ibrahim. How, then, did these terrorists obtain the Cloudburst fuel-air mine and the Sevruga plastique explosive? They are both of Russian manufacture."

It was Buskin who answered. "The situation in the Army's Far East Military District is bleak."

"Yes. I understand the scarcity of food supplies nearly triggered a nuclear civil war in the region a few weeks ago."

A surprised Buskin eyed Faisal warily. "*Da.* Some of the senior commanders have taken to selling the only thing they have—armaments—to obtain food for their troops. North Korea will provide hard currency for what it wants. Based on my knowledge of the situation, I would guess the North Koreans obtained Cloudburst and Sevruga from a senior officer within the Far East District, and they, in turn, sold it to this Musa Kousa. For a profit, I'm sure."

Faisal nodded, then turned to Romanenko. "Why tell me all this? Having the Bloodstone circuit design was a potential SIGINT coup. If the Bloodstone was deployed, you could have read our mail for years. Why tell me about it?"

Romanenko looked at Buskin, and Faisal sensed the two men were sort of, well, embarrassed. Then Romanenko spoke. "As I mentioned, our country has suffered great upheaval these past few years. Our economic situation has deteriorated, month by month, day by day."

"No argument there, I must say."

"We need help. From any quarter we can get it. Your Prime Minister has been instrumental in promoting a new economic aid package from the Europeans and Americans. The other nations are reluctant, but she has remained adamant. If you are successful in bringing down this 'invisible government' around her, we ask that you bring our assistance to her attention. Please. We need the package . . . desperately."

Faisal could not escape a feeling of guilt as he looked into the eyes of a man who felt alien to begging. He rose from the chair and nodded, saying, "General Romanenko, General Buskin, I thank you for your candor. Rest assured that if I am successful, I will not forget those who helped me. Now I must leave for Paris. I have only ten days to find the Maidenhead. Good day."

CHAPTER TWENTY SIX

T he black depths of the Irish Sea churned like a cauldron as the ferry plowed through the whitecaps toward Belfast. Faisal stood on the upper deck and welcomed the saltwater mist as it peppered his face, for it kept him wakeful. He'd slept little during the last forty-eight hours, as the sands of time slipped through his fingers.

Barney had picked him up on the *Sea Crest* at Arromanches, and they had repeated their infiltration drill in reverse, making landfall on the Devon coast near Plymouth. Barney then rowed back to the *Sea Crest* and made flank speed for Dublin, while Faisal found his way to a train station and took the first compartment to Liverpool. Using his Egyptian passport, he booked a room in the St. George's Hotel and waited. The call from Barney came late that same afternoon, with the snapshot message that the meeting was on for the following day.

As the vessel continued inexorably toward Belfast, Faisal groped for who or what was behind Mittleditch and Stoneleigh. Surely they were not alone. Surely there were others. But who? And more importantly, why? What was their agenda? Their purpose? Why had Prince Ibrahim and dozens of innocent people died? Why, exactly, was Faisal's life now perched on a razor?

The ferry terminal approached and Faisal made his way to the lower deck to join his fellow voyagers as they disembarked. Although there were no passport checks, Faisal knew the Royal Ulster Constabulary had raised surveillance to an art form, so he put on hat and sunglasses as he stepped onto the quay. He stayed with the crowd as they queued up for the taxis, and when his turn came, he jumped inside and said, "Sperrin Peak pub."

"Right," said the cabby as he kicked in the meter. They drove through the Protestant section of Belfast, passing through streets with prosperous shops and genteel housing. But Faisal knew that not far away were the grim tenements of Falls and Shankill roads.

Nothing exemplified the problem of Northern Ireland as did the "peace line" fence between the Catholic Falls and the Protestant Shankill neighborhoods. The steel barrier was a kind of Jordan River with brogue—the fault line where two peoples, driven by their bloody history and tribal instincts, coveted the same piece of real estate. It was a land a half-step removed from anarchy, and at the same time ensnared by an Ulster Mafia. It was into this land that Faisal ventured to seek his salvation.

Upon reaching the pub he flipped the surprised driver a twenty-pound note and exited the cab. A quick street reconnaissance revealed three Black Watch soldiers patrolling the sidewalk with their SA-80 rifles at the ready. For a terror-laced moment Faisal wondered if he'd been made, but the soldiers left him alone. His pulse racing, he quickly crossed the street and entered the Sperrin Peak.

The smoky chamber was indistinguishable from the hundreds of other public houses on the island, replete with its well-stocked bar, dark paneling, and tufted-leather stools. Since it was midafternoon, the few patrons and the barkeep gave Faisal a side glance as he made straight for a booth in the rear. The buxom waitress eyed him curiously, then brought his order for coffee and left him be. Faisal stirred the black liquid, hoping it would have more kick than tea. His watch told him it was early yet, and at this point waiting was something he was loath to do.

In the Republic of Ireland, internal security is the responsibility of the *Garda Siochana*, or "Guardians of the Peace," which is a police force of eleven thousand that reports to a police commissioner appointed by the minister of justice. The Garda handles the day in, day out crime-fighting work like any police force—such as robberies, burglaries, theft, drugs, and answering questions from tourists. Within this largely unarmed force, however, is the Irish Special Branch, whose sole purpose is to deal with "internal threats," which is a euphemism for the Irish Republican Army. To combat the IRA, the Special Branch maintains border security, keeps reams of dossiers, and operates a network of IRA informants, and the level of cooperation with their British counterparts is greater than you might imagine.

Given the massive terrorist threat posed by "the Troubles" in Ulster, efforts by the British security services there are nothing short of massive; and GCHQ, of course, figures prominently in this enterprise. There is the Northern Ireland Working Group within Cheltenham, and with regard to electronic surveillance, suffice to say GCHQ had turned Ulster into a rather large microphone. That is to say, when an IRA suspect farted in Londonderry, it eventually came through the headphones of a GCHQ analyst in Cheltenham.

In a similar vein to GCHQ, the Irish Special Branch had an electronic surveillance division to combat the IRA. Since this division was smaller than GCHQ's presence in Ulster, the Irish had to do more with less. They achieved this by recruiting some of their brightest people into the SIGINT division and putting a capable man in charge. He was an Irish half-Jew by the improbable name of Paddy Brillstein.

When Brillstein was appointed to his position within the Irish Special Branch, he was given a courtesy orientation tour of GCHQ, and during this tour he received a briefing by Faisal Shaikh. As you can imagine, with Irish and Jewish bloodlines, Brillstein was received at Cheltenham tepidly at best, but in Faisal Shaikh he found a kindred spirit. They shared a passion for chess and latakian tobacco, and over the chessboard their friendship grew. Faisal found Paddy's chess dazzling and quickly learned the soft-spoken Irishman was tough as maplewood, as well as twelve times smarter than the Brits who looked down their noses at him. From that time on, when Brillstein made an occasional business trip to Cheltenham, he and Faisal would renew their friendship over dinner and the chessboard.

As he waited in the pub, Faisal now hoped to trade on that relationship. It was certainly possible that instead of Brillstein a dozen RUC constables could come through that door. Faisal could only hope that their friendship would keep Brillstein's finger off the panic button until he had a chance to explain himself.

Paddy Brillstein entered the pub on the leading edge of evening regulars. A little shy of medium height, he possessed a round face with a swarthy beard, and when he took off his hat, a shiny bald head reflected the pub's dim light. He wore a black turtleneck with windbreaker jacket, and he surveyed the chamber methodically until his dark eyes met Faisal's. He made his way to the booth and slid onto the leather seat, remaining silent until the waitress appeared.

"What ya be havin'?"

"Irish whiskey," muttered Brillstein, and the waitress left.

Staring at Faisal, he remained silent while firing up a cigarette with a Zippo lighter. When the drink came, he took a long pull, then spoke in a low voice. "Bloody Christ, Faisal. What in God's name have you *done*? Anyone in the Western Hemisphere with a badge is after you. Scotland Yard, MI-Five, RUC, FBI, Interpol, the lot."

Faisal pointed at Brillstein's pack of smokes. "Mind if I have one of those, Paddy? It has been a long time for me."

Brillstein shoved the pack over and waited for an answer as Faisal lit up.

After inhaling, Faisal said, "Nothing quite like a latakian blend. I always found it cleared the mind like nothing else. Do you know who initiated the arrest bulletins on me?"

"Home Office. London. You are to be held incommunicado for prosecution under the Official Secrets Act. But something queer about all this."

"What's that?"

Brillstein sipped his whiskey, then lowered his voice even further. "The old boy network is in play on this one. In a big way. We get arrest bulletins every day. They're routine. But yours has been given top priority. Phone calls were made, very high up.

Markers called in. All to push you to the top of the list—and it's all hush-hush. I've never seen anything like it. If you're apprehended in Ireland, your arrest is to be brought to the personal attention of the police commissioner."

"It appears you stepped out on a limb to keep this appointment with me."

"Farther out than I would like, I can tell you. So what's it all about?"

Faisal pointed at Brillstein's drink and said, "You might want a refill. It's a long story."

The crowd had trickled away. One by one they'd bade farewell to the barkeep and left the Sperrin Peak for the home fires. Only a few die-hard stragglers remained at the bar, watching the telly through an alcoholic haze. In the sequestered booth, Brillstein had listened to Faisal with rapt attention, forcing himself to believe the unbelievable. When Brillstein ran out of cigarettes, he methodically tore a series of paper napkins into tiny pieces, and as Faisal neared the end of his soliloquy, a small pile of torn paper lay on the table. Finally, Brillstein could contain himself no longer and blurted out, "Good God, Faisal, couldn't you have blown the whistle on this thing? Called in favors from your friends in government? Don't you know someone in Parliament or the press? This whole madness is outrageous!"

"Outrageous, yes. But if I tried to blow a whistle without evidence and, more importantly, not knowing who was behind all this, I would be dismissed as a lunatic. Whoever is pulling the levers would go to ground until I was put in prison, or in the grave. Once I was in custody I'm quite certain my fate would be sealed. Shot while trying to escape, or something equally convenient."

Brillstein tossed down the remnants of his Irish whiskey, then said, "Well, if you're in such a box, why come to me? Why aren't you on the run?"

"As I explained, I was able to break the final Black Cipher message in Moscow, and since there is an IRA connection, I wanted to know if it made any sense to you." Faisal reached for an inside pocket and withdrew a folded sheet of paper, which he passed to Brillstein. The Irishman opened it and read:

TO: **PAGEBOYS**

FROM: **SANDCASTLE**

SEVRUGA FOR MAIDENHEAD WILL ARRIVE LONDON SAFE HOUSE OCTOBER EIGHTEENTH.

MAY THE GHOST OF GUY FAWKES BE WITH YOU ON HIS GLORIOUS DAY.

END MESSAGE

"Although I was able to decipher it," explained a pensive Faisal, "the message uses code words."

"Umm. 'Pageboys'—that be the Provos?"

"Correct."

"And 'Sandcastle' is this Arab fellow Musa Kousa?"

"Yes."

Brillstein tapped the paper. "Guy Fawkes Day—that's November fifth, isn't it?"

"Yes. Six days from today."

"We Irish always held Guy Fawkes in high regard. That is why I remember the date."

Faisal swallowed. "Is there anything else in the text that rings a bell?"

Brillstein rubbed his chin, then tossed the paper back across the table. " 'Fraid not, old man. Except for the part about Maidenhead."

Space and time froze for Faisal, and his mouth dried up like a dead oasis. "Maidenhead?" His voice was a scratchy whisper. "What is Maidenhead?"

Brillstein looked at Faisal as if he were a daft schoolboy fumbling over a simple arithmetic problem. "Why, everybody on the far side of Falls Road knows who Maidenhead is."

"Well, I'm not everybody. Tell me."

Brillstein was a bit startled by his friend's intensity. "Why, it's the Prime Minister, of course."

CHAPTER TWENTY SEVEN

He was back in the Belgravian mansion, pacing the sitting room like an entrapped Bengal tiger, his mind consumed by the final Black Cipher message. The IRA meant to top the Prime Minister on Guy Fawkes Day with a ghastly plastique explosive called Sevruga. Exactly where it would happen he'd no idea. Trying to assassinate prime ministers was nothing new to the IRA, of course. Margaret Thatcher had escaped death by the narrowest of margins at a party conference in Brighton, and John Major had survived a poorly aimed mortar shot during a cabinet meeting at No. 10 Downing Street.

Now another attempt was approaching, and behind it was a dark force that went beyond the IRA. Who was orchestrating this deathly dance? And for what purpose? The answers still eluded him. Whipped by the riptides of anguish and impotence, Faisal was at the end of his tether. If he went to the press, would they print his story? Would his old friends help him now that he was a wanted man? If he walked into a police station and said the Prime Minister's life was in danger, they would reply, "Ah, yes, Mr. Shaikh. Seems there is a warrant for your arrest. Just come along. We're sure the PM is quite safe, thank you." And he would be dead. Just like that. He racked his mind for some course of action to take, but time and again he broke his shins on the insurmountable stumbling block: if he raised the alarm, Mittleditch, Stoneleigh, and the invisible forces would simply remain invisible and wait for another day. What was the word Paddy Brillstein had used? *Outrageous.*

His pacing and smoking was so frenetic that to settle himself down he snapped on the telly. The image that appeared did nothing to calm him, for there in living color was the Prime Minister at the ballot box in the House of Commons, taking on the opposition during Thursday's question time. Faisal became transfixed as he watched the PM parry and lance her opposition with the same verve and style she'd always mustered. Sitting behind her on the front bench were her two closest advisers—the professorial defense minister, Michael Downs, and the rakish foreign minister, Stephen Whittier, who looked as if he'd stepped off the pages of a fashion magazine in his Savile Row suit. The ministers for defense and foreign affairs were appearing in a supporting role as the PM fielded questions about the latest bloodbath in the Balkans.

Faisal was paralyzed by his outlandish situation. There on the screen was the intended victim, and he was powerless to stop the oncoming fulmination that would turn her into a funeral pyre. It all caved in on him now, and his shoulders sagged. He was beaten, at the end of his game. He'd played his final chip and lost it all, and his body began to rack with the sobs of a defeated man.

Then the telephone rang.

The peal of the bell startled him so badly he jumped off his chair. He was alone in the house, and Barney was mooring the *Sea Crest* at Southampton. The ring persisted. Who could it be? Did the police know he was here? Had they ferreted him out already? Should he answer or no? Unsure, he swallowed hard and picked up the receiver, saying, "Hullo."

There was a pause, then a feminine voice, also cautious, said, "I thought I had a fiancé seven weeks ago. Now I'm not so sure."

Like a drowning man breaking the surface, he gasped, "Razia."

"Yes, it most certainly is Razia. Where on earth have you been? I've been worried sick."

"I've been all over the earth and then some. Where are you?"

"At my office at the school."

He had to see her. If nothing else, to forewarn her. He whispered urgently, "Hyde Park. The Serpentine bridge. I'll meet you there in half an hour."

As he peered over the bridge rail, Faisal mused that the waters of Serpentine Lake looked cold, dank, and dark—much like his prospects. His emotional reservoirs were spent, and the emptiness he felt was profound as he descended into a sea of despair.

Then he saw her.

She wore a black woolen cape and carried herself with such self-assurance that when they fell into an embrace, he genuinely felt he'd reached safe harbor.

After a long, lingering kiss, Razia pulled back and touched his face, seeing that the lines were deep, his eyes troubled. She went back into his embrace, and as he held her close, she felt fluttery and giggled, saying, "You started smoking again."

He found himself still capable of laughter. "Justified under the circumstances, I assure you."

Razia drew back again and searched his brown eyes. "Circumstances? What circumstances? Where have you been? What has happened?"

Faisal felt the weight of his situation return as he led her to a nearby bench and they sat down. After a protracted silence, he said, "I don't know where to begin."

"Why not try the beginning?"

Becoming lost as he looked into her eyes, he said, "Of course. The beginning."

It came out of him like a torrent. His life at GCHQ, the assassination of Prince Ibrahim, his sacking, Investment Research, his global quest to break the Black Cipher, and the shocking identity of the Maidenhead.

As it grew dark and cold in the park, they moved down to Piccadilly, to the tearoom of the Athenaeum Hotel. Once refreshed by the warm brew, Faisal continued his dialogue with renewed urgency, describing in precise detail his dilemma. "So if I try to raise an alarm—go to the press, ring up Scotland Yard—I still lose. The

invisible forces will simply remain undercover and wait for another day while I am taken into custody. I'm a wanted man, you
see. If there was some way I could get to the Prime Minister. Quietly. Privately. To warn her, then perhaps she could flush the
quarry. But, alas, I am at a loss. Guy Fawkes Day is only five days
away and I find myself powerless to stop an assassination." He
paused and caught his breath. "So there you have it, my love. The
entire story, with all the ugly warts. I have withheld nothing."

As Faisal had progressed through his story, he expected Razia
to be shocked, appalled, and aghast. He would not have been surprised if she dropped her engagement ring and bolted, never to
look back. But she registered none of these things. Instead, she sat
there attentively, listening to his story and nodding occasionally
like a schoolgirl absorbing a lecture. In fact, her lack of reaction
began to vex him a bit. Did she not understand all that he had told
her? Did she not comprehend what was at stake? The Prime Minister's life. Their life together. Everything hung in the balance. Yet
through it all her high-cheekboned face retained a soft, even gaze
as she sipped her tea. "So what do you think of this whole affair?
I'm a hunted man, you know. I could be apprehended at any moment. I may have even put you at risk."

With the self-assurance Faisal found extraordinary, Razia placed
her teacup on the coffee table and gently patted his knee, saying,
"Not to worry."

The blue Peugeot sedan and the Vauxhall made a small convoy
as they cruised along the Buckinghamshire road near Wendover.
Faisal sat in silence next to Razia, occasionally squinting when a
pair of oncoming headlights caught him in the eyes.

"There's a turnout just ahead."

"Good a place as any," sighed Faisal. "Pull in there."

Razia expertly wheeled the Peugeot into the turnout and pulled
to a stop, and the Vauxhall followed suit. Not wanting to linger,
Faisal leaned over and kissed her, then held her, fearing it might
be for the last time. "I must go now. Rest assured I will do my
best for God and country—and for us." Razia knew she'd gone as
far as she could and must now say farewell. They exited the Peu-

geot and walked to the Vauxhall, where the driver held the boot open. Even in the dark, Faisal could sense the man's tension. "Are you ready, Hassan?"

He bore a slight resemblance to his cousin Razia, although he was a bit on the plump side. With unveiled apprehension he swallowed, then stammered, "I, I suppose so."

Razia spoke to her cousin in a hard voice. "No supposing, Hassan. You must do this. Do you understand?"

Cousin cleared his throat and replied, "Very well. Get in and let's move on."

Faisal couldn't help himself and embraced Razia one last time, then wearing the butler's waistcoat, he climbed into the boot and let Hassan close him up into total darkness. He heard the crunch of gravel as the cousins parted, then the Vauxhall's door slammed, the engine started, and Faisal felt the sense of motion. A few turns followed, then Hassan's muffled voice came through the backseat. "The gate is just ahead. For God's sake remain quiet."

The car stopped and Faisal held his breath, hoping that Hassan's staff-identification bumper sticker would vouchsafe them through the security gate. It apparently did because the car began moving again. Once more there was the crunch of gravel as the tires rolled along the entry lane called Victory Drive. Then the car slowed and Hassan's muffled voice returned, saying, "We are almost there. Stay in place until I come fetch you."

Faisal didn't have much of a choice, so he remained silent and curled up in the fetal position as the car came to a halt. The door slammed again, the gravel crunched, and Faisal was left in what seemed a dark, cold, silent abyss. He put his nose close to the airholes Barney had drilled beside the taillight and waited.

It was all up to Hassan now.

Chequers.

It was first mentioned in the Domesday Book of 1086, that remarkable inventory of England's properties, as an estate of fourteen and a half hides (about 1,250 acres). Some fifty years after that Domesday entry the property passed to an Exchequer official, Elia de Scaccario. The Norman-French version of de Scaccario was de

Chekers, or del Checker, and from this the property's name evolved to Chequers.

In 1917, Lord and Lady Lee of Fareham bequeathed the grounds and Tudor mansion to a trust that would allow Chequers to serve as the country home of Britain's prime ministers. Here they could find solace from the pressures of office and take the curative elixir of country life. Every prime minister since Lloyd George (except for Bonar Law, who had a hang-up about the countryside) has reveled in the beauty and tranquillity of Chequers, including Churchill, Attlee, Eden, Macmillan, and, of course, Margaret Thatcher.

Faisal was starting to shiver from the chill. It had been two hours. He'd heard several cars start their engines and drive away. Then silence. Had Hassan changed his mind? Was he going to be left here? Faisal started to wonder about the kind of security afoot in this place. It had to be the best in the world, surely. Perhaps any moment the boot would fly open and Faisal would face a platoon of Royal Marines with fixed bayonets.

The gravel crunched.

Faisal held his breath at the approaching footsteps. A key was inserted and the boot opened, but it was only Hassan.

"Come quickly. There's no one about."

Stiffly, Faisal pulled himself out of the boot and stretched as Hassan closed it back up. He'd been in total darkness for so long he could see quite well under the moonlight, where he found himself standing in the gravel parking area of a classic Tudor mansion. Hassan took him by the arm and said, "Stay close to the wall and you won't be seen." He pointed to an object that Faisal guessed was a surveillance camera atop one of the mansion's gables. Stealthily he slipstreamed Hassan around a corner and into the service entrance of the kitchen. Faisal examined his watch, which read nine-fifteen P.M. "What do we do now?"

Hassan was breathing rapidly, and like Faisal he was wearing a butler's waistcoat. "The Prime Minister and her husband dined alone this evening. She has asked me to set up coffee and cake in the Hawtrey Room while she works her boxes. It's a frequent routine."

"Are there any staff on the premises?"

"Yes. About a half dozen administrative and security staff will be in the house during the night, but they stay in the far wing for the most part."

"Will my butler uniform fool them?"

Hassan shook his head. "No. Not a chance. I only had you wear it in case we ran into the exterior security men. The grounds are crawling with them."

"Well, let's get on with it."

"Yes. Of course." Hassan handed Faisal a tray of cakes and steaming coffee, then led him out. They traveled through a well-appointed dining room, then through the Long Gallery, which was an extended narrow library.

Offhandedly, Hassan said, "During the war Churchill watched movies in this room."

"I didn't know that," whispered Faisal, while thinking, *When I want the tour, I'll ask for it.*

At the end of the Long Gallery, Hassan paused and peeked through the doorway, then whispered, "Come on." They entered a parlor that looked like any you might find in an English gentry's estate. Wood paneling, a bay window, marble fireplace, and such. Between two easy chairs was a table with a Dictaphone, a pad, and writing implements. Hassan motioned Faisal to put the tray on the table while he struck one of those long matches to torch the fire. "This is the Hawtrey Room," whispered Hassan. "This is where the Prime Minister likes to work in the evenings."

Faisal nodded in understanding. "I must confess I was quite surprised when Razia told me of your position."

"Yes. A lot of people are. That is why we keep it quiet. People ask all sorts of intrusive questions."

"I can imagine. By the bye, how did you secure this position anyway?"

Hassan shrugged. "I cannot say. I'd served on the cabinet staff for years. I waited on the Prime Minister during a luncheon one day and for some reason she liked me. Had me transferred to her immediate staff when an opening came up at Chequers."

Voices. Two of them. Masculine.

Hassan turned white and motioned to Faisal. "Come along. Quickly!"

They went through a far doorway and into the reception foyer (known as Stone Hall), then up a flight of stairs, through a camouflaged door secreted in the wood paneling, up a spindly spiral staircase, and into a small bedroom that was lit only by the moonlight coming through the windows. Hassan paused, his chest heaving. "Those had to be the staff or security people down there. They were male voices."

"What do we do now?"

"I will go down and make sure they have cleared out. You remain here. You'll be safe. No one ever comes up to the Prison Room."

"Excuse me?"

"I said, you remain here—"

"No, no. What was that part about this being a prison?"

Hassan sighed, exasperated. "Lady Mary Grey, sister of Lady Jane Grey, was imprisoned here for two years by Elizabeth the First. Punishment for marrying without the Queen's permission, or some such thing. Now it's a seldom-used guest room."

"I see."

Hassan nodded in the darkness. "Now keep quiet. I'll be back."

Faisal waited in the moonlight of the small room, somehow feeling an empathy for Lady Mary Grey. Finally Hassan reappeared and they retraced their steps back to the Hawtrey Room. Everything was the same, except under the fireside table were three of the red boxes reserved for state papers. Faisal guessed the voices they'd heard belonged to the staff people who placed them there for the Prime Minister.

"She should be here any moment. All we can do now is wait."

"I see. Well, thank you, Hassan. I am deeply in your debt. I will take it from here. You may return to the kitchen."

"What!? You can't wait here alone."

"I fear I must, Hassan, for I may have to speak some words intended for the Prime Minister's ears only."

With apoplectic shock Hassan stared at Faisal, convinced he'd made a stupendous blunder in bringing him here. "I, I cannot leave you alone with the Prime Minister."

"Go, Hassan. Now. Or there is no chance for either of us."

Hassan swallowed, then left, whispering, "Razia has made a terrible mistake."

Once alone, Faisal felt a soggy dampness in his armpits and realized that if the PM appeared with a staff member in tow, it could be a problem. Or, rather, a bigger problem. Quickly he crossed the room and took a position behind the draperies of the bay window. He stood there waiting . . . waiting . . . waiting . . . until he heard the soft padding sound of bedroom slippers on the carpet. Carefully, Faisal peered from behind the draperies and beheld the Iron Lady.

Margaret Thatcher had been consigned to the political slag heap. After eleven and a half years at No. 10 Downing Street, three electoral victories, and a decade that included the Falklands War, union busting, privatization, strikebreaking, and ultimate prosperity, her hold on No. 10 seemed unassailable. But a series of bruised cabinet ministers, high interest rates, and an imperial style ultimately led to the unthinkable, and she was deposed by her own party in the fall of 1990.

Made Baroness Thatcher by the Queen, she took her seat in the House of Lords where she chafed, reduced to lobbing an occasional verbal hand grenade into the other chamber. And when her memoirs were published, she succeeded in alienating even her closest supporters.

And so, it seemed, her political fortunes were stone dead.

But in the bizarre skein of politics—where anything can happen and usually does—a stunning chain of events took place. The country that was home to the world's oldest monarchy didn't seem to fancy the "classless society" much, and the Conservative Party was savaged in a series of local and by-elections. The Tory cardinals smelled blood in the water and decided if they continued to back the sitting Prime Minister they would pass into the realm of the shadow cabinet. By cardinal thinking, the party's only hope was to change horses in midstream and hope to invigorate the electorate (and their hold on power) with new leadership. Prizing self-preservation above all, they dumped the PM at the party conference and rallied behind the chancellor of the exchequer as their new leader. Spot polls soared on the news, and the cardinals felt smug in their role as kingmakers. But then, as the chancellor stood to deliver his acceptance speech, he slumped over the dais—dead from a massive coronary.

The very next day China announced it was fed up with Britain's unilateral libertine actions on the Hong Kong transition and began massing troops along the city's border.

The cardinals now had to come to grips with the Mother of all Blunders. They'd dumped their leader, only to install a new one who was dead on arrival. They were caught between a power vacuum at No. 10 and a menacing Chinese tiger. A confidence vote loomed. It was in this cauldron of crisis that someone, somewhere, floated the idea: "What about Maggie?"

At first it seemed absurd. Margaret Thatcher? Recalled from the House of Lords to form a caretaker government? To save the bacon of a bunch of used-up old men who didn't like her very much? Yes, it was absurd. But two heavyweight backbenchers named Stephen Whittier and Michael Downs promoted the idea until it gained enough currency to reach critical mass.

Since the House of Lords possesses all the political verve of a cemetery in eastern Yorkshire, it took Margaret Thatcher approximately three nanoseconds to make up her mind when the offer was tendered. Strictly a caretaker government, said the cardinals. Of course, replied Lady Thatcher. We regroup, and at the next party conference you step aside. Certainly, came the response. Wouldn't dream of doing otherwise.

But once Margaret Thatcher was back in the saddle, well, you can imagine. The Hong Kong crisis faded as the Chinese shifted their attention to the oil field on the Vietnamese border. The economy rebounded and the people seemed to warm to the idea of Thatcher back at No. 10. Polls proved it. So the cardinals swallowed hard and asked the grocer's daughter to stand for party leader at the next Conservative conference.

A stunned press corps asked her, "Weren't you supposed to administer a caretaker government?"

"Yes," replied the grocer's daughter icily. "I intend to take care of the government."

It seemed Margaret Thatcher had returned with a vengeance—in the most stunning political comeback since Churchill returned from the wilderness.

Faisal peered from behind the drapes. She was wearing a quilted dressing gown and eyeglasses as she poured coffee from the pot and read a piece from the *Economist*. Even in this manner of dress and within these surroundings she seemed to have an imperial style about her. She was totally absorbed by the magazine as she raised the cup to take a sip. Faisal figured it was now or never, so with moist palms and a dry mouth, he stepped out from behind the curtains and said softly, "Good evening, Prime Minister."

Margaret Thatcher spun round, slopping some coffee onto the carpet and dropping her magazine. They stood there for a moment, looking at each other. Then once she'd recovered from the initial shock, Faisal found himself drilled with a pair of laser-beam eyes. Eyes that belonged to a woman known to have the mind of a computer and the forgiving nature of a shark.

"I apologize most profoundly for startling you, Prime Minister, but I had no alternative but to seek an audience with you under these irregular circumstances."

She eyed the butler's waistcoat. "Who are you?" The voice was sharp and commanding. "Where is Hassan?"

Faisal's palms were absolutely dripping now as he spoke with a cotton mouth. "Hassan is at his station in the kitchen. It was by his assistance I am here."

"And you are?"

"My name is Faisal Shaikh and I am the former chief cryptanalyst of Government Communications Headquarters. I come to you on a matter of great urgency concerning the defense of the realm, and I must ask you to hear my plea."

Her gaze was flintlike as she slowly lowered her coffee cup back on the saucer. A few moments of silence ensued, then almost imperceptibly she started moving her hand to the edge of the table. Faisal had not noticed it before, but on the side of the table a small white button protruded.

A panic button.

Faisal spoke quickly, mustering all his powers of persuasion. "Prime Minister, I doubt you remember me, but we met once when you made a clandestine visit to Cheltenham in May of '87. You were given a briefing by the director, Sir Reginald Bloom, in the senior conference room and I was among those present."

The movement of Thatcher's hand stopped for a moment as she contemplated him, then it started moving again.

"Prime Minister, I come to you on a matter of great urgency that you alone can correct. If you summon your security people, that opportunity may be lost forever. For your own safety I implore you to hear me out."

The hand hesitated, but the laser-beam eyes never wavered.

Faisal pressed his case. "Prime Minister, I know these circumstances are irregular. Bizarre, in fact. I'm sure you question who I am, so please listen carefully. In the spring of 1990 Muslim-based riots had broken out in the region of Kashmir occupied by India. India blamed Pakistan for the unrest and moved large numbers of troops into the Rajasthan region near the Pakistani border. Pakistan responded by moving their own forces to the border and commenced assembling nuclear weapons at their research facility at Kahuta. Once assembly was complete, these weapons were transported to a storage facility at Balochistan, in the mountainous region of southwest Pakistan."

Faisal saw he had her attention so he forged ahead. "Pakistan knew there was no way they could win a conventional war with India. They'd lost Bangladesh in 1971 and feared India would try and split the country with a new offensive. In view of this, we at GCHQ and the Americans of the National Security Agency increased our surveillance of Indian and Pakistani signals traffic—from our jointly operated base at Diego Garcia in the Indian Ocean.

Due to my facility with the languages, Sir Reginald sent me to Diego Garcia to personally supervise the on-site codebreaking efforts. In early May our Anglo-American team broke an encrypted message sent from the Pakistani military command in Islamabad to the storage-facility commander at Balochistan, ordering him to move the 'Storm Clouds' to a nearby Air Force base. The meaning of the message was obvious. The Storm Clouds could be nothing but nuclear weapons. Shortly thereafter, additional message traffic indicated that Pakistani F-sixteens were armed, prepositioned, on full alert, with pilots in their aircraft, ready to launch at a moment's notice—probably to deliver a nuclear strike on Delhi itself. A CRITICOM message to this effect was sent to the White House and to you at Number Ten. I assume you conferred directly with President Bush on this matter before he sent his personal emissary, Mr. Robert Gates, to Delhi and Islamabad to confer with the governments. As I understand it, Mr. Gates was able to diffuse the situation. The F-sixteens stood down, the troops were withdrawn, and the nuclear weapons returned to storage."

Margaret Thatcher looked at Faisal curiously for a moment, then sighed and sat down in her easy chair. "You have impressive credentials, Mr. Shaikh. Few people outside of H Division at Cheltenham could have known about those events. Particularly the Storm Cloud code words."

Faisal was similarly impressed by her memory and knowledge of GCHQ's organizational manual.

She inspected him more closely. "How did you obtain that butler's uniform?"

"Hassan secured it for me."

"And what is your connection to Hassan?"

"He is my fiancée's cousin."

"Ah, a family matter."

"In a manner of speaking, yes."

The Prime Minister's gaze stayed on him a bit longer, taking his full measure, then she said, "Well, since you are playing the part, the least you could do is refill my coffee."

"Of course, Prime Minister. I am so sorry about the carpet."

With dispatch Faisal refilled her cup, then stepped back, not wanting to crowd her. She took a sip. "Well, now, Mr. Shaikh, what is it that I, and only I, can do for you?"

Faisal felt the tension ebb from his body, and for the first time in ages he found himself able to relax. That it was at Chequers made it all the more remarkable. "If I may, Prime Minister, I should like to sit down. It will take some time to tell you about it."

The clock was nigh to two A.M. when Faisal wrapped up his story. She had listened attentively, interrupting with an occasional technical question that surprised Faisal by her grasp of GCHQ's operations. He made no attempt to gloss over the illegalities of Investment Research, and to his relief she did not press him about it. When he finished, she sat in silence for a time, then rose and paced the room, absorbing the extraordinary story. When at last she halted, Faisal noticed the iron veneer had melted away. She was a woman vulnerable and more than a little afraid. Faisal sipped the tea a bewildered Hassan had brought him.

Margaret Thatcher peered out the bay window, but saw only darkness as she absorbed all that Faisal Shaikh had told her. It was an extraordinary story, told by an extraordinary man. Certainly a capable man. She knew nothing about the technical intricacies of codebreaking, but like Napoleon, Margaret Thatcher could size up a man in a glance, and her instincts told her this man was most capable.

"Maidenhead," she said with a trace of poignancy. "That is what they call me in Ulster. I've heard it many times. And they've tried to kill me before, you know. In Brighton. Escaped by a scratch."

There was genuine fear in her voice, but Faisal did nothing to reassure her. "The IRA are simply the means to an end, Prime Minister. Someone within the government wants you dead."

Thatcher sighed. "Yes, yes. But the question is who? And why?"

"Sir Vivian Mittleditch is a party to it for certain, and Graeme Stoneleigh, but he is only a lapdog to Mittleditch. There has to be more firepower behind it than just those two."

"Yes, of course, but who?"

"On that question, Prime Minister, I am totally at a loss. I was hoping that after you heard my story you could identify the, ah, dark forces."

She shook her head. "There are legions of people who do not like me, Dr. Shaikh. Hate me, in fact. The IRA would like nothing better than to put me in the grave. But something like this *within* Her Majesty's government—that is too bitter to contemplate."

"But contemplate it we must, and quickly. Guy Fawkes Day is almost upon us."

The Prime Minister's back straightened. The Iron Lady had returned. "You are quite right, Dr. Shaikh. However, I must confess that I am at a loss as to how we can flush our invisible quarry."

Faisal placed his teacup on the saucer and said, "Why, I thought it was obvious how we should flush them out."

The Iron Lady was perplexed. "Obvious?"

"Why, yes, Prime Minister," replied Faisal, while helping himself to a cake from the tray. "The answer is most obvious. We are going to have to kill you."

CHAPTER ✛ TWENTY-EIGHT

The slick black door of No. 10 Downing Street swung open, allowing Prime Minister Margaret Thatcher to step outside to her waiting Jaguar limousine. She was wearing a navy blue dress with white jacket and navy blue piping. She also wore a wide-brimmed white hat and, unusual for her, a pair of sunglasses. A few photographers were behind the press barricade, but the PM did not pause—as she usually did—to give the snappers a wave and a photo opportunity. Instead, she kept her head down and entered the sedan as an aide closed the door behind her. Had any of the snappers paid attention, which they didn't, they would have noticed the tint of the Jaguar's windows was much darker than usual.

The limousine took off, and at the end of Downing Street the bobby opened the security gates to let the car pass. The Prime Minister was on her way to a speaking engagement at the annual convention of the Association of Electrical Contractors where she was expected with great anticipation. The car turned right onto Whitehall, went past the Cenopath, and was humming along Parliament Street when it passed over a manhole cover. There was an eruption as the hood of the Jaguar blew off, the tires exploded, and the skies over Whitehall became filled with a dark, acrid smoke.

Miraculously, there was no other traffic on the road at the time, and no pedestrians or tourists happened to be near the kill zone.

∎ ∎ ∎

The airwaves lit up with the news as cameras and microphoned reporters crawled over Whitehall to the drumbeat of news and police helicopters hovering overhead. The nation was seized by profound shock. Their prime minister had been slain, almost on her own doorstep. Scotland Yard issued a terse statement, declaring that the murderers would be hunted down "to the ends of the earth" and brought to justice for this heinous crime. Denis Thatcher appeared on television devastated with grief. Yes, the family was coming together to bury their mother. Condolences rolled in from heads of state around the world. A memorial service was planned for Westminster Abbey, and out of the shock came The Question: Who would lead the nation? The situation called for a swift resolution.

Stephen Whittier, Her Majesty's minister of foreign affairs, was something of a political phenomenon himself. Born to a moneyed family in East Anglia, he had long bankrolled Tory causes and was approaching fifty when he first stood for Parliament. Once inside Westminster he passed on a junior minister's post to become a force on the backbench. Granting favors and support to fellow members of lesser means, his stock rose—to the point that during the Conservative leadership crisis he was considered a long shot for the PM's post. He withdrew his name from consideration, however, and became the driving force behind Margaret Thatcher's return from Lords. He even shepherded the "fine print" legislation through the Commons that allowed Lady Thatcher to return from the House of Lords. For his ardent support she rewarded him with the post of foreign minister, which he humbly accepted.

In his highly visible post at the Foreign Office his star continued to rise.

Two days after the assassination, in the teeming, surging mass of people within Waterloo Station, Sir Vivian Mittleditch squeezed his elephantine girth off the train and walked as quickly as he could toward the taxi stand. He hated to rush because his breathing became heavy and the effort caused him to perspire. But time was of the essence now, so he hurried along. Preoccupied to the point of distraction, he hardly noticed when a petite Pakistani woman bumped into him and deftly dropped something into his pocket.

"Out of the way, woman," he wheezed.

"Sorry," replied Razia.

He said nothing further and hurried to the taxi stand. Climbing on board, he rasped to the driver, "Number Ten Downing Street."

The slick black door had a simple "10" in brass letters above the lion's-head door-knocker, and both were polished to a gleaming finish. Stephen Whittier walked through the doorway and onto the Persian rug that covered the black-and-white marble floor of the foyer. He was dressed in morning coat in anticipation of the impending call from Buckingham Palace. To Whittier's right was a marble fireplace, to his left was the Chippendale porter's chair, and ahead was the long-case clock crafted by Benson of Whitehaven. The doorkeeper closed the door behind Whittier as the foreign minister soaked up the atmosphere. He'd been here many times, of course, but never like this.

A slender gentleman in a double-breasted Huntsman suit emerged from the gold-carpeted corridor and approached Whittier with a deferential manner. He possessed a bony face, an angular nose, and a few strands of black hair combed over a bald cranium. This was Sir Anthony Stone, the principal private secretary of No. 10 Downing Street and the epitome of the British civil servant. He extended a hand. "Good morning, Minister. I hope you realize that we are still in shock over the Prime Minister's death, but as I told you over the phone, the palace feels we should move forward swiftly with a new government."

"I quite understand."

Sir Anthony bowed. "Very well, Minister. Please follow me."

The principal private secretary led Whittier down an immense corridor with portraits of actors and actresses on one side and a bank of high windows on the other. They entered the anteroom where ministers gathered with their red boxes before cabinet meetings. Churchill's blood, sweat, and tears portrait looked sternly down upon them. From the anteroom the principal private secretary opened another door, which led into the surprisingly modest room that was the vortex of power in Great Britain. This was the Cabinet Room and it seemed to be alive with history. Somewhat overcome, Whittier inspected the chamber as if he were there for the first time. The white walls, the high windows, the long table, and the mahogany chairs where the ministers of Gladstone and Disraeli had sat. Above the fireplace was a portrait of Robert Walpole, the first Prime Minister. Taken as a whole, the chamber was understated, yet awesome.

"Please be seated, Minister," said Sir Anthony. "The call from Buckingham Palace should come at any moment. Ring this button when you are ready to depart, and I will come and fetch you. These calls are always taken in private so I will leave you alone."

"Very good, Sir Anthony. Thank you."

"Yes, Pri—er, I mean, yes, Minister. I regret that your ascension to the leadership has occurred under such tragic circumstances, but with that caveat may I offer my best wishes as you embark upon your new duties."

"Thank you, Sir Anthony. We are all trying to cope with this devastating situation. I appreciate your kind remarks. That will be all for the moment."

Sir Anthony bowed and withdrew.

Once alone, Stephen Whittier took a moment to savor the atmosphere of the room. Its decorum. Its history. But most importantly, its power. His fingers caressed the arms of the mahogany chair, the only chair in the room with arms and a subtle reminder of who was in charge. He fingered the blotter with the gold-embossed EIIR cipher and the citation CABINET ROOM, 1ST LORD, for the Prime Minister was officially first lord of the treasury. He touched the candlesticks that had been owned by Pitt and Disraeli, and the William IV silver wafer box. At his elbow was an antiquated phone that he could soon use to summon an aide, an MP, or whomever he wished to summon within Her Majesty's realm, for the power was within his grasp. His calls would be taken at the Élysée Palace, the Kremlin, and even the White House. No doubt he would soon be spending a weekend with the President at Camp David. The Americans always invited a new PM over. It was all part of the "special relationship." There would be a motorcade, of course, and a state dinner. Pomp and circumstance. All for him. With those delirious thoughts dancing in his head, Stephen Whittier clenched his fists on either side of the blotter and uttered a low, menacing growl from the deep, wicked regions of his soul—a growl that transformed itself into the single word "*S-u-c-c-e-s-s!*" A trace of foam appeared at the corner of his mouth, and his eyes held a rabid intensity. It had been such a long, hard road. Fraught with peril at every turn. But slowly, meticulously, his syndicate of like-minded men had grown like a spider's web into the key corners of the government. A web that was now his to command. A pity about Margaret, but she was simply in the way. She never understood it was time to go.

The phone rang, startling Whittier out of his reverie. He straightened his cravat, then lifted the receiver and said in a silkened baritone voice, "Stephen Whittier."

"Ahem, terribly sorry to disturb you at this moment, Minister. Anthony Stone here. It seems Sir Vivian Mittleditch of Government Communications Headquarters has just arrived from Cheltenham. Unannounced. He insists upon seeing you immediately. I tried to explain the sensitivity of the timing, but he is adamant."

Whittier cleared his throat. "That is quite all right, Sir Anthony. Show him in."

"Very well, Minister."

The door opened and Mittleditch lumbered in, wheezing and sweating profusely. As Sir Anthony closed the door, Whittier rose and went to him, grasping his corpulent arms and whispering, "We've done it, Vivian! We've done it!" He made a sweeping motion with his arm. "This is all ours now. With the Society in place we can call the tunes, Vivian, and call them we shall. Now that the nettlesome woman is out of the way."

Mittleditch wheezed out his words in a jumble. "That's why I came. I made the scheduled call to O'Banyon from a phone box. He said it wasn't their doing."

Time and motion froze for Stephen Whittier as he tried to comprehend what his coconspirator had said. "What do you mean?"

"Just that. He said the Provos had hidden some Russian plastique into one of the wooden planks beneath the speaker's platform at the convention. They were going to top her when she started talking. He said the blast would have taken her out and half the convention hall. Said he didn't tell us beforehand because of security. After we rang off I caught the first train to London to tell you straightaway."

The room seemed to shift for Whittier, like a vessel does when it takes a torpedo amidships. "Wha . . . what does this mean?"

"I, I, don't know," gasped Mittleditch. "I thought you might."

The ring of the phone pierced the air, causing the two men to grasp each other like frightened children. It sounded a second time, causing Whittier to disengage himself and grab the receiver. "Yes? I mean, Stephen Whittier here."

"Yes, Minister, this is the Queen's private secretary calling. Her Majesty commands your presence at the palace to discuss the formation of a government."

Whittier cleared his throat. "Yes. Of course. I will depart forthwith."

"I shall inform Her Majesty to expect you."

And the line went dead.

Whittier replaced the receiver, his mind racing. This was not the time for panic. Margaret Thatcher was stone dead and that was all that mattered. By whose hand was irrelevant. *He* could control events now. The Society could get to the bottom of it. Bottle up whatever needed to be. That was power, wasn't it? He turned to his coconspirator. "I must leave. You remain here. Speak to no one. We can deal with this, Vivian. We weren't the only ones who wanted the old woman dead. Perhaps it's an extraordinary coincidence. Maybe some militant Orangemen did it. Who knows? But we *can* deal with it, Vivian. We *will* deal with it. Now I must leave for the palace."

Mittleditch wheezed acknowledgment and dabbed his forehead with a linen handkerchief.

Outside No. 10 Downing Street, in St. James's Park across Horse Guards Road, a tall, dark-haired man fed the ducks along the pond bank. Apparently he was a music lover because a cassette recorder was strapped over his shoulder and an earphone was stuck in his ear. As Stephen Whittier departed for Buckingham Palace, Barney Slickman tossed a final crumb to the ducks, turned off the recorder, then extended the antenna on his handset radio and spoke into the microphone.

The Daimler limousine pulled up to the Privy Purse Door of Buckingham Palace. Stephen Whittier exited the vehicle and was met by an equerry, who escorted him into a nearby lift. He went up to the Principal Floor of the palace where an official with the title of "gentleman usher in ordinary" greeted him. He led Whittier down the marbled King's Corridor, which was adorned with elegant paintings, to a pair of double doors at the entrance of the Audience Room. The usher knocked once, did not wait for a reply, then opened the doors and intoned, "Your Majesty, Your Majesty's secretary of state for foreign affairs."

Stephen Whittier straightened his morning coat and stepped into the presence of the diminutive woman who was, by the grace of God, Elizabeth the Second, Queen of the United Kingdom of Great Britain and Northern Ireland, her Realms and Territories, Head of the Commonwealth, Defender of the Faith. As he executed a deep bow from the waist, the Sovereign rose from behind the Chippendale desk and extended her hand. "Stephen, so good of you to come."

"I am honored, Your Majesty. Were it only under other circumstances."

"Quite. It was a tragedy. Such a beastly tragedy. We are all in shock. Mrs. Thatcher and I had our differences, of course, but I did admire her." She motioned to two chairs by the fireplace. "Please, do sit down." She was struck by what a dashing figure he cut in morning coat. So tall, so broad. The auburn hair, the jawline, the green eyes. He would make a telegenic prime minister if not a capable one. Once settled, she twisted and untwisted a long strand of sixteen-millimeter pearls. "Stephen, I shall come directly to the point. Although the Conservative Party conference does not convene for another month, my advisers tell me we must move forward immediately to form a new government. This will demonstrate continuity of leadership and our resolute stand against terrorism. After a vote is taken at the party conference the government can reform again, but I have it on authority that you"—she smiled here—"are certain to be chosen party leader. Therefore, I believe it is most sensible that you be the one to form a new government at this critical time. I am asking you to be my next Prime Minister."

Stephen Whittier bowed his head. "Your Majesty, this task comes to me under a veil of sadness, but I shall not shirk my responsibility. I am humbled and honored by your request; and you may rest assured I shall endeavor, with all the resources at my command, to fulfill my duties as your Prime Minister. And— if I may speak on a personal level—in the times to come I hope we shall develop an enduring relationship of mutual respect and trust." He had rehearsed the speech many times and he sensed it went down well. Inwardly he was smiling to himself, savoring the moment, when a talonlike voice sliced into his soul like a scythe, saying, "I think not, Stephen."

If it were possible for a man to part company with his skin, Stephen Whittier nearly jumped from his as he leapt from the chair and spun round to behold the Iron Lady. "Margaret," he gasped, "it, it can't be . . . "

Standing by the drapes that had concealed her, the Prime Minister replied, "Reports of my death have been greatly exaggerated, Stephen."

Whittier stood frozen, as if caught naked in a floodlight, when the gentleman usher opened the double doors to reveal two men. The first fellow was rather muscular and athletic, while the second was a gentleman of—what?—Mideastern descent.

"This is Mr. Blakemore from Special Branch, Stephen," explained the Queen. "We have a special detachment of Special Branch people in palace security. Did you know that? Not many people do. We call them 'special Specials.' Ha, ha. Now do be a good boy and run along with him."

Whittier was numb as the athletic man took him by the arm and led him out of the Audience Room. At the doorway he resisted and glared at the Prime Minister. "How . . . how did you know?"

Margaret Thatcher glanced at Faisal, then replied, "We are not the fools you and your conspiracy took us for, Stephen. I must confess you were the last person in the government I would have suspected, but the facts turned out differently. Her Majesty and I look forward to your telling us more about this monstrous plot for a secret coup d'état."

Whittier glared at her. "You'll get nothing from me."

The Special Branch man pulled Whittier along as the Prime Minister's stony gaze drilled into his back. "You'll talk," she said icily. "You bloody well *will* talk."

The venom that dripped from her voice caused Faisal to shudder.

Margaret Thatcher went on television that night to speak to a stunned nation. In a matter-of-fact tone she explained how a volunteer policewoman had impersonated her by climbing into a specially rigged Jaguar driven by remote control. Once inside, she dropped the backseat and crawled into an armor-plated box in the trunk, where she rode out the explosion unharmed. The driver was a mannequin.

The Prime Minister went on to explain that she was compelled to undertake this illusion in order to smash a ring of IRA bombers. Arrests had been made. The accused would stand trial. She was confident the people of Great Britain would understand that the subterfuge was taken in the national interest.

She did not mention a word about Stephen Whittier, Sir Vivian Mittleditch, a sinister "Society," or a remarkable codebreaker.

CHAPTER ✛ TWENTY·NINE

He was a burly man, with hairy forearms bulging forth from rolled-up sleeves. As he loaded up another spool of recording tape onto the machine, Stephen Whittier's indignant voice rasped, "I want to see my solicitor."

The burly man's face contorted, as if he were on the business end of a poorly done rectal exam. "Solicitor?" he asked rhetorically. "Solicitor? No, no, no. You've got it all wrong, boy-o. Solicitors, habeas corpus, and all that other tommyrot is for lawbreakers. You, boy-o, stepped *outside* the law. When you did that, you pissed away all that solicitor nonsense—in particular that part about the right to remain silent." He hit the RECORD button on the machine. "Now, then, let's start again, shall we? Tell me everything about this little coup of yours."

Whittier was sullen. He sat on a spindly wooden chair, under a spotlight in a darkened cellar. Just like in the movies. It was a chamber within a quiet country house in Kent not terribly far from Chartwell—which was, perhaps, appropriate. Winston would have understood.

"Come on now, boy-o, let's get along, shall we? Who else was in league with you?"

Stephen Whittier was unshaven, had received nothing but water for three days, and was now stripped of everything but his dress shirt and morning trousers. "I have nothing to say," he said lamely, his defiance having ebbed with sleep deprivation.

"Oh, yes, you will, boy-o. My mother, heaven bless her, used to say, 'One way or another, Archie, you are going to eat your spinach.' And I bloody well did. So one way or another, boy-o, you are going to tell me everything." Archie put an edge on his voice. "Now let's have it. Who else was involved? We know about Mittleditch and Stoneleigh. Who else?"

Whittier stared at the floor. "I need to pee."

"Who else was involved?"

The defiance returned. "I *said*, I need to pee!"

Archie drummed his fingers on the table as he considered the request. Then he said, "Do it in your pants."

Whittier looked aghast. "What?"

"I said, do it in your pants."

Whittier's face betrayed his consuming anguish. Cut off from his power base, his friends, his office, his banker, his tailor, there was no lifeline to seize. After three days of no food, no sleep, and no bath, the release of his warm bodily fluid into the crotch of his morning trousers caused Stephen Whittier to break, and he began sobbing like a child with a broken tricycle.

Archie pursed his lips and nodded to himself. You could take a Yorkshireman out of the fields and beat him three times a day before breakfast and he wouldn't tell you the time of day. But rob a silver-spoon public-school man of a little sleep and his bath—well, they became putty, didn't they? The interrogation had reached the crossover point, so he punched a button on the table. A guard opened the door and Archie said, "Take our guest back to his room for a shower, then give him a spot of dinner and a good night's sleep. We'll reconvene after he wakes up."

Whittier looked at his interrogator with surprise.

Archie smiled benevolently.

Whittier drained his coffee cup and placed it on the saucer by the microphone. Archie had moved the interrogation into the bright and airy breakfast room of the country house, where a refreshed Stephen Whittier seemed relieved, even eager to talk. He wanted to please his master.

"Now then," said Archie, smiling, "let's take it from the top, shall we?"

Whittier looked out the window at the pastoral scene and wistfully said, "We called ourselves the Hastings Society. Rather dramatic, isn't it? We moved slowly, carefully, and the capstone of our plan was to install me as prime minister. We didn't feel I could capture the reins as party leader in an open conventional race. I mean, I would have to grapple with the likes of Heseltine, Portillo, Hurd, Lamont, and all the others. Too many entrenched longtimers to deal with. But when our new leader dropped dead at the party conference, we saw a golden opportunity, and that's when I had the idea—it was my idea by the way—of bringing Thatcher out of retirement. I would slipstream her while solidifying my position as her heir apparent. The Society worked to that end as well, and everything was going superbly until . . . "

"Until?"

Whittier shrugged. "The old woman refused to leave. I always despised her, by the way. Such a common type."

"Terribly common."

"Exactly. Well, she simply wouldn't go. So we decided the best action to take was to make the government fall. That way Thatcher would be forced to resign. By that time my position was firm. We felt confident I could win the party leadership and even come out of a general election with a stronger majority."

"So that was why you topped Prince Ibrahim with the fuel-air bomb?"

Whittier shrugged. "Had to be done. A number of backbenchers were dissatisfied with Thatcher. All they needed was an excuse to dump her. It would have worked, too. We just missed it by four votes. Razor thin, wouldn't you say?"

"Razor thin."

"So having missed the ring, we had to regroup. Thatcher had to go this time."

"So you struck another deal with the Provos?"

"What would you say? A confluence of goals? Yes, that's what it was—a confluence of goals."

"What was in it for them?"

Whittier leaned back and clasped his hands behind his head. "Since that peace initiative fell through—no surprise there, was it?—Thatcher had cracked down on the IRA to the point they were feeling the pinch. So we cut a deal. They top her, then I become prime minister and call for a 'new political dynamic' in Northern Ireland. I withdraw the troops from Ulster, let the Northern Ireland Parliament reconvene to keep the Orangemen happy, and the IRA lays low . . . for a year, maybe two. Ulster is quiet. I look like a bloody political genius. Then when the IRA starts up again, I hand the problem off to the Ulster Parliament and say, 'You wanted your Parliament back, you deal with it.' Brilliant, wasn't it?"

"Oh, yes. Brilliant, indeed."

"And, of course, once the troops were out, the IRA made us agree to keep the Union Jack flying over Ulster. That was the crux of the deal."

Archie blinked. "I'm sorry, Stephen. Could we back up? I think I missed something here? You said the IRA wanted you to keep Ulster British? I thought they wanted us out."

Stephen looked at the ceiling. "Mythology, Archie. Pure mythology. You see, the IRA cast themselves as heroes, patriots, that sort of thing. More fools than you could imagine believe them, especially in America. But since the Troubles began they've chucked the united-Ireland rubbish and evolved into a crime syndicate, pure and simple. They skim the peacekeeping money London pumps into Belfast, Londonderry, and the like. They've become hooked on it, like addicts. Did you know the IRA and the Loyalist scum rags—the Ulster Defense Association and all that—often work *together*? No? Well, they do. They make cease-fire pacts, define boundaries, share munitions and intelligence, and even trade enforcers from time to time. You wouldn't believe the collusion! They shake down construction companies, shopkeepers, pubs, and all that for protection money. The ones that don't pay get kneecapped, right? Know why all those bombs go off? It's nothing to do with politics. It's just a means to keep everyone in Ulster scared shitless when the shakedown man comes a calling. Why do you think Gerry Adams got a Semtex shower and the peace initiative went down like the *Titanic*? If peace ever came to Ulster the

'Hard Men' of the IRA and the UDA would lose their gravy train. They couldn't allow it. Topping Adams was an act of self-preservation."

Archie cleared his throat. "I, uh, can't say I knew all that."

"Most people are fooled by the IRA mythology, but the Hastings Society wasn't. So we decided to make the reality work for us. We made a deal that once Thatcher was killed we would keep pumping Exchequer money into Ulster and not reintroduce troops, and we would let the IRA keep the blood flowing at a trickle so they could continue their extortion game. We get what we want while they get the troops out and the money keeps rolling in. Thatcher, of course, had gotten on to their game. She was cracking down on one hand and squeezing the Ulster funding with the other. The Provos were feeling the pinch. That's why they were willing to do a deal with the Hastings Society."

Archie leaned forward on his elbows. "Which brings me to my next question. Why?"

Whittier looked at him, not comprehending. "Why?"

"Yes, Stephen—may I call you Stephen? Why? What was this Hastings Society all about?"

Whittier spoke as if he were explaining the obvious. "Well, I mean, it's a rabble out there, isn't it? The country ruined. Everyone on the dole. I tell you, whores in Soho should command more respect than MPs in Westminster. I've seen it on the inside. The Empire broken up and given to those jungle monkeys in uniform. South Africa showed a little spine for a while, then slacked off. The country is crying out for a firm hand. England needs to regain her rightful place in the world! Just like the Battle of Hastings led England into a new age, our Hastings Society would do so again. With a small group of like-minded men on the levers of power, you'd be amazed what we could do."

"What, exactly, would you have done, Stephen?"

Whittier shrugged. "Well, I thought it was obvious. Deport all the coloreds for a start. The blacks, the Abs, the slope-eyed vermin. They've poisoned our island. Yank their passports and send them all packing to where they came from. Give England back to Englishmen."

"You mean, a little ethnic cleansing?"

"Exactly."

Archie's eyes lit up as he comprehended. "I understand now, Stephen. Of course, I should have seen it all along. You're just a bleedin' Nazi."

Whittier looked indignant. "Hitler was misunderstood from the start. If it hadn't been for that bugger Churchill, we could've worked wonders with him."

Archie sighed. "Stephen, forgive me, but in this day and time wouldn't it have been a little difficult to pull off a scheme like this? I don't think Parliament would go along. Let alone the press."

Whittier brightened. "But don't you see, Archie? That was the beauty of the Hastings Society. The state has awesome powers when you think about it. To make our plan work, all you needed were men with the will to pull those levers of power. You don't believe me? Well, then, let me explain. We started out by creating the right political climate so our policies would seem reasonable, even welcomed. You know all those militant groups of Africans, sand wogs, and skinheads that have sprung up over the last two years?"

"What about them?"

"The Hastings Society bankrolled them all. Covertly, of course. It was hard to turn on the BBC without seeing them breaking windows or torching a car. People were surprised, then scared, then angry. Manipulating public opinion is so devilishly easy, don't you think?"

"Devilishly so," conceded Archie.

"I mean, everyone likes a good lynching, don't they? It's all in giving people what they want." Whittier was becoming energized now. "Anyway, once we'd reached critical mass on public opinion, we would introduce our policies and make the trollops in Parliament and government knuckle under. The Hastings Society has well-placed men in the security services. We had dossiers on over three *hundred* MPs. Many more on press people, executives in business and finance, Civil Service, BBC, the lot. Once in power, we'd use those dossiers to bend Westminster, and the country, to our will. And don't think it couldn't be done! I must confess my idol has always been the American FBI director, J. Edgar Hoover. A great man. Ran the country for decades, he did. Hoover knew how to use dossiers, and so did we. Would have, had things not tripped up. How did you fellows get on to us anyway?"

Archie smiled. "We read your mail."

"Read our mail?"

"Something like that. Now then, Stephen, let's have the membership list of your Hastings Society."

Whittier sighed and gazed out the window, knowing it was the end game. All his wicked hopes and dreams had ended at a breakfast table in the countryside. And being the public-school type, his misery craved company. "Michael Downs," he said softly.

"The minister of defense?"

"Yes."

"My, my. Who else?"

"Arthur Vines."

"Permanent secretary of the Home Office?"

"Yes."

"Extraordinary. Who else?"

"Philip Darman-Greaves."

"I say, the deputy director of MI-Five? Incredible. Who else?"

"Roger Hartwell."

"Chief of staff of the Joint Intelligence Committee. Who else?"

"Aubrey Phelps."

"Deputy chief whip in Parliament. Who else?"

It was twilight when Whittier finished his debriefing, and Archie's demeanor turned from warmly conversational to stone cold. He arranged his notes and said, "Now, Whittier, we come to the matter of your future."

Whittier swallowed, recalling that Archie used to call him Stephen.

"You have a choice. You can liquidate your family's estate in East Anglia, plus all your investments and assets, and donate them to the National Trust." Whittier made a choking sound as Archie continued. "You get to keep a hundred thousand pounds and go into exile, never to set foot in Britain for the rest of your natural life."

The prisoner exploded. "Whittier Hall has been in my family for two centuries!"

"And it will make a fine addition to the National Trust, I'm sure. You can do that, or . . . "

The prisoner became wary. "Or?"

Archie smiled. "Or you can have an accident on your yacht while sailing in the Channel."

Whittier swallowed again, then tested the water. "I suppose you're making the same offer to Vivian?"

Archie grimaced. "Well, to be honest, Stephen, I'm awfully sorry to tell you this because I feel terribly embarrassed. I mean, not all of us inquisitors have the experience I got, see? If I told my junior staffers once I told them a hundred bleedin' times, always, *always* take away the belt and the shoelaces. Well, wouldn't you know it. They had Mittleditch and that bugger Stoneleigh in a safe house just down the road. Forgot to take their belts, and, well, you know. Sort of a lovers' leap, you might say. Now what will it be, Stephen? Exile or the Channel option?"

Whittier's mouth was dry as he whispered, "Exile."

Behind the see-through mirror on the breakfast-room wall, Faisal crushed out his last cigarette, muttering, "You're lucky the choice wasn't mine, you bastard."

aisal surveyed the township of Cheltenham from his new perch and was struck by how tranquil it all seemed. He'd been near this window many times before, of course, but he'd never taken the time to drink in the view. Since the Oakley campus was set into the hillside, the elevation provided a much better panorama of the valley than his old office across town.

He examined his new surroundings and decided he didn't care much for the decor. He'd put something in the budget to have the place refurbished. Better yet, perhaps it was time for a new headquarters building. If MI-5 and MI-6 could get gleaming new structures on the banks of the Thames, then certainly there were funds to bankroll something similar for GCHQ.

The intercom buzzed and he pressed the button. "Yes, Geneviève?"

"Burdick is here to see you, Sir Faisal."

"Very good. Send him in."

Jamie Burdick walked in looking well-pressed in his coat and tie. A bit older and wiser, but a trace of the boyishness had returned.

"So how is the new chief of H Division holding up?"

"Not bad for the first week." Was there a trace of cockiness in his style? "Trying to learn your knack for delegating."

"Of course. That's absolutely essential. Otherwise you get overwhelmed."

Faisal led him to the liquor cabinet where he poured an Evian water for both of them. Passing the tumbler to his protégé, he said, "You know, Jamie, I've been thinking. Perhaps it's time to embark on a capital upgrade here at Cheltenham. Our people often work in facilities that are positively grim. It's time we made them a bit more user-friendly."

"I'm all for that."

"I want you to accompany me when I attend the next Joint Intelligence Committee meeting. We'll float a trial balloon there."

"We'll encounter some resistance, surely. Scarce budget resources and all that."

"Then I'll float it on up to Downing Street. We have a friend there. But enough about that. Let's get along to the dining room and have some lunch. There is some unfinished business from our trip to Moscow I want to discuss with you."

"Really?"

"Yes, really."

EPILOGUE

The Hastings Society had eighteen members in all, and as Stephen Whittier had pointed out, they were "like-minded" men (although there was one woman among them—the ambitious, Cambridge-educated daughter of London's leading Mafia don). They brought treachery to a high plane, and it was frightening how close their plans had come to fruition. The intelligence-security community in Britain is much more intimate and clubby than in America or Russia. By manipulating public opinion, then applying the J. Edgar Hoover principles of coercion and blackmail, plus close ties to organized crime—well, it might very well have worked.

No one in the press correlated the series of remarkable donations to the National Trust with the early retirements of a number of public servants, captains of industry, and MPs.

A half dozen small fry IRA bombers were put on trial for the attempted assassination of the Prime Minister. Despite their protestations of innocence, they were found guilty. And they were guilty—just not of the attempted murder of the PM.

The people of Great Britain forgave the Prime Minister her feigned assassination. Indeed, her popularity ratings soared. Denis, especially, was given high marks for his performance.

Margaret Thatcher's health started to decline and she announced her intention to step down for good after the following year's party conference. However, before her departure she browbeat the Western powers into providing a healthy economic aid package to the former Soviet block.

Barney Slickman, OBE, bought the *Sea Crest* and started up a charter service off the Côte d'Azur.

Stephen Whittier moved to Barbados where he eked out a living trading in local real estate.

The American NSA pulled Mason "Tex" Mattea out of Alice Springs and was on the verge of prosecuting him when the Prime Minister placed a private telephone call to the White House. Shortly thereafter he was reassigned as senior U.S. liaison officer to GCHQ at Cheltenham.

Razia took her doctorate in economics and settled down to her unofficial duties as the wife of the GCHQ director. She redecorated their house in Battledown Estates and taught two classes a week at the London School of Economics, which were the same days Faisal traveled to No. 10 Downing Street to brief the Prime Minister.

As to the matter of Investment Research, Limited, after enormous pressure was brought to bear by the Americans and the European Commission, the Principality of Liechtenstein forced the Grobert und Dortmünder Bank to open their books to a special investigative unit of the EC and U.S. Treasury Department. One vigorous EC investigator examined a series of wire transfers, stock option orders, and cash withdrawals involving a gentleman by the name of Katami Mousef and a firm called Investment Research, Limited. The investigator wanted to question the director of the bank—one Anton Grobert—about the transactions, but Anton had been felled by a heart attack. Apparently from stress.

One wire transfer was traced back to London, so the EC investigator forwarded the data to the financial-offenses division of Scotland Yard, asking if the British police wanted to pursue an insider-trading investigation. Since the Prime Minister trusted the European Commission about as far as she could throw a Daimler, every shred of paper dealing with the EC had to pass her review. Therefore, the request percolated up the chain to No. 10 where it found its way into the PM's box. It quickly came under the scrutiny of her prodigious paperwork skills, and she brought the matter up at her Tuesday-evening audience with the Queen. They discussed the matter and found themselves in agreement. The EC request was returned to Scotland Yard with a note scrawled in the Prime Minister's own hand: *Her Majesty and I do not wish this matter to be pursued further.*

So the inquiry died a swift and silent death.

And finally, as to Faisal, he embraced his new position as GCHQ director with energy and verve, and his peers in the other security services were consistently amazed at how the PM approved his budget requests while cutting back theirs. He missed some of the hands-on cryptologic work, but taking the reins of GCHQ into his hands helped compensate for the loss. With his new wife and renewed life he was genuinely a happy man.

Now all he had to do was find that Russian mole.